SLEEPERS, AWAKE

EDEN BARBER

OMNIFIC PUBLISHING

DALLAS

Omnific Publishing
10000 North Central Expressway, Dallas, TX 75231
www.omnificpublishing.com

First Omnific eBook edition, June 2013
First Omnific trade paperback edition, June 2013

The characters and events in this book are fictitious.
Any similarity to real persons, living or dead,
is coincidental and not intended by the author.

Library of Congress Cataloguing-in-Publication Data

Barber, Eden.
   Sleepers, Awake / Eden Barber – 1st ed.
   ISBN: 978-1-623420-18-5
   1. Death — Fiction. 2. Loss — Fiction.
   3. Love — Fiction. 4. Fantasy — Fiction. I. Title

                10 9 8 7 6 5 4 3 2 1

Cover Photograph ©Ayal Ardon/Trevillion Images
Cover Design by Micha Stone and Amy Brokaw
Interior Book Design by Coreen Montagna

Printed in the United States of America

To my darling elltea.
How could I have known when I began writing
that this story would be for you?
Wherever you are in the universe,
I hope the people in charge know you're pretty great.

ONE
AWAKENED

I can't see. I can't move. I'm less alarmed by this than you'd think. My arms are pinned to my sides. Slowly I realize I'm wrapped tightly in some sort of shroud. I try to raise my arms. The fabric is old, decaying. After an initial resistance, it tears easily, like ripping through cobwebs. The scraps of fabric fall away with only a whisper of protest, and despite the fading day, I'm squinting, my eyes unaccustomed to the light. How long have I been asleep?

It's an oddly familiar place, overgrown with briars but still somehow recognizable. I can't remember the last time I was here. It's all Spanish moss and vines and crumbling stonework. When have I been here? Who was I? It was something important. I can almost remember, the memories murky shadows in my subconscious.

You can tell this place used to be majestic. Perhaps hundreds of years ago it might have been the center of an advanced civilization. Now though, it's wild and overgrown. Savage. Still, it's impressive in its own way, beauty in its rawest form.

I stretch my arms above my head and walk in a slow circle, taking in my surroundings as I step over the cloth scraps that once held me prisoner. I'm standing on what must have been a courtyard, tiles of thick granite with grass and weeds now growing through the cracks. Nature always reclaims what we've built with our hands.

I step off the edge of the granite slabs onto the hilltop. The grass beneath my bare feet is damp and soft, and the air smells sweet. The wind kicks up, whipping my long brown hair across my face, and I reach up to tuck the errant strands behind my ears.

I have the strangest feeling that I've returned home.

"...shortly after takeoff from Chicago O'Hare. There were no survivors. Investigators continue to search Lake Michigan for the aircraft's black box recorders. Wintry weather conditions are likely to have been a factor in the crash—"

I'm jolted from unconsciousness by NPR. The news report washes over me like an incoming tide, covering me with a general feeling of dread. Even under ideal circumstances, that is, when I coldly comfort myself with the statistically proven safety of air travel with my feet solidly and safely on the earth, I have an almost disabling fear of flying. I've tried everything: books, meditation, hypnotherapy, regular therapy, biofeedback, expensive courses taught by entrepreneurial exiles from the airline industry, and still the only thing that gets me on a plane is the trusty anti-anxiety medication prescribed by my doctor. It relaxes me just enough so that I can make it through the jet bridge on wobbly legs and take my seat, but even so, every second inside the titanium coffin is a kind of agony. I'll sit in my narrow seat, fists clenched, seatbelt secured so tightly that if the plane stopped suddenly, I'd probably bisect myself. I'll sit in my tense ball, wondering if this will be my last moment on the earth. Or maybe this. Or the next. And on and on until the wheels touch ground at my final destination. *Final destination.* Even the term for the endpoint of the journey has a terrifying ring to it.

When I fly, I always find myself thinking of that line from *Julius Caesar*, "Cowards die many times before their deaths; The valiant never taste of death but once."

I have died many, many deaths.

So whenever there is a plane crash, I obsess over the details. Have I ever flown that route? That carrier? Is there significance in the flight number? Can that have been me? I read every article, pore over the news photos on my computer screen, and slowly break out into a cold, clammy sweat. Sometimes I make myself so sick and lightheaded that I have to stop what I'm doing and sit with my head between my knees. The blood will rush to my head and pound in my ears. I pick apart the details of every crash, as if somehow by knowing everything about it, I'll be protected from suffering the same fate.

No, it doesn't make sense to me, either.

It seems my semi-conscious self, at least, is more protective of my mental health. My arm, practically of its own volition, swings out and smashes the snooze button before I can hear more details. It also knocks a book off my nightstand, and the ensuing clatter startles me into full wakefulness. I sit up and rub my eyes. For some reason I feel like extending my arms by my sides, as if I am stretching out wings. The movement feels familiar and important, so I do it again slowly, my fingers swollen from sleep.

My perception still fuzzy, I vaguely recall listening to something important before I woke up. What was it? I close my eyes and try to remember, and then it comes to me: *There was another plane crash.* I'd normally feel tempted to fire up my laptop and get on the news sites, but something stops me. I'm immediately distracted by my morning routine. *Cereal. Make lunch. Pack your bag.*

There'll be time later to Google to the brink of a panic attack.

I sit with a bowl of Cheerios and gaze out at the colorless day. I've been living in Boston a long, long time, and I feel far away from my family and old friends, on the opposite coast of the country. I came here for college, stayed on for grad school, and I guess I never made my way back home.

Being afraid to be on a plane for nearly seven hours might also have had something to do with it.

I'm from a place in California called Poppy Beach. It's a tiny town about four hours north of San Francisco by car. If you've never heard of it, it's probably because it's on the so-called Lost Coast, a stretch of California's coast so rocky and treacherous that no one ever bothered building any major highways near it. Sometimes I wonder if the Lost Coast is so geographically isolated from everything else that we've evolved into entirely different species of people, like we're the duck-billed platypuses of the United States. The only people who used to live in Poppy Beach were the people whose families had always lived here — *lifers,* we call ourselves. We would have stayed that way, isolated and insular, except that in the seventies, an eccentric billionaire (is there any other kind?) named Théophile

Butler invested a lot of money in the town, built a golf course and a luxury hotel and a country club, and put his name on it all. He would have renamed the town Butler Beach, but even his billions weren't sufficient to convince the town officials to change the name, although they were happy enough to allow him to invest and develop the land as much as he wanted. He, however, liked the exclusivity that the remote location gave and purposely didn't work to improve the roads into town from the main highway. He wanted to keep Poppy Beach his secret garden.

Once the Butler Golf Course and Country Club were built, Butler and his friends invaded. The town residents were grateful for the steady flow of tourist money, but the socioeconomic divide between lifers and visitors was steep, about as ridiculous as in a John Hughes film with Molly Ringwald. After Butler died, though, Poppy Beach fell out of vogue, and the tourists who remained and eventually moved there permanently were the ones who fell in love with the unspoiled beauty and slower pace of the town. There's still a big economic difference between the lifers and the newer residents, but it's not as bad as it used to be, at least not from what my dad tells me.

My dad, Pete Larch, is the kind of tall, handsome older guy you can tell was gangly and too angular as a kid. My friend Vivian says it's like Kiefer Sutherland, how he was weird looking in his twenties and grew up hot. (I try not to think too much about how hot Vivian thinks my dad is.) My dad runs the Larch Bait and Tackle Shop, which has been in our family for four generations. When Butler and his entourage came to town, my grandfather expanded and added a convenience store, although he never changed the name to reflect that. Despite the loss of Poppy Beach's richest clientele, the shop still does steady business. Enough to pay the bills, anyway, but not much extra. But that's okay; we never needed all that much.

I've got friends here in Boston, a good life, all things considered, but I miss the salt-tang of the air in Poppy Beach, my dad's smile, the fit of my childhood bedroom's ceramic doorknob in my hand. Sometimes I wake up in the middle of the night, feeling so strongly the distance between me and the place of my birth, like a hollowness in my stomach. I wonder if everyone feels this, like there's an invisible string connecting each of us to the womb where we were made. Maybe you always feel the ghost of your umbilical cord the same way amputees feel the phantom of a missing limb.

My high school classmates mostly stayed on the West Coast; if they left for college, they came back west to settle down. If they wake up in the middle of the night, their umbilical ghost has to stretch only a few dozen miles, a couple hundred at the most. I think mine stretches over three thousand.

I put my bowl of cereal down on the kitchen table and draw my feet up to the seat. I lean my face against my knees for a few moments before starting my day in earnest. We're having one of those crazy cold snaps, so I pull on tights, long underwear, and flannel-lined khakis. I consider wearing two sweaters but decide that would be overkill. My puffy winter coat will have to bear the brunt of the cold.

There are still patches of untramped snow as I pick my way through the Fens to get to the E line. I have a thermos of canned chicken noodle soup, my sketchpad, and my notebook in my fraying backpack. Boston in February can be pretty desolate. You almost forget what it's like to be warm, what it's like not to have layers of sand and grit on your floor. The snow in the tread of your boots melts into puddles that evaporate and leave amorphous salt shapes that surely hold important messages if only you knew how to interpret them.

February in particular always seems the worst. Even though December has the shortest days, February seems drearier, more bitterly cold. My knitted mittens do nothing to keep out the chill. The cold air makes my fingers feel like they are being bitten. In February, frostbite never seems more literally a possible affliction.

I stamp my feet to keep my toes from going numb as I wait for the E train. I gaze down Huntington Avenue, looking for headlights of the little green trolley car. The E train is always late. I dream about moving away from the Green Line on days like today, to somewhere with a legitimate subway line. But then I wouldn't live so close to the Museum of Fine Arts, and I wouldn't be able to stroll home late at night in the summer, the smell of grilled sausages in the air, the lights from a nighttime game at Fenway Park making my neighborhood as bright as day. With my windows open, I can hear the crowd cheering.

The E train finally arrives, already packed and steamy inside. I tap my Charlie Card against the reader and find a small corner to tuck myself into. I've been temping this week at a commercial real estate company. I rewrite contracts, get the coffee orders for meetings, and spend a lot of time staring at the cubicle walls, wishing I had real walls and maybe a window. My skin, already pale away from the West Coast sunshine, looks even more sallow and sickly under the fluorescent lights.

My ears pop as the elevator zooms up to the sixteenth floor, and I'm reminded of the plane crash. If things are slow today, I'll sit at my borrowed computer and do my usual obsessive examination of news stories. Fate is against me, though, because the office manager is waiting at my cubicle.

"Agnes," she says, frowning slightly, "Frannie can't come in—she's got the flu." Frannie is the receptionist. "I know you're supposed to cover Karen, but would you mind filling in for Frannie today?"

What can I say? I cheerily assent and follow her to the receptionist's desk. The company gets a lot of phone calls. A lot. The computer on Frannie's desk is really just a fancy phone, a way to connect with the hundred or so extensions in the office. It's not even connected to the Internet. I didn't even think such things were possible in this day and age.

The phones ring all day, and I'm sweating bullets trying to connect everyone. I hate asking people to repeat their names and who they're trying to reach, but I've been here only four days so far, and I haven't come close to knowing who everyone is. I can barely grasp what commercial real estate is. Before I know it, it's five o'clock.

It must have started snowing in the afternoon, because there are already several inches on the ground as I make my way home. I take the T to Hynes and walk from there. It's a little farther, but I don't cut through the Fens after dark. No matter how long I live here, I never feel *safe*, not the way I do in Poppy Beach. I know it's such a cliché to say you come from a place where no one locks their doors, but it's true. Poppy Beach is safe, and quiet, and I've never seen anything as beautiful as the shore with its dark, volcanic sand.

I hope one day I'll see it again.

When I get home I start peeling off layers, stripping down to my long underwear. I make some pasta, changing into my pajamas while the water's on to boil. I know it's Friday, and most people in my demographic are hitting the bars on Lansdowne, but that's never been my thing. And tonight I know I need to draw. My fingers tingle, feeling empty without the blue and black Staedtler Mars pencil in them.

I eat dinner on my couch in front of the TV. Cartoon Network is showing *The Iron Giant* again, and I can't stop watching, even though I itch to flip to the news to find out more about the crash. This movie breaks my heart.

Later I sit with my sketchpad, drawing the wolves, these silly little anthropomorphized creatures I've been drawing for as long as I can remember. I've always been writing and illustrating their adventures with a five-year-old girl, Aggie. Yes, I lack imagination in naming. The wolves were something I'd doodle in margins, and when I expanded the media in which I worked, I'd do them in charcoal, watercolor, acrylics, oils. When Tricia, my best friend from home, had kids, I'd periodically send them little books of the wolves.

"It's just so amazing that you made this!" she'd said when she called to thank me for the most recent wolf book I'd made for her boy Patrick's birthday. "You should get these published!"

Yeah, that. Maybe one day I'll have the guts to submit them for publication, but it seems like such a daunting prospect. I don't think I can handle any more rejection. It's what made me drop out of grad school, the constant scrutiny of my teachers and my classmates. I hated having my work tacked onto the boards for twenty pairs of eyes to study and point out where I'd failed.

"You need to develop a thicker skin, Ms. Larch," my advisor had said. I was sitting in his cramped office, dark and dusty, and my portfolio was laid out on his desk. I was fighting hard not to cry in front of him. *Maybe you're just not cut out for this, Agnes.*

I'd nodded glumly. "Yes, sir."

"You're going to face much harsher criticism when you're out there," he noted.

"I know," I mumbled, looking past his head. If I focused on the dark wood paneling, I could pretend I wasn't really here, that I wasn't on the verge of flunking out. Flunking out! Who knew you could flunk out of art school?

He looked at my cartoony wolves. The buckled watercolor paper had made a distinctly un-paper-like sound as he shuffled through them, more like that hollow wobbliness of disposable aluminum pie plates. I was wondering how paper could sound so much like metal, trying to recreate the sound in my memory.

"Ms. Larch, are you listening?"

"What?" My eyes refocused on his shiny, balding head.

He looked annoyed. "Your instructors have told me that you don't listen to their suggestions. And all you do is draw these wolves. These are fine for a side project, but for your thesis…I just don't know.

They don't show enough depth or range. Anyone from the street could have done these. As we made clear, we don't often accept non-art majors into our graduate program, and we have time and time again given you the benefit of the doubt. But given your work here in the last semester, I don't know if you'll be able to finish the program."

"Oh." I felt like the air was getting sucked out of my chest.

I tried to do what I was told. I tried to find new subjects, but even as I attempted to paint a trite still life of a bowl of fruit, my hands had other ideas. All they wanted to make were the cartoon wolves. And five-year-old Aggie. I dropped out before I could be kicked out, unable to face another rejection.

I couldn't think about art for some time after that, too filled with shame, too embarrassed about my failure. But my hands did what they wanted. At a restaurant, I'd look down at my paper placemat and see a wolf staring up at me. Where had I even found a stub of a pencil? I'd wake up with fingers blackened from charcoal, wolves on the walls. It was a good thing my apartment was painted in that glossy stuff that wiped clean. Eventually I gave up trying not to draw, because if I consciously did it, at least I could control where my drawings ended up.

Tonight I draw with newfound vigor, not the usual resignation of putting paper and pencil in front of me to avoid destroying property. Tonight, it's not wolves. I keep drawing trees waving with Spanish moss, a hilltop, a crumbling tower. This place...*this place*. Why do I know it? Furrowing my brow, I tap my pencil neurotically against the paper. *Taptaptaptaptaptaptap*. The tapping pencil is a blur, the frenzied beating of insect wings. I stare at the black and blue ghost streaks in the air and tap faster, hoping to make the solid *thereness* of the wood disappear altogether. I lose control, and the pencil flips out of my fingers, clattering onto the wooden floorboards and rolling behind the TV stand.

I drop to my hands and knees, crawling to the stand. I can see the pencil peeping out, and I reach my hand into the crazy bird's nest of RCA cables and extension cords. I feel around the smooth, round cables, the plastic-covered wires, until my fingers close around the hexagonal wood of the pencil. Success.

As I pull the pencil out, I feel whispery resistance against my hand, sticky and dusty all at once. My hand is covered in spider silk when I pull it out from behind the TV stand, clutching my pencil. I wipe the web bits off on my pajama pants, and as I feel an echo of the sensation of pulling apart the spider web, I remember tearing through the shroud in my dream.

My dream.

I dreamed.

Last night I dreamed. I have not dreamed in over a decade, not since my mother walked out on my dad and me. When she left our lives, so ended my dreaming. I know, I know, they say if you don't dream, you eventually go crazy. I must do something like dreaming, something involving REM, because when I wake up, I feel like my brain has reset. But I never dream. I imagine my brain just shuts down with nonsense, like a TV tuned to nothing, a screen filled with snow.

I settle back into the couch and begin drawing again. Without warning, the power goes out. I exhale slowly and set my pencil down, folding my hands together as if in prayer. In the dark, without the drawing to distract me, I realize how cold I am. Feeling my way to the closet, I dig out my old sleeping bag. I slither into it and potato-sack-race hop back to the couch. I sit in my sleeping bag on the couch in the dark and listen to myself breathe.

All is dark and still, even in the city. The falling snow muffles everything. *Hush, hush,* it seems to say. My nose is quite cold. I imagine a thermal photograph of the room, my body an explosion of oranges and reds, with a humorous yellowish-green spot at the tip of my nose.

My cell phone on the coffee table chirps, breaking the stillness. Tricia is calling me. I haven't heard from her in ages. "Hey, stranger," I say.

"Oh, Agnes," she says, sounding troubled.

"Is everything all right?" I ask.

"Have you heard the news?"

"The power's out," I say, not understanding.

"Did you hear about the plane crash?" she says. I can feel the cold clamminess return.

"Yeah, I heard something about it this morning. Out near Chicago, yeah?"

"Agnes, didn't you hear?"

"What?" Why am I suddenly afraid?

"Do you remember Ian Millbrook, from school?"

It's a name I haven't heard spoken aloud in years, and my heart thuds unevenly just having the familiar syllables beat against my eardrum.

"Of course," I say haltingly, wondering what on earth this has to do with anything.

"He was on that plane."

"Wait, what?" I don't understand how her two sentences can possibly fit together. These puzzle pieces are defective.

"He was on the plane, Agnes. He's dead."

With a swish and a beep as the appliances in my apartment take a deep breath, the power comes back on, the TV loud and embarrassing like a drunk uncle at a family reunion. I blink at the sudden and painful light, and it's as if my heart has stopped. My ears still ring with the remembered silence, Tricia's last words echoing in my mind.

Ian Millbrook is dead.

TWO
THE FIRST TIME

I was thirteen years old the first time I saw Ian Millbrook. I replay the moment a lot in my head. I stand behind thirteen-year-old me, hair pulled back in an unassuming low ponytail, right as she's about to push open the door to the music room. Her palm, damp with nerves, lingers for just a moment on the cool metal door. *Do you know that your life is about to change?* I ask her, but she never hears me. She always just pushes open the doors, disappearing into the mouth of the classroom, and I'm left standing alone in the dark hallway as the music room doors swing back and forth in an irregular rhythm, leaving smaller and smaller slivers of light and room visible as the swinging slows and eventually stops.

No matter. I know what happens. She goes in. The music teacher makes her introduce herself. Face on fire, she stumbles over her name, but no one notices, too bored to bother snickering. And then she looks up and sees him sitting in the front row, a mop of dirty-blond hair falling over his wire-rimmed glasses, uniform shirt untucked, tie loosened, sleeves rolled up. His face is soft, almost feminine, his nose covered with a dusting of freckles. He's bent over his guitar, grinning madly but not at her. She doesn't know why he seems so happy.

Cute, she first thinks. *I wonder if I'll like him.* She scoffs, finding it highly unlikely that she'll fall *in* *like* with the first boy she sees.

No, that's silly, she thinks. *You shouldn't just go crushing on the first boy you run into. Don't be such a girl.* She's not used to being around boys her age, which is why her father has forced her to join this extracurricular activity in the first place. He wants her to be socialized, worried that she spends too much time at home, looking after her poor, abandoned father. Of course, only her dad would be clueless enough to think that the school liturgical music group would be a good way to be "socialized."

"Agnes? Agnes? Are you all right?" Tricia sounds worried, a tiny buzzing in my ear. I'm so lost in my thoughts that I nearly swat it away like a mosquito. I'd forgotten I was on the phone.

What were we talking about? My brain seems stuck. Something bad. And then I remember: *Ian Millbrook is dead.*

The walls begin to melt around me. See, when I think about death and the finality of it all, the concreteness and consistency of this world don't make sense. If I can die today and disappear forever, then why shouldn't I just float up to the ceiling now? What is stopping this couch from becoming misty and immaterial or transforming into a dragon? I clutch the phone in my hand so tightly that my fingernails are turning white. I grip it as if it's the edge of a cliff I'm about to fall over. The solidness of this piece of plastic and wiring and circuitry held in my hand is the only thing keeping me tied to this reality. Everything seems so ridiculous that I have to bite my lip to stop myself from laughing maniacally.

Tricia's still waiting for my response. I've got to say something, anything. I quickly try to calculate the amount of sorrow that won't arouse suspicion: enough to sound sympathetic but not so much that she'll question my reaction.

"That's…just so horrible," I say. But my attempt to rein in my emotion results in a flat, robotic tone.

Tricia doesn't seem to notice. "Isn't it, though? I just can't believe he's gone."

I need time to myself. I am liable to slip up and react too strongly. Although Tricia is my best, my oldest, friend, she doesn't know everything about me, certainly not about Ian Millbrook. Even just thinking his name makes my heart skip a few beats, my cheeks redden. I'd die before I let her know how deeply her news has affected me.

I can't have her asking questions. I've got to end this conversation. I feign a headache, and Tricia tells me to go to bed.

"I'll talk to you soon," I promise.

I get up and pace, padding along in thick woolen socks on the hardwood floors. My hand hurts, and I realize I'm still clutching the phone. I lay it down on my bedside table.

I'm fully aware that I'm avoiding thinking about the fact that Ian Millbrook is dead. With Tricia off the phone, I'm free from trying to work out how I'm *supposed* to feel. But I'm still not sure how I *actually* feel. I guess right now I'm stunned, maybe a little numb, still frozen from the bone-cold of the Boston February outside. Besides, Ian Millbrook has existed in my imagination for so long that some days I wonder if he was *ever* real. So does it matter that he's gone? Would I even know the difference?

Of course it matters. I chastise myself for even thinking so selfishly. That's not what I meant, anyway. It's just that I have trouble believing that I didn't just imagine him, that he really exists. *Existed*, I immediately correct myself.

Shit.

Existed, past tense.

With that, it hits me. I start sobbing. I seem to have leapfrogged over a few stages of grief. Which stage is "motherfucking devastated"? Because that's where I am.

I wander from room to room aimlessly, barely seeing through my tears. My arms hang limply at my sides, and I don't have the energy to pick up my feet. I'm howling like a wounded animal, and I hope that my neighbors are out for Friday night, because I'm fairly certain the thin walls are doing nothing to muffle my cries. I end up in the bathroom, and I wonder where Ian Millbrook is now. I imagine his spirit swirling around the infinity of time and space, and I am hit with vertigo. Even my tiny bathroom seems too large. It's like I'm walking in an Escher woodcut—I can't tell which way is up. Every way is up.

I'm going to slip away. I need to be contained. I climb into the free-standing bathtub and sit down in my pajamas. Better. Safer. I hug my knees to my chest and cry awhile, my sobs echoing a little against the tiles. My sobbing sounds ridiculous against my ears.

Why are you crying, Agnes? You have no right to cry.

I don't. I don't have a right, not to cry as if my world were ending. Not like his parents. Not like his siblings.

He doesn't even know who you are.

The sentence is devastating enough without being in the past tense. I don't bother correcting the tense in my head, because it will always be true in an eternal present. He doesn't know who I am. And now he will never know. Not now, not ever. No matter if I'm able to make something of myself and someday end up someone worthy of knowing.

And selfish as it may be when people in the small town of Poppy Beach, thousands of miles away on the Lost Coast of California, are mourning the loss of their son, their brother, their friend, maybe even their lover, I weep because Ian Millbrook will never know me. I cry until my eyes throb and ache and my breath catches raggedly in my throat. My face burns, and I lean it against the coolness of the side of the tub. Exhausted, my eyes drift closed.

I am not alone. I can feel eyes on me. Who is watching me? I turn around, glancing up and down, left and right, trying to see who is there. I realize I haven't spoken aloud since I've arrived here, wherever *here* is.

"Is that you, my princess?" I jump, hearing a voice. It's a man's voice, deep and rich and smooth like bittersweet chocolate. Did I really hear that? Was it just in my head?

"Who's there?" I call out, trying to mask the fear in my voice.

I hear a rustling in the copse of trees behind me. The hair on the back of my neck is standing on end, and my body is poised for fight or flight. I see shadowy forms beginning to emerge.

If I screamed in this place, would anyone hear me?

Would anyone save me?

I awake with a crick in my neck from falling asleep in the tub. Christ, what time is it? It's pitch black in the bathroom. I get up slowly, my limbs stiff and creaky. I perfunctorily brush my teeth without bothering to find the toothpaste. I go to bed with my socks on. I'm too tired to cry again.

"Goodnight, Ian Millbrook, wherever you are," I whisper to the darkness, hoping he can hear me.

The silence feels more empty than usual.

I'm running now, running as fast as I can from the trees. Whoever is out there, I am afraid. I don't remember how this works, the dreaming. It has been so long since I have been here, and I don't remember the rules. I'm running down the hillside. The grade is steep, but amazingly I don't lose my footing. I'm also not out of breath. I'm flying down the side of the hill, and it feels phenomenal: the wind in my hair, the grass under my feet, the sun on my bare arms. It's warm here, and I am strong and graceful. I grin and run faster.

I keep running down, down, down the hill, feeling more alive than I have in a long time. My fear is slipping away. I run for hours, my body a well-oiled machine. I don't even remember what I was running from. Why was I afraid?

Abruptly, I stop running, not because I'm tired but because I feel victorious and want to celebrate. I didn't know I was so strong. I raise my arms high as if I'm trying to embrace the sky. I close my eyes and let the sun bathe my face.

When I open my eyes, I'm back at the top of the hill, back by the copse of trees, the shadowy figures. How…how did this happen?

"Have you returned, my princess?" the dark voice says again. *"Is that really you?"*

I see movement in the trees. Someone is coming toward me. I am frozen with fear.

A rhythmic pounding wakes me from my dream. I am drenched in sweat.

"Agnes! Ags! Come on! Get up, loser!"

Why am I afraid? Was I dreaming again? Two nights in a row, then? What does it all mean?

"Ags! We're going to miss all the good shit!"

It's Vivian. I shuffle over groggily and open the door. Without being invited in or even taking off her snow-covered shoes, she pushes past me and plops down on the couch.

"Lamb Aggaloo," she says, "we made promises to each other at commencement. I promised to be there to hold your hair if you were going to puke, and you promised you'd be ready at nine a.m. on the dot on Saturday mornings to get our starving grad student hobo breakfast on. Are you reneging?"

I roll my eyes. "On the contrary, you know I never promised any of that. Besides, I'm a grad school dropout loser, so technically for me it's a *grad student dropout loser* hobo breakfast. And I haven't puked in ages," I add, narrowing my eyes at her.

Vivian and I were roommates all four years at Longfellow University, yes, *the* Longfellow University, pinnacle of the Ivy League, home of the best and brightest, training ground of the future leaders of the world. Vivian and I were thrown together freshman year along with Tina the Conspiracy Theorist, Joanna the Howard Hughes-esque Loon, and Rachel the Easily Offended. Sure, Vivian was crazy too, but in a mild, fun way. We clung to each other as the only relatively sane inmates in our little corner of Ivory Tower Bedlam.

I'm not sure we would have been friends otherwise. Six feet tall, Asian, and simply gorgeous, Vivian made a formidable first impression. "The minute any of you call me *Crouching Tiger* I'm going to kick your ass, but pointedly non-martial-arts style," she'd announced during our freshman dorm's orientation week social. "More of a Great Depression-era fisticuffs kind of thing. Very *Newsies*. Don't test me." Even if I weren't so intimidated by her stature I would have cringed away from her after that outburst. But when Tina would cover all the common room windows with tinfoil to "block the surveillance equipment from the Russians" and Joanna would spend the evening clipping her fingernails, measuring them, recording her findings in a small notebook, and then carefully dropping little keratin half moons into an empty jelly jar, Vivian and I would exchange horrified glances from across the common room as if to say, "That's...not normal, is it?"

When things in our common room got too weird (which was fairly often), Vivian would drag me to the basement of Thoreau Hall, where they sold frozen yogurt until two in the morning. "I have to get away from those nutbars," she'd whisper in my ear, pulling me out of our suite and down the entryway steps. She'd yank me by my arm, laughing as we'd run across the quad to Thoreau, the sky an odd, bright shade of orange despite the late hour. I'd shriek, a little from fear and a little from the thrill of belonging. Sometimes I'd purposely trip on the flagstones, just to see if I could take Vivian down with me, which was no easy feat—Vivian's a good foot taller than I am, and built like a solid oak. She sometimes calls me her "Caucasian pocket-buddy," a term of endearment I've unsuccessfully tried to dissuade her from using in public.

We both stayed in Boston after we graduated. Viv took a couple years off, working as a paralegal while she figured out if law was really the thing for her—she only just started law school in the fall. Meanwhile, I went seamlessly from undergrad into art school but dropped out before she even got around to filling in her name with a number two pencil in Scantron bubbles on the LSATs. But Vivian loves tradition—at least, she loves any tradition she's started herself. And tradition, ever since we've graduated and moved into our own apartments, is to forage for breakfast on Saturday mornings at the Trader Joe's across from the Prudential Center.

Today, being assaulted with her bizarre routine is soothing, even anesthetizing. I let her energy infiltrate me and make me numb. She's got her hair pulled into a sleek ponytail on the top of her head, and she's wearing pink Hello Kitty earmuffs. She's also wearing rainbow-striped legwarmers over tight jeans, and a puffy rainbow vest from Goodwill. She looks like the Korean Rainbow Brite of your nightmares. And yet, on Vivian, this look works.

"Come on, come on, come on!" Vivian claps her hands as if I'm a trained dog. "Chop, chop! Shake those tail feathers!"

This is exactly what I need. It's hard to wallow in death when there is such vibrancy around me.

I wash my face, for once grateful for the icy coldness of the water from the ancient taps. My eyes are still sore. I know precisely why, but I'm choosing at the moment not to think about It. I'm choosing instead to cloak myself in Vivian's bright light. I force out the thoughts of last night, draw up the barrier. I'm afraid to think about It, worried that my mind and heart will break. I pull on stockings and jeans and then a big peasant skirt. Today I don't care if I look like the Michelin Man—I pile on two sweaters and a fleece pullover. I finish off my outfit with giant moon boots.

"You dress like a homeless person, you know," Vivian says, eyeing my ensemble with disdain.

"Are you ashamed of being seen with me?" I ask, stepping into the hallway and locking my door behind me. "And you're one to talk, Homeless Sailor Moon."

"I just don't want to draw too much attention to us at TJ's," she complains as we clomp down the carpeted stairs. "You know how crabby I get if they shoo us away from the samples counter before I'm full."

"Are you *ever* full?" I ask, quickly shutting the apartment door in Vivian's face and leaning against it as hard as I can as she swears and pounds on the glass with her fists. I make a break for it down the sidewalk. Vivian's legs are about twice as long as mine, but the race is over before it's begun as I slip on a patch of ice a few feet from the front door and land flat on my ass. Boston sidewalks are treacherous in February.

"That's what you get," Vivian nods primly once she makes sure I'm not hurt. She does stop to help me up, and we shuffle down Boylston Street with our hands jammed in our pockets. I've got a scarf wound again and again over my face, only my eyes visible. With our height difference, I wonder if passersby mistake me for a child.

I'm already pretty numb by the time we reach the escalators leading down to Trader Joe's. Despite the scarf, my cheeks feel inhuman, plastic. Vivian sprints down the escalator steps, but I'm too scared my boots, wet with snow, will slip on the slick, grooved metal. I cling to the railing and breathe as shallowly as I can. With my luck, I'll get my scarf caught in the teeth at the bottom and be slowly strangled while employees in loud Hawaiian shirts stand around helplessly and flail their arms.

By the time I reach the samples counter in the back corner of the store, Vivian is on her third tiny Dixie cup of coffee. I opt for a thimble of apple cider. There are tiny squares of a nutty coffee cake, and little pleated paper cups are filled with some sort of tapenade that makes no sense in any context at ten in the morning. It's no Grand Slam breakfast, but it's free, and it's tradition. It's actually a good day, because an employee is slicing up little cubes of smoked Gouda and impaling them on festive wooden toothpicks, the kind with the little colored cellophane flags.

We hover around the free samples until the grumpy Trader Joe's samples lady gives us the hairy eyeball. That's our cue to leave. I end up buying a bag of soy sauce flavored rice crackers. We call them "crack crackers," because once you have a taste, you end up inhaling the whole thing and twitching on the floor until you can get your hands on another bag. I imagine Joe the Trader has quite the arsenal of cracker-whores in the storeroom. Maybe that's where all the Hawaiian-shirted employees come from. I should be nicer to the TJ's sampler lady. Next week I will smile more.

"Have time to go to the Common?" Vivian asks.

"Sure," I say noncommittally, still afraid of being by myself, still afraid of where my thoughts might lead me if I'm alone.

We wind our way through the Back Bay to the edge of the Boston Common, cutting through to Frog Pond, which has been converted for the season to an ice rink. I like watching the kids on their double runners, clinging to the wall, falling on their well-padded bottoms. It's nice to sit on a park bench, ass freezing off, listening to the happy shrieks of the kids, the scraping of blades on the ice. Vivian and I share the bag of crack crackers. I hold my big mitten under my chin as my hand digs around the bag for the little sesame-seed-studded rounds of crack.

A sudden peal of laughter draws my attention. I look up, and I see Ian Millbrook in the corner of my eye — his camelhair overcoat, shaggy hair, John Lennon frames — skating effortlessly toward the middle of the rink. I drop the bag, the brown crackers pockmarking the mostly white snow around and under the park bench.

"What the fuck?" demands Viv, crouching down and trying to salvage as many crackers as she can.

I look up again, and Ian Millbrook is gone. Must have been a trick of the light. I do see a guy in an overcoat, but it's grayish, and he's wearing one of those hats with earflaps. The hat is floppy and made of shearling, so it's possible that that's what it could have been. Just my active imagination. It's not the first time I've imagined seeing him.

It doesn't matter though, because my carefully crafted isolation chamber has been compromised. Last night comes flooding back. First my lip quivers, then my vision goes blurry, and the next thing you know, I'm sobbing into my hands, trying to muffle the sound as much as I can behind my chunky-knit mittens.

"For fuck's sake, Aggles, I'll buy you another bag of the crack crackers," Vivian says, trying to lighten the mood.

I don't stop crying.

"Agnes, what is it?" she asks more gently, reaching over and giving my hand a little squeeze.

I feel like an utter ass as I mumble, "A guy I loved died in that plane crash yesterday."

"Oh, honey," Vivian says, wrapping her arms around me. "Why didn't you say something earlier?"

I don't answer her. I've already said too much. I don't deserve her sympathy. I am so selfish, trying to claim even the tiniest sliver of grief over the death of Ian Millbrook.

My behavior sickens me, so I stand up and adjust my scarf back around my face.

"I think I should go home, Viv."

"Hon, are you sure you want to be alone?"

Of course I don't *want* to be alone, but I am disgusted with myself. *I am not fit to be around people*, I think. *I took someone else's grief and pretended it was mine.*

I can't get back to my apartment quickly enough. I race up the stairs and do what I do best: Google the shit out of the crash. The black boxes still haven't been found. Nearly two hundred people dead. Ian Millbrook's name is mentioned in most of the articles, because he was probably the most famous guy on the plane, part of the B-, C-, or possibly D-list of up-and-coming musicians. I check out online papers, going from the Associated Press and Reuters to the bigger Bay Area newspapers right on down to the *Poppy Beach Dispatch*.

Of course it's the main headline on the *Poppy Beach Dispatch* website. This is huge news. Ian Millbrook is the town's biggest success story—Théophile Butler excepted, of course. My eye zones in on a small paragraph near the end of the article on Ian Millbrook: *A memorial service for Ian Millbrook will be held on Tuesday at Butler Academy, in the auditorium.*

He doesn't even know who you are, I remind myself.

I don't care. I need to say goodbye.

And before I know it, I've booked myself a plane ticket.

I'm going back to Poppy Beach.

THREE
RETURNING

I am living in a state of extreme nausea. My head is a hot explosion of disaster images, worst-case scenarios, and prickly panic, but below my neck I'm cold and numb. When I walk, I can't feel my feet, only the vibrations that travel up my body. I feel like the Tin Man, hollow inside, which makes me think of T. S. Eliot's "The Hollow Men," which is fitting, as my head feels filled with straw. Alas!

Am I the Tin Man or the Scarecrow, then? Or maybe I'm the Cowardly Lion. That's the most likely. Where will I find the courage to do what I have to do? There will be no *Wizard ex machina* for me. Oh, but didn't he tell the Lion that he didn't need the Wizard? That he'd had the courage all along?

Bullshit.

I'm going to get on a plane. I'm going to get on a plane on a flight path roughly over where Ian Millbrook died. But I will do it for him. I will do it because I need to say goodbye. I will do it because I want to be sure that this has happened. If I see the casket, if I see the freshly dug grave, the dark, moist earth, then maybe I will believe.

I call my dad right after I've clicked the confirm button on my flight. My keyboard is slick with sweat from my clammy hands, and I'm already exhausted from booking the plane ticket. It's is no easy task, obviously, given my phobia. There's a regional airport about two hours north of Poppy Beach, but not even Ian Millbrook could get me to step foot on a propeller plane. No way. So I've got to fly to the nearest big airport, San Francisco International, a four-hour drive away.

I've done a lot of research over the years. Your chances of being in a crash rise dramatically the more takeoffs and landings you add onto your itinerary, so it would logically follow that it's better to take a direct flight. But nothing is ever that simple. Three carriers fly nonstop from Boston to San Francisco International, but only one of those is a major airline. Smaller carriers are less safe than the major ones, which have flights in the millions, not tens of thousands. Then again, the larger carriers often outsource to smaller companies to save money, so just because you have a reservation with one of the big four or five doesn't mean you have the numbers and statistics of the big company behind you. I had to check all the airline fatality incidents on Airsafe.com and weigh my options.

Of the three airlines that fly directly to SFO, two have a pilots' union, and one does not. I know these things because I lurk on fear-of-flying message boards. I've been told it's safer to go with unionized airlines. But the major airline has had more fatal "incidents" (that's their term, and makes it sound more like a bar brawl or finding out your friend has been sleeping with your boyfriend than a catastrophic loss of life) in the last couple years than I am comfortable with. The smaller airline with the pilots' union hasn't been around long enough for me to feel the statistics mean anything. And nevermind just picking an airline—I've got to consider aircraft. The Boeing 757 is fatality-free in the US. Airbuses scare me, but the accident on that A300 a while back happened due to a rudder problem from flying in the wake of a larger plane. So, with a little hesitation and a lot of dread, I picked the airline without a pilots' union. It's not a 757; it's an Airbus. But it's an Airbus that is, so far, fatality-free in the States. I hate this so much. Every time I book a ticket, I feel like I'm playing Russian roulette.

There are times I hope that I am just being paranoid about it. Of course flying is safe. How can the plane *not* fly? It's pure physics, not subject to the frailty of human inadequacy. It's the infallibility of the Bernoulli effect and other stuff I don't understand. But I also don't understand how such a large, heavy piece of machinery can stay in the air. And because I don't believe in it, I worry I'll be punished—punished for my lack of faith.

Maybe he was afraid too. Maybe lack of faith is what killed Ian Millbrook.

"Dad?" I say, after he gruffly answers on the fifth ring. His voice sounds rough, like maybe he hasn't spoken to anyone all day. He's not much of a phone person, so we don't talk too often. I don't have much to say to him either, actually, but I do miss him a lot. I miss being in a room with him, just sitting quietly together. Of course, I haven't been home in years, but I remember high school, how I'd sit on the couch with a book or my homework, and Dad would be walking through on his way to refill his drink or grab his checkbook to pay bills, and he'd just…pat me on the head or something as he walked by. Like, "Hey, kid, I may not be able to talk to you, but I sure love you a whole lot." All that in a little pat, a little ruffle of the hair, a hand gently laid on a shoulder.

When I call him on the phone, it's not the same. We both feel obligated to speak, and that's just not who we are. I wish it would be okay to call him up and just sit in silence for an hour, listening to each other breathe. I would be able to hear the TV in the background, no doubt tuned to some sports channel, and I could imagine Dad sitting there with a TV dinner and a crappy beer my Longfellow classmates would drink only with hipster irony.

I hope he isn't lonely, but I never ask. I'm pretty sure he is.

He's come out to visit me a few times, once it became clear that I wasn't coming home because I was too afraid to fly. I've managed to take short flights, nothing more than two hours. But I could not bear the thought of flying seven hours over lakes, rivers, mountain ranges. Too many places to die. So Dad would come to me. As if it were better, somehow, to place my dad in danger. When it comes down to it, I guess I'm pretty selfish.

He came every Parents' Weekend at Longfellow, looking bewildered but so proud that his daughter was attending the most prestigious university in the country. He'd stop by the school bookstore and stock up on *I'm a Longfellow Dad* sweatshirts, key rings, and coffee mugs. He bought overpriced Longfellow University bumper stickers, although I couldn't imagine them on the back of the old bait shop truck. I'd show him around campus and point out the buildings where famous poets and scholars, patriots and presidents had studied, had slept, even supposedly had lost their virginities. He wandered, wide-eyed, reverently taking everything in.

But it killed me a little to see him struggling to fit in when my friends, our parents, and I would all go to dinner together. Dad would wear his one faded, outdated suit—his go-to suit for weddings and funerals—the pants hemmed just a little too short, the blazer cuffs a little too long. While the other parents would try to decide which wine would go best with the meal of dishes Dad couldn't even pronounce, he would sit and stare at his hands folded neatly at his place, jiggle his knee under the table, and wish he were invisible. He never said as much, obviously, but I knew that look, because I did it too.

Dad clears his throat. "Agnes! I was just watching the game."

I smile a little to myself, because of course he is. That is home. That is familiar. "Dad, I'm coming home on Monday."

I can hear Dad choke and sputter a little. I wish I were there to pound his back hard. "Are you okay, Dad?"

"Ags—really? Do you think you can do it?"

No. No, I don't, actually. But I know I have to.

"I'll be there Monday. Do you think you can pick me up from SFO? I know it's far. I'm sorry I can't fly into Arcata, but I—"

"Of course, Ags, no problem. It…it'll be good to see you."

Hanging in the silence is the question he is wondering but won't dare ask. He wants to know why. Why now? What's changed?

Everything. And nothing.

I figure I'm going to have to start answering some questions sooner or later, so I just offer, "Uh, you heard about that guy from Poppy Beach? In the plane crash?" I can't even say his name out loud. It's too precious, too secret. I button it up somewhere deep in my chest.

"Isn't it awful?" says Dad, echoing Tricia's words almost exactly.

"I…I think I'd like to go to the memorial service. He was in my class."

"Of course, Ags. That's…good of you. I'm sorry," he offers awkwardly in sympathy. Even over the phone I know he's not sure where to look, like he's avoiding making eye contact even though I'm not in the room with him. He's probably wondering why, after all this time, the death of someone he thinks I barely know would be the reason I'm grappling with my phobia to fly home. I bet he is wondering, on a level deeper than words, why *he* isn't enough for me to be so brave.

It breaks my heart to think of him sitting alone in our joyless house, thinking he's not good enough, so I just say, "I miss you, Dad."

"You too, kiddo."

"See you Monday." And that's that.

I love you, Dad, I add in the silence of my heart after he's hung up the phone.

I lie in bed for hours and stare at the ceiling. I can't sleep, too upset about Ian Millbrook and too scared about the flight. I keep thinking of "The Hollow Men" and scarecrows and wondering if death feels cold, if Ian Millbrook is freezing at the bottom of Lake Michigan.

I drift asleep, shivering.

I'm here again on the hilltop. Why can't I escape? The shadows hover in the trees. I can hear branches snapping underfoot, and soon I see a pair of eyes glowing like embers. I no longer am capable of running. I am fixed to this spot on the earth like a scarecrow on a stake.

"It is you; I am sure of it now," says the voice, and the shadow emerges.

Incapable of phonation, I find myself whispering, "I am here."

He is here too.

Sunday morning. I don't want to get dressed. I don't want time to move forward, because if time moves forward, I will eventually be on a plane. I eat nothing but cereal all day. And I draw. Vivian calls around lunchtime, but I don't answer the phone. I'm ashamed to be around her right now. I know she'll ask me how I'm doing, how I'm coping, because she is a good friend like that. I don't want her to know how ridiculous I am.

I do, however, leave a chickenshit voicemail with my temp agency, telling them that I have to leave town suddenly and won't be able to work next week. "There's been a death," I say, free to pretend that I'm remotely involved and mourning legitimately when I talk to these strangers. I probably won't be welcome back at the commercial real estate place for leaving on such short notice, but there'll always be another job. There's always another job — another job for the easily replaced — the same way it'll be easy for the commercial real estate place to replace my unremarkable self.

I let the pencil fly over the paper, barely even looking as I sketch. It's that place again, the place from my dream. I'm still shaken about the sudden return of my dreaming. Why now?

Poppy Beach is already hidden behind rocky hills and impenetrable forests, but when my mother Shelly walked out on us, she didn't just take away her duffel bag crammed with her ridiculous, trying-too-hard clothing; she took with her the very light from inside the house. We were plunged into darkness, one that seeped even into my sleep, leaving my mind as dark and silent as a black hole.

I was just five years old.

As children will do, I thought it was something I'd done that had driven her away. If only I'd been smarter, or prettier, or less *me*, maybe I would have been enough to make her stay. Dad was no help. I couldn't articulate what I was feeling, and even if I could, Dad wouldn't have been able to comfort me with his words. He was practically catatonic anyway.

What he could do was take me to the lake to fish, as boring as it was. I think he felt sheepish about it, helpless, unable to think of any other activity we could do together, but the truth was that I liked to be by him, to sit in the boat, lean against his warmth. I would be exhausted from having to get up before the dawn, and having no interest in the actual act of fishing, I'd eventually curl onto my side in the little rowboat and rest. The gentle rocking made me feel like Shelly was lulling me to sleep the way she'd still done when I was sick. Five years old wasn't too old to be babied when I had a tummy-ache. I'd doze off, rocked to sleep by the lake, in a gesture that felt like maternal love but was only the ambivalence of nature. And I would sleep without dreaming.

I glance down at my sketchpad, and I see I've drawn myself: long, limp hair with messy ends, my pale, round face with dark circles under eyes open wide. I'm tied to a wooden pole stuck in the earth. I am a scarecrow, waiting for something. The question is, what am I there to scare off? And who would possibly be afraid of me?

I fling the sketchpad away. Like it or not, I have to pack. Light is falling, and soon I will have to make my way to the airport. I'm staying only through the weekend, so not even a whole week. I take the largest suitcase that will still fit in the overhead compartment and throw clothes in it haphazardly. My panic mounts by the minute.

Eventually my panic outweighs my disgust, and I call Vivian.

"Can you come over?" I ask.

"Of course," she says, not asking details, and she's at my door within the hour.

She surveys the mess of my apartment, clothes flung around, the open suitcase.

"Agamemnon, what's going on?"

"I'm, um, I'm flying home." Oh God, I said it out loud. That means it's happening. My chest tightens, and I lie down on the floor before I can fall over. I don't trust my legs.

"Are you serious? Are you going to be okay?" Vivian has known me for so long that she knows this is a really big deal.

"Sure. I've got my meds. They help. Millions of people fly every day without dying, right?" I joke weakly from the floor.

What I don't say out loud is an important exception to that rule. *Some* people don't fly without dying.

"Listen, Viv," I ask, still on my back and staring at the ceiling. "Do you think you could stay with me overnight? Like do an old-school slumber party?"

"Yeah, that's cool." She shrugs, like it's no big deal. "I brought my reading."

I don't want to talk, but I don't want to be alone. I think Vivian must know this because she doesn't pry. She knows how I am. So we order a pizza, but I just watch her eat. My hands are so cold that I doubt I have the dexterity to feed myself. My stomach feels hollow and sour anyway.

Then I watch her do her reading for classes the next day. I'm too fidgety even to draw. I stare at the drawing of me as a scarecrow until Vivian yawns and says she can't possibly read another word of Con Law.

"Take my bed," I say. "I'll take the couch."

"Are you sure?"

"I don't think I'll be able to sleep tonight." When my voice starts to quaver, Vivian gives me a hug. "You know I love you, right?" I say. "You know, just in case I...I don't make it back?"

"Now shut the fuck up about that, Agnes. You'll be back before you know it. Nothing is going to happen to you. And I love you too. Asshole," she adds.

Her profanity is oddly comforting. I sit in the dark for hours in my sleeping bag, on the couch, listening to her impressive snoring. It amazes me how quiet the city can be this time of night. I do hear a couple of cabs go by, but they are few and far between. I'm watchful, keeping vigil. I imagine I'm keeping vigil for him, as if I were his widow in another time. I wish I had candles to light, a photograph to hold.

Pink light begins to creep through the dirty windowpanes, and Monday is upon me. Maybe this will be the day I die.

I don't bother showering, but I do finally change out of the pajamas I wore all day. I zip up my bag, kiss the sleeping Vivian on the forehead, and pull on my boots.

I have a plane to catch.

FOUR
A POINT IN THE SKY

It's snowing again as I leave my apartment in the faint morning light. I drag my rolling bag behind me on the bumpy, iced-over sidewalk. I'm walking to Hynes, not relishing the idea of trying to take my bag through the uneven terrain of the Fens. One rolling bag, one tattered backpack, one quivering heart. My legs still feel hollow and numb as I pick my way across the sidewalk.

Snow. As if it weren't scary enough getting on a plane today, it's snowing steadily. Maybe the flight will be canceled, a stay of execution granted by the heavens. But why should the heavens be merciful to me and not to *him?* What makes me more worthy?

My suitcase thumps painfully against my leg as I go down each step into the Hynes station. Step, thump, step, thump. It makes me think of the first sentence of *Winnie-the-Pooh*, the *bump-bump-bump* of the back of the bear's head on the stairs. I miss the last step and nearly fall on my head, but someone catches me. I see a tailored camelhair coat, strong, wiry arms. *Ian Millbrook*, I think with a burst of hope, but when I look up at the face of my savior, it's an older gentleman with a full beard and a friendly, laugh-lined face. I look down, and his coat isn't even taupe. I must be seeing things from not having slept all night.

"Thanks," I mumble, walking away quickly, embarrassed.

The platform is crowded with people heading to work, but since three different subway lines pass through the station, I don't have to wait long. At Government Center, an airport-bound train rolls in just as I go down the stairs to the Blue Line platform. Of all the days I'd like the trains to be slow, so slow they cause me to miss my flight entirely, the *T* runs smoothly, effortlessly, the transfers as seamless as a trapeze artist leaping, full of trust, from her swing to the strong, outstretched arms of her partner. I am not surprised that the shuttle to the terminals is waiting right outside the doors of the station at the airport. Of course.

I clamber on board on wobbly legs, and a kindly man about the age of my dad hurries to carry my bag up into the shuttle without my asking. "Do you travel a lot?" I ask absentmindedly, before I realize he's in a uniform and doesn't look like he's about to go anywhere. His uniform and ID badge indicate that he's some sort of custodian. He's just coming here to work, just another ordinary day.

"No, miss, nowhere to go."

So this man comes here every day to Logan Airport, and it's just a job. He commutes with travelers humming with excitement and anticipation and grasping their suitcases, skis, briefcases: the corporate types traveling for business (despite having to work, they still must look forward to a change of scenery); the families with shrieking children traveling to Disney; the chatty, European teenagers backpacking through the States and heading back home to their envious classmates; the lovers eloping or heading to their honeymoons; and yes, even the pathetic girl returning home to say goodbye to her the boy she's loved for what feels like forever. And through it all, this man stays behind to clean the bathrooms. Life changes around him, and he is the fixed point, like the sun. It's just a job. He doesn't seem unhappy, but I still want to cry a little when I think of it, that life is all around him in this transitional place and he is destined always to stay the same.

"Thank you for my bag," I say.

He nods in acknowledgment, a little uncomfortable at having to make conversation. He pointedly turns to look out the window, signaling the end of our small and awkward chat.

Terminal C is busy, travelers and employees milling around like bees in a beehive. As I take the escalator up to ticketing, I am struck with the realization that only three days ago, Ian Millbrook was doing these very things. He went about his business like it was any other day, another trip to another gig. *Ho, hum.* I know he traveled so much that it probably wasn't a big deal to him. How could he have known that this time would be the last?

Unaware, he walked up to the ticketing counter, sliding across his confirmation and driver's license with his polite smile. Or maybe he went to a self-serve kiosk. I find myself wondering if he'd been the type to be able to breeze through the touch-screen instructions to print out his boarding pass, or if he were flummoxed by technology, accidentally canceling his transaction and having to begin again several times. I am disappointed that I don't know, that I'll never know.

Still, I am retracing his final steps. I'm terrified but also feel strangely like I am honoring him, taking a pilgrimage, my steps atop his ghostly ones, like Good King Wenceslaus's servant: *In his master's steps he trod, where the snow lay dinted.* I know he wasn't in this airport, but all airports seem the same.

As soon as I get through security and sit down near my gate, the true panic begins. This is happening. This is really happening. I shakily reach into the front pocket of my backpack and get my prescription bottle of lorazepam. I fumble with the childproof cap, nearly spilling the precious tablets all over the nasty institutional carpeting. I manage to catch the explosion of pills in my skirt and get them back in the bottle. I place one under my tongue, tasting the strange sweetness of the dissolving pill. It's still a little gritty as I swallow the pasty remnants down. Only half an hour before I will start feeling the chemically induced calm.

The ceiling-mounted, flat-panel TVs in the boarding area are all tuned to CNN. But it's that pussified, edited-for-travelers version of CNN. They remove all the news about plane crashes, air disasters. It's so ridiculous. Do they really think they're fooling us? It doesn't make us safer. And just because the airport CNN pretends air crashes don't happen doesn't make them imaginary, does not stop these thoughts in my head of my impending death.

I know I'm not supposed to, but I take another pill.

When they call my section of the aircraft to board, I am hit with quiet resignation. Time to face my fate. The flight attendant scans my boarding pass, and I'm numbly aware that my name's been added to the manifest that they'll consult to notify next-of-kin — my dad — should my plane go down. I shuffle forward with a grim determination. But the minute I step onto the jet bridge, my resignation yields again to panic. I hate jet bridges. They are deceitful. They pretend they are comforting hallways, the sort you might encounter in a safe building on the ground, but they are meant to trick us, to lure us into the plane, a human roach motel. The floors feel flimsy and hollow, reminding you that it's all only an illusion of normalcy, of security.

I make my way to my seat, and a flight attendant helps me lift my bag into the overhead bin. I make sure to count the rows between my seat and the nearest exit row. I saw on a news program once that it greatly increases your chances of surviving a crash if you can feel your way to the emergency exit, since the first thing that usually happens is that the plane fills up with smoke. *Three rows. Three.* I commit the number to my memory and visualize myself feeling around for the seat-backs, one, two, three seat-backs, in a smoke-filled plane. *Deep breaths, deep breaths.* I'm trying to push my panic back down my throat, into a safer place somewhere in my stomach.

I take my seat with my backpack and pull out my sketchbook and a pencil. In the front pocket I also find one of Vivian's scrunchies. I bring it to my nose and am immediately comforted because it smells just like her. I smile just a tiny bit when I consider Vivian is probably the only person on earth still using scrunchies in her hair. When I slip it around my wrist, it's like she's holding my hand, helping me get through this. Maybe I can't die on this plane if she is waiting for me back on earth.

It's a nice thought, but I know that's not how these things work.

While I'm waiting for everyone else to board, I flip open again to the sketch from last night: there I am, tied to a wooden stake, my arms spread wide and lashed onto a horizontal beam. My eyes look crazed, and there is a dark figure hunched in front of me. My mind spins thickly as I try to imagine his face. I shiver and turn the page. I don't want to look at that picture any longer.

I glance out the window, and the snow is still swirling about. I think about the ice accumulating on the plane, subtly altering the shape of the wings, messing with the Bernoulli effect that lifts the plane into the air. The de-icing truck comes by with its incongruously festive pink goo. It may as well be snake oil. I don't trust the process of de-icing. I don't want to die today. I clench and unclench my fists, the pencil making a groove in my right hand.

The flight attendants shut the aircraft doors, and I suddenly feel cold all over, as if I've touched a piece of ice-nine. The fear spreads along my skin, slips down my throat, through my blood, freezes my organs. I'm not going to make it. I'm not going to make the long flight. I'm trapped. I'm frightened. I'm so, so cold. I'm going to feel like this for hours, unless the plane plummets out of the sky first.

I try to remember the coping techniques I learned in my fear-of-flying class. Centering thoughts. All I can think about is Ian Millbrook. I close my eyes and try to remember.

I'm trying to remember the first time I realized I was in love with Ian Millbrook. Since the start of eighth grade, I'd dutifully been going to liturgical music practice at Butler Academy every Wednesday after school. Butler Academy is a private K-12 Catholic school, founded by—guess who—Théophile Butler sometime in the seventies. The eccentric Butler wasn't himself Catholic but had been educated by nuns and always saw them as somehow responsible for his economic success (nevermind that he'd been born into money and had always had his own trust fund). Butler Academy separates boys and girls for all academic classes. It's basically an all boys' school and an all girls' school fused at the hip like conjoined twins. We even had separate lunchrooms, and you were expected to stay in your side of the building unless you had a note from a teacher. The only communal area was the auditorium where we'd gather for announcements, award ceremonies, performances, dances, and masses on Holy Days of Obligation. And even for those co-ed gatherings during the school day, we were separated by gender. It made the boys forbidden and mysterious. And, if you were completely shy and tongue-tied like I was, akin to aliens or strange animals at the zoo.

The other girls found ways to be around the boys. They all seemed to know each other, not just because we went to the same school. Their parents ran in the same social circles, all were members of Butler Golf Course and Country Club. They might have stopped into Dad's shop for a quick soda or bag of chips, but the newer residents of Poppy Beach didn't know my dad on a first-name basis, not like the Poppy Beach lifers. To them, he was just a step above "the help."

I was at Butler Academy on scholarship, as were the other few lifers in the school, and my dad definitely was not of the elite social circle—unless selling bait and junk food to the town's wealthiest made you part of the circle by association, and I suspected it did not. He'd enrolled me there for third grade because my second grade teacher, Mrs. Colby, whose own daughter attended Butler, thought I was too bright to stay in the public school system with its crumbling facilities and underpaid teachers. (Mrs. Colby herself was underpaid, but she was a new Poppy Beach resident and certainly didn't need the income—she just wanted to "give back" to the community.) She was also concerned about my quietness and thought maybe a specialized school would suit me better.

See, once Shelly—*I do not call her Mama anymore*—left, I just didn't feel like talking, not unless someone asked me a question directly. I'd never volunteer information. I would just read at lunchtime, or doodle my wolves in the margins of my notebooks, or stare out the window at the rain streaking down the windows like tears. Weeks went by when I wouldn't speak at all. The other teachers were just relieved that they didn't have another hellfire chatterbox in the classroom, but Mrs. Colby worried. She wanted to help. So she sent me home with a Butler Academy brochure and called Dad to talk about what she thought might be best for me.

It didn't occur to Dad to be offended at her boldness. In fact, I think he was relieved to get the outside guidance, as he must have been bewildered at the prospect of raising his little girl singlehandedly. He knew how to take care of my basic needs—food, clothing, shelter—but as far as what I might need emotionally, intellectually, he was worried he was deficient, stunting my growth. He was a little concerned about the whole Catholic school thing, since our family had never been particularly religious, but Mrs. Colby assured him that it wouldn't really matter, that there were mandatory services, but you could just sit there quietly and not participate. So he welcomed the advice, closing the shop one day to take me to the Butler Academy campus.

I spent the day in interviews with the headmistress and teachers, took a few written tests, and the administration looked me over and decided I'd do. I was given a full-tuition scholarship, renewable every year provided I stayed in the top of my class. That was the easy part. Books, studying, understanding—that was like breathing for me.

I was surprised at what a relief it was to be around just girls, even if they weren't Poppy Beach lifers. I hadn't realized how much the rambunctiousness of boys my age had made me uneasy. To their credit, the Butler girls were, for the most part, friendly and inquisitive. They were too young to notice yet the difference in our socioeconomic classes, and the new girl, one noticeably absent from their extravagant birthday parties at the country club, was a curiosity.

I came out of my shell about as much as I was able to, and I smiled more. I talked a little, very softly. I liked sitting with the girls at lunch and listening to their happy chatter, like the songbirds outside my bedroom window in the morning. Then Tricia, Mrs. Colby's daughter, sought me out—I never knew if her mom had made her "be nice" to me, but she always saved me a seat at lunch and on the bus for field trips. Eventually we were whispering secrets together, laughing uproariously at recess, making friendship bracelets, teaching each other hand games. She'd invite me over to spend the night, and Mrs. Colby would let us paint our nails with glittery polish.

Still, Dad worried as the years went on. I was reaching an age when I should have been interested in boys, in going to the mixers that had started in junior high. "It's okay, Dad," I'd say, when he'd asked if I needed a ride to school for the dance. "I'd rather just stay here with you."

So, he scratched his stubble, looked over the worn brochure Mrs. Colby had sent home with me all those years ago, and decided I would join a co-ed school group.

Only certain extra-curricular activities were co-ed: drama club, Model UN, yearbook, and liturgical music. He picked the one that he thought I could handle, the one that would let me hide the most. He knew I liked to sing, how I'd warble erratically while doing the dishes, and he thought that performing only during school masses and in a group would be less pressure, since he figured the kids would be bored and not paying attention anyway. I was angry with him at first for forcing me into a new, stressful situation, but that was soon forgotten as I began to look forward to Wednesdays.

It turned out that Ian Millbrook grinned so madly because he loved music down to his bones, down to his blood. He didn't care that no one would be paying attention when he played. I would hide behind my folder of music and try to peek at his left hand moving in a blur on the frets of his guitar to change chords, his right hand pumping forcefully when strumming or skittering erratically like a spider when picking. I couldn't imagine ever loving anything so much that everything else would disappear around me the way it seemed to for him when he played.

He was good at everything. He played guitar, piano, trumpet, and probably any other instrument you'd throw in front of him. I could have watched him all day, but rehearsal was just an hour and a half, and when Mr. Stefano would dismiss us, I'd feel my heart deflate. I'd purposely dawdle, packing up my music and bag distractedly just so I could stay in the room a little longer with Ian Millbrook, who would glance at me and smile politely as he passed, pushing open the door with his guitar case and heading for his mom's Lexus outside.

I tried to memorize that smile and pretend it meant a lot more.

Once the doors had stopped swinging and I'd heard the car door slam outside, I'd whisper, "Bye, Ian," to the now-empty room and wonder if I'd ever have the courage to say it to his face. It even felt too familiar and intimate to say his name to the vacant room, my mouth spread wide in a secret smile for the "I," the tip of my tongue on my alveolar ridge for the "n." As soon as my whisper had dissolved back into silence, I'd shuffle out, scanning the parking lot for Dad's truck. And I'd count down the days until the next rehearsal.

The captain's voice crackling over the speakers jolts me out of my memory. "Flight attendants, please take your seats for takeoff."

Oh God. Here it comes. I lift my feet off the floor of the plane. Like the jet bridge, the floor of the airplane feels false, hollow, insubstantial. When the plane is in the air, I don't like my feet to touch, worried they'll punch through the floor and cause the plane to go down. I slide my sketchbook into the seat pocket in front of me, tuck my pencil behind my ear, and grip the armrest with my hands. I glance around the plane, and everyone else seems calm, even bored. I would give anything for that kind of serenity or annoyance. Instead, my insides are churning, and I'm bracing myself for the inevitable fall. I consider taking another pill, but getting another one would mean letting go of the armrests. And I don't think I could let go if I tried.

It's choppy going up because of the snow, and I find myself analyzing every sound coming from the engine. The loud noises make me worried something is wrong, and when the loud noises stop, I worry even more. Eventually the plane levels out, and I can let go of the armrests for a moment. I take out my sketchpad and pencil again, flip my tray table down, and open the pad to a clean page. I stare at the whiteness of the paper while the blood pounds against my ears.

When the flight attendant comes by with drinks, I find a handful of crumpled bills in my backpack and get a gin and tonic. I pound it back as soon as she hands it to me, my teeth chattering from the sudden chill, my face flushing from the gin. My eyes start to swim, so I lean back against the headrest and close my eyes. The booze and the two pills collide into each other, and I can feel myself slip away. Finally serenity has come, because I have forced it with my hand.

I'm waiting. He is here, a huge beast, not a man at all. Who was talking, then? He is as big as a horse, but he seems to be some kind of wolf. *My wolves*, I think, remembering briefly another life, the one that is hazy and strange when I am in this place. His teeth are bared, and he noses the ground, sniffing where I have trod. I'm still immobile. He circles me slowly, sniffing the whole way.

"*You look different, my princess, but you smell the same.*" I can feel his voice boring into my brain.

I don't think he will attack me, but I am not certain.

"Do you know me?" I ask haltingly. My voice crackles like crumbling ash.

"*I have known you since before I was born,*" he says.

"But have we met?"

"*You Named me, so you created me.*"

I have no idea what he means. "And what is your name?" I ask.

His glowing eyes seem to fade a little. "*You do not remember my name?*"

"I...I'm sorry, I'm just so confused. I feel like I've been here, but can't remember for sure." It's rather strange conversing this way, as I speak out loud to this gigantic wolf and he answers directly into my head. Maybe I'm imagining it all.

"Are you really speaking to me?"

"*Are you?*"

"Of course I am. I'm speaking out loud. I'm not even sure I'm hearing you, or if I'm making it up. Can you really talk? Is this real?"

"*What is real?*"

I don't have an answer for that, as nothing in this life or that hazy other life seems real. Nothing I know is concrete or solid or unchanging, except for death.

I decide to ask something else that's been bothering me. "And why do you call me *princess?* Why am I *your* princess, or any princess at all?"

"*You created me. I serve you. I protect you. You are my princess,*" he says simply.

None of this makes sense. "Why can't I remember anything?" I ask, sitting down and holding my head in my hands.

"*You've been gone a long time,*" he says with a little bit of a snarl.

The plane drops sickeningly, and I wake up, gasping, my heart stuttering. It's happening. It's happening now.

"Don't like flying, huh?" says a voice on my left. I turn and see a man about my age looking at me with an amused expression.

I shake my head. I can't form words.

"Don't worry. It's just a little turbulence. The pilot even came on and said something about it a few seconds ago while you were asleep. You've been sleeping a long time," he adds. His words sound oddly familiar.

I nod and look out the window. The plane's leveled out again. Outside I see a carpet of blindingly bright white clouds not so far below the plane, and I can imagine I am skimming over Antarctica, an expanse of snow and ice, and it's kind of bleak and beautiful all at once. I put my hand up to the window and am surprised at how cold it feels. I can see the shadow of the plane on the clouds, and I am struck by how small the plane looks. I look around me again, and from the inside, the plane seems so large. I imagine myself hurtling through the sky, a tiny point in this large plane, the plane a tiny point in the enormous sky, the earth a tiny point in the universe, and beyond that? It is too frightening to contemplate.

"How do you do that, anyway?" the man cuts in again.

"Do what?"

"Draw while you sleep."

I look down at my sketchpad, and I've drawn a majestic, gigantic wolf with enormous fangs. *I know him*, I think. "Some people sleep-walk," I reply with a shrug, knowing I haven't answered his question.

He is quiet the rest of the flight.

The flight attendants scurry around and get us to put our tray tables and seat-backs up, as we begin to make our descent into San Francisco. I slip my sketchbook again into the seat-back pocket, the pencil in my hair. It will be over soon. When the pilot commands the flight crew to take their seats as we make our final descent, I want to cry with relief. Statistically I know that descents are about as dangerous as ascents, but I am just so glad to be coming down toward the ground slowly, gently, like drifting snow. After all, it's not the dying itself that I'm afraid of most—it's the falling. It's the falling and being aware that I'm about to die.

I shudder, thinking of Ian Millbrook and his last moments, the falling, the terror he must have experienced. I don't want Ian Millbrook to be afraid. A few tears escape my eyes, and I dab at them with Vivian's scrunchie. I smell the scrunchie deeply, closing my eyes and trying to see her face, imagine her bravery, pretend to hear her call me *fuckface* or *cuntwad* or *twatwaffle* to make me laugh.

The plane rattles in a horrific way, and I think we are crashing, but I look out the window and see we've already touched ground. As the wing flaps come up, I'm forced against my seatbelt. It strains painfully against me as the plane decelerates quickly. We're here. We've made it. I'm back in California for the first time since I was eighteen.

I remove the sketchpad from the seat-back pocket to put it into my bag, and I look at my drawing again before flipping the pad closed. The wolf stares at me with shining, menacing eyes. I look into them for a long time, brow furrowed, trying to make a connection. A name pops into my head.

Ash. His name is Ash.

I scrawl his name in the corner of the drawing and pack him away in my bag. I don't want to forget.

The seatbelt sign turns off with a bright chiming sound, and with the precision of a first-rate orchestra, all the other passengers simultaneously flip open their seatbelt clips and begin to stand in the aisles, waiting to walk through the deceitful jet bridge on this side of the country.

I slip my arms through my backpack straps and stand up. My seat companion helps me get my rolling bag down from the overhead compartments, and I walk, foot in front of foot like a tightrope walker, down the narrow aisle of the airplane. At the edge of the plane, looking down into the jet bridge, I take a deep breath, because I know my next step will start my journey to Ian Millbrook's farewell.

FIVE
THE SOURCE

Dad's waiting for me by baggage claim, anxiously studying everyone's face as if he's worried he's forgotten what I look like.

"Dad!" I shout, running when I see him. My legs are still wobbly from the double lorazepams and the gin and tonic, but I manage to keep it together. As soon as I'm close enough, I let my rolling bag fall over and I slam into him, standing on my very tippy-toes so I can throw my arms around his neck. It's so good to see him, so good.

He does that Dad thing where he's momentarily paralyzed, embarrassed at the affection, before raising his arms almost mechanically and patting me awkwardly on the back. His familiar gesture brings tears to my eyes. God, I have missed him so much.

"Well, kid, how much luggage do you have?"

"This is it," I say, picking up my rolling bag again.

"Good girl," he says, "not dealing with checked baggage bullshit."

I raise my eyebrows a little when he swears around me, and he just shrugs in response. Part of me is kind of proud that he thinks I'm grown up enough to swear around, but part of me is sad that I'm growing up and not a kid anymore in his eyes. Dad takes the rolling bag from me, and I loop my arm through his and lean against him as we walk outside. It's at least thirty degrees warmer here than it is in Boston. Even though it's unseasonably cold for the Bay Area, it feels balmy to me. I stop and take off my coat.

"Aren't you cold?" Dad asks, watching me hang the coat over my arm, and I'm glad he still worries about the little things like that.

"This is like spring in Boston," I explain, and Dad nods. We walk in silence to short-term parking, and Dad hoists my rolling bag into the back of the truck. I take my backpack up front with me. I quickly text Vivian: *Am on ground. Not dead. Love u.*

She texts back immediately: *Told u, loser. Con law sucks donkey dick. Love u too.*

Once we're on the road, I try very hard to keep my eyes open. But I've been up all night, and the relief of being safely on the ground again floods through me like an opiate. I lean my face against the stained webbing of the shoulder harness of my seatbelt and let sleep take me.

The wolf is still watching me when I lift my face from my hands. My face is twisted in thought. There is something I'm supposed to remember. I tap my finger against my forehead, trying to jog my memory.

"Ash," I say. "You are Ash."

"*You do remember me, then?*"

"Not exactly. But I know your name is Ash. It *is*, isn't it?"

"*Yes.*"

"Why couldn't you just tell it to me?"

"*I do not have the authority.*"

"Well, who does?"

"*I do not make the rules here.*"

"Then *who does?*" I demand. I feel like I'm a skipping record. I'm beginning to get irritated that he won't ever give me a straight answer.

"*YOU used to have some power, long ago. Before you went away. Before you left us.*"

What? Left…I…what? I don't leave people. That's Shelly. Shelly leaves people. "I don't remember doing that."

"*Does memory negate fact?*"

"I guess not," I say, still not convinced. How do I know I can trust him?

"*Shall we walk to find the others?*"

"The others?"

"*I am not the only one.*"

"How do I know that you won't hurt me?"

"*You don't.*"

"Oh." I swallow and rub my sweaty palms on the fabric on my thighs. I haven't yet stopped to notice what I'm wearing here, a short linen dress, knee-length, loosely gathered at my shoulders. I've never worn anything like this before. In fact, I've never seen anyone wearing anything like this before. It reminds me of something I learned about in an early history of drama class. Chi-something. What was it? *Chiton.*

I can tell Ash is growing impatient. He paces back and forth in front of me.

"*Will you follow?*"

"You might kill me."

"*I cannot promise that I will not. But you are my princess. I can tell you that much.*"

Since I can't think of anything else to do, and since I know there is no way I could protect myself if Ash should choose to attack me, I walk with him. The grass is springy and fresh, and his paws pad silently next to my dirty bare feet. I can feel heat radiating from his body. We walk in silence for some time. It feels like hours.

The light is fading, and the moon rises in the crystal clear sky.

"*We're almost there,*" he says, nudging my hand with his wet nose.

"Where is 'there'?" I ask, but then I see a big, rushing river below. We've been walking at the top of a valley ridge. I begin to pick my way down the valley's edge, and I lose my footing a little.

"*You had better hold onto me, my princess,*" says Ash.

I'm not sure if it's a suggestion or a command, but I plunge my hands into the thick fur on his back and let him guide me to the water's edge.

"Agnes? Ags?" Someone is shaking me. My hands twitch in my lap, trying to grab something in the air. "Ags, we're here. We're home."

With a sharp intake of breath, I open my eyes wide. Dad's already gotten out of the truck and opened the door for me. For a second I am reminded of all the times I'd fall asleep on the way home from those fishing trips, how I'd wake up partway up the stairs as Dad carried me up to my bedroom.

I wish I were small again, small enough to be carried. I wish I could feel that safe again.

"You must have been tired, kid. You didn't move a muscle the whole way here." He stretches and groans a little as his joints pop from the long drive. I feel guilty, thinking of how he's been driving all day just to see me. He takes my bag up the walkway to the house, and I follow him with my backpack slung over one shoulder. I realize that the last time I was standing in this driveway, we had just finished packing up the truck with all my things and were about to start the big cross-country drive to Longfellow for my freshman year. I suddenly feel as though my life is a palindrome and I've reached the midpoint, when everything will start going in reverse, in a perfect reflection of what has come before.

The house looks exactly the same, which is upsetting in a way. I almost forget that the place exists when I'm going about my day in Boston. After being away for so many years, I'd expected it to seem unfamiliar and unsettling, but what's unsettling is how *ordinary* it feels, as if I have been here the whole time. As if my life in Boston is the dream. How can both places exist at once?

I walk through the open front door after Dad. The familiar smell of the house nearly knocks me over as I am transported back in time to a past version of me. Me as a child. Me as an awkward teen. Me just beginning to fall in love with Ian Millbrook. I remember walking up these stairs after rehearsal each week, lightly trailing my hands on the banister, trying to picture his long, sinewy fingers dancing on the frets of his guitar.

I remember the first time he spoke to me. I'd gotten to rehearsal early, running all the way from my last class to the other side of campus in my penny loafers. My hair had come out of my barrettes in my eagerness to get to practice, and some strands clung to my neck, damp with sweat. Outside the music room, I smoothed my hair and patted down my plaid uniform kilt. Ian Millbrook was already there, tuning his guitar. Sometimes, now, if I find myself in front of a piano, I'll play the notes of the open strings of standard tuning: E, A, D, G, B, E. I let the notes ring, and I'm back in the music room with him again, watching him tune.

I felt my face turn red as soon as I walked in, and I quickly took my assigned seat and tried to look busy, pretending to search my bag for my folder. He finished tuning and started playing something familiar, not something for the next service. Something popular, classic rock. It was a little riff on a rich, lower string, a quick turn around a note followed by a bright chord, the tonic. Another quick turn, and another bright chord, this time the dominant. I hummed along a little. God, what was the title of this song?

"You like Zeppelin?" he asked, looking up through the hair falling over his glasses and freckled nose.

"Y-Yes," I whispered, quickly looking down at my scuffed shoes.

I glanced up again as he smiled and turned back to the guitar, continuing to play that song whose title was on the tip of my tongue.

My mind was racing, searching desperately in every crevice of gray matter to find something else to say to him, but neither of us said another word. I was too shy, and he was too engrossed in his music. I listened to him play, amazed that at thirteen he could recreate real songs from the radio. Soon the other kids burst in, and I'd lost my opportunity to impress Ian Millbrook.

When I got home that evening, I tore my room apart, looking for the shoebox of Shelly's old cassette tapes I'd hidden in the closet. When I found it tucked behind a box of my school papers, I picked out her Led Zeppelin cassettes. I listened to them all until I found the song he'd played: "Over the Hills and Far Away." *If only I'd remembered*, I thought. If I'd remembered, I could have said, "Oh, I love that song. *Houses of the Holy* is my favorite." Maybe we would have started a conversation, an actual conversation where he'd say something, and then I'd say something, and then he'd say something back, and we'd keep talking, the way normal people did. But instead I'd just said, "Yes," and stared at my shoes, and Ian Millbrook probably didn't even remember my name.

I spent that night listening to all of Shelly's Zeppelin tapes, trying to commit each song to memory, so the next time we were alone I would be prepared. I fell asleep with my headphones on, slipping into dreamless slumber while Robert Plant growled and sighed and wailed into the darkness.

Dad opens the door to my room and puts my carry-on bag by the foot of my bed. "You need anything, kiddo?" I shake my head and smile. "I'm good. Thanks." I lean back against my door and let my fingertips brush against the ceramic doorknob. I've always loved this doorknob, so delicate, like something from a dollhouse, tiny roses painted beneath the crackled glaze.

"Well, I have to go back to the shop."

"Okay." I'm unzipping the bag and taking out the black dress I've brought to wear to the memorial tomorrow. I go to hang it up in my closet, which is empty except for a tangled mess of wire hangers and a long-forgotten semiformal dress still in a vinyl garment bag. I try to extract just one hanger, but they're all interconnected like a misshapen Slinky. I finally pull one out, and about seven others clatter to the floor, sounding like an out-of-tune music box.

After I've hung up the dress, I turn around, surprised to see Dad still standing there.

"It's good to have you home, Ags," he says, nodding once and heading back down the stairs before I can say goodbye.

I watch him from my window as he gets into the truck and drives back to the bait shop, leaving me alone with my thoughts. I sit cross-legged on my bed, trying to understand what I'm doing here.

I sit on my bed, unmoving, until darkness falls.

SIX
THE BEGINNING

"I'm home!" Dad calls up the stairs the way I always remember him doing when I lived here. I wonder if he says this every day, whether or not I am here, just to feel less alone, or maybe out of habit. I wonder if he just says it in his heart, hoping I'll hear him from wherever I am in Massachusetts. I wonder if he's been thinking of saying it all day today while he was at the shop, because I've finally come back home.

"Hey, Dad," I say from my position cross-legged on the bed. I slowly stretch my legs out. They're a little stiff from my strange afternoon game of statues. I don't know how the time went so quickly. I was just thinking about how exhausted I was, and my mind went to nothingness. I wasn't even aware of my body. Maybe this is what it was like all those years when I wasn't dreaming.

I get up cautiously, making sure my legs haven't fallen asleep, and creep down the stairs. Dad's already flipped the TV on. Since I was here last, he's upgraded to a nice flat screen. *Good for you, Dad*, I think. He works so hard; he deserves a toy.

"So, Ags, thoughts on dinner?" He's got a stack of takeout menus in his hand, and he's waving them around a bit like a pompon. I momentarily picture Dad as the "Most Unenthusiastic Cheerleader in the World," and I smile to myself.

"Oh, well, I was thinking that maybe I could make dinner. You know, like the old days."

"Aw, no, don't go to any trouble. We should be celebrating because you're home, kid."

"I want to make dinner, really. And it's celebration enough getting to be here, you know, with you," I say, looking down and feeling stupid. This is more than I ever really share my emotions with Dad. I'm not sure which of us is more embarrassed by the display. Dad clears his throat and rubs his hands on the side of his jeans, suddenly feigning interest in the beer commercial on TV.

"Do you think those bottles really turn blue when the beer is cold enough?" he asks.

"It's like we're living in the future, isn't it?" I say, heading off to the kitchen to see what non-processed foods Dad might have in the refrigerator.

Luckily, Dad is a cheese fiend, so there are a few unopened bricks of cheese. I'm able to put together a massive homemade mac and cheese casserole. We settle in front of the TV, balancing the hot plates on our knees. We eat in silence, but I still feel my dad's love all around me like a warm and well-worn blanket. I sneak peeks at him out of the corner of my eye from time to time and catch him looking over at me with a rare, open tenderness, like he can't believe I'm really here sitting next to him. When something exciting happens during the hockey game he hoots and claps and punches the air. I'm too distracted thinking about the memorial tomorrow to be paying attention to the TV, but I hoot and clap and punch the air along with him, like a little girl pretending to waltz by standing on her daddy's feet.

Before the game is over, I start yawning. The three-hour time difference is wearing on me, so I excuse myself to go to bed well before ten.

"So, Dad," I say, standing up and collecting our dinner plates, which look like lunar landscapes with their formations of congealed cheese, "I've got that memorial tomorrow for...that boy." God, I still can't say his name in front of my father, or basically, anyone else who knows him. I hope he cannot see how much I am blushing.

Dad nods, eyes still on the game.

"Does Bessie still run?" I had seen my mammoth Oldsmobile Cutlass in the driveway when I got here, but as far as I know she's been untouched since I left for college when I was eighteen.

"Sure, I drive her once a week to get groceries. Bessie's running fine."

"Okay, then, I'll just take myself tomorrow…unless you're planning on going."

"I'm closing the shop for the day, you know, out of respect, and the school asked for volunteers to help direct traffic, so you'd better go on your own."

As I get ready for bed, I'm struck by how much smaller everything seems: the bathroom, the sink, the medicine cabinet, even the chipped soap dish. Have I grown so much, or is it just from living in the city for so long? Are people like goldfish, adjusting to fit the size of their habitat?

I pull back the covers and slide in. The sheets smell fresh, and my heart catches a bit thinking of my dad doing the laundry and making up my bed for my arrival. He shouldn't have gone to all that trouble for me.

The moonlight behind the fir trees casts strange shadows on my walls, feathery, claw-like, alive. Are these the shadows I remember from my youth? While Dad's house feels smaller, the trees have grown in my absence, and I feel dwarfed by these shadows. I curl onto my side, feeling like Gretel, lost and alone in the woods with her brother. As I wait for sleep, I can hear Dad hooting it up downstairs. Something good must have just happened.

His unbridled joy is the best lullaby in the world.

We are right at the water's edge, watching the stream swirl and eddy. "So, what now?"

"*You must come closer to the water.*"

I take two tiny steps forward. The land is damp and muddy and squishes between my toes.

"*What can you see there?*"

I lean in, careful not to slip, and I can see my reflection on the rippling surface of the stream.

"Just me. And a lot of water."

"*You are not close enough,*" he says sternly, and I take another tiny step. "*Look again.*"

As I lean forward again, the wolf gets up on his hind legs and leaps at me with his front paws. Against that force, I have no choice but to tumble into the water.

I don't have time enough to figure out if I feel betrayed or merely surprised before my body slaps hard against the water, knocking the breath out of me. The shock of the cold nearly stops my heart, and I've already taken in a big gulp of water into my lungs. *I am going to die here*, I think.

I'm choking and trying to come up for air, but eventually I stop struggling. I stop breathing. My linen dress floats up and around me like swirls of cream poured into a cup of coffee. I begin to sink to the bottom. I am dying. And I begin to see.

I can remember who I am.

In my mind's eye I see the hilltop where I woke up in my shroud a few nights ago, but it's no longer in ruins. The place is built with some sort of white stone, so bright that I'm squinting. *Oread's Keep*, I think, and I know that is the name of this place. I am just a child, a small child, but I have a bow in my hand and a quiver of arrows slung across my back.

I am not afraid of anything. I stand on top of the tower with an arrow on the string, always ready. I am the guardian of this place, and this place and its creatures are mine. I am Princess Aggie.

As I continue to drift in the current, I see again the hilltop as it appeared when I awoke: the rubble, the ruins, the vines, the sinister weeds. What happened here? Was this my fault? Where are all the other inhabitants?

What have I done?

I feel a sharp pain in my shoulder and a tearing, a tugging. Something pierces my skin, but the cold river makes it somewhat bearable. My eyes open underwater, and I see my blood tinting the swirling stream, little ruby curlicues almost too dainty and charming to be the visual manifestation of the pain in my body. I'm being dragged backward out of the water until I find myself on the riverbank on my back, looking up at the starless sky.

I turn on my side and vomit up the cold water. My lungs, for all the icy water they inhaled, are burning. The cool night air feels like knives in my throat. I see Ash standing over me, staring at me with his glowing eyes. My shoulder is still bleeding from where he bit me to drag me out of the stream. The wolf starts to lick my bleeding shoulder, and I'm getting ready to jump up and try to run away when I notice that the wound is closing up and no longer hurting.

"*Don't move,*" he says.

He howls once, twice, three times, and I hear rustling, leaves crackling, twigs snapping.

"Why did you do that?" I rasp.

Licking the blood—*my* blood—off his lips, he says, "*I needed to stop the bleeding.*"

"I don't mean about the shoulder. Why did you push me into the water?"

"*You needed to remember.*"

"Remember what it's like to be betrayed? To be nearly killed?" I raise my voice, increasingly furious at the danger he's put me in, and my heaving, angry breaths start me coughing all over again, vomiting up another stream of water.

"*It was the only way. These are the laws. You remember now, do you not? Where you came from? What you used to be? What this place used to be before you left us?*"

"Yes. Some of it."

"*The rest will come.*"

"Will it come if you try to drown me again?"

"*The Source works only once.*"

I'm afraid to ask how else he will try to make me remember.

"*The others are coming—can you see them?*"

I can't lift my head up yet, too exhausted from my ordeal in the river, but I hear footsteps approaching. I sense two more wolves as large as Ash, and I somehow know they are approaching me with teeth bared, suspicious, hackles raised. With my eyes closed, I feel the heat-print of their bodies.

"*Are you sure?*" asks one of them. A female voice. "*She was a child. This one could be an imposter,*" the voice says.

I look around but can't see who is speaking.

"Who is that?"

Ash growls. "*You cannot see her?*"

"No," I admit.

"*Can you see me?*" asks a third voice. Male, I think. Young, puppyish.

"I'm sorry, no. I can't."

"*What good is she to us?*" demands the female.

"*In time,*" says Ash. "*She has begun to remember.*"

He starts to circle me, and I can hear the footfalls of the two others going around me as I lie on my back, soaking wet, still staring up at the night sky. They are chanting something over and over as they circle faster and faster. I can see only Ash, but I feel wind rush past me, chilling my skin, as the others circle behind him. It takes me a while to separate the chanting into separate words, but eventually I tease apart the phrase like a tangled ball of string until I understand.

"*You are ours, you are ours, you are ours, you are ours, you are ours,*" they say.

The slamming of Dad's truck door jolts me awake. I can't stop coughing. My room is probably extra dusty from having been vacant for so long. I go to the bathroom and drink water from the tap out of my cupped hands.

I take a long, hot shower. I just can't seem to warm up today. The bathroom is unrecognizable, mysterious with steam when I finally pull the shower curtain back after toweling off. I brush my teeth in the mist, unable to see myself in the mirror clearly. My reflection has no eyes.

When I return to my room, I take the lone black dress off its hanger in the closet and lay it on my unmade bed. Once again, I am dressing for Ian Millbrook.

Vivian once asked, as we lay on our backs in the common room, eating Fritos and sour gummy worms while trying to make sense of our weekly problem set for Calculus III, how you knew you had a crush on someone. She was speaking hypothetically, as Vivian didn't have crushes. She didn't need to have crushes. If she liked someone, she pretty much told the guy, and the guy would be damn grateful she'd picked him. But she did like having these faux-philosophical conversations. I think it was, to her, part of the college experience.

"I don't know," I'd said. "When your heart does that thing when the person walks by and you want to barf?"

"Hmm," she said, biting the head off another gummy worm. "No. It's got to be more specific than that. I mean, you could want to barf because someone was really rank or fug."

"When you have fantasies of marrying the person and having a million babies?" I offered.

Vivian rolled her eyes. "Ugh, too cliché and heteronormative. Keep throwing out ideas."

"When you sneak into the person's residential college dean's office and bribe the dean's aide to let you see the person's schedule, so you can be sure you'll run into the person during the day?"

"Agnes, you evil stalker freak! Have you done that?"

"Um, *no*," I said, offended and throwing a Frito at her.

"You bitch, you got, like, corn dust in my *eye!*" she shrieked.

"It's exfoliating," I said, grabbing the Fritos bag and tub of gummy worms to avoid retaliation as Vivian chased me around the room.

After we'd settled down, I tried again. "Maybe," I said, remembering and blushing, "it's when you dress up and wear makeup and do your hair nice just in case you run into the person. And you always look for that person no matter where you are."

"Bingo," said Vivian. "You are like Samuel Fucking Johnson but way cuter. Way less like a melting-bladder-like old dead British dude."

"That guy is British? And dead? Like, the motherfucking snakes on the motherfucking plane guy?"

"Not Samuel *Jackson*," Vivian said, laughing. "Samuel *Johnson*, the dictionary dude."

"Of course," I said, bursting into giggles. Eventually we went back to our problem sets, our stomachs sore from laughter and junk food. I was distracted, though, remembering Butler Academy.

A few months after I met Ian Millbrook, Wednesdays — that is, rehearsal nights — became dress-up days for me. I wonder now if anyone else noticed. I brushed my hair — one hundred strokes — scrubbed my face until it glowed, made sure to wear earrings and lip gloss, and even dabbed a little tween-marketed "cologne spray" from cvs behind my ears. Times like this, I'd wished Shelly had stuck around to advise me.

There wasn't much I could do about the school uniform, but I spent Tuesday evenings ironing my shirt and kilt. I shined my scuffed shoes. I probably had looked like a colossal dork. I think of all this now as I look at my black dress on the bed, as I prepare, for the last time, to dress to meet Ian Millbrook.

I step into the lined silk dress and zip up the back. I hop and slither into the unworn pair of pantyhose I purchased a few years ago for an interview I never bothered showing up for, the one for an academic publisher in Boston. I brush my hair, one hundred strokes, and slick on some lip gloss. I even curl my eyelashes. *Who do you think is going to see you?* I ask myself, but I put on mascara anyway. I pull the comforter back up on my bed and sit on the edge, breathing deeply for a few minutes before I slip on my black heels and head out the door.

Bessie the Oldsmobile, boat-like and majestic, waits for me like an old friend. As I climb in, my leg catches on a rusty patch by the door, and my pantyhose runs. No big surprise there. Pantyhose and I are often soon parted.

I sit with my hands on the wheel for a long time, the key in the ignition. It could be any day in high school. I could be driving to a long, boring day in AP English, AP calculus, AP everything, hoping to catch sight of Ian Millbrook in the parking lot, trying to spot his blond floppy bird's nest of hair across the auditorium toward the boys' side of the room during announcements.

Instead, I am driving to Butler Academy to say goodbye forever. I am driving to see him and not see him. Or rather, to see him, but with the knowledge that he will not see me.

And in that way, this day is already very, very familiar.

SEVEN
LOOKING FOR THE BODY

The parking lot at Butler Academy is, predictably, jam-packed. Dad once told me that the younger you go, the more people show up to your funeral. Is it because more people you know are still alive? Is it because people want to gawk? Or is it because they want to convince themselves that you bear no resemblance to them, that they are not destined to follow in your footsteps to such an early grave?

The lot is filled with expensive foreign cars, and my old junk heap sticks out like it always has: the loudest, plainest car shielding the quietest, plainest girl. It was hard being a scholarship kid. Even with school uniforms, it was easy to tell who had money—a white collared shirt from Target will never look like a white collared Polo shirt. My car may have been the only used car in the entire school lot. And it couldn't be, say, a cute little used Honda or Toyota, which would have been different enough from the brand new Porsches and BMWs, oh no. Bessie was like Yosemite Sam, six-shooters blazing, in the middle of the Louvre. There was no blending in.

When I turned sixteen, I didn't expect to get a car, which seemed the traditional sixteenth-birthday parental gift at Butler Academy. I knew we were too poor for that. But Dad had other ideas. He must have scoured the classified ads for months to find something he could afford that was still functional. Who knows how far he traveled—I can't imagine there were cars in his price range in Poppy Beach. I woke up on my sixteenth birthday because some asshole was obnoxiously blaring a horn outside at six in the morning. I groggily made my way to the window to discover that my dad was the asshole, honking the horn of my new-to-me car. He'd even put a bow on the windshield—not one of those giant bows you see on luxury car commercials at Christmastime, but a tiny, plain, ninety-nine-cent, drugstore-greeting-card-aisle bow. It looked both cute and ridiculous, like false eyelashes on a hippo. I ran out of the house in my pajamas, my slippers quickly soaking up the morning dew on the lawn, and hugged him. And then I punched him in the arm for being so extravagant. He rubbed his arm as if I'd hurt him, but the corners of his mouth twitched with a smile.

"I've been calling her *Bessie*," Dad said, patting the car's side fondly.

"Bessie is perfect," I said, and I meant both the name and the car itself.

But when I'd pulled into the parking lot, I'd felt self-conscious. I'd never felt so much like an outsider. I mean, as a Poppy Beach lifer, I knew my clothes weren't quite right and that I was the only girl in my class who didn't even carry a purse, but the uniform skirt let me blend in somewhat. But there was no blending in with Bessie, and I hated that Dad's spendthrift gift should embarrass me so. I hated to be ashamed of him, of what we were. I'd loved Bessie until she sputtered and coughed her way onto Butler Academy's property.

One of the rougher boys, Dex Wayman, sniggered as I slid out of the car. "Nice ride, Larch. Can you even see over that dashboard?" I was surprised he knew my name.

Ian Millbrook was standing with him, rubbing an apple clean on his uniform shirt. "Don't be an asshole, Wayman," he said. I stood there ashamed, staring at my feet. *Aren't people supposed to be nice to you on your birthday?* I wondered.

"But check out that bumper! It's rusted to shit!"

My hands clenched into fists, and I was trying to decide if I was going to cry or deck him.

"Fuck off, Wayman," Ian Millbrook said, and he peeled the little sticker off his apple and pressed it onto the most dented part of the bumper. "Seal of approval," he said with a small smile before turning and walking away, leaving me staring and open-jawed at his retreating form.

What had just happened? I walked to the bumper of my car, and after making sure no one was around, ran my finger over the apple sticker. He'd never given me anything before—what reason had he? I knew it was just a stupid little sticker from his apple, but already it was like a holy relic to me.

I had a banana in my brown bag lunch, so I peeled the Chiquita sticker off of that and put it next to his apple sticker. Every morning I put another sticker on there, and pretty soon everyone in the school was doing it, whether or not I was by the car. The bumper was soon covered with fruit stickers of all kinds, and Bessie became a sort-of mascot for the school. No one ribbed me for it after that, and even people who didn't know my name knew I was "the girl with the bumper."

And it was all because of Ian Millbrook.

I spent ages thinking about it. I still wondered now. Why had he done it? It wasn't because of me, I don't think. I think it was because he hated injustice. That was right around the time his parents had adopted that little girl—Meg, I think her name was. I'd heard that Mr. and Mrs. Millbrook had always wanted a girl. Ian Millbrook had a brother, Benjamin, a few years behind us.

I don't know how Meg Millbrook came into their lives, but something wasn't right about her. Her eyes were haunted. Word on the street was that something awful had happened to her birth mother. She acted like a frightened, wild thing, and she did not speak. I didn't see her much because she needed to go to a special school, but I always felt drawn to her, or at least the *idea* of her, remembering too well what it was like not to want to talk to anyone.

At lunchtime, I'd try to sit near the girls who knew Ian Millbrook better: the country club girls. Although Tricia was a country club girl too, I didn't dare ask her questions about the Millbrooks, and Tricia, I think, didn't volunteer country club gossip because she didn't want me to feel left out—not to mention that she was too nice to spread gossip anyway. Most lunches, Tricia and I would sit together, and my back would be toward the popular girls' table. I'd pretend to be listening to Tricia, but I'd really be eavesdropping, trying to find any crumb of information about Ian Millbrook that I could hoard away in my heart. It was like I was trying to make a portrait of him in my mind, a mosaic made of overheard snatches of conversation.

"She's totally weird. Kind of creepy," Butler's queen bee had said. "My mom and I were over the other day, and she just stared at us."

"Is she retarded or something?" The queen bee's second-in-command was not known for her compassion.

"I don't know. Mom said the doctors told the Millbrooks that they didn't think there was anything physically wrong with her, just that she didn't talk. No one's ever heard her say anything. They called it something...*something* mute *something*."

Elective mutism, I filled in for myself. After Shelly had left and I talked less and less, it was a term I'd heard thrown around about me by concerned doctors and school counselors. But I didn't fit all the criteria. I was just sad, I think, too sad to make the effort to talk. *Poor girl*, I'd thought. I felt a kinship with little Meg though we'd never met.

"Freaky mute." I could hear the queen bee audibly shudder. "How can Ian and Benjamin stand to be around that?"

I heard a lot of people gossip about poor, mute Meg, and it made me furious. She was only five years old, the same age I was when Shelly left us. I probably over-identified. I saw Dex Wayman with a black eye one day, and I heard it was because he'd said something insulting about Meg within earshot of Ian. I was a little shocked, since Ian Millbrook seemed like such a pacifist. I also couldn't believe he'd do anything that might hurt his hands, his musician's hands. But I had to believe it when I saw him in the parking lot with his fist bandaged up.

I loved him even more that day, knowing he'd put all that on the line to protect his family, to defend this defenseless girl who wasn't even his family by blood. He'd given up playing guitar for as long as it would take for his hand to heal, maybe even risked never playing guitar again. He probably hadn't given thought to the danger, of what he might be giving up. And I found myself a little jealous of Meg, to have such fierce love and protection, to have Ian Millbrook's love.

I found myself jealous of a traumatized, mute orphan girl.

People are streaming in from everywhere into the auditorium, and there are even a few news vans from the bigger cities hours away. Ian Millbrook had just been starting to make a name for himself on the indie scene, singing and playing his guitar. Sometimes he'd play piano. Sometimes there was a mournful cello played by a friend of his from conservatory. He had a website for his music with thousands of subscribers and commenters. I listened to his sound clips there a lot—an embarrassing lot. I would even check out his personal Facebook profile for the slivers of information he had viewable to the public. I sometimes imagined friending him there. But he wouldn't remember me, or he'd find it creepy. Either way, I couldn't bear it. I'd let the cursor hover over the *Add Friend* button, palms sweating, daring myself to click. But I never did, and now it's too late—another entry on my list of regrets.

It's sunny today, unusually sunny for Poppy Beach in February. Blades of light pierce through breaks in the clouds, and it seems wrong, just wrong. The heavens should be weeping today. I blink back tears as I file into the auditorium. I can barely see, just focusing on the legs of the people in front of me.

I am startled as someone grabs my arm.

"Agnes? Oh, Agnes, is that really you?"

Crap. It's Tricia. How am I going to explain myself?

"Hey," I say sheepishly.

"Why didn't you tell me you were coming?"

I just shrug.

"Did you…oh God, did you *fly* here?"

"Yeah. Yesterday." My stomach flips over, remembering.

"I can't believe you flew! God, Agnes, it's so good to see you!" And she squeezes me hard, and I'm sobbing, because I suddenly realize I have not let myself miss Tricia these years as much as I really do. She is like my sister. She is *home*.

"I've snotted all over your sweater," I say when I'm finally able to speak again.

"Please, after two kids? That's nothing. And I mean *nothing*." She smiles warmly and takes my hand. "Come inside. I think there's room in my row. And you can meet Carla and Patrick."

I feel like the worst friend in the world that I have never met her babies. I did make it to her wedding, but only because she and Todd decided to get married at his grandmother's place in North Carolina. I doped up enough to fly the two hours there. She said it was the best present I could have given her, as I stood weaving from side to side in front of her in the receiving line, trying my best not to vomit on her satin bridal shoes.

I shuffle sideways into the row and nod to Todd, who looks exactly the same as he did in high school but with an "I'm a Serious Dad" beard. He's holding a wriggling toddler on his lap while a little girl stands, using the seat next to him as a desk as she colors furiously on a sheet of paper, getting crayon on the chipped, splitting wood. Tricia says, "Patrick? Carla? This is your Auntie Agnes. Can you say hi?"

Patrick chews on his chubby fist thoughtfully, and Carla doesn't stop coloring. "Hi, Agaga," she says, furrowing her brow and leaning into the paper with her purple crayon.

"Carla, Auntie Agnes made you and Patrick the wolf books!"

She stops coloring and looks at me with serious eyes. "I yike da wolfs," she says. "I yike da yiddle girl. She hazza pwetty dwess." She turns back and colors some more. Tricia shrugs, smiling.

The memorial service is beginning. I crane my neck around. *They're going to bring in the body*, I think, and I brace myself. His precious body, can a wooden box contain it? Can his beauty be confined within six flat planes? Can the joins hold together and not break apart from grief?

But there is no body, only a large framed photograph of him on the stage. As his family files in, I whisper to Tricia, "Where is the body? Where is…he?"

Tricia whispers back, "They haven't recovered all the bodies yet, I guess. The Millbrooks said they'll have a proper burial later, if they find any…parts matching his DNA."

My heart sinks. *He's not even here. Where are you, Ian?*

His family sits at the front, facing us: the mourners, the spectators, the gawkers. Where do I fit in? Benjamin has puffy eyes, and Mr. and Mrs. Millbrook look absolutely shell-shocked. I can't imagine their grief. I look at Mrs. Millbrook, and the pain in my chest is unbearable. *She carried him inside her for nine months*, I think. *She felt him flutter and stretch and kick and watched him grow into this amazing person. And now she will never see him again.* I think of the ache in my belly, my umbilical ghost, and I wonder if mothers feel it too. How far does her umbilical ghost stretch now? Or is it severed completely? *He was her little baby*, I can't stop thinking, *her sweet little baby*, and I put my head in my hands and sob. I really should have brought tissues. I don't know what I was thinking.

Tricia, the ever-ready mom, pokes me in the arm and hands me a purse pack of tissues. "Thanks," I mumble and dab at my eyes. Christ, my mascara. The tissue comes away with splotches like India ink. I look over to see if she thinks my behavior is odd—am I crying too much? Does she know?—but she only looks concerned about me. Her eyes are just a little misty. She's got Carla on her lap now, and she's kissing the top of her head. Watching this tender little scene of motherhood tears me in two. I weep again, thinking of Mrs. Millbrook. How many times did she hold Ian in her lap, kiss the top of his head? And I weep, remembering, as if in a dream, what it was like to have Shelly's arms around me like that, her lips on my hair. Maybe it was only a dream. I can't even remember. I can't remember if she ever loved me like that.

I don't know where Shelly went when she walked out on us. Was there someone else? I don't know if Dad knew, but I do know that he never would have told me if there were. But I was pretty sure she was still in the area, and she would usually send a card for my birthday and Christmas. She never left a return address, but the postmark always was somewhere in California. So I knew she was in the same state—to be fair, a pretty large one—and chose not to be with me, not to see me.

Sometimes I hate her a lot for that, but it doesn't stop me from feeling the ache in my belly when I wake with a start in the middle of the night. I still want my mommy. And I hate myself for needing her so much.

I rub my eyes dry, trying to get off all the mascara. I lean over to Tricia and say, "How do I look? Raccoon eyes?"

"No, sort of heroin chic," she says with a small smile. "It's okay." And she gives Carla another little squeeze.

"Thanks."

And I focus again on the service. I look at the slight, dark-haired young woman at Benjamin's side, and I wonder if that's his girlfriend. She seems awfully young for him. And then I realize, of course, that this must be Meg. I do some quick math—she is now thirteen. Her other childhood ended with something so horrible that it took her speech, and she enters adolescence now with the loss of her brother, her protector. Her eyes look even more hollow than I remember, and she's chewing the end of her long braid and wringing her hands and rocking back and forth a little. But she isn't crying. Mrs. Millbrook puts her arm around her shoulders, and Meg leans against her mother's shoulder. *Oh, Meg.*

I think of one of my favorite, secret memories of Ian Millbrook, of spotting him and Meg in the playground at the local park. I was on my way to the public library to work on a research paper, and I saw his familiar shape on the hill, his familiar Ian shape. I could always find him, because his shape was always an absence in my retina. There was an ache in my eyes until his Ian shape slid back into its retinal outline.

He was pushing Meg on a swing, and she was smiling, really smiling. I'd never seen her smile. I mean, I hadn't seen her much, not ever. I stayed at a distance and watched them from behind a tree, my hand lightly leaning on rough bark. He pushed her for such a long time, never tiring, never complaining, and she just smiled and laughed silently. So different from that haunted girl. He transformed her.

And now I look at her, once again hollow, empty. Will she ever smile again?

"Is that Meg?" I whisper to Tricia. She nods. "Did she ever start talking?"

"No," she says, giving Patrick a small Tupperware of Cheerios. "She's never said a word. She goes here now, and the teachers just let her do everything in writing. The other kids leave her alone."

I'm glad no one is tormenting her, but if they are leaving her alone, it means they're also not trying to be her friend. Who makes her smile? Who takes the time to know her? Who is going to help her figure out how to grow up?

Benjamin gets up to talk. He's got a stack of papers, and Mr. Millbrook kind of claps him on the back as he walks up to the podium.

"Hi, um, as most of you know, I'm Ian's little brother, Benjamin. My family thanks you for coming here to support us. The last week has been a shock, as you can imagine." It's weird seeing Benjamin after all this time. He definitely looks like Ian's brother, but there's nothing about his combination of Millbrook features that makes my heart stutter. It reminds me of how often I'd picture Ian's face before I went to bed, picking it apart in my head, wondering why it would have such an effect on me—hoping that if I could figure out the secret of his face, that maybe I could just get over this debilitating crush. His face wasn't perfect. His lips were kind of thin, and his unkempt eyebrows were severe, too dark for the rest of his coloring. His freckled nose was cute, but freckles alone shouldn't have disarmed me. Was it the glasses, which made him seem bookish and sensitive and *artistic?* That he still wore glasses at all, even though by then most Butler Academy kids had transitioned to contacts? If I'd just seen a picture of Ian when I was thirteen, I don't think I would have given it a second glance. So why did my breath catch every time I saw that face in person?

Benjamin breaks me out of my self-indulgent musing. "Ian was the best brother a guy could have. He knew everything, he protected the ones he loved, and he poured his soul into his music. He was going to be a superstar. Everyone knew that. Even his hair knew that."

There are a few sob-tinged chuckles. Ian's hair did have a life of its own, messy, erratic, an unruly mop. How I dreamed of putting my hands in his hair, wondering if it would be soft, or thick, or fine like baby hair. What did it smell like? Another thing I would never find out.

Benjamin clears his throat and continues, looking at his papers. "I don't really know what I'm supposed to say. I never imagined I would have to write a speech like this, at least not until I was old and incontinent and wearing my pants up by my armpits.

"Ian, I always thought you'd be there for me. You lived life a few steps ahead of me, stamping out a path so my way would be easier. So I'd know the way. And now, now I'm...totally lost."

Benjamin starts to cry. It is hard, so hard, to watch an otherwise low-affect guy like Benjamin break down. God, why did I come here? The pain around me is practically tangible. I've got a tissue balled up, and I'm pressing my fist against my mouth, trying to hold in my keening. It is taking everything in me not to cry audibly. I try not to breathe, not wanting to fuel my sobs. The French have such a better word for *sob*, I think: *sanglot*. It captures more of the sorrow, the desperation, the catch in the heart, the breath that is ragged from being torn on the edges from grief. I find a little comfort meditating on the word. *Sanglot*. The word fills, a little, the emptiness.

"I...I'm sorry, I can't finish. Just...thank you for coming. We appreciate it. Ian, I love you, big brother. I hope you're out there, still looking out for me."

He shuffles back to his seat, and the Millbrooks surround him, hugging him, weeping. Meg's face crumples, but her eyes stay dry. For a second I think she is looking right at me. I wonder if she knows.

There's a receiving line of sorts after the service, and I get in line. I don't know what I'll say. Tricia's kids are fussing, so she says she and

Todd had better go and feed them lunch. We make tentative plans to meet up before I go back to Boston. She hugs me again, and I thank her for the tissues and kiss her on the cheek.

I shuffle forward in the line like I'm waiting to get through security at the turnstiles into Fenway Park for a baseball game. If only this were an ordinary line like that, one with something wonderful on the other side, walking through the tunnel and emerging in that magical world of emerald green fields, bright lights, so much happiness and palpable excitement. But no, at the other end of this line is only despair and loss.

I'm finally at the front, and I don't know what to do. Do I hug his parents? Do they know who I am?

Stupidly, I hold out my hand like I'm at a goddamn cocktail party. "Hi, I'm Agnes, Agnes Larch. I was in Ian's class," I blurt out in one frenzied breath. It feels strange, too revealing, to finally say his name out loud. Mr. and Mrs. Millbrook look at me blankly. They don't know me.

"Thank you for coming," they say, pressing their palms to my hand in turn. I walk over a step or two to Benjamin.

"Hey, Benjamin. It's Agnes. I'm so, so sorry," I say.

"Agnes," he repeats mechanically, taking my hand. He looks at me, his expression unchanging — not a flicker of recognition. He doesn't remember me either. My heart sinks. I am invisible. I ask myself for the hundredth time why I have come here.

I feel increasingly stupid as I continue down the line. "I'm so sorry, Meg." I don't bother holding out my hand. She looks at me, practically right through me, eyes so pale and blue they make me think of frigid Lake Michigan and Ian's unfound body. I shiver. She doesn't move.

There's one more person in the line. "Agnes," I say, holding out my hand again. "I'm...I'm so sorry."

"Thank you," an elegant woman with corkscrew curls and red-rimmed eyes says. "I'm Gillian."

Gillian. Who's Gillian? My bafflement must be easy to read, because she adds, "Ian and I had an apartment together." She sucks her breath in suddenly, and I think she looks embarrassed to have to clarify — no doubt, embarrassed for my sake.

I walk in an imitation of calm to the auditorium exit, and then I run as fast as I can to my car. I need to be alone. I need to be away from everyone. I make it to Bessie and gaze at the bumper, covered still with hundreds of little fruit stickers.

Frantically I scratch through years of accumulated dirt and bird shit, peeling off a few layers of stickers, looking for the one that Ian gave me. I can't find it. I wouldn't recognize it if I found it; they're all the same. *If you were meant to be together, you'd be able to find it*, I think. I sink to my knees in front of Bessie, wailing. The parking lot is fairly deserted, people still milling around, waiting for the reception the school has provided. I put my finger in the deepest groove of the bumper, knowing that his sticker is there, and the knowledge somehow gives me the strength to get back into the car and drive home.

My knees are gritty, my pantyhose completely ruined. I kick off my shoes in the foyer of the house and go up the stairs in my stocking feet. I curl onto my bed on top of the covers, draw my knees up to my chest, and close my eyes. Why am I so upset?

I hadn't realized how much I'd been hoping that I'd introduce myself to his parents and they'd say, "Oh, *you're* Agnes Larch. Ian loved you, you know." Or at least, "Oh, Agnes, he talked about you all the time."

They didn't even know who I was.

The last bit of hope I had held in my heart, a tiny candle against the hurricane winds of my doubt and self-loathing, snuffed out with their empty glances. My pillow is soon hot with tears, and exhausted, I let myself slip away.

Ash and the invisible wolves are still circling me. Slowly I sit up.

"Willa," I say, and I'm not sure if my eyes are playing tricks on me as I see a lithe, graceful wolf materialize, knit itself together molecule by molecule, in front of me.

Now there are two.

"*Good*," says Ash. "*It is coming back to you.*"

"*I still do not think she is Princess Aggie*," says Willa.

"I go by *Agnes* now," I say.

"*Imposter*," she hisses.

Ash growls at Willa. "*I believe her. She has drowned in the Source. She will remember in time.*"

Ash focuses his eyes on me. "*Come.*"

"Where?"

"*You have much to rebuild.*"

You, he said. Not *we*. Which means I'm responsible for whatever ruin has happened here.

"*Come*," he says again, with a little more force.

Ash and Willa watch me as I slowly get to my feet. My lungs still burn from the water of the stream, the *Source*, as Ash called it. We walk along the riverbank, Ash to my right and Willa to my left. The third one, the invisible, follows behind.

The water rushes by us, a murmuring witness as we walk in solemn silence.

EIGHT
THE BRIDGE BETWEEN

I walk with the wolves—*my* wolves—until the sun begins to rise. It's amazing that I do not need to sleep in this world. I guess that makes some sense, though, because if I dreamed here, where would I go? Nevertheless, it feels wonderful, despite my still-burning lungs, not to feel tired.

I spy something as the river widens. Ropes and rotted wood. It's familiar but in a cellular and inexpressible way, like something coded into my DNA.

"What is that?" I ask, pointing and walking to the water's edge.

"*What is it now, or what was it once?*" asks Ash in his annoying way of answering every question with a question.

"Are you allowed to answer both questions?" The irony of answering his question-answer with a question does not escape me.

"*I will have to consider.*" And he is silent for a long time. I sit down on the damp grass and study my mud-caked feet.

"*I do not think I am breaking any rules.*" He looks toward the ropes and decaying planks of wood. "*This is what remains of the Bridge Between.*"

"The bridge between what?"

"No, that is, that was, its name: the Bridge Between."

"It's not much to look at, is it?"

"If it is not much to look at, that is your fault, my princess."

I? I did this? Is this part of what I must rebuild? "How do I fix this?" I ask, crawling on my hands and knees to get a better look at the fraying ropes. I wonder if Ash will push me into the water again.

"You must remember your nature," says Ash, and I see Willa shake her head in a most human way, as if she knows it's already a lost cause.

"Why are we bothering with her?" she asks, glaring at me.

Ash snaps his jaw dangerously close to her face. *"Have you forgotten too? You live, you breathe, only because of the princess."*

"What about you?" I ask the silent, invisible presence behind me.

"Me? You care what I think? You don't even remember my name."

"I'm sorry. I wish I could. I…I know I'll remember. Why can't you just tell me?"

"We are beholden to the rules. We follow you because you made us, but we may not remind you of who we are."

"I'll remember you," I address the empty space. "I don't know when, but I will. I promise." He sounds hurt that he's the only one I still cannot see.

"That's not a promise you know you can keep," the invisible voice says, and I know he's right.

"Are there more of you?" I ask suddenly.

"There used to be," Ash says, and his voice is tinged with sorrow and regret. And maybe, even, a little bitterness.

"What happened?"

"You left us."

I still don't understand, but I am beginning to believe he tells the truth. I can't think of anything to say except, "I'm sorry. I am so sorry."

"Thank you."

Willa crosses in front of me. *"Just because she is sorry does not change what she did."* She looks at me with such hatred. I almost wish she were still invisible. I can't stand the way she looks at me — her eyes bore into my heart, and I feel the weight of the world, this world I've somehow managed to destroy.

"How can I make things right again?"

"*You cannot restore our fallen,*" says Willa, looking away from me, looking far in the distance.

Ash growls at Willa, and she walks a bit away from us. He gazes at me. "*You can rebuild. You* must *rebuild.*" And he indicates the Bridge Between with his head.

So how do I do this? What is my nature? What do I have to remember? "I'm sorry, I don't know how. Isn't there a way around the rules? What happens if you break the rules?"

Ash shudders in fear, and he is so large and frightening that I am suddenly more afraid than I've yet been in this world. What is out there scarier than Ash?

"*Let me think a moment,*" he says, pacing. His eyes light up, and he says, "*Come.*" He leads me to a large rock. "*Look.*"

I gaze at the rock face, and in the morning light I can make out some grooves in the rock, too regular to be the work of nature. I crouch down and trace my fingers along the grooves. *Aggie.* That's my handwriting, my childish scrawl.

"*If you rebuild the Bridge Between, you will remember,*" Ash says, and I'm not sure if he's broken a rule by telling me this much.

Maybe he hasn't. He hasn't told me how I can possibly rebuild this bridge. Is this something hidden in my memory? I continue to trace my old name in the rock, over and over again until my fingertip is raw. Why can't I remember? I grind my fist into my forehead. *Come on, remember — remember* something*, damn it.*

I will myself to remember. I mentally put myself back in the stream, the Source, try to bring back the flood of images that hit me as my lungs filled with water.

I see me, five-year-old me, my eyes closed, my palms to the sky. My eyelids, so pale they are almost violet, are delicate veils of living tissue, smooth and tranquil, my face a mask of calm and concentration. My mouth is open. What am I doing? There is no sound in my memory. Am I singing?

I mimic the pose in my mind, standing with my arms out at my sides, my palms up. I sense Ash sidle up to me, his body pressed against my leg. I can feel his hope radiating like heat through me. Maybe this is right.

I open my mouth.

And to my surprise, I begin to sing.

There is gentle knocking at my door. I wake up, momentarily confused. *Where am I?* But here I am lying on top of my childhood bed in my grown up funeral dress. I'm freezing. I've been sleeping lying on my side with my knees curled into my chest. I should have gotten under the covers. My legs are cramped from being curled up so tightly. I have no idea what time it is.

Another knock. "Agnes? Ags? Are you okay?" It's my dad.

I'm not sure what my voice will sound like, but I'm hoping I sound fairly normal as I say, "Yeah, everything's fine. I was just napping."

"Want to come downstairs? I brought some donuts on the way home."

"Are they from Helga's?" Helga's is the bakery around the corner from Larch Bait and Tackle.

"Yeah."

"Be right there." I peel off my ruined tights, still sandy from kneeling in the parking lot, and walk to the wastepaper basket by my desk. I hesitate a moment before I drop them in the trash. Do I want to save these? Do I want to save the pantyhose I wore to Ian Millbrook's memorial? I realize I'm being silly, so I let the balled-up pantyhose slide off my fingers and into the can.

They don't make a sound as they fall, and I have to look into the can to make sure I haven't just imagined throwing them away.

I slip out of my black dress, leaving it in a puddle on the floor before changing into pajamas. I begin to turn the doorknob to go meet Dad in the kitchen, but then I feel a pang of guilt leaving the dress like that. I turn back around and hang it up properly in the closet, lightly fingering the closet's permanent occupant, the abandoned semiformal dress, while I have the door open.

"Come on, Ags, the donuts miss you." I can tell my dad is impatient to get his donut on, and I know he wants to wait until I am there. He has to. This is understood.

This used to be our late-night ritual in high school. I'd be studying in the living room or at the small desk in my bedroom, and Dad would come home with a box of donuts from Helga's.

"Ags?" he'd call from the foyer. "Want a study break?"

I'd run down to the kitchen where there would be a twine-tied box on the table. I'd use a knife to cut the twine, and after a moment of reverence, thanking the fryers at Helga's for bringing us this bounty, Dad and I would dig in. Dad would end up with powdered sugar all over his cheeks, and I'd invariably get a big glop of jelly on my lap from biting into my donut too hastily. We'd look at each other and laugh, and I loved the way Dad's eyes would crinkle at the corners, even if the laugh lines meant that he was growing older. It still did my heart good to see him so happy.

When I go into the kitchen, the box from Helga's is there, as it has been so many times. So many reincarnations of so many donuts, so many late-night study breaks. It feels almost like a religious ceremony as I get the knife from the drawer and walk to the table to cut the twine. I use the serrated edge to saw back and forth, and the twine is winnowed down, fiber by fiber, until finally giving way. I remove the twine and hold it in two hands, idly trying to match up one frayed end to the other, as if it somehow contains the secret of the universe.

"Ags? Jelly?" Dad offers me my favorite. I take the donut from his hand and lift it to him in tribute. We clink our donuts together as if we are toasting each other with champagne, and take greedy bites. It's like we're working off a script, because Dad ends up with powdered sugar all over his face and I'm laughing so hard at him that I don't notice until it's too late—the big blob of jelly oozes out of the end of my donut onto my pajama pants.

Dad laughs, watching the jelly fall, and I notice new crinkles—a lot of them—by his eyes. I'm not a little girl anymore. I can't bear the thought of losing Dad. My donut is good, but not as good as I remember, and I'm suddenly finding this ritual kind of empty, like we are animatronic versions of ourselves in a museum exhibit of the Larch Household, circa 2002. I gulp down my bite of jelly donut, which suddenly feels like sand against the lump in my throat.

"Oh, hey, kid," Dad says, pausing to get a napkin to wipe some of the powdered sugar off his face, "I keep forgetting to tell you. I, uh, I ran into your mom."

What? The room's gone out of focus.

I put my donut down onto the table, and a bit of jelly oozes out of it onto the unfinished wood.

"How...?" I can't even finish my thought.

"Sunday, darndest thing, I was heading to Fortuna; she had a flat tire right off the highway. Her hair's different. Boy, we were both shocked when I pulled over to offer to help. I said you were coming to town. She wants to see you."

"She does?"

"Told her about Longfellow, and she's so proud, Ags."

I feel bile in my throat rise. How dare she? How dare she feel fucking proud? She had nothing to do with my achievements. I suddenly feel like the Little Red Hen.

He pats the pockets of his jeans. "She gave me her number. Said it would be up to you to call."

He finds a slip of paper and leaves it on the table next to my bleeding donut.

I recognize her loopy handwriting from grocery lists that I've saved and from the cards she's sent me through the years. Why now? Dad and I have always lived in this house. She knew where to find us. And what was she even doing near Poppy Beach? Has she always been nearby?

I put my hand on the table over the note and close my hand on it. The paper crumples in my hand like a dead leaf. My jaw is clenched.

Dad continues eating his donut, getting powdered sugar all over his face again, but I'm not laughing. He sighs. "Maybe I shouldn't have said anything."

"No, Dad," I say, trying to smile. I know this isn't his fault. "I'm glad you told me. I'm glad you left it up to me."

"Are you going to call her?"

"I don't know." I really don't. Part of me wants to set this balled-up piece of paper on fire, see Shelly's name and number burn up and disappear into ash. And part of me, well, I'm just curious. I want to know why. Why wasn't I good enough?

"Either way's fine with me, kiddo."

"Yeah, I know."

We sit in silence for a while, and I listen to him chew. Finally he says gently, "Hey, Ags, aren't you going to finish your donut?"

I reach for a napkin and wrap my donut up, putting it back into the box from Helga's. "Maybe later. I'm not so hungry right now."

He looks at me like he wants to say something, but instead he takes another bite of donut and stares out the window.

Our silences are usually comfortable and familiar, but this one feels different. I can't stand it. I ask, "So how was the rest of the memorial? Anything interesting happen?"

Dad furrows his brow in concentration. "Not really. It took a long time for everyone to clear out. That kid must have been pretty special."

He glances over at me, trying to read my face. I'm sure he's still wondering what it was about this guy that made me get on a plane and come home. How can I explain it to him? I just shrug my shoulders and say, "He was always nice to me."

He nods, as if this explains everything.

"I'm still kind of tired from the traveling," I say, pushing my chair back from the table. "I think I'll lie down a bit before dinner, if that's okay."

"Of course, Ags. How does pizza sound?"

"Great."

We like all the same toppings, so I don't have to say anything before I trudge back up the stairs to my room. I put the crumpled ball of paper, which has been in my fist this whole time, on my desk. I let it sit there for a moment, contemplating how it can be possible that such a tiny little ball of paper can throw my world upside down. Eventually I smooth it out onto the desk's painted wood surface. The paper is soft now, pliable and quiet.

I wish Dad had told me why she left. I guess I could ask him one of these days. Maybe I'll ask him while I'm home. But I don't want him to relive the pain of when she walked out. I don't know. He seemed so casual about it just now—maybe he's over it. Maybe it was mutual. I'm trying to picture Dad being the Good Samaritan and changing her tire, the two of them talking about me and what I've been up to while he loosened and tightened lug nuts.

I bet he didn't tell her I dropped out of art school, though. He doesn't like quitters.

I remember the panic I felt those last months of school, when I felt like everything I did was being judged, that they were just looking for one more thing that I'd do wrong so they could toss me out. It felt kind of like when you're losing a board of Tetris, as you watch the blocks pile higher and higher, and all you need is that long skinny piece to buy yourself some time, but the skinny piece never comes, and you know you are going to lose; the blocks are going to reach the ceiling. I just bailed before the last brick could fall. It was inevitable, but at least I felt like I had some control.

I briefly wonder if my mother saw her marriage like that, somehow, like a Tetris board about to fill up, and maybe I'm more like her than I want to be. Maybe there's a whole world inside her that I don't know about. Maybe I should call her to find out. I stare at the ten digits written on the wrinkled scrap of paper, trying to decide.

Maybe I don't want to find out how alike we really are.

I tell myself I don't have to make up my mind right now. I leave her number on the desk and sit on my bed, feeling paralyzed. Should I call? Should I ignore her? What if this is my only chance to know why? To know her? For her to know me? My mind whirls in crazy circles until I hear the pizza guy ring our doorbell.

I know Dad won't call me to dinner because he thinks I'm asleep. I come down the stairs as he's bringing the pizza box into the kitchen.

"Nice nap?" he asks.

"I was just lying down, but I wasn't sleeping," I say, wrestling with a gooey string of cheese on the slice I'm trying to get on my plate.

"Anything you want to do while you're in town, Ags?" Dad asks as we walk to the living room with our plates.

"I'm supposed to call Tricia. I ran into her today at the service."

"Tricia Colby? Is that your teacher's kid?" asks Dad. He's funny, the way he doesn't remember who my friends are—it's not as if I had a parade of them coming through every afternoon. It was pretty much just Tricia. The guy can memorize sports stats without even trying, but when it comes to names and faces of real people in his life, he's sort of lost.

"Yeah. She's Tricia Shepherd now and has two cute kids." I don't bother trying to remind him who Todd is.

"Man," says Dad, "you kids sure grow up fast."

"Not me," I say, leaning my head against his shoulder. I feel stuck. I feel perpetually thirteen years old, always pushing open the doors to the music room and seeing Ian Millbrook for the first time.

"No, Ags, you are. Look at you, living on your own in a big city like Boston! You don't need your old man for anything."

"I'll always need you," I say, giving his hand a squeeze. Dad clears his throat, and he excuses himself to get a beer from the fridge.

I have room only for one slice of pizza, the grief of this day draining me of appetite and energy.

"I'm going to go to bed," I announce and put my dish in the sink. It's not even nine, but I am wiped out. This morning's tears feel very far away now, a distant memory, a shadow of sorrow. I am reminded of Emily Dickinson: *After great pain, a formal feeling comes.* There's a formal, heavy feeling in my heart while I go up the stairs again to ready myself for bed.

"G'night, kid," Dad calls after me as I disappear into the darkness of the second floor.

My eyes are closed, and my palms face heavenward as I sing. I'm not even *trying* to sing, but music is pouring out of me, music without words, without a familiar melody. I'm just the vessel for this song. I do not think this is my voice. My singing voice is scratchy and thin and full of air, but this voice coming out of me is pure white light.

I can still feel Ash's body heat against my leg, and soon I feel Willa pressing against me on my other side. I don't know where the other one is.

In my mind, I picture the ruins of the Bridge Between and try to remember what it used to look like. I can't, but I say to the bridge in my mind, "*Be whole again. Be what you were. Be what you were meant to be.*" I don't stop singing until I can feel rope fibers coming together, time moving backward, moss and mold being stripped away, wood becoming new.

And when I open my eyes, there is a tremendous bridge in front of me, whole and complete. I can't even see the end of it. It disappears into the clouds. I *did this?* I ask myself in wonder.

I look to the wolves to see their reaction. Willa sort of sniffs as if to show she's not too impressed, but Ash says, "*Well done.*" I feel the third one nudge me with his moist nose, and I know he is smiling a wolfy smile. I step back to look at the restored bridge and am filled with hope.

I have begun to rebuild.

NINE
TRAVELING BETWEEN

I wake up suddenly but without alarm. My eyes just flicker open, and I'm in my bed, wrapped under my blankets and looking at the ceiling. *I rebuilt the Bridge Between*, I think, and I'm surprised at how incredibly sharp my dream is. It's not like a murky thing in muddied water that I'm groping around, hoping to find what's hiding beneath the surface. It's a crystal clear memory, as clear as going to Ian Millbrook's memorial yesterday.

This is different.

I remember now: the wolves, Ash and Willa, and the third, whose name I don't know but whose warm, wet nose I can still feel on my skin. *I was a princess*, I think. *And Oread's Keep was my kingdom.* That part is still hazy, since I remember only through visions from my dreaming, a copy of a copy, the crispness of the memory degraded. Somehow I left Oread's Keep behind and caused its ruin. They keep telling me I left them. Did I leave willingly? Or was I forced out?

They're just dreams, I tell myself. *Why does it matter?* But I can't help feeling, deep within me, that it does. That it's terribly important. After all, these dreams were locked away for years, ever since Shelly left.

Shelly.

I glance toward my desk at the piece of paper I know is there. I can't see it from where I'm lying in bed, but I feel its presence there like a pulsing, living thing. I have to decide. I'm in town only a few more days, and then who knows when I'll be back again, when I'll be able to make the long flight?

I should call her.

I swing my legs out from under the covers and stand up slowly, walking over to the desk and looking at the rumpled bit of paper. I dial her number, but I hit the cancel button and toss the phone on my bed. No need to make this decision right this minute. If I call her, I might know why she left. If I find out why she left, I might stop blaming myself.

Or, if I find out why she left, my heart just might break.

Little steps first, maybe. Maybe today I will call Tricia. I go downstairs to get some cereal. Dad's long gone. It's raining today, and at least that makes more sense to me, the drops streaking against the kitchen windows. I think about how, just a few days ago, I was in my apartment three thousand miles away, eating cereal, looking out at the snowy wasteland outside, and thinking Ian Millbrook was still alive. How different things are now.

I pick up the old land-line in the kitchen and dial Tricia's number. An older woman answers the phone. I ask for Tricia.

"Oh, she doesn't live here anymore."

I'm confused until I realize I've dialed Tricia's parents' house. Stupid autopilot. "Mrs. Colby?"

"Yes?"

"Hey, it's Agnes Larch."

"Oh, *hi*, Agnes! It's nice to hear your voice. Tricia mentioned you were in town."

"Yeah, I dialed your number by accident, sorry."

"Terrible about that Millbrook boy, isn't it?"

I watch the last few Cheerios bloat up in the milk. "Yes," I say quietly. *Yes, my world has ended now.*

"So much promise. Did you know him well?"

"I...I wish—" I cut myself off. "Well enough," I end up saying. "He was a good guy."

"Seems like it," says Tricia's mom, sighing. She changes gears. "So, do you need Tricia's number?"

"No, I have it. I just am so used to dialing this number from this phone," I say, giggling nervously and hating the sound of my voice. "I'm sorry to have bothered you."

"Oh, Agnes, it's no trouble, and it's nice to hear your voice again."

"You too, Mrs. Colby."

Since I actually don't have Tricia's number memorized, I have to go back upstairs to get my phone. I sort of miss the days when I knew everyone's phone number. Sure, it's convenient having people on speed dial, to be able to call them with a tap on your phone, but it's relying too much on technology, outsourcing your memory to cold circuitry. Are we losing our humanity somehow by having our communication, our connections, dictated by wires and binary code and fiber optics?

I sit cross-legged on the bed and hit Tricia's number. She answers right away.

"Agnes! Hey!" Caller ID has changed the way people communicate, I think. There's no surprise anymore in answering a phone call.

"Hey. Hi. So, listen, did you want to get together today? Are you busy?" Tricia is a stay-at-home mom these days. She says she'll go back to school when Patrick is in kindergarten.

I can hear clanging and singing and happy shouting in the background. "You know, nothing too exciting around here," she says.

"Poppy Beach, you know," I say by way of explanation.

"Yeah, always the same. Do you want to have lunch, maybe?"

"Sure—the diner?" There really aren't that many places to go in Poppy Beach.

"Sounds good. I could probably have the kids mopped up and relatively non-grubby in an hour or so. Want to meet around noon?"

"Sure."

We're about to hang up, but I blurt out, "Hey, could you bring the wolf book I made for Patrick for his birthday?"

Tricia sounds distracted but agrees. When we disconnect, the absence of the children's happy playing noises makes me realize how quiet and lonely the house is. *Poor Dad*, I think. How does he stand it? At least I have the sounds of traffic, loud sidewalk conversations, and, come baseball season, cheering and the booming announcer's voice at Fenway Park.

I take a quick shower and walk back to my room wrapped in a towel. As I get dressed, I realize how relieved I am that I don't have to put on three pairs of pants to stay warm. Being in Poppy Beach is practically a vacation in the tropics after February in Boston. Of course, I imagine that tropical vacations usually don't involve hysterical sobbing and awkward silences and fears of losing your dad and being alone in the world. At least, as far as I'm led to believe from the brochures. But then again, I've never been to the tropics, so I could be wrong.

It takes me only five minutes to get dressed. How nice not to have to put on my puffy winter coat! Now I have a while to wait and nothing to do, so I get my sketchpad. I flip through the pages, seeing if anything makes more sense to me now that last night's dream is so sharp and present in my memory.

The ruins of Oread's Keep. *Flip.* Ash looking at me through the trees. *Flip.* The picture I turn past quickly, of me lashed to the stake like a scarecrow. I flip to the beginning of the sketchpad to see the drawings from before I returned to my dreaming.

There are wolves on almost every page, packs of wolves. I don't know their names. I think I can spot Ash, though — he is the biggest by far. He seems to be the leader. There's a drawing of a younger version of me, a child in an antiquated costume, with a bow in my hand and wolves around me. Three wolves: Ash, Willa, and…and the other. I *will* remember his name. I will. I promised him. I remember clearly that I promised him.

And, oh. Here's something new, something I don't remember. I'm standing on the tower, little child me, Princess Aggie, maybe, with the bow in my hand. Something is in the distance, but even from the distance, this thing is huge. Monstrous. I am filled with terror just looking at this shadow, but I look at Princess Aggie on the page, and her face is determined and not afraid.

She's braver than I am, I think, and I am a little bit ashamed.

I get a pencil, turn to a clean page, and sketch. As always, I'm barely looking at the paper, just letting my hand go where it wants, and when I look down, I see the Source, the raging river, the Bridge Between halfway rebuilt, and there I am with my eyes closed, my palms up, my mouth open. The wolves are at my sides, and behind me, where the third, the unnamed one, stood, I've sketched just a feathery outline. In the margin I've done a detail of just a wet, warm nose. I'm drawing more the *feeling* of it on my leg than I am drawing the actual thing, since I didn't see it. *Who are you, mystery guy?* I think.

The ropes of the bridge are flying through the air like something alive. I didn't see this happen, but I saw it in my mind. What else did the wolves say to me, that I called them into being? Maybe I did something like this for them too.

Maybe the book I gave Patrick will have some answers.

I glance at the old clock radio by my bed. It's almost time to meet Tricia. My hands are covered in graphite, so I go wash them off in the tiny bathroom, so much smaller now that I am grown.

I walk out to Bessie and run my hand along her front bumper. "Hi, Ian," I say with my finger resting in the dent. His sticker is under there. He touched that sticker. The apple he ate that day is gone; even his body now is gone, but that little bit of plastic and adhesive is under there. Funny how that little sticker might outlive us all. Maybe in thousands of years, archeologists will dig up this old car, and these stickers will still be there, undamaged, and they'll wonder what the significance was of covering an entire bumper in tiny stickers. *A religious ceremony, perhaps? A sign of status or vanity? A charm to ward off evil?* But they'll never guess that once there was a boy named Ian Millbrook and a girl named Agnes Larch who loved him with her life and breath. They'll never guess that it's the only thing that Ian Millbrook ever gave to her, at least, the only tangible object.

It's my whole world, and when we are all gone, no one will remember what it all means. I am the only keeper of the secret.

I barely pay attention to the road as I drive to the Poppy Beach Diner. I've driven this path many times. We even came here for homecoming one year instead of taking the hour and a half to get to a real restaurant in Fortuna, the closest big town. I can feel my face crumple a little at the memory, a delayed reaction, perhaps, of having to wear a mask of indifference that night.

Tricia is already here, which is rather impressive given that she had to haul two small, squirming children with her. She's settled in a booth, Patrick in a high chair, Carla in a booster on top of the greasy vinyl bench. She gets up as soon as I walk in and gives me a hug before we sit down.

The kids are already eating goldfish crackers and string cheese. "Hi, Agaga," says Carla with the string cheese clutched in her fist. I'm impressed she remembers me.

"Hi, Carcar," I say back with a little wave.

"It's Car-LA," she says, pouting.

"Sorry, Carla." I don't think I'm good with kids. I tend to piss them off in my attempts to banter with them. I glance at the menu. It's new, the laminated pages still sharp in the corners. Of course they wouldn't have the same menus from high school. Why should the menus freeze in time for me? There are other little changes, new lighting fixtures, reupholstered booths. Sometimes I wish everything would stay the same. Home things, at least. This place is no longer familiar.

I order chicken fingers and a side of fries, and Tricia smiles. "Ah, the Agnes special," she murmurs. She orders a salad for herself and grilled cheese for the kids.

"So." Tricia studies me with her chin resting on her folded hands, reminding me a lot of Mrs. Colby. "Why did you come back? I mean, after all this time?"

I fiddle with the napkin dispenser on the table. "I don't know," I say honestly. "I just sort of ended up booking the ticket. And here I am."

"There were a lot of our classmates at the memorial," she says. "The usual suspects. Did you see them?"

No, I was a little too busy crying my eyes out and feeling like I would die of grief. "Where were they sitting?"

"Oh, around," she says with a vague wave of her hand.

I hope she won't mention how much I was crying. I'm embarrassed about it now. Not embarrassed that I cried that much or that hard—Ian Millbrook deserves to be mourned like that—but because it was in such a public place.

"Did you go to the reception thing afterward?" she asks instead.

"No, I was suddenly really tired."

"Hmm," she says, stirring her straw in her iced tea. "Oh hey," she says, reaching into her diaper bag, "here's that book you made for Patrick's birthday. The kids just love it."

She slides it over to me. I can barely remember what I put into this book, only that I made it.

I didn't give the book a title. *Untitled Wolf Story #1, by Agnes Larch, watercolor and India ink on paper.*

I turn the pages slowly, looking for some hint. These are watered-down versions of my sketches, less feral, less frightening. Aggie is cartoonish with big anime eyes. She stands on the tower with her bow. "I will protect you!" she says to the wolves, who pile around her when she sleeps and bring her hot chocolate when she wakes up hungry in the night. This…does not seem accurate. I don't think I will find the answers here.

I keep turning the pages. "Oh no, Princess Aggie, the Stone One has returned!" says this cartoon version of Ash, who wears a permanent grin even when he is supposedly terrified.

"Let him come. I am not afraid," says Aggie, and I've drawn sort of a stubborn jutting of her jaw.

Carla's watching me as I turn the pages. "I no yike da page wid da stone ding," she says with solemn eyes.

"Sorry," I say. Man, I scare kids. I suck.

I turn the page. Even in Disneyfied cartoon form, this is pretty scary—a giant Golem-thing, a stone beast as tall as the tower. Taller.

I've drawn his dialogue in shaky scrawl, and I can even hear a voice in my memory that is unsettlingly not human, a voice like stone against grindstone, of a stone rolled in front of a grave. "*I have come to devour your city.*" Jesus fuck, what was I thinking, giving this to kids?

Aggie stands on the tower with her bow. "I am not afraid! You are just stone! You cannot harm us!" She's looking the Stone One in the eye.

"*Goodbye then, Princess Aggie,*" he says, giving up without a fight and slouching toward…wherever he came from. Beyond the mountains.

The wolves all cheer and run around her, and then it's time for a party and ice cream, and all the wolves wear pointy party hats and sit at a grand banquet table, paws on the damask tablecloth. *The end.*

Perhaps Tricia is lying through her teeth when she tells me the kids love this book. Maybe it's because they know it was written just for them. Still, I'm glad I got to see it. I'm beginning to put it together. Maybe now I know what happened to the other wolves, to Oread's Keep. Maybe.

"Thanks," I say, handing the book back to Tricia. Our food is here, and the next few moments are spent making sure the kids have their sandwiches cut up into handy strips, that lids are tightly screwed onto their sippy cups. My chicken fingers are too hot from the fryer for me to eat right away, so I watch Tricia pick at her salad.

"Do you remember homecoming?" I ask. This may be my only time to ask.

"What?" She's got a dollop of dressing on her lip, and she grabs the napkin off her lap to dab it away.

"Sophomore year, you know. When we came here, to the diner?"

"I…you know, I get a lot of those dances mixed up," she says. "And anyway, you know, I get mom brain now—can't remember all that stuff from so long ago."

But I remember.

It was our first semiformal dance, and the whole school was abuzz. Of course I hoped Ian Millbrook would ask me, but I knew that was like wishing I could sprout wings or become a mermaid or something. Fantasy world. I didn't expect him to ask me.

But I also I didn't expect for Ian Millbrook to ask Tricia to the dance, either.

They'd known each other for ages, again, swim classes and tennis lessons at the country club. Why wasn't I in swim classes and tennis lessons? I'd probably die of embarrassment anyway, and *Ian Millbrook seeing me in a bathing suit, just, no,* but maybe learning how to serve and volley would have thrown us together. We would have been forced to converse. Maybe we could have hated the instructors together, had inside jokes.

I remember sitting in the girls' lunchroom, dreamily thinking of the dance, when Tricia sat down, a funny look on her face. "What is it?" I'd asked.

"I…I just got asked to homecoming."

"Hey, that's great!" I said. I knew she was sort of shy like me, and I was glad for her that some boy had taken notice. "Who is it?"

Tricia sighed. "Ian Millbrook—do you know him?"

Inside I was disintegrating, like I'd just taken a swig of carbonic acid. I swallowed thickly before I replied, "Yes, I know him."

"I mean, he's nice and all, but I've known him forever. He's like my brother." She sighed again.

"He's in liturgical music with me," I lamely added. "He seems cool."

"Yeah, he's all right. I was kind of hoping Todd Shepherd would ask me."

Todd was tall and gangly, all limbs and elbows and joints. His arms were way too long for his body, and he had a face full of pimples. How could anyone prefer him over Ian Millbrook? It was baffling. "So what did you tell him?" I asked, hoping she'd turned him down.

"Well, of course I said yes. I can't leave him hanging." I was reappraising Tricia as she talked, trying to see her as Ian saw her. No one was as kind as Tricia, and she did have those huge baby doe eyes. *So that's what he finds beautiful*, I thought.

No one asked me to the dance, but that was no surprise. "I'm going to stay home," I told my dad when he asked about it.

"What? No, Ags, you have to go to homecoming! It's your first dance!"

"I don't even like dancing," I said.

"Oh." He rubbed the back of his neck.

I knew that gesture well. "*What* did you do?"

"I kind of already bought you a dress," he said sheepishly.

"Oh, Dad," I sighed as he trotted to the hallway closet and pulled out a dress in a dry cleaning bag. It was from Goodwill, as many of my things were, and I knew I would have to go to the dance now.

"I, uh, I took one of your dresses to the store with me, and a nice lady there helped me. She said she was pretty sure it would fit." It was actually quite nice, almost off-the-shoulder black velvet, slim all the way down. "I can take it back, I guess," Dad said, a little crestfallen.

"No, I love it. Let me go try it on." So I went to the bathroom and got into the dress. It fit me perfectly. The dress was practically new, probably purchased for one occasion and quickly donated.

"Oh, Ags," Dad said when I stepped out in the dress, my feet still in thick socks. "You look so grown up."

I tried my best to smile for him. "I love it, Dad, really. So much. You didn't have to do this. I can't wait for the dance now," I lied.

He beamed, and that almost made everything worth it.

I'm sure Ian Millbrook wasn't pleased that I tagged along with Tricia and him to the dance, but Tricia had insisted. "If you're going stag, you are still sticking by me," she'd said. Mr. Millbrook picked me up from the house, and I sat shotgun so Ian and Tricia could sit together in the back. I stared straight ahead, trying not to get eaten alive by jealousy. Mr. Millbrook made polite conversation about school, but I was flushed and tongue-tied and gave monosyllabic answers.

Mr. Millbrook waited for us in the parking lot of the diner with a book while we had dinner. If you look up "awkward" in the dictionary, there might be a picture of the three of us sitting in a booth at the Poppy Beach Diner for sophomore year homecoming dinner. Ian Millbrook clearly wanted to be alone with Tricia, and Tricia clearly was thinking of Todd. And I clearly wished I were someone else, someone lovable.

The dance itself was loud and dark. I did notice that I was the only girl there without a corsage. I felt naked and awful in my secondhand black velvet, as if everyone else could see the lack of flowers on my body and know that no one had asked me to be here. If there were other girls who hadn't been asked, they stayed at home or brought pity dates. I should have done that, but the thought of making conversation with someone's brother or cousin or neighbor for an entire evening made me want to hide under my bed.

I danced some of the faster songs with Tricia and some other couples. I noticed her craning her neck the whole time, looking for Todd. He was fairly easy to spot since he was so tall. He had brought a small redhead, shorter even than I, and I wondered why all the tall guys always dated the tiniest girls. I could see Tricia's face fall, and I think I had a pretty good idea of what she was feeling.

During the slow songs, I sat in a folding chair on the side of the auditorium and was glad for the blackness of the velvet, hoping it helped me melt into the shadows. Tricia claimed her shoes were pinching her, and she went to sit next to me.

"Are you having a good time?" she shouted over the music.

I shrugged. "Having fun watching people, I guess."

"Who *is* that redhead?" asked Tricia.

"Don't know."

Ian Millbrook came to us then with glasses of punch. "Thanks," I tried to say, but no sound came out. I probably just looked like I was chewing gum. Even though the school uniform was already dressy, it was a whole new world to see him in a suit. His tweed blazer was tailored perfectly to accommodate his narrow shoulders. He'd also made an effort to tame his wayward hair. It still flopped over his glasses in waves, but they were all going in roughly the same direction. He sat down in the free seat next to me, close enough to touch. I snuck a look at his eyes long enough to notice he had surprisingly long eyelashes, so blond that they weren't visible from a distance. Great, just more for me to obsess over. I drank down the punch and crumpled up the cup, tossing it in the bin a bit away.

"Two points," said Ian kindly.

The DJ announced the last song of the dance—another slow song, Eric Clapton's "Wonderful Tonight." Ian stood up, holding his hand out to Tricia. Tricia shook her head. "I'm sorry, Ian, my feet are killing me."

He looked a little disappointed, but he turned to me and asked, "Do you mind?"

Did I mind what? I stared at him dumbly.

"Dance?" he asked. Oh. *Oh!*

I tried to sound breezy and say, "Sure, why not?" but again, no actual sound came out of my mouth. I took his hand—my skin was touching his skin!—and we walked out to the dance floor.

I'd never slow danced before. I put my hands on his shoulders, and he put his around my waist, and we maintained a huge, proper distance (as the nuns would say, "Enough space for the Holy Ghost") between us as we stepped from side to side and in a slow circle. Ian sang along absentmindedly, not looking me in the eye. When he and Clapton together sang, *"How much I love you,"* my whole body thrummed.

God, how I wished he were really singing those words to me, but I knew him and how he was around music, and I could feel his hand forming the guitar chords to the song on my back through the velvet. He was just appreciating Clapton.

Still, as much as I tried to stay practical about it all, my heart was fluttering like hummingbird wings, a blur of nonstop motion. My hands were sweaty, and all I could notice was this one coarse hair sticking out of his tweed blazer. I wanted to pick it out of his jacket. And I was angry with myself for spending my time thinking about that coarse hair and not taking the opportunity to look up at his face and study those curious, almost colorless long eyelashes I'd just discovered or try to memorize the feel of his hands around me, even if I were only a placeholder for Tricia or his guitar.

When the song ended, he just shrugged and said, "Thanks," and walked back to Tricia. I was frozen in place, and the lights came up, showing the institutional dreariness of the auditorium that had only in the dark been a convincing illusion of glamour with its crepe paper streamers and helium balloons, already beginning to sag.

I called Dad to take me home because I thought maybe Ian Millbrook and Tricia wanted to be alone. I sat on a bench outside the auditorium until Dad drove up.

"Have a good time, kiddo?"

"I guess so," I said, looking out the window just in time to see Ian Millbrook kiss Tricia lightly on the lips as they made their way back to Mr. Millbrook's car.

"You don't remember the year Ian Millbrook asked you to the dance?" I say to Tricia, who has been looking at me inquisitively.

Tricia chuckles a little to herself. "Oh, man. I seriously had totally forgotten that. I don't remember much before Todd and I started dating. That was weird."

"Did anything happen between you guys that night?" I ask as casually as I can.

"Gosh, Agnes, I don't remember that far back."

Ian Millbrook kissed her, and she doesn't remember. I can remember the feel of that coarse hair between my fingers, his hands forming chords through secondhand velvet on my back. And she can't remember his *kiss*.

Patrick starts shrieking and banging his sippy cup on the table, and Tricia waves down the waitress for our tab. "Let me get this, Agnes," she says. "You're never here. I want to treat you."

I carry Carla to Tricia's car so she doesn't have to walk. She buckles her kids into their car seats and then leans on the open driver's side door. "It was good to see you, Agnes."

"Yeah. I miss you."

"You, too."

We stand there awkwardly for a while, wondering what else there is to say.

"Well, see you when I see you, I guess," I offer, going in for a hug. My eyes are welling up with tears, because I honestly don't know when I'll see her again. She was my childhood, my years when I saw Ian Millbrook every day, when I slept each night down the hall from my father, safe and secure. Will I remember less if I don't see her face?

"Oh, you'll be back before you know it," Tricia says, squeezing me and rubbing my back, but we both know that's not true.

I cross my arms against a sudden breeze and watch Tricia drive away. I don't get in my car until she's long out of sight.

When I get home, I go straight to bed. This three-hour time difference is killing me. Or maybe it's just all these memories about Ian Millbrook. I have no energy. I just want to sleep all the time. I get under the covers, close my eyes, and find myself humming loose threads of "Wonderful Tonight."

I'm gazing at the Bridge Between, and I am full of pride. I made this. I also feel a heavy burden inside. A line from "Wonderful Tonight" escapes my lips.

Oh.

Oh, now I see. I remember going to bed. I remember the diner. I remember that Ian Millbrook is dead. I remember all of my waking life, and I know I am dreaming. It's as clear as my dream was in my waking. I can carry my thoughts back and forth from one world to the other. Maybe this is what Ash meant, that if I rebuilt the Bridge Between, I'd begin to remember.

"Ash," I say, "tell me about the Stone One."

He stiffens, his hackles raised, and I hear Willa whine a little.

"*It is time*," he says, and I shiver.

TEN
A PIECE OF HER

"What is it time for, exactly?" I ask Ash, who has begun to stride away from me.

"*It is time to return to the damage,*" he says.

"Where are we going now?"

"*Back to the ruins.*"

"To Oread's Keep?"

"*Yes. Good, you remember the name.*" Ash continues to lead the way, and Willa trots right behind him. I hurry to keep up. The third wolf, the invisible one, stays close by my side. I can feel him, still remember the feel of his damp nose against my leg. Even though I can't see him, I feel this immense love and am sorry I don't remember his name.

I walk a ways with the invisible wolf next to me. "Hi," I say.

"*Are you talking to me?*" he asks with surprise.

"Yes."

"*Why do you bother? You don't even know who I am.*"

"I do and I don't. I don't remember your name, but I remember loving you." And I do. I remember his face in the drawings I examined in my room before I went to meet Tricia. I remember the wolf, perpetually grinning, not just in the watered-down illustrations for the children's book, but in the darker sketchpad drawings as well. This one was always smiling, lean, with limbs too big for his body, as if he hadn't yet grown into them. Almost grown up, but forever a child to me. I feel such tenderness toward him, almost as if I were his own mother. Did I create him the way I repaired the Bridge Between? If so, maybe I am his mother, in a way. I reach down and stroke his fur.

I feel slightly foolish petting the empty space by me, but I can feel his warmth, his coarse hair. He leans into me as we walk. I hope he can sense in my touch how sorry I am that I can't remember his name. I pat around to find his head and try to scratch behind his ears. His tail thumps against my leg.

"*I've missed you,*" he says, and I feel forgiven.

"I'll remember you soon," I whisper to him, and I feel him lick my palm. His breath is hot in my hand, and I scratch him under his invisible chin. I wish I could see him. I wish I could just remember his name. Why am I so blocked?

"*We are here,*" says Ash, and we're at the hilltop where this all started. I suppose it's a good rule always to return to the beginning, to the source. Maybe the answers are here.

"Can I rebuild this place too?" I wonder aloud.

"*You can try,*" he says, looking worriedly into the distance. Is he searching for the Stone One? I realize that Ash never answered my question.

"Tell me about the Stone One," I ask again.

"*I am not sure what you want to know.*" It's hard to tell if he's evading the question because he is afraid, or if it's just his standard, infuriating evasiveness.

"Did he destroy this place?"

"*Yes.*"

"Did he harm the others of your kind?"

"*Yes.*"

I steel myself and in a lowered voice ask the question I've been dreading the answer to. "Is it because I left that the Stone One did these things?"

Ash hesitates. "*Things aren't always that simple, Princess.*"

"But I had a part in it."

"*Yes.*"

"I used to protect this place, didn't I?" I think of the illustration in Patrick's book of brave little Aggie facing off the monster.

"*You were the princess and the guardian and the creator of this incarnation of the land.*"

"Am I those things now?"

"*Only you can answer that.*"

"I don't understand."

"*You are always given a choice. You may take it, or you may not. Your path is always changing. That is why you were able to leave. We could not hold you if you no longer wanted to stay.*"

Is that a clue? That I didn't want to stay? "So why am I back, then?"

"*Only you can answer that,*" he says again.

"I…I wish to rebuild Oread's Keep," I say, but I am afraid. I worry that my actions will somehow draw the Stone One to us.

"*We serve you; you are ours,*" say all three wolves simultaneously, their three voices together somehow amplifying in my head, the sum greater than its parts. It's so loud I can feel it vibrate through my bones. It sends a tremor down my spine, and I know somehow that it's my cue to begin. I stand at the center of cracked marble on what remains of the courtyard. With my palms up, my eyes closed, I take a deep breath. I brush my bare feet along the stone, appreciating the cool roughness against my soles.

I don't know if it will work twice.

But I open my mouth, and the Voice pours out of me again, sunlight and honey and steel all at once, and I will Oread's Keep to re-form, brick by brick, the alabaster tower once again reaching toward the sky. "*Be what you were meant to be,*" I think, coaxing it back into existence. "*Be your best self, your most perfect self,*" I humbly ask of the dust and rubble that used to be Oread's Keep.

I can feel time turning backward again, moss peeling away, vines disappearing back into the soil, sand fusing back into rock, rock into brick, brick into wall. I should be exhausted from the concentration—I'm raising an entire building, after all—but instead I feel alive, as if every particle in my body is singing with me. In the back of my mind, I think, *This is what I was always meant to do. I am a creator. I love this place. I will make it whole again.*

And when I open my eyes, I am not surprised to see Oread's Keep restored, reflecting the sunlight so brightly that I can hardly bear to look at it.

My joy is dampened as Ash sniffs the air with alarm. *"He is near."*

I did it, I think, waking up from my nap, my arms at my sides, palms up as they were in my dream. I have summoned the Voice twice. Is it always in my control? Is it me — *my* voice? Or am I just a channel for something deeper? I can fix this world, I think. I can make things right again, make it right for those wolves. But why should I care so much about them? They aren't real. And yet, I feel such a connection, such concern for their well-being. I rush to find my sketchpad and draw what I can remember.

I'm drawing a castle, but it's not like anything I've seen in storybooks — part European with arches and flying buttresses and towers, and part…Eastern, I guess, with minarets and strange, twisted spires. I'm standing in the middle of the restored courtyard, Ash looking into the distance. Who is near? The Stone One? Someone else?

I know nothing more about the Stone One than I did before I went to sleep. What if I've left them in danger? Should I hurry back into the dreaming? I realize, of course, that I sound like a crazy person. *They're just dreams.* The wolves will be all right, waiting for me the next time I fall asleep.

I get out of bed and jump up and down a few times to get the blood moving. I am so tired. I have been so tired ever since I've gotten here. I know staying up all night before flying cross-country had something to do with it, but it can't explain this weariness in my bones. This is more than traveler's fatigue, more than jetlag. More, even, than mourning Ian Millbrook.

Being in my tiny childhood home has enveloped me in a shroud of my childhood. I've missed my dad, sure. And it's good to be back, to see him. But this house, this house is also where my world fell apart, where I had to learn to make do with just one loving parent. Of course I wouldn't trade Dad for anything else in the whole wide world. If I had to choose which parent stayed, maybe as a child I would have said Shelly, but I now pick Dad. *I pick you, Pete Larch, now and forever.*

I think again of his new laugh lines, the silver hair shooting up like weeds on his head of thick, dark hair. He's aged a lot since the last time he flew out to visit me. I think of a world without my father, and I am terrified. *Don't be foolish*, I chide myself. *Dad isn't going anywhere*. Even if it's a lie, I tell myself that he'll be with me for a long time. He'll be with me as long as I need him. Which is always.

My eye is drawn again to my desk, to that little scrap of crumpled paper. The paper is practically a live thing, sweeping across my brain like a searchlight with its repeated *Look at me, look at me, look at me, look at me*. I know I'll get no rest until I make a decision about Shelly.

I will call her after dinner. But not now, I can't think of it now. I can prepare myself. Can she really have wanted to talk to me, or was she feeling obligated for Dad's help with the flat? Then again, she's sent all those cards over the years. My dad forwards the cards to me in Boston in a big manila envelope along with the rest of my mail, since of course Shelly doesn't have my current mailing address. I rather dread the mail around my birthday. I know that if I see her loopy script on a brightly colored envelope, I'll think, *She loves you enough to remember your birthday, but not enough to try to find you or to know anything else about your life*. And I worry every year that *this* will be the year that she forgets to send a card, the year that I am finally and completely erased from her memory or crossed off her list of obligations. I don't know which I fear more.

I can ask her these questions myself if I call the number on that scrap of paper. But do I really want to know the answers? Am I ready to hear the truth?

I go downstairs to see if there is anything to eat. The cupboards are fairly bare, as is the refrigerator, aside from the blocks of cheese. I'll make a quick trip to the grocery store, maybe make a meatloaf. Dad likes meatloaf. I check the cabinet for spices. *Oh, Dad*. Salt, pepper, garlic salt. He's such a stereotypical bachelor. I'll have to restock the kitchen.

In five minutes I'm out the door and back in Bessie. I try not to look at the bumper as I pass by, but my eye is pulled to the dent. I choke back the lump in my throat and drive to the grocery store, a bit past Butler Academy. I wander up and down the aisles, struggling with my cart. I always somehow choose a cart with a bum wheel. Is it a special gift, or are all the carts in this sleepy town somehow defective? In any case, today is no exception. It takes far more effort than it should to navigate the cart around the store without clipping other shoppers in the leg or knocking over entire displays.

Despite my cautiousness, I run over the foot of a guy restocking the dairy case. I can tell he is biting his tongue, trying his hardest not to swear a blue streak at me. "Sorry, sorry," I mumble, my face on fire. He just shakes his head, angrily dismissing me before turning back to his stacks of yogurt quarts. I feel about six inches tall. It's hard to believe that an hour or so ago, I was recreating a world. Here I am bumbling and all wrong.

When I get to the meat aisle, shivering slightly from the chill despite my long sleeves, I close my eyes on a whim and lift my hands, palms up, by my sides. I open my mouth just to see what might happen. Nothing, of course. I'm just ordinary Agnes. No princesses here.

I open my eyes and sheepishly glance around, hoping no one has seen my weird behavior. I don't know what I was trying to do or what I thought could happen. To be honest, I don't understand much of my behavior lately. I shouldn't even be here in Poppy Beach. I should be working my silly temp job in Boston, tramping home on the frozen ground, eating alone in my tiny little apartment near Fenway Park. I should be living the same day again and again, the only difference being the clothes I wear and what time the sun sets.

It's already dark when I leave the grocery store. As I pass Butler Academy, I notice a moving truck and spy Mr. and Mrs. Millbrook and Benjamin and Meg and Gillian illuminated under the orange streetlamps by the school. What's going on?

I pull into the lot a bit away from them, turn off the ignition, and observe, hoping they don't notice my gigantic old sedan. They're holding hands in a circle. Their heads are bowed for a second. Eventually they all reach in together for a big hug for a moment before breaking the circle and parting ways with wet eyes. Mrs. Millbrook hugs Meg tightly and kisses the top of her head while Mr. Millbrook claps Benjamin on the back. Gillian stands a bit away from the family, fiddling with her purse. Ian's parents and Meg go back into one car, Benjamin and Gillian get into another, and they all drive away.

I see some guys heading back to the moving truck with blankets, and I hop out of my car, the door making a horrid squeaking sound as I open it. "Hey, what are you guys doing?" I ask.

"Just moving a piano," the bigger guy says, in a total meathead *what's it to you?* manner.

Normally that tone of voice would make me shrink and want to disappear, but my curiosity makes me bold. "But, but…the Millbrooks?" I turn around, looking where their cars have disappeared into the inky night.

"They donated it," the guy says, bored.

Ian's piano. Of course he would have had one. I imagine a piano in the Millbrooks' house, which I have never seen the inside of. It's in one of the fancy developments for newer Poppy Beach residents, and I'd driven by it plenty of times in high school even though it was way out of my way, just to get the thrill of being close to him, to see the outside of the place where he slept and dreamed. As far as I know, he had been on the road a lot the last few years, his career as a musician slowly taking flight. It must have been a comfort at the time to have a tangible reminder of their talented son in the house, the piano a cumbersome but welcome stand-in for their traveling son. But now, now the piano must seem to them like a coffin, a reminder of everything they've lost, its cheery, glossy finish incongruous with their grief. I can understand why they'd want to donate it so quickly.

"Shit, forgot my coat," says the smaller guy, and he jogs back inside.

In that moment, I hurry back to the car, grab one of the bags of groceries, and wait by the door for the smaller guy to come out. I stand there, looking casual, like I'm waiting for someone to pick me up, and when the door is almost closed, I stick my foot in the doorway to keep it from shutting all the way. When the truck pulls away, I sneak into the building like a vandal. I rush down to the arts wing, my hand grazing along the painted cinderblock walls, back to the room where I would wait breathlessly every Wednesday night for Ian Millbrook just to look at me. I push open the doors, and the motion-sensor lights switch on.

After my eyes adjust to the blinding fluorescence, I see it. In the middle of the room is a glossy black baby grand piano. I sit on the bench and open the lid. I brush my hands over the keyboard and imagine I feel a buzzing under my palms, as if his essence is still trapped in the hammers and strings and keys. He loved this instrument, I am sure. I'd like to sleep here tonight, near something he loved so much, but I know my dad would be looking for me. I realize also that it is a totally crazy notion.

But I can do for him what he once did for me. I reach into my grocery bag and pull out an apple, peeling off the sticker. I stick it underneath the piano, somewhere out of the way where it won't be noticed, my secret little mark. I press it into place, buffing down the edges with my fingernail until the sticker is smooth. "I'll always be here with you, Ian," I say out loud, not caring if I feel a little foolish.

Before leaving, I play the open strings of standard tuning: E, A, D, G, B, E. I know his fingers must have touched these very keys in this very order many times as he tuned his guitar. I close my eyes and let the chord ring, and I can almost imagine that it's just a normal Wednesday evening ten years ago, that Ian is alive, tuning his guitar, not knowing that I'm hanging on his every word and gesture.

Huh, it *is* Wednesday, I think, the weeks lining up exactly, so if I took a big pin and pierced it through this day, through this moment, if I poked back far enough, I'd find myself back here with Ian Millbrook for Wednesday night rehearsal. I'm not sure if this thought is comforting or unsettling. I pick up the sack of groceries and shuffle back outside, taking deep breaths of the cool night air.

Dad's truck is in the driveway when I get back to the house. I run in, hoping he hasn't already taken care of dinner.

"Hey, Dad," I call as I push open the door. "I'm going to make meatloaf—is that cool?"

"Ags, you know you don't need to do anything like that."

"I know," I say, unpacking the groceries.

The meatloaf is mixed quickly, but it takes so long to bake. "I'm sorry I didn't start earlier," I say to Dad, who is parked in his usual spot in front of the TV. "You must be starving."

"Late lunch," says Dad, patting his belly and never taking his eyes off the TV.

I watch my dad eat his dinner while only picking at my slice of meatloaf. I'm not really hungry. I can't stop thinking about what I've vowed to do after dinner: I am going to call Shelly. The thought of talking to her fills me with a cold dread. I'm not even sure I remember what her voice sounds like.

I enjoy watching Dad eat, though; I enjoy feeling like what I've made with my hands is nourishing him, helping to sustain his life. I feel so much guilt about not being here to take care of him. This is the least I can do.

After Dad's plate is clean and my meatloaf is cold, I clear my throat. "Dad? I…I think I'm going to call Mom now." My mouth gets a little stuck on the word "Mom." I want to call her "Shelly." She is not my mom. But I have a feeling that Dad would still insist I show her respect.

"All right, Ags, if that's what you want to do," he says, reaching over and giving my hand a squeeze. I smile tightly and nod, feeling braver from his touch. I can do this. I can survive this.

I walk up the stairs like a condemned man climbing the gallows. In my room, I flip on my lamp and get the piece of paper off my desk, where it's been waiting for me all day. I sit on my bed with my phone in one hand and the piece of paper in the other, my hands clammy and shaking.

It feels almost as if I'm out of my body when I finally get the guts to dial all ten digits of her number and hit the button to connect the call. What am I going to say to her?

The phone rings four, five, six times. "*Hi, you've reached Shelly Kent. You know what to do.*" Kent? A shrill beep interrupts my confusion over her outgoing message, and I stammer, "H-Hi, this is Agnes." I'm tempted to say, *This is Agnes Larch, the daughter you abandoned,* just in case she doesn't remember. "Dad said you wanted me to call. So this is, uh, me calling." I leave my cell number with her, and that's that.

A mother should already know her daughter's cell phone number, I think bitterly.

I flop back on my pillow and consider my mother's voice on the outgoing message, the waves of the vibrations of her voice captured, a ghost of her presence. Does this electronic representation of her voice match at all the organic print buried deep in my memory? Her voice sounds deeper, scratchier. Maybe she's been smoking. Maybe my memory is faulty. Maybe it's a little of both.

After all the buildup, it is a bit anticlimactic to get Shelly's voicemail. I put the phone on the bedside table and crumple up the piece of paper again. I crush it into a tight wad and leave it next to the phone. I should just throw it away, but I let it sit, a blight on my bedside table.

I curl onto my side. The thought of getting ready for bed right now exhausts me. I have no ability to get into pajamas. Maybe I'll just rest my eyes a moment, take a little nap before I go to bed. I used to do this all the time, fall asleep on the couch downstairs while Dad watched the Giants go into extra innings. He'd just cover me with a blanket and let me sleep until I had the energy to climb the stairs to my room. I'll just close my eyes for a moment. Just a short moment. And then I'll have the strength to get ready for bed.

I close my eyes, both eager and fearful of what I may encounter in the newly restored Oread's Keep.

ELEVEN
FREE WILL

"I'm back! I'm here! Is everyone all right?" I ask breathlessly, looking around for my wolves. Ash and Willa are lazing about in the sunlight in the courtyard. There's a fantastic fountain in the center, the serenely cascading water incongruous with the anxiety churning inside me.

"*We are fine,*" says Ash, speaking for the others.

"So, what happens when I wake up? Does time stop? Or do I disappear?"

"*You live only in our memory then,*" answers Ash, rolling onto his back to let the sun shine on his belly.

"Are you in danger now?" I ask, looking past him.

"*Why would you ask that?*"

"Well, you said, *He is near.* And you seemed worried."

"*I am not so afraid now that you are here,*" he says.

How can he be so confident, when I am filled with terror?

"*Hi,*" the third wolf says, nudging me with his nose.

I scrunch up my face, trying to wring his name out of my memory. "Your name, it begins with a J. *Jason?*"

The invisible one makes a noise that sounds suspiciously like a wolfy version of blowing a raspberry.

"Okay, it's not Jason. But I'm close, aren't I?"

"*You promised,*" Not-Jason says.

"I know. I'm sorry. I'm trying."

"*Jason's a stupid name,*" he huffs.

The wind changes, and Ash's ears perk up. "*I can hear him. You must get ready. Hurry!*"

"What? What am I to do? Who's coming?"

"*The Stone One comes, he comes.*"

Willa is on her feet at once, cowering behind Ash's large body. "*She is not prepared to face him. We are all in danger.*"

Ash approaches me. "*You must have your weapons.*"

"I...I have weapons?" I close my eyes and remember. "The bow, the arrows—where are they now? Must I sing again?"

"*That is not necessary. Give me a moment.*" And Ash takes off for the woods beyond Oread's Keep.

I'm pacing, worried about coming face to face with the monster I can remember only in sketches. I'm terrified of his two-dimensional, monochromatic incarnation—how can I possibly face the real thing? How was it that as a child I could stare him down? *Calm yourself,* I think. *Remember what you are capable of here.* I sit down, cross-legged, on the stone floor with my hands resting palm up on my knees.

I will wait for Ash to return with my weapons. I will face the monster.

The invisible wolf nudges one of my hands off so he can rest his head on my knee. I stroke his head. "It's going to be okay, Jay—" I clap my free hand over my mouth. "Sorry. I know your name isn't Jason. Something like Jason. I'm sorry. I do love you though, you know."

Not-Jason whimpers a little. I know his feelings are hurt.

Ash appears, dragging something backward out of the woods in his mouth. It looks like a mummy. He deposits the corpse-like object at my feet. "*Here. We have kept this for a long time, waiting for your return. Hurry. There is not much time.*"

The object is covered in damp earth, recently exhumed. I touch the wrapping: more decaying strips of linen, just like the shroud I woke up in. I tear away at the fabric, and inside is a fine longbow nearly as tall as I am. How the hell did I handle this thing when I was five?

As if reading my thoughts, Ash says, "*The bow always adjusts to the size of the guardian and protector.*"

"Oh." I continue unwrapping and find the quiver and arrows. "I'm not sure I remember how to use this thing," I say, slinging the quiver onto my back. The arrows are sharp despite their many years of storage. I think back to my other life, of gym class at Butler Academy, of my adequate but certainly not extraordinary displays of athleticism. How can I be a warrior here?

The trees seem to shiver, but not from wind. The ground is vibrating.

"*He comes,*" warns Ash. "*Go.*" I grab the bow and run through the wooden tower door, up the stone spiral stairs, and emerge at the top of the tower. The wolves wait below, ears laid flat against their heads. From up here they look tiny, like plush toys.

I'm scared. I'm so scared. How can I possibly do this?

I try to think of Princess Aggie and her anime eyes, bold and unafraid. How was that ever me? My hands are so clammy that I am struggling to hold onto the smooth wood of the longbow. I can feel the Stone One's approach rippling out from the epicenter of his footfalls; the aftershocks of his steps travel right up through the brick of the tower.

What do I do? I can't fail them again, I think in a panic. I let my eyes close and try to let my mind go blank, to let my body take over. *I am tranquil. Show me; lead me to my duty.* My arm reaches behind my head for an arrow. When I open my eyes I see I have already notched an arrow on the flaxen string. I am thankful that my muscles are able to hold a separate, secret history independent of my mind.

I hear him before he is visible. "*So you have returned after all these years, Abdicator?*" The voice sounds just like the monster's jagged lines of dialogue in Patrick's book, like stone rubbing against stone, like a heavy stone rolled in front of a tomb. I will stand firm. I will not back down.

"I am not afraid," I call out, but my voice quavers.

"*I can smell your fear, sweet as honey,*" says the Stone One.

I fight my urge to tremble. It seems that when I let my mind go quiet, my body knows what to do, even though my mind has the power to override everything else and make my body freeze up and disobey. *Empty your mind. Trust your body.* But oh, I am so afraid.

I hear branches snapping, cracking, whole trees going down, and soon I see the beast emerging from the trees. He has a face almost like a man, but misshapen. If his face were somehow less human, his deformity would be less disturbing, because then he would be wholly Other and I would not be able to find any reflection of myself in him. Instead, the traces of humanity in his face completely unsettle me. It brings to mind the Freudian concept of the *uncanny*. He is something that ought to be human but isn't quite. As he draws nearer, I see he is taller than the highest tower of Oread's Keep.

We are doomed, I think.

I look down at the wolves, who gaze up at me anxiously. I must protect them. They are all that are left here with me. They strengthen my resolve. I lift my chin defiantly at the beast, now right in front of me.

"You may not destroy anything today, Stone One," I say, in language that seems to flow from deep within my body. My voice does not waver. I hold firm.

"*So you have returned, as I felt in my bones. Will you stay this time, then, Princess?*"

When he calls me *Princess*, it sounds mocking and cruel.

"I'm here, aren't I?"

"*You won't beg for them to bury you again?*"

I have no idea what he is talking about, but I shiver. "No," I say with some uncertainty.

"*I can feel your weakness. I will be back.*" And with that, he turns and goes away. As I watch him disappear into the woods, my legs finally give way, and I collapse onto the floor. I weep with relief while I wait for the feeling to return to my legs. Once I feel steady on my feet, I make my way down the stairs, running my hand along the polished stone walls for balance.

When I emerge back into the sunshine of the courtyard, the wolves are waiting. Ash, Willa, and the third one nearly knock me over in their exuberance. "*Thank you,*" says Ash.

"*Yes. You did well,*" Willa admits, nodding.

"*I knew you would protect us,*" says the third one, licking my face.

I hug them each in turn. "Does he come around here often?"

"*Not so much in recent years,*" says Ash. "*But since you've rebuilt Oread's Keep, he will be here more often, waiting for you to make a mistake.*"

The invisible one asks, "*You won't leave us again, will you?*"

"I...I don't think I will. No. I want to stay." I don't think I have a choice anyway, despite what Ash said to me earlier: *You are always given a choice. You may take it, or you may not.*

"What do we do now?" I ask, now that the danger has passed. "What did we normally do after the Stone One retreated?" I think of Patrick's book. I don't think we really wore party hats and had hot chocolate afterward.

"*We just enjoyed being alive for another day,*" says Ash.

"*That's not true,*" says the invisible one. "*We had fun too. You used to play hide and seek with us,*" he says to me.

"I think I remember that! I'd be frustrated that you could always find me by sniffing me out. I told you that it was cheating to use your nose."

"*You were a sore loser,*" he laughs.

I playfully grab where I think his head is. "I was *not*, Jason." The wrong name slips out again, and I can tell that it's like I've slid a knife right into his heart. He howls in pain and hurt.

"*Not Jason! My name is Joshua. Joshua!*" he shouts into my head.

I feel stupid. "Of course it's Joshua! Of course!" And he materializes before me. I'm so happy to see him that I don't notice for a long time that Ash and Willa have grown still as statues.

"*What have you* done?" Willa shrieks. Is she talking to me or to Joshua?

"*There is nothing we can do for you now,*" says Ash.

Joshua paws at the ground. "It's going to be okay, Joshy," I say.

I hear alarm bells in the distance. Joshua whimpers.

"*He is coming back,*" says Ash. "*He knows when the rules have been broken.*"

"I'll protect you," I say as Joshua cowers behind me.

The alarm bells grow more persistent. I cover my hands over my ears, but the alarms continue to sound until I feel myself getting pulled out of this world.

"No!" I cry out. "No! Not now! I need to stay!"

The alarm bells are unrelenting.

My phone is ringing. I have no idea what time it is, but my lamp is still on and I'm still curled on my side on top of the covers. I can hear my dad snoring down the hall. I glance at the number. It's almost familiar, but a name doesn't come up—whoever it is isn't in my address book. I'm filled with a sense of dread. I don't like when the phone rings late, and the display on my phone says it's just after midnight.

"Joshua!" I yell into the phone.

A throaty chuckle answers me. "Expecting your boyfriend, sugar?"

"M-Mom?" Can this be Shelly? Her voice is so different.

"Aggie, it's me." I bristle at her casual tone and have to bite my tongue not to correct her. I don't like being called Aggie. I haven't been Aggie in a long time. But again, she doesn't even deserve to call me Agnes. She doesn't get to know me.

"Oh." I have no idea what I want to say to her. I mean, I have so many questions, but I certainly don't have the guts to ask her them right now. I sit up in bed with the phone against my ear, just listening to the static on the other end. I cup my hand over my other ear and hear the sound of the ocean.

"You sound so grown up, shug," she says.

"I guess so." I mean, I'm sure I sound older than when I was *five fucking years old, Shelly*. I'm rolling my eyes so hard that I nearly hurt myself.

"So I guess Pete must've told you about our run in. He hasn't changed a bit." She chuckles again.

"Dad's *constant* like that," I say through gritted teeth.

If she's noticed my veiled insult, she doesn't let on. "Well, when Pete mentioned you were in town, I thought I should see my little girl."

"I'm not."

"What?"

"*Your* little girl." I'm less upset by being called a child than I am by her use of the possessive pronoun.

"Now don't you be a sourpuss, Aggie-waggie. You didn't have to call me."

I think of the crushed wad of paper with her number on it, how it pulsed and buzzed like a malfunctioning fluorescent light, like an angry wasp trapped in a jar, until I decided to call her. I don't feel like

I had a choice. Ash's words come back to me again: *You are always given a choice. You may take it, or you may not.*

"Didn't I?" I ask. "I mean, you walk out with no explanation when I'm just a tiny *child*, and you never even try to see me for nearly twenty fucking years?"

"Language, Aggie."

"What is it, then? Am I grown up or am I not? Am I allowed to use four-letter words or am I just a child? You can't tell me how to behave. You lost that right." I'm sort of shocked at my words, at the viciousness in my tone. I must still be half-asleep, missing my filter.

Shelly sighs heavily. "Okay, maybe this was a mistake. I just, you know, when I got that flat and Pete drove by, it sort of felt like a sign. You know? I never stopped thinking about you."

"Gee. I'm so moved. Oh, I guess I'm all better now."

"Come on, don't be like that. I…I made some mistakes, I admit it."

Way to own up and take the blame, Shelly.

"I thought maybe we could talk," she tries again in a bright tone. "You're old enough now to know the truth. I mean, I take it that Pete never told you."

Never told me what? My mouth hangs open, and I don't say anything.

"You still there?"

"I'm listening," I croak out. Oh, Dad, Daddy, what have you been hiding?

"Pete never talks to you about me, does he?"

"Not so much, no. You kind of broke his heart, *Mom*."

"Oh please, he knew what he was getting into."

I have no idea where this conversation is going, and now I have far more questions than before Shelly Fucking Kent waltzed back into my life.

"So, listen, *kid*," she says, sounding suddenly icy. "Do you want answers or not? Pete says you're in town for a few more days. Do you want to meet? Talk it out? Get some answers?"

I may take this choice, or I may not.

No. I don't have a choice. I *have* to know. I have to know now that she's made me doubt the one solid, the one given, the one *forever* in my life, Pete Larch. My dad. My flawed father, somehow more perfect *because* of his flaws.

"Fine. When?" I pick up the little wadded bit of paper off the bedside table and roll it between my thumb and forefinger. I wish I'd just set it on fire like I first wanted to when Dad gave it to me.

"Are you free tomorrow?"

I have no plans. I don't know why I'm still here or why I even came out here in the first place. "Let me check my calendar." I pretend to fumble with a datebook, but I'm just turning pages of my sketchpad. A grinning wolf draws my eye to the page. *No, Joshua! Is Joshua all right?*

"I have some time tomorrow," I say, eager now to get off the phone so I can protect Joshua.

"You want to meet at the diner? Brunch? Like eleven? That crappy diner's still there, right?" Shelly laughs a little. "As if there's anywhere else to go in that shithole town," she mutters under her breath.

"Yes, it's there. Yes, that time works. See you then, I guess."

"See ya tomorrow, kid," she says, and I don't know if I can believe her.

"I guess," I say again before hanging up, the little ball of paper still pinched between my fingers.

I creep downstairs, feeling my way in the darkness. I flip the lights on in the kitchen and find a book of matches. I light one, enjoying the sudden brightness and the smell of phosphorous. I let the flame lick the side of the little ball, setting it down in the sink before it singes my fingers. For a second it doesn't seem to take, but soon enough the little piece of paper is burning, the flame consuming, reducing the paper to ash. "You are dust now, Shelly," I say, but I don't feel much better.

The phantom of the flame still dances behind my eyelids as I make my way back upstairs to get ready for bed.

I'm about to get under the covers when I hear Shelly's voice in my head again: *I take it Pete never told you.* It could be nothing. Maybe she's just manipulating. She could just want to take everything from me, make it a clean sweep. Maybe it wasn't enough for her to steal my childhood away. Maybe she wants to take away my foundation too, leave me with nothing.

I go to the hallway and tiptoe to Dad's room, the room where he and my mom used to share a bed. He's still snoring like a lumberjack, so I know it's safe to push open the door. As my eyes adjust to the darkness, I notice that he sleeps right in the middle of the bed, arms splayed wide. I wonder how long it took him to sleep in the whole bed, not stay corralled on "his" side, afraid to stray into the Shelly side of the bed. I realize that I don't remember what side of the bed Shelly used to sleep on. There's so much I've already lost.

I hate Shelly even more for making me doubt my father. She's already planted the seed. What does he know? What hasn't he told me? I sit on the floor next to his bed with my knees drawn up to my chest. I rest my head on my knees and listen to his even, noisy breathing. I start to nod off but shake myself awake. I mustn't fall asleep here.

"You're perfect, Daddy," I whisper before tiptoeing back out of the room and shutting the door behind me again.

I get under my covers finally, turning off the lamp, plunging my room into darkness. I hope I'm not too late to save him.

TWELVE
CONSEQUENCES

I've been tossing and turning for hours. The red numbers on my old clock radio glow and taunt me. It's after two in the morning. I don't know what's keeping me up—knowing that I have to meet with Shelly in a few hours, or being so worried about Joshua that I want to dig my nails all the way through the palms of my hands. One or the other. Both. *Just go to sleep, already*, I tell myself. *You can't help him from here. You can't help him if you stay awake.*

I keep nearly being pulled under, but the moment I think, *Aha! I'm falling asleep!* I'm jerked back into wakefulness. My heart's pounding like crazy as I think about Joshua. Poor Joshua. If anything happens to him, it will be on my head. If only I could have remembered his name. What good is it if I can remember every last detail about every encounter I had with Ian Millbrook, and I can't remember the name of the sweet wolf I created?

Well, there's the fact that Ian Millbrook is a real person and Joshua is a figment of my imagination. But still, it feels like some horrible betrayal. I can feel his pain. His pain is my pain. And his fear eats away at me. I know he's afraid. And I know I have to get back to him. So why can't I just fall the fuck asleep?

I'm so frustrated that I kick the covers off my bed. I get up and feel around in the dark for my backpack and sketchbook. I turn the lamp back on, the light stabbing my eyes. I push the heels of my hands against them to relieve the pressure. When they finally adjust again, I flip through from the beginning, looking for Joshua. There he is on almost every page, so sweet and trusting, so full of life. He seems like a baby compared to the other wolves, such an innocent spirit. He was too young to understand the rules, to control his impulses. And I provoked him. I had to call him *Jason* over and over again.

He just wanted to exist. He just wanted me to know his name, to care enough to remember him.

I think I know how he feels.

No more dawdling. I shut off the light and close the sketchpad, laying it across my chest. The weight of it against me is comforting. I lie on my back and lay my hands, palms up, a bit away from my sides, like a prone version of the position I take in my dreams when I let the Voice flow through me. I try to let my mind go quiet. *Help me be where I am needed. Help me get there. Please don't let me be too late.*

I'm not sure if it's the physical proximity of the Joshua sketches to my heart, or lying in the position when I invoke the Voice, or the exhaustion of being up so late, but in a few moments I'm sound asleep.

"Joshua? Joshua?" I cry out even before I can see anything, while I am still slipping between my worlds.

"*Good. You are here finally. I was waiting for you.*"

No. Oh no. It's the gritty, sepulchral voice of the Stone One. Even before my eyes open, I know I don't have my weapons. I don't feel the weight of the quiver on me.

"*You need not worry about being unarmed, Abdicator. I am not here for you.*"

We are both on the hilltop outside Oread's Keep. I am among the wolves. I stand protectively in front of Joshua, poor, sweet, darling, innocent Joshua. I think I already know the answer, but I still ask, "Then why have you returned this day, Stone One?"

"*The rules have been violated. I have come to claim the transgressor.*"

"I can't say I know what you mean," I say, trying to stall him.

"*You know the wolf has broken the rules. He may not speak his name if you remember him not.*"

"But I do! I did remember him!" *Just not in time,* I think guiltily.

"You did not remember his name."

"You shall not hurt him! He is an innocent." What can destroy a stone monster? How can I fight?

"Princess," he says in that same mocking tone, *"you may have some power here, but these rules hold more power than you. You must step aside and allow me to take the wolf. He is my prize, my bounty. It is the law."*

"I will fight you. I am not afraid to fight," I say, even though my legs are beginning to shake with terror.

"You may fight me if you wish, but the result will be the same. There is no escaping this rule. His life is mine to take. If you try to stop the natural order, then your other wolves will suffer. Would you have that, Princess? Would you allow the others to suffer for the sins of one? Would you have others punished for the sinning that you provoked with your own shortcomings?"

"Then punish me instead of him," I say. "Do what you must to me. I offer myself in his stead." What am I saying? I…I'm not ready to…I don't want to…I can't even think it.

The Stone One laughs, and it is a sound like old bones exhumed in a long-forgotten potter's field. *"I am afraid I cannot take your life for his. The time when you could have helped him has passed. Your faulty memory has condemned him."*

I am ashamed, so ashamed, of the relief that floods through me when my offer to sacrifice myself is rejected. I am such a coward.

"If you do not step aside, the others will suffer, and I still will take him in the end," he says.

What do I do? What *can* I do? I'm biting my lip in concentration, hoping for some sort of *deus ex machina* to save us, when I feel a warm nose nudge against my hand.

"It's…it's okay. I'll go with him. I don't want Ash or Willa to get hurt. I don't want you hurt. Don't be afraid, Princess."

"No, no, Joshua, you can't do this," I say, my voice catching with a sob. I get to my knees and throw my arms around his neck. "This is entirely my fault. I should have remembered your name. It is *my* failing, *my* lack. You are perfect and wonderful."

"I think I will be all right," he says bravely, trying to remove himself from my embrace.

"No!" I scream. "You can't go! You can't go to him!"

"What other choice do I have?" he asks quietly. *"I can't have anyone else hurt because of what I've done. I knew the rules, and now I must live with the consequences of my actions."* He speaks like he's already given up, like the rules are some sort of creepy wolf catechism they've had to memorize since they were pups.

"But it wasn't your fault, sweet one," I sob, dampening his fur with my tears.

"Please don't cry, my princess. It makes it harder for me. I can feel your pain. Just let me go. It will be all right. I'll…somehow be all right. I…I am not afraid."

But I know he's just putting on a brave face for me.

"Now," says the Stone One.

"And I am ready," answers Joshua. Joshua, whose name I will never, ever forget, now that it is too late. Joshua, who I will never be able to think of without knowing that I caused his destruction. Joshua, who never gave me anything but warmth and wet-nose nudges and games of hide-and-seek, and paid for his love of me with his life.

He walks with resolution toward the Stone One, who has hunched down in order to claim his prey. As Joshua nears, the Stone One opens his monstrous mouth. I watch his gaping maw but force myself to look away as Joshua stands before him, ears back, tail down. I feel a sudden chill, but Joshua doesn't make a noise, and I think that I could never be so brave as he is in this moment.

When I can bear to look again, the Stone One is back on his feet, and there is no trace of Joshua. But I know that he is gone, because my heart feels empty, scoured raw by his absence.

"He did not suffer," says the Stone One. *"He just ceased to be."* I can't tell if he's trying to comfort me or taunt me.

"Why do you do this?" I yell. "Why can't you leave these innocents alone?"

"It is my purpose. It is why I was created. I am acting only according to my nature and duty."

Before I can argue further, he turns and leaves us. I sink to my knees and sob. Oh my Joshua, what have I done to you?

I can't even look Ash or Willa in the eye. "I'm sorry. I'm so sorry," I mumble over and over, as I watch my tears plop onto the ground.

Ash is silent, but Willa says quietly, *"You promised him. You promised you would remember."*

"I know."

Ash has walked some distance away from us, and Willa goes to join him. She rests her head on top of his. *And now we are the only ones who remain,* she says. Ash stays silent.

"What…what happens if I try to rebuild him?"

Their heads snap toward me. *Such things cannot be done. You cannot use your power in that way,* says Ash, finally breaking his silence.

"But what would happen?"

It has never been done.

That's not an answer to my question. I stand in the pose, eyes closed, palms raised, mouth open. Something like the Voice comes out of me, while I think, *Return to me, my sweet Joshua. Return. Be again. I Name you again, as I Named you when you were born.*

I can feel him forming within me, but something is not right. *No!* I feel him cry out. *Please. Just let me rest. Don't disturb the order for me. Your pain is my pain. Your grief ties me here and pulls me until I will break in two. Let me go. Please. You can help me by letting me go. If you love me, you will release me.*

Well, what can I say to that? I stop singing and open my eyes. Ash and Willa stare at me with horror.

That was foolish and selfish. You should have let Joshua go. You do not challenge the order.

"It was my fault," I say, scrubbing my face with my hands. "I had to try. I failed him."

There's not even a body to mourn or bury, no gravestone to mark his final resting place. "How do you mourn your dead?" I ask.

They live in our memory, with honor, says Ash.

That's not enough. I close my eyes again and think of Joshua, of his sweet, goofy grin, the body he never had a chance to grow into, his trust, his warm eyes, his damp nose, the way his tongue would loll out of his mouth when we'd chase each other when I was a child. I try to crystallize each memory in song, make each a perfect object in my mind, perfect as he was perfect.

"Oh," I hear Willa gasp.

When I open my eyes, I see a beautiful weeping cherry tree before me. I walk forward and let the blossoms brush against my face in the breeze. "You will be remembered and loved forever," I say, patting the trunk, "my beautiful and perfect Joshua." The wind picks up a little, scattering pink petals around us like a sudden, gentle snow-shower. I look up, and the petals drift down slowly, kissing my face.

"Now," I say, turning to the others, my eyes glittering with fury. "Tell me how I can kill the monster."

I feel empty as I sit up in bed. My pillow is damp, and I realize I've been crying. *Oh, my sweet Joshua*, I think. Now the memories of my childhood dreams with him come rushing back, flashes of his toothy grin, of dancing, images flickering by more and more rapidly like a Soviet montage film until the images blur into a haze of grief and loss, a kaleidoscope of pain. Getting out of bed, I hear a crash and find my sketchpad on the floor, open to a new drawing which I must have done in the night. A noble weeping cherry tree, Joshua's tree.

I failed him.

My hands are blackened with graphite, but it may as well be his blood. He was the dearest one to me; how could I have forgotten his name?

When I go to the bathroom to get ready to meet Shelly, I see my face is smudged with graphite as well. I look bruised. I turn on the water and let the bathroom fill with steam, feeling too heavy and numb to undress for my shower. *He's just a made-up thing in my brain*, I try to reason with myself, but I can't stop the tears from coming.

I can hear his words float back to me: *If you love me, you will release me.* I wonder if he also means carrying around my sorrow for him in the waking. Joshua would want me to be strong, to live my life as if nothing had happened. *I will honor you, sweet Joshua*, I say, finally finding the strength to peel off my pajamas and step into the rapidly cooling water. By the time I rinse the shampoo out of my hair, the water has gone cold. My teeth chatter uncontrollably as I dry off.

What are you supposed to wear to have brunch with the mother who abandoned you when you were five? Do you try to look pathetic to make her feel bad, to show how emotionally stunted you are because you lacked a strong mother figure? Or do you dress to kill and exude self-confidence to show that you turned out far better because she wasn't around to screw you up? And, perhaps more importantly, do you have any items of clothing in your hastily packed suitcase that could possibly touch either end of this spectrum?

I don't know what to do. I sit on the bed in my towel, teeth still chattering. I'm staring daggers at my suitcase, even though I know that it's me I'm angry with. I can't remember Vivian's Thursday schedule but chance it and give her a call.

Two rings. "Hey, Aggie-baba. How's it going out there?"

"Awful. I suck."

"Ridiculous. You are incapable of sucking."

"I ruin everything."

"What are you talking about?" I realize I can't exactly tell her about how I accidentally got my childhood dream-world wolf friend killed, so I try to change the subject.

"I'm about to go see my mom."

I can hear Vivian make a strange gurgling sound.

"Viv! Are you all right? Did you swallow your gum?"

She coughs a few times, hard. "Fuck, are you serious? Your mom? How did this happen?"

I tell her about the flat tire and the scrap of paper and brunch in a few hours. I don't mention the weird last name or her insinuations that Dad has not been telling me the truth about something. I tell her that I have no idea what to wear.

"Well, Agnamaniac, what sort of impression are you trying to make? What do you want her reaction to be?"

"If I knew that, Vivian, I would already be dressed." I add, "I just wish I knew what she wanted."

"Armor, baby. You need armor. Don't let her in. She is bad mojo. Be like, I don't know, like a fucking armadillo. Or horseshoe crab. Or like a crazy spiky echinoderm."

"And which of my assortment of ironic T-shirts and unwashed jeans exudes an echinoderm vibe to you?"

"Fuck if I know. Don't wear anything cute. Be severe. Merciless. Echinoderm power!"

"I have a brown turtleneck."

"Fine." I can almost hear Vivian's eyes rolling. "Did you bring any of those enormous hippie skirts of yours?"

"I may have."

"There you go. You're going to be great." She's silent for a few moments, to the point where I'm wondering if my crap-ass network dropped the call. I'm about to hang up when I hear her say, "Agnes?"

"Yeah, Viv?"

"Are you okay?"

Am I okay? I think of the last few days in Poppy Beach, of my flight, of the emptiness in my heart since I learned of Ian Millbrook's death. Of my impending reunion with Shelly. "I don't know," I answer, feeling very small.

"You can tell me anything, you know." I know Vivian means it, but somehow I fear if I told her of all the blackness in my head, all the sorrow and regret saturated in every part of my body, that she would look at me differently. Maybe she would see me as a burden. She'd distance herself bit by bit until one day I'd run into her and she'd have a last name I wouldn't even recognize. No.

"I know," I say. "Sometimes it's enough for me just to hear your voice. Tell me something distracting."

"I have to head to Torts now, and every time I walk in there and the prof starts talking, I feel disappointed that the class isn't about cake. It's like Charlie Brown and the football, man. I fall for it every time."

I have a good belly laugh over that, and I say, "Thanks, Viv."

"Anytime, dollface."

"I should let you go, I guess."

"Yeah, time for my cake/Torts bait-and-switch. But, Agnes-fish, call me later, okay? Let me know how it went? I'll be thinking of you when I can distract myself from cake rage."

"Okay. Love you."

"You too, Agnesthesia."

I feel stronger now, infused with a little of Vivian's light, the gift she gives me unknowingly. Her energy, her courage, her lack of fear, all give me the strength to put on my armor and gird myself for battle with Shelly. I will not let her destroy me.

When I arrive at the diner exactly at eleven, I scan the parking lot before realizing I have no idea what kind of car Shelly drives. I wonder if she'll recognize me. Will I even recognize her? I pull open the door, trying to imagine Vivian feeling misled in Torts class and wanting cake. It keeps me from running back into Bessie and driving home as fast as the old girl will let me.

A waitress holding a pot of coffee asks me if I'm there to eat in or get takeout, and I say, "I'm supposed to meet someone here." She shrugs and continues making the rounds of the diner, going from cup to cup and refilling. She reminds me of a bee in a meadow, alighting on flower after flower.

I scan the room, my heart pounding, looking for someone resembling the hazy image of Shelly in my brain. Even the few photographs I have of her are faded, discolored. But no one seated in the diner is alone. She's not here yet. I settle in on the padded bench by the door and wait. Maybe she won't show at all.

I feel like I'm waiting at the dentist, dreading the shot of Novocain and the smell of singed tooth and the high-pitched whirring of the drill. My ears are tuned to every car door slam outside, and with each my head snaps around to see if Shelly is here.

It turns out I needn't have been looking so hard, because as soon as her car pulls in, I can feel it, our severed umbilical connection, my phantom pain. I turn slowly and see Shelly taking a final drag on her cigarette before flicking it away and crushing it under her foot. She's older, a lot older, her face way too tan to be healthy, her skin a weird leathery quality. Her hair is big with hairspray and looks damaged. I can't see her eyes behind her sunglasses. It's not even sunny today.

I glance at the clock on the diner wall. Shelly is forty-five minutes late. I'm not surprised, but I do feel a bit the fool for having shown up on time. I'm already on my feet by the time she opens the door.

She looks me up and down, pushing her sunglasses up and into her hair. "Aggie?" Her voice is even raspier in person.

"Hi, Shelly." I make a conscious choice that today I will not call her *Mom*.

She doesn't flinch. "So, kid, let's get a table. I'm starving."

We sit in the same booth where Tricia and I had lunch yesterday. I remember how Tricia, even while talking to me, was always tuned in to her children, ready to respond with napkins or goldfish crackers or soothing pats, and then I look across the table and see Shelly absentmindedly twirling her chemically frosted hair around a finger while she squints to read the menu.

The waitress comes by for our order, and Shelly barrels in without asking me if I'm ready to order. "Coffee, and the lumberjack special. Give me the eggs scrambled." She shoves her menu at the waitress, who hasn't even finished writing.

"What would you like, sweetheart?" the waitress asks me kindly.

I give her a small smile back. "Just pancakes, I guess. And orange juice."

"You got it," she says, taking my menu and walking away.

"Let's look at you," says Shelly. I sit still, unsure of what she wants. "Longfellow University, man. Really! So you must be making the big bucks now, some high-powered executive or something. Bet you make six figures a year. You probably have a corner office and a terrific view."

"I'm a temp," I say.

"Oh."

"I dropped out of art school."

"Art school? What the heck were you going to do with that?"

The waitress is back with Shelly's coffee and my juice. "Here you are, hon," she says to me. I wonder if she can sense the totally messed-up vibe at our table.

"Thank you," I say, smiling again.

Shelly rips a packet of Sweet'N Low into her cup, gives the coffee a couple of stirs, and drums her fingers on the table while she waits for the coffee to cool enough for her to drink. Her nails are long and make a hollow, rattling sound. It reminds me of dead leaves in the fall, dragging slowly across asphalt in the wind.

"Why did you leave?" I ask, my voice louder than I intended it to be.

"Cutting right to the chase, I see," she says, chuckling humorlessly.

I shrug. "I'm only in town for a few more days, and this might be my only chance to find out. It's kind of important."

"Do you want the short version or the long version?" I can't believe she is going to tell me.

"I don't have anywhere to be for a while."

"Well then," she says, reaching into her purse for a cigarette and her lighter.

"You can't smoke in here," I say.

"This fucking town," she says with the unlit cigarette still in her mouth. It moves as she talks like a waggling finger.

The waitress comes back with our food. "I'm sorry, you can't smoke—"

"Yeah, yeah, I know," Shelly says, spitting the cigarette out. It lands on her plate. "Fucking bullshit," she mutters, taking the cigarette out of her scrambled eggs.

"Thank you—the pancakes look great," I say to the waitress, trying to balance out Shelly's atrocious behavior with stilted politeness. She smiles at me sympathetically before disappearing again into the kitchen.

"So, kid," Shelly says, pouring ketchup all over her plate. "You know Pete and I went to the same high school?"

I nod. "High school sweethearts," I say.

Shelly cackles. "Is that what he told you?"

I clamp my mouth shut. I don't want to share anything about Dad with her.

"Pete mooned after me all through high school, but he was a loser," she says, shoveling eggs and home fries into her mouth. "Bobby and I, now we were an item. Homecoming king and queen, prom king and queen, we were *it.*"

"Bobby?" Pete has never mentioned anyone named Bobby.

"Bobby *Kent*," she says, and I notice finally that she has a wedding ring on. "Shit, Pete really didn't tell you anything, did he? Bobby was captain of the football team. I was head cheerleader. Pete was nobody."

My pancakes have soaked up all the syrup I poured onto them, but I am no longer hungry.

"Bobby and I were perfect, had our lives planned out: he'd already been scouted by a bunch of colleges, and I'd follow him wherever. But senior year we got in a fight about something, something stupid. I don't even remember now—isn't that funny?" She looks over at me, but I'm not laughing.

She begins cutting up her sausage links into little pieces. "Anyway, we broke up. We'd do this all the time, have these stupid breakups, fume for a few days, come back, and have hot make-up sex."

I push my plate away from me.

"Oh for fuck's sake, kid, don't be such a prude. Your mama got some in high school. A lot of some." She laughs, no doubt reminiscing.

"Why are you telling me this?"

"Hey, kid, you asked. You wanted to know why I left. Are you enough of a big girl to handle it?"

"Of course," I say, pulling my plate back toward me and using the side of my fork to cut into the syrup-saturated pancake. I cut a tiny little slice out like a pie chip from Trivial Pursuit.

I'm reminded suddenly of the end-of-year parties we'd have for liturgical music. I'd never know what to wear. It was one of the few opportunities I had for Ian Millbrook to see me out of my uniform. Maybe, when I wasn't dressed like all the other girls in school, I'd have a chance to be noticed. But my Goodwill clothes were outdated, boring. I felt so drab. But still, I'd try.

Dad would drive me over to the party, hosted by whichever parents had agreed to it that year. I hoped he didn't notice how much effort I'd put into my appearance; I wouldn't want to explain it to him. My hand would tremble as I rang the doorbell, and I'd be dizzy thinking I could be spending the next few hours playing board games and eating chips and dip in the same room with Ian Millbrook. I think that moment before I walked into the party was the best, because the evening was full of such possibilities. Anything could happen. If I wore the right clothes, if I had my lip gloss on just so, if I told the right story or smiled the right way, maybe he would notice me. Maybe he would brush his hand across my back as he walked by. Maybe he'd ask me out. Maybe he'd kiss me in a dark corner of a hallway.

Before I walked through the door, a romantic, feel-good comedy waited on the other side, with me as its quirky heroine, Ian Millbrook as the matinee idol.

Sometimes I stood on the doorstep longer than necessary, too drunk on the images of what could happen. I stood there because I knew deep down that nothing would change, that the minute I walked through, I would be just ordinary, invisible Agnes again. Half the time Ian wouldn't even bother showing up (*of course he'd have better things to do with his Saturday nights*), and I'd feel deflated and foolish for taking so much time to try to pretty myself up. I'd wipe off the lip gloss off on the back of my hand and try to salvage the evening, lose myself in the board games.

But when Ian was there, all I could see was him. I'd blush later, remembering how I'd laughed too hard at everything he'd said, worrying I sounded like a braying donkey. I'd hope he hadn't noticed that I'd trailed after him all night as if there had been an invisible tether between us.

He showed up at the party after freshman year, and I was a total spaz in my attempt to act casual. We ended up on the same team for Trivial Pursuit, less fate than being in close proximity when the room had been divvied up into teams. I was mesmerized by his fingers as he cupped the die to roll, as he moved our pie dish around the board. I answered nearly all of the questions correctly, and our team easily won. Ian whistled through his teeth. "You're *smart*," he said admiringly. I smiled so much that my cheeks hurt.

So I'm staring at this little piece of pancake shaped like a Trivial Pursuit pie wedge, hearing his compliment again in my head, clutching the memory like a worry stone. Shelly's gritty voice is a harsh contrast as she continues, "So I was mad at him this time, really mad. There was a party that night—a girl's parents were out of town. You know how it gets."

Actually, I don't, but I nod.

"So I get wasted, and I stumble into a room and see Bobby making out with some slutty freshman. And I see Pete sitting in the corner with a beer, and he's watching me with those moony eyes. And I think, *I'll show Bobby, that bastard.*"

I can't imagine Dad at a party like this. I can't imagine him going to a party at a house of someone whose parents are out of town. But then I think, *Well, if he loved Shelly, he could have gone hoping she'd be there.* I can understand that.

"I waltzed over to him and sat on his lap. I said, 'Hey, I've seen you watching me. You're crazy about me, right?' And he nods, too drunk to try to lie. And I say, 'Well, come with me, and let's make all your fantasies come true.'"

This can't be real. This can't be how they got together. And her and this Bobby? Head cheerleader and captain of the football team? What a fucking cliché.

"I took him upstairs to an empty bedroom, and we screwed on top of a pile of coats on this bed." Shelly chuckles. "I had a zipper in my back the whole time, and Pete looked like he'd won the fucking lottery." She considers what she's said and slams her hand on the table a few times. "The literal *fucking* lottery," she cackles.

I'm still staring at the pie wedge of pancake. She is horrifying.

"Well, turns out, we made you that night, that meaningless drunk-fuck. When my pee stick turned up positive, I told Bobby, who dumped me. He knew it wasn't his."

"How…how do you know it was that night? How could *he* be sure I wasn't his?" How do I know that anything she is telling me is true? I'm also in shock that she referred to me as an *it*.

"I mean, look at you. You look just like Pete. Anyways, Bobby and I always used protection. I was just so damn mad at him that night that I just wanted to hurt him as much as I could. It was stupid, an accident. It shouldn't have happened."

There's really nothing quite like hearing the woman who gave birth to you describe you as an *it*, stupid, an accident that never should have happened. I think of Tricia again here yesterday, making Patrick squeal with delight by chomping up and down his chubby arm.

"I went to Pete next. I was really just looking for him to give me enough money to get rid of it, but he got down on one knee and proposed, and I was so torn up over Bobby that I said yes. I... sometimes I liked the way he looked at me, like I was the center of his world. It wasn't hot like me and Bobby, but, you know, it was all right. And you were born, and I thought that life wasn't too bad."

So I didn't imagine the maybe-tenderness from Shelly when I was a child. Maybe she did love me, a little, once upon a time. "So what happened?" I ask, still staring at my tiny, perfect slice of pancake.

"Fate, Aggie. Fate happened. I bumped into Bobby when I was visiting my cousin in Portland, and he was so sorry, said he'd always missed me, and I realized that I missed the fire, the spark. I never had that with Pete. He was just...predictable adoration. That gets boring, kid. You'll understand some day."

"I'll never be like you," I say. "I'd never leave my baby behind."

"Kid, you were already in kindergarten. You knew how to take care of yourself. I'd already let you ruin my body. It was time for Shelly to live for Shelly."

She disgusts me. I wish I could tear out all the parts of me that come from her genes.

"I can see you judging me, kid. And you know what? I don't care. I raised you good. I fed you, drove you to school, took you to the doctor. And you're probably more like me than you think. You'd drop everything for the right guy. I can see it in your face."

I can't help but think of Ian Millbrook. If I were married with a kid, and Ian Millbrook showed up on my doorstep and said he'd always loved me, would I leave everything I knew behind?

I am ashamed to realize that I probably would.

Shelly laughs and slaps her hand on the table again. "I knew it. I can see it. You've got a Bobby too. So don't you judge me."

"But…then why did you send the cards? Why not just make a clean break?" I ask.

"I'm not a monster," she says. "You're still my kid. I always know when your birthday is coming up. I can feel it here." Shelly uses her fork to point at her stomach. "So I send a card to let you know your mom remembers you. I do think of you sometimes." *Sometimes*. So generous of her.

"Well, you don't have to bother," I say coolly.

"You've got a Bobby too," she says again, jamming a triangle of toast in her mouth. She glances at her watch and reaches into her purse, throwing a couple of bills on the table. "Listen, can you take care of the tab? Bobby's waiting."

"Sure," I say in a flat voice.

She looks me over and chuckles to herself. "You really look just like Pete. Strong genes, that stubborn bastard."

"I'm glad," I say, picking up the bills. It's not nearly enough to cover what she's ordered.

"Well, Aggie, it's been real. You grew up nice. Longfellow University, definitely smarter than either of your parents." She pulls her sunglasses back down, fluffs her hair, and stands up.

I stand up to be polite, and she reaches in for an awkward hug. Her touch feels foreign to me, and I recoil.

"I'm glad you know the truth now," she says, and I sort of want to hit her. "All right, kid. See you around." She gives me a little wave as she goes to the door, immediately lighting a cigarette as soon as she's outside.

I sit back down, and our waitress comes by with the tab. "Are you all right, sweetheart?"

I nod numbly, pulling napkins out of the dispenser to dab at my eyes — no. This is a good thing. I'm *glad*. I'm glad now that I can close the door on Shelly. My mother is dead. I had a mother who loved me a little, who loved me enough to keep me alive, and when I turned five, she died. This will be my truth now.

I don't know what Shelly wanted. If she wanted me to doubt Dad, to steal everything from me, she failed. I only love him more than I ever have. He only wanted me to have a mother that I loved. He was just doing his job. He wanted to protect me.

I feel a gentle hand on my shoulder, and the waitress is back. "Cherry pie," she says, sliding around the used plates on the table to make room. "It's on the house. You look like you need it."

The slice of pie matches my little slice of pancake, and I think that love can come to us through unexpected ways. "You're *smart*," I hear someone say, and I look around, because that's Ian's voice, that's his compliment.

But of course he isn't there.

I take my fork and pierce the slice of pie, and the lattice crust crumbles. The piece loses its form, turning into a messy blob of startlingly red filling and broken bits of pastry, reminding me again how easily I can destroy something perfect. I put a forkful of pie in my mouth and close my eyes, letting the tears stream down.

When I use a napkin to mop up my tears, I remember the feel of cherry blossoms on my face.

THIRTEEN
TWO SISTERS

The waitress gives me another slice of pie to take home before I go, and I leave her a huge tip for being kind to me, decent. Even if my mother — no, I will not call her that ever, ever again — even though *Shelly* is more selfish and cruel than I ever could have imagined, there are still caring, nurturing people out in the world. And I am lucky to find kindness where I may: an apple sticker, a slice of pie, a pair of steady arms when I'm falling down the stairs. I still believe in this world. I won't let her poison me.

I shuffle back to my car with the little plastic container of pie. I bet Dad will like it. He's a sucker for baked goods. I should make him a cake before I leave. I step in gum as I cross the parking lot — Shelly's, I bet. It feels like she's clinging to me, dragging me down with her with every step I take.

"Let's take you home," I say to the pie in the car, feeling goofy about talking to dessert but wanting to speak to someone or something that doesn't fill me with hatred.

After putting the pie in the fridge at home, I try to decide what to do with the rest of my day. I'm not sure why I made my trip for so long. Maybe I felt guilty about not being home for all this time. Maybe deep down I fear that this is the last time I'll make it back here. *If I knew this were my last time in Poppy Beach, how would I spend my time? What would I make sure to do or see before I go?*

I don't even know. Poppy Beach is home, but there isn't a lot to do. Fortuna was the big place for us to hang out on the weekends, but I'm not nostalgic for it at all — it's such small potatoes compared to everything Boston has to offer. Do I miss anyone else from school? Not so much. Tricia is wonderful, and I love just *being* with her, but we don't have much to talk about, and my hidden feelings for Ian Millbrook weigh on me whenever I'm with her, even more so now that he's gone and will forever be a gigantic question mark. And I know I will never speak about it with her, though I'm not quite sure why. Maybe knowing that she was his first choice, of being rejected by someone Tricia didn't think was good enough for her, or maybe being embarrassed to love so much and so deeply a person she barely remembers. Maybe because I feel pathetic for harboring such feelings so long after we saw each other on any regular basis.

I text Vivian once I'm back in my room: *Back frm brunch. Shelly=Lifetime Channel Movie Event. Can u talk?*

She calls me right back. "Viv, how's the cake rage?" I ask.

"Abating slowly. I'm eating a Twinkie. That helps. It's like cake methadone." Her words are muffled, and I wonder if she's jammed an entire Twinkie in her mouth at once. I have no idea how Vivian can eat the crap she does, but I love her for it. I love her for appreciating the inherent awesomeness in severely over-processed foodstuffs. She can find something worthwhile in everything, which is why I need her so much in my life. She brings out a side of me that I never knew I had before I met her — she makes *me* feel worthwhile. When I'm with her, it's like I get a sense of the person I might have been if Shelly hadn't left, messing everything up. Carefree Agnes. Fun Agnes. Wisecracking, smartass Agnes. I'm not like this around anyone else. I wonder if she brings that out in me, or whether I am just a mirror, reflecting back some of her brightness.

After today's brunch I wonder now what Agnes I would have become if Shelly *had* stayed, if she hadn't run into her Bobby. Would she have loved me? Would she eventually have grown resentful of everything I'd cost her? If I hadn't been conceived that night, maybe she and Bobby would never have broken up, so maybe she would have thought of him every day, hating me more and more. I used to mourn the person I could have been if she'd stayed, but now, now I just don't know. Maybe the only way I could have been another, better Agnes was if Shelly hadn't been my mother at all.

"So, Agraba, tell me everything. Lifetime Event, eh?"

"Ugh. She's horrid. She's rude, and her skin's like old football leather."

"What did she want?"

"You know, I don't even know. She said that she thought it was some sort of sign that she'd run into my dad, but she seemed way less interested in me when she found out I wasn't controlling the world yet as a fresh Longfellow alum."

"The keyword here is *yet*," says Vivian, making me laugh. "I know you've been working on the nude ray."

"Dude, you are *so obsessed* with that nude ray! It's never going to happen!"

"Not with that attitude," she sniffs. "But seriously, Agnes, what a colossal bitch. You know my thoughts on the matter. Bad mojo. I never met the woman, and I use the term *woman* quite generously, but anyone dumb enough walk away from you isn't worth the black market fee for their stolen kidneys. Not that I still wouldn't harvest them if I ran into her. You know, just out of spite. I wouldn't even try to sell them. I'd leave her in the ice-filled bathtub with the kidneys *just* out of reach."

"Thanks," I say, but it's still so hard to shake the feeling that it's my fault. "I mean, I'm glad—uh, not about the kidney harvesting out of spite. I'm glad I saw her, so now I can stop with the *what-ifs*. I'm pretty sure now I'm better off without her. But—" and here I think about what she said to me, about *having a Bobby of my own* "—I hate that she's a part of me. I hate that half of everything in me comes from her."

"Oh, hon," Vivian says. "Biology isn't destiny. I've never seen you be anything but kind. And Pete's the cat's pajamas. He's so stubborn: I bet his genes are a force to be reckoned with. We should pretend that Pete just asexually reproduced, like a fucking hammerhead shark. Or, rather, like a *non-fucking* hammerhead shark."

"Is that shizz true?" I ask. "About hammerhead sharks?"

"Yeah. I think so."

"And also, could you never use the words *Pete* and *fucking* in close proximity ever again?"

"Life is long, Agnes, and I cannot in good conscience make such a guarantee. Pete's hot. It's just a fact of life."

"You suck," I say, but I'm laughing. I'm grossed out, but I'm laughing.

"Love you too."

"How's Boston?" I ask.

"Cold as fuck. Drab without Agnes Larch. You're my bedazzled space heater, babe."

"I...I don't even know what that means."

Vivian laughs. "I don't either. I think this Twinkie is messing with my brain."

"I don't know what I'd do without you, Viv," I say, getting a lump in my throat. God, I've been away only a few days, and I miss her *so much*. I think about how much I miss Dad when I'm in Boston, and I hate how I'm always feeling like I'm missing somebody, my heart torn into pieces, pulled in so many different directions at once. It's impossible to have everyone I love in one location, and I don't know how I can handle feeling this pain in my heart for the rest of my life. I feel so Holden Caulfield about it all, doomed to start missing everybody.

"Are you getting emo on me, Aggles?"

I'm quiet for a while, soaking in the day and feeling echoes of Shelly's viciousness. "Why do you put up with me? Be honest. If our freshman year roommates hadn't been such freaks of nature, would you even have talked to me?" I say it with a light tone, but I'm dead serious, my insides teetering on collapse, afraid that Vivian is going to tell me that she never intended to be my friend at all.

"Agnes," she answers sternly. She rarely calls me just *Agnes*. I can hear her exhale in exasperation. I knew it. I'm a burden.

"Forget it," I mumble.

"Agnes," she says again. "Do you have any idea how amazing you are?"

I feel like she's making fun of me, but it's not like Vivian to be cruel in this way. Still, I'm bracing myself for mocking laughter.

"I'm waiting, Agnes. Do you know?"

"I guess," I say flatly. "I mean, you're the amazing one. I'm just your sidekick."

"Goddamn it, Agnes, don't make me get on a plane just so I can beat your ass. You know I fucking love you. No matter how afraid you are, you always do the thing you fear most. You've never told me to piss off even though I know I'm crass and annoying and an attention whore. You make me feel like those are good things to be."

"What? How could you be annoying?"

"I'm just saying that sometimes we don't see ourselves the way others do. But I see you, Agnes. I want you to remember that."

"Okay," I say with a sniff. "You're the shit, Viv."

"No, *you are*," she says in her best thick Boston accent. It sounds like, "*No, you ahhh!*" God bless Viv.

"Wicked pissah," I say back. I drop the accent and say, "Thanks. I miss you."

"You too."

"I'll see you in two days," I say, and we hang up. For the moment I am not going to think about flying back, about the terror that awaits me. I'm just going to try to make it through my last days home. The house is quiet, so quiet. I can't stay here; it's like a tomb. Vivian's sunlight has already slipped away from my reflective surface, and I'm drowning in the silence and darkness of the fading day.

I run back outside and into the car. I start to drive. I don't know where. I'd like to see the ocean, the *proper* ocean. But first I'm just following my heart. Turn left here, right here, right again.

I'm on Briar Way in front of the Poppy Beach Cemetery. *Follow me*, something says, so I park and get out. It has stopped raining, and the ground is spongy under my boots, which I've shoved my feet into without socks. I close my eyes and just walk where I feel pulled. *This way*, I feel a voice tickling the back of my brain, and I step carefully, my hands in front of me as if I'm *It* in a game of Blind Man's Bluff.

Like a dowsing rod, I feel a strong pull down, and I know this is where I need to stop. I open my eyes. I'm in front of a gravestone that says MILLBROOK. I walk around to the back:

EMMY ELIZABETH MILLBROOK

AUGUST 22, 1997–AUGUST 30, 1997

OUR BORROWED ANGEL

Surely this can't be the same Millbrook as…but I keep reading the gravestone:

IAN CHRISTOPHER MILLBROOK

JULY 5, 1984–FEBRUARY 6, 2009

IN DIESEM WETTER, IN DIESEM SAUS, IN DIESEM BRAUS,

SIE RUH'N ALS WIE IN DER MUTTER HAUS,

VON KEINEM STURM ERSCHRECKET,

VON GOTTES HAND BEDECKET.

~FRIEDRICH RÜCKERT

I haven't taken German since sophomore year at Longfellow, but I remember enough to get the gist: "In this weather, they rest as in their mother's house, fear no storm, covered by God's hand." I don't know what *Saus* or *Braus* means. I can imagine, though, why they'd be drawn to this inscription, losing their son in a storm, wanting to think he is safe and warm and unafraid wherever he is, even if his body is frozen, lost in the icy waters of Lake Michigan. *Bedecken* makes me think of *Decke*, the German word for *blanket*, and I like the idea of a divine blanket out there to keep Ian warm. *May he be rocked to sleep by your hand*, I think.

I look at the other name again. I didn't know Ian had a sister before Meg, one who died so young. I start to cry again, feeling like no mother should ever have to endure the sort of loss Mrs. Millbrook already has. Once would be enough for several lifetimes, but now she has had to endure two. How can this world be so cruel? How can it take away two very wanted children from one woman, and let thrive the unwanted child of another?

My eyes feel hot, and I sink to my knees and put my finger in the grooves of the letters on the tombstone. I trace Ian's name, the way I had always wanted to trace the contours of his gentle face. I know his body isn't here, but it—*he*, I correct myself—will rest here some day. I pray that at the very least they find him. The only thing harder to bear than the grave of your child must be the empty grave of your child.

The wind kicks up, blowing my hair across my face. I'm still kneeling by the gravestone, the damp earth soaking my skirt. I'm thinking about doing laundry when I get home when someone or *something* brushes against my shoulder.

I stifle a scream and slowly turn my head, hoping I've just imagined it. When I look, I see a small hand there. I look up, and I see a pale face, wild eyes, and a tangle of long, unbrushed hair.

"Meg? Meg Millbrook?" I say.

She nods.

I look at my watch. "Shouldn't you be in school?"

She nods again.

I wonder how long she's been here, how long she's been watching me.

She touches Ian's name on the stone, just as I had a few moments prior, and big tears roll down her face. I remember again her open-mouthed, silent laughter as Ian pushed her on the swings. I reach up and wipe a tear away from her cold cheek, and I drape an arm around her shoulders to pull her to me.

"I'm so sorry, Meg." She turns her head toward my shoulder, and her little body is shaking. Soon I feel her hot tears soak through my turtleneck. I wrap my arms around her and rock her a little. Her body stops shaking, so I stop holding her, feeling a little awkward, like maybe I've crossed some sort of line, but she slips her icy little hand into mine and squeezes it. We sit there for a minute in silence, squeezing hands.

For some reason, I say to her, "Meg, you don't know who I am, but I loved your brother. I loved him with my whole heart and my whole soul. I faced my greatest fears so I could come here to say goodbye to him. He was kind to me when he had no reason to be, and I loved him. I still love him. I will probably always love him, until the day I stop breathing."

She pulls away from me, and I feel like an idiot. But then she reaches into her pocket for a small notepad and a little pencil. I hear her scratching away and tearing the paper out. She presses the paper in my hand. I'm about to read it when I hear a voice shout with worry, "Meg? Meg, are you here? I wish you wouldn't run away from me like that!"

It must be Mrs. Millbrook. I feel embarrassed. I know I could not possibly explain to her my presence here, so I stand up, give Meg a hug, and run away, hiding behind the thick trunk of a nearby tree.

"Oh, Meg, why did you jump out of the car? You could have broken your neck! I promised you we were going to stop here on the way back from the doctor. Come on, darling—come back to the car. We'll come see Emmy and Ian after your appointment. We can have a nice long visit then." She tries to sound soothing and chipper, but her voice wavers a little as she says his name. In my mind's eye, just saying his name aloud lights up the fissures in her heart, red and raw. I lean my forehead against the rough, fragrant bark of the tree and sob silently for her loss.

I wait until I hear doors slam and their car drive away before I emerge from behind my tree. I walk slowly back up to the road. I'm clutching Meg's message in my hand, but I vow not to look at it until I'm back in the car.

It's not until I shut the door that I realize that I'm soaked and freezing from kneeling on the wet ground. I turn the car on and turn the heat up as high as it will go, trying to warm up a little. I'm still clutching Meg's note. I unfold it slowly and read.

She's written just two words: *I know.*

I know? What does it mean? Does she mean she already knew, or she can tell from my presence? Or…or something else entirely? I read the note again before laying it on the seat beside me.

I puzzle over her note as I drive to the shore. I park up on a hill and sit on Bessie's hood and watch the sun set over the Pacific. The sun's so big and red and close, and the water goes from a reflective, jeweled sapphire to near darkness, where it's only sound and not sight that lets me know I'm so near the ocean's edge.

When I get back to the house, Dad's truck is in the driveway. Maybe he shut the shop down early again. I hope everything is all right. I fold Meg's note back up and tuck it into my hand.

"Dad? Hey, Dad?" I call as I come in.

"Ags! I was just wondering where you were."

I look at him with new eyes, hoping that most of me comes from him and not from Shelly. We *do* look a lot alike, with our dark features and round faces, although I'm just a wisp of a thing compared to Dad, who, even though he's not basketball-star tall, is strong and broad from a lifetime of hard physical work to run the bait shop.

I run to him and give him a big hug, soaking wet and smelling of the sea. "I love you, Dad. I love you so much. Thank you for being my dad."

For once he doesn't cough or try to change the subject. He just hugs me back.

We're quiet for a long time, until finally he says, "Ags, you'll catch your death of cold. Maybe you should get into some dry things."

"You're right. I'm going to take a shower."

I pull my muddy boots off and run upstairs. I take Meg's note and tape it onto a blank page at the end of my sketchpad before heading to the bathroom and peeling off my wet clothes. As I'm under the hot water, I think, *I'm rinsing off Shelly from me; I'm scrubbing her from my genes. I am saying goodbye to her.* I feel clean when I get out, lighter, somehow.

When I go back downstairs, Dad is sitting at the kitchen table with the newspaper.

"Hey, Dad, I brought you a slice of pie from the diner," I say, going to the fridge and getting the plastic container out.

"Pie," Dad says with a smile. Actually it sounds more like "Piiiiiiiiie." I laugh, and it feels so good to laugh at my dad's elongated vowels of pie love. I kiss the top of his head before going back to get a fork out of the drawer for him.

He digs into the pie, not caring that it's cold. When I offer to nuke it for a few seconds, he waves me away. "Piiiiiiiiiiiie," he says again. I think now he's just trying to make me laugh.

I watch him enjoying the slice of pie, that unexpected kindness from the waitress, as I sit down across the table from him and lean my head on my hands. "So," I say.

"Mmm?" Dad answers through a mouthful of pie.

"I, uh, had brunch with Shelly."

He stiffens and furrows his brow. I don't know if he's upset that I'm using her first name, but I don't care—I will never refer to her as my mother again. He's still got that mouthful of pie, though, so he doesn't say anything.

"She told me everything," I say, putting careful emphasis on the last word, and he flinches. I reach my hand out and pat his free hand. "No, it's okay. I don't care. It doesn't matter."

He swallows hard. I stand up to get him some water. With my back toward him, I casually say, "So, is it true? What she told me?"

"Well, I don't know what she told you, now, do I?" He avoids my eye as I put the glass of water beside him.

"She told me about Bobby, about high school, the party after the fight. And, uh," I stammer with burning cheeks, "a bed covered in coats."

He pushes the plastic container of pie away, and I think, *I really am his daughter.*

"So, is it true?"

"Ags, I…I didn't want…"

"Dad, it's okay. I just need to know. Is that…where I came from?"

He sighs. "I'm sorry, Ags."

"How…how can you not hate her?" I ask after a long silence.

"Well, now," he says. We have never spoken this honestly about anything, least of all Shelly. He drops his voice and doesn't look at me. "I still love her," he says. "I thought I was the luckiest guy in the world that night, and every day she was with me. And she brought you to me, didn't she?"

I kind of gape at him, and he finally meets my eyes.

"I know, you must think I'm crazy. Sometimes *I* think I'm crazy for still loving her. I knew she never loved me, not like she loved Bobby. But every day she was with me was like an unexpected gift. A little over two thousand unexpected gifts."

I do some quick math in my head. He'd counted the days.

"When she left, I guess I wasn't surprised. I couldn't complain—that would be ungrateful. I always knew, deep down, she wasn't mine."

"Oh, Dad." I want to tell him that he deserves better, that she's *awful* and mean, but I can't. This is the woman he loves. He still loves her. *Yeah*, I think, *Dad's constant like that*. "You're too good for this world," I say, squeezing his hand.

"I'm the luckiest guy in the world," he says, "because I have you."

"Likewise," I say. "Go on, finish your pie."

Dad smiles and says again, "Piiiiiiiiiiiiiiiie."

I kind of laugh and cry at the same time, and I realize that there's nowhere that I'd rather be in this moment than sitting here, patting my dad's hand, watching him eat pie.

FOURTEEN
SHE KNOWS

Dad and I eat cold meatloaf sandwiches and watch *Blazing Saddles* on TV, and it's a perfect night. We laugh at all the same parts.

"I miss Madeline Kahn," I say as she sashays on stage in her black lingerie and feather boa.

"Me too, kid," he says, and he seems sad and far away. I wonder if her bleached hair reminds him of Shelly somehow, or, more likely, if he sees reminders of her everywhere he looks. I can understand that. I wish I knew how to take away that pain. I wish I could absorb it like a charcoal filter.

And I think of how strange it is, that being called "kid" can feel like a loving shoulder squeeze coming from Dad but like a curse — not just a swear word, but an actual incantation attempting to undo my existence — coming from Shelly. It's the same simple, monosyllabic word. How is that possible?

I start nodding off on the couch as the movie ends, and I force myself to stand up and put the dirty plates in the sink, too tired to deal with them now. My legs feel as heavy as sandbags as I climb the stairs. I brush my teeth first, knowing that if I go to my room, I'll fall asleep before getting ready for bed. I pull on my pajamas with wooden, numb limbs as I think about the day. Shelly, Vivian, Ian Millbrook's gravestone. And Meg. Meg, whose eyes I can still feel boring through me from across the room at the memorial on Tuesday. Meg, who seems to see right through me with those haunted eyes.

I sit on top of the covers with my knees up, the sketchpad resting against my thighs. I flip through, looking at Joshua again. He won't be waiting for me tonight. How can I miss so palpably something that I created in my head? I turn to the end of the sketchpad, to Meg's cryptic note. *I know.* Did she know when she saw me from across the room? Did she mean she didn't doubt the sincerity of my confession?

Next to her note, I sketch us, what we must have looked like from the back: two girls holding hands and grieving at an empty tomb. I flip back to Joshua's tree and touch the trunk in the drawing with my fingertip. *I miss you so much already, sweet boy,* I think. I leave the sketchpad with me in the bed, just in case, turn off my lamp, and prepare for a world without Joshua.

There's a heavy weight in my chest as I wake up in the dreaming, because I can already feel Joshua's absence. I'm standing by his tree. "How are you, Joshua?" I ask, patting the trunk.

"*He cannot hear you, you know,*" says Willa.

"How do you know for sure?"

"*Because he has gone beyond. He feels no pain, but he is also unaware of our trivial lives.*"

"I don't know about that," I say. "And even so, it's important to *me* to be able to talk to him. Does it matter if he can hear?"

"*That is a self-centered way to think about it,*" remarks Willa.

They are practical wolves, and I am so *human,* so petty.

"I'm going to kill him," I say quietly, reaching down for my quiver of arrows and my longbow. "Is there anything in the rules about not killing the Stone One?"

Ash and Willa both look at me. "*It…has never been spoken about. We do not know. It is not forbidden, but it may not be possible,*" Ash says as Willa continues to stare.

"Did I make him?" I ask.

"*He existed here long before you ever came to us. You protected us from him, but he has always been, as far as the wolves remember.*"

"But how can that be?" I ask. "Didn't I create you?"

"*You created us—Ash and Willa and Joshua and our lost breth-ren—but we have always been and have always been ready to be called. We have been here forever, and we are newly born. When we die, we disappear, but we live on when you call us again, the same, but new.*"

I can almost understand what they are saying. I can always call new wolves into being, but wolves have always lived here, wherever *here* is. Maybe their memory stretches back too, the way Ash is al-ways saying that things live on in their memories. Is each wolf born already knowing the entire history of this land?

"Did I come to this place willingly, or was I called?"

"*We do not know, and even if we did, we would not be able to tell you,*" says Ash.

My brain is flooded with memories of my day in the waking, my horrible reunion with Shelly. I feel a strong desire to find the scraps of linen that wrapped my weapons and me before I awoke here. *Where are you, my burial shroud?* I think. *Let me feel where you are.* The longbow in my hand begins to hum a little, and just as in the graveyard this afternoon, I close my eyes and walk where I feel pulled. The bow leads me around into the forest, stopping at a tall redwood tree with a large hollow in its trunk. I reach in and pull out the scraps. I don't know how the scraps ended up here, but since the hilltop where I first became aware again now holds the rebuilt Oread's Keep, I suppose the scraps had to go somewhere. Although I also have a feeling that normal, waking logic does not hold in this world.

I get down on my knees so I can better pull out the strips of linen. I don't know what I'm looking for, but it feels vital. My body is tell-ing me to keep searching. I'm almost at the bottom of the scraps in the hollow, my arm in past my elbow, when I touch something that does not seem to belong in this world at all. I roll the soft, cylindrical object between my fingers as I pull my arm back out. In the muted sunlight of the forest I see that it's a cigarette butt with a lipstick stain.

Shelly.

I touch the print Shelly's mouth made where she sucked on the filter. So many things I've forgotten from my childhood, but as I touch this bit of trash, images begin to flicker in my mind like little jolts of electricity. I see again the ashtrays all around the house, cigarette butts, her lipstick always marring the ends.

I know from all his stern talks that Dad thinks smoking is a dis-gusting habit, for me anyway, but he never said anything judgmental to Shelly. At least, I can't remember that he did. There were ashtrays on every table in the house, on the countertops in the kitchen, even on the back of the toilet.

Of course Dad would have let her smoke all she wanted. He wanted her to be happy. He couldn't try to contain her spirit, although I don't even like using the word *spirit* for Shelly — nothing so light and ethereal and infused with good could come out of her. Are there bad spirits? I suppose there are. I imagine Shelly's like a polluted fog, like the exhalation of carcinogens after Shelly sucked on the cigarette butt in my hand.

And just like that, I remember now, how it happened, how I left the dreaming. It's all in this cigarette butt with the lipstick stain, repressed memories stinging my brain awake like jellyfish tentacles.

I walked out of my kindergarten classroom, swinging my red Snoopy lunchbox. I was surprised to see my dad, instead of Shelly, waiting with the other parents. Once Grandpa died, Daddy was always still at the shop when I got out of school.

"Daddy!" I ran to him and hugged his legs, the force of my swinging arm bringing my lunchbox around and banging into his shin, but he didn't seem to mind. He absentmindedly patted me on the head like a dog, taking my hand and walking me to the truck.

He got the booster seat out from the back and put it in the cab. I could buckle myself in. "Where's Mama?" I asked when he'd started the car. I tried to look at his eyes in the rearview mirror, but he was looking away, lost.

"She...she's going away."

"Going away? Like on a trip?"

"Something like that," he said in a strained voice.

When we were home, there was a strange car in the driveway. Shelly was dragging an old, dirty duffel bag down the front stairs. The unfamiliar car was packed to the gills. There was no driver.

She swore under her breath when she saw me.

"Mama, are you going on another long trip?" The car seemed too full, and she'd just gotten back from Portland.

Shelly wouldn't look at me. She had a cigarette dangling from her lip, the end glowing brightly as she took another puff, flicking away the ash. She hoisted the bag into the backseat of the car. She slid into the driver's seat and was about to pull the door shut when my dad stopped the door with his hand.

"Look, I know I can't make you stay, Shelly, but goddamn it all to hell, you *will* say goodbye to your child." I'd never heard him sound this angry or even say so many words at once.

I heard Shelly laugh coldly. "Are you *threatening* me, Peter Larch?"

The fight went out of him. "Do what you have to do, Shelly. You can treat me however you want. But she's your *daughter*, your *baby*."

I remember standing in confusion while watching this exchange. These people looked like my parents, but they behaved like strangers. I clutched the Snoopy lunchbox in my hands tightly, the plastic handle digging into my palms like the monkey bars at recess.

With an exaggerated sigh, Shelly got back out of the car in her ridiculous heels and brightly colored capris.

"Aggie, sweetheart," she said, crouching down to be eye level with me, "Mama loves you, but Mama needs to go away."

"You need to?" I asked, puzzled.

"Someday you'll understand, Aggie."

"Are bad people trying to get you?"

"No, Aggie. I'm going away because I want to. I need to, but it's my choice. And that's what being a woman now is all about, Aggie. Choices. And I'm making this one."

"Can I come with you?" I asked. I was hardly ever alone with my dad; Shelly was my constant. I glanced over Shelly's shoulder and saw Dad watching us, his face perfectly still, his eyes glassy and unseeing, like the dead fish he'd bring back from his weekend expeditions.

"No," she said flatly. Just that. Just "no." Not an explanation, not an excuse, just block letters ten feet tall in my brain in flashing neon. *NO.*

She hadn't touched me, but I recoiled as if I'd been slapped. I clutched the Snoopy lunchbox more tightly.

"When are you coming back?"

She sighed. "I'm not. I won't be coming back."

"Shelly!" my dad snapped. He still hadn't moved from his spot by the unfamiliar car. "She's just a child!"

"What do you want me to do? Give her false hope? Did that ever help you?" she spit. My parents were strangers to each other and to me. Maybe this was all just a dream.

"You're a big girl, Aggie, so I'm not going to lie to you. I'm not coming back. But Mama loves you. Don't forget that." She took a final puff off the cigarette and tossed it onto the front walkway. I watched the stub fly in an arc until it landed, still lit, on the concrete. I stared at the wisps of smoke bleeding out of the dying cigarette.

"Well, kid, I guess this is goodbye." Shelly opened her arms to hug me, but I was frightened. This woman, she could not be my mother. Who was that man who looked like my dad but spoke so sharply? They were strangers. I was not supposed to trust strangers. I dropped my lunchbox and ran into the house, up the stairs, and hid under my bed.

I heard more shouting, a car door slam, and squealing tires. The door opened, and I heard my father's voice. "Aggie, honey? Are you in here?"

I was crying, but I didn't know why. I didn't understand anything that was happening. Dad sounded more like Dad, but like something was missing. I didn't answer him in case he was still a stranger, some sort of alien creature. *Had they been kidnapped and replaced with monsters who had their faces?*

I heard him clomping up the stairs in his work boots. I scrambled farther away from the door. "Honey? Honey?"

He knew my hiding spots from weekend games of hide-and-seek, so he squatted by the bed and peered in. I screamed. "Oh, there you are." He looked tired. "I'm going to lie down for a bit. You stay there as long as you want, okay?"

That sounded more like my dad, but again, like part of him was missing. I wasn't afraid of him any longer, but I still waited until I'd heard their bedroom door close before I ventured back out.

I walked cautiously down the stairs to see if Shelly was still outside. I'd heard a car drive away, but I wanted to see for myself. There was only his truck in the driveway. My eye was drawn to something bright red on the front lawn. My Snoopy lunchbox. I went out to fetch it. As I bent down to pick it up, I saw the cigarette butt Shelly had flung away before trying to hug me. I stepped on the end and twisted my foot on top of it the way I'd seen her do countless times. I reached down to pick up the butt. Her lipstick had stained the end, as always. She was always reapplying her bright red lipstick.

I closed my hand around the cigarette butt lightly, as if I'd caught a firefly. I walked inside, put the lunchbox on a kitchen chair, and went back upstairs. I sat on my bed and stared at the cigarette butt in my hand. "You are the last one," I said to it solemnly. I don't know how I understood it, but I did. I knew from my father's face, his dead fish eyes, that our lives would never be the same.

I touched the lipstick-stained end to my cheek, pretending it was Shelly giving me a goodbye kiss.

Dad ordered pizza that night, when he finally emerged from his room. I thought it was a terrific treat, but I didn't know then that it was the first of many nights of pizza, leftover pizza, and new pizza again. Dad sat numbly in the living room and watched TV, not even telling me to go to bed. This also felt a little like a holiday, but somehow not right either.

When I started yawning, I went upstairs to my room. The cigarette butt was still on the bed, and I closed it into my palm as I went to sleep without brushing my teeth. No one had reminded me to.

When I woke up in the dreaming, the cigarette butt was still in my hand. I wondered what it was at first, because I hadn't seen anything like it in my wonderful play world of talking wolves and castles and pretty dresses.

It wasn't until I was in the dreaming that I realized, fully, what had happened. *Mama is gone, and she is never coming home.* In the dreaming I somehow understood more clearly that she had thrown me away. She hadn't wanted to take me with her.

The wolves were eager to play games again, to help me practice my archery skills, but I stood with the butt in my hand.

"*Why won't you play with us, Princess Aggie?*" they asked.

"Shh," I said, still staring at my palm. I needed to figure something out.

Finally, I said, "I need to go away. I love you, but I need to go away."

"*What?*" The wolves seemed to speak in unison, one whole lupine unit of confusion.

"I am going away now," I said, holding the cigarette butt cupped in my hand, as if that explained everything. "Being a princess means making choices, and I choose to go away forever. I am going away forever now."

"*But who will protect us from the Stone One?*" they asked.

"Someone else," I said.

"*There is no one else.*"

"Then you'll have to do it."

"*We cannot protect ourselves from him.*"

"You'll have to find a way."

"*Who will play games with us?*"

"You will have to play them without me."

"*But why? What did we do?*"

I had no answer. I just started to cry and scream, pushing wolves out of my way. My scream pierced the sky, and it began to rain, something that never happened in this world. As I screamed, the stone walls of Oread's Keep began to crack. I ran until I was by the Bridge Between, shrieking the whole way, some weird spirit moving through me. The ropes began to fray and unwind until the planks came loose, falling into the river, breaking against the rocks.

"*What are you doing? Why are you doing this?*" the wolves asked as they ran after me, confused and hurt. I could sense their fear and bewilderment coming off of them in almost visible particles. I did not answer them. I was a wild thing, wilder than the wolves, my hair tangled and matted with branches and leaves from running through the woods.

I waited until I was in the center of the courtyard in Oread's Keep before speaking again. The rain had soaked the stone, and everything smelled of wet rock and earth. The wolves filled the courtyard around me. The hair on their backs bristled, and a few wolves looked up at the skies, confused about the wetness coming down. They blinked as raindrops fell into their open eyes.

"I won't be coming back. Wrap me up. Wrap me up and bury me. I won't return."

"*But, but, Princess Aggie—*" they started to protest.

"*No!*" I shrieked. "No. You do what I tell you. I made you. You have to do what I say. Wrap me up. Bury me. I won't come back. I don't want to be here anymore." As a wolf advanced on me, I stamped my foot and screamed, "*I don't want to be here anymore!*" I found my bow and tried to snap it in two over my leg. Ash stopped me.

"*Princess, please. Please leave us this. The bow has always belonged to the land. We will let you go.*"

"You'll *let* me go? *I* tell you what to do," I said. I didn't know who was speaking through me. These were not my words. I felt almost as if I were watching the whole scene from far away.

Ash let out a sharp bark, and several wolves ran off, coming back with a bolt of fabric. I held onto the end of it as they wound me up tightly, exactly as I had asked. I felt no fear. I just knew this is what I needed to be doing. The process seemed to take hours, and the little butt fell out of my hand part of the way through, ending up somewhere by my leg, tangled up in the linen. My breathing slowed as the wrappings grew tighter, and I was soon damp all through from the rain, which had not stopped falling.

I remembered being dragged through the courtyard, through the grass, and I had a vague memory from another life of someone — a woman — dragging a large bag into the back of a car. Something so familiar, but so hazy…what was it? Did I know her?

The earth was soft underneath me, and I could hear the wolves digging. *Goodbye*, I thought, not sure what I was really saying goodbye to.

"*We obey you; you are ours*," Ash said, barking again. I felt noses and paws nudging me, and then I was falling, falling, landing in rich, damp earth. I felt clods of dirt kicked onto me from above, soft little pats. *Good*, I thought.

The dirt was soon heavy on me, and my mind became empty. Who was I? Why was I lying here? What was this pressure on my chest? What was that muffled sound? It was like the howling of something in pain. Of many things in pain. Before I could wonder about it too much, everything went to white, a blank sheet of paper, bright in its nothingness. I saw nothing and felt nothing. This was peace.

When I woke up the next morning and went downstairs, the TV was blaring, my father still asleep in front of it, the half-eaten pizza from the night before lying cold on the coffee table.

I nudged my father awake and said, "I don't want to be called *Aggie* anymore."

I think of all these things as I roll this long-forgotten cigarette butt between my fingers. I did all this. I made them bury me. I caused the destruction. I create, and I destroy. I tear the cigarette butt into shreds with my fingers. I dig a hole with my hands, dirt crammed under my nails, and I bury this piece of filth. I stand and stomp on top of the loose earth, pounding it down until it is firm. "Be forgotten, Shelly," I say with a cold finality. "No longer pollute the land."

I run out of the woods back to Joshua's tree. "Ash! Willa!" I call out. "I remember everything, all of it."

"*Do you?*" asks Willa skeptically.

"I do. Willa, I am so sorry. I never should have left you. I never should have said those things. I destroyed the bridge. I left you unprotected." I'm crying now. "I made the rains come." I look up at Joshua's tree. "And Joshua and the others are dead because of it. I will never leave you again. Never."

For the first time, Willa looks at me with something other than contempt. She cautiously comes forward and licks my hand. "*It is you,*" she says, lying down at my feet.

Ash is sniffing the air. "*He is coming back. Are you ready?*"

"The Stone One?"

"*Yes.*"

"How do I kill him?"

"*I do not know.*"

"I will find a way. He won't hold you prisoner any longer. He will pay for what he did to Joshua."

"*The price may be high, my princess.*"

"I am not afraid," I say, even though my heart is quaking.

"*I will stand with you,*" says Ash.

"*As will I,*" says Willa, getting up and pressing her warm body against my other side.

I can feel the ground rumbling as the Stone One returns. This time, this time I will be ready. I will honor Joshua. I will have my vengeance.

"*Will you?*" laughs that voice, like bone scraping against bone. He is coming. He is here.

This meeting will be our last.

When I wake up, my hand is cupped. I sit up and slowly open my hand, expecting to find nothing. A shredded cigarette filter rests on my palm, traces of a lipstick smear still visible on one end.

FIFTEEN
BEING HESTIA

I stare at my hand and at the impossible piece of trash cupped in it. A cigarette butt, shredded as in my dream, with a lipstick stain on the end. Shelly's cigarette butt, the last one. How is this possible? I put the cigarette butt down on my bedside table and hold my head in my hands. *This is not happening, this is not happening,* I think over and over.

I have finally gone completely crazy.

Let's think logically about this, I say to myself. I mean, I draw in my sleep. It's possible I do more than that. It's possible that I walk around, maybe pick things up. There might have been a cigarette butt under my bed or something. I could have just found it in my sleep, and then dreamed of it because it was in my hand. I could have shredded the filter in my hand when I shredded it in my dream. That must be it, because the alternative is…impossible.

Isn't it?

I consciously decide to stop thinking about it. I found the cigarette butt in my sleep in a long-forgotten corner of my room, end of story. I think of the rest of my dream, of learning why I left the dreaming, why I couldn't remember.

It was me. *I* was the monster. I destroyed the Bridge Between. I shattered the walls of Oread's Keep. And I left the wolves unprotected from the Stone One. Any pain, any suffering they felt, that they still feel, was because of me. It's hard to realize that you're the destroyer of such a beautiful and perfect world.

Fictional, Agnes, I remind myself, glaring at the bit of cigarette butt on the table. What should I do with it? I can't throw it away, much as I'd like to. It's important. I tape it into my sketchpad on a new sheet of paper and spend time drawing what I remember, the hollow in the tree, the scraps of cloth. Swirling around the big tree I have quick sketches of the wolves wrapping me, burying me. And at the roots of the great redwood, the actual remnants of Shelly's cigarette butt lie quietly menacing like some sort of fairytale snake, the filter leaching all the color off the page like a straw, the lipstick stain at its tip bright and startling like a bruise.

I flip back a few pages to see Joshua again. I miss him. How can I miss him so much? He's not real. He never was real. But I feel like I've lost someone dear to me. He's about as real as Ian Millbrook, at this point, maybe more so. *At least Joshua loved me,* I think, and then I shake my head to stop this train of thought. This is a train of thought that leads to Crazytown. They're just dreams. Dreams are important, sure, but they aren't real. I created this world because I needed to. I mean, why do any of us dream?

Don't let the dreams poison your waking, I tell myself, and I have to laugh. I'm laughing because I'm admonishing myself for putting too much stock in dreams, in memories of my imaginary wolf friend, when I've traveled across the country for the first time since I left home for college just because some boy who barely knew I existed died in a freak accident. What's more ridiculous? I don't know. I just feel pathetic and sad.

Today is my last full day in Poppy Beach. We'll have to leave pretty early tomorrow, and traveling days are so weird anyway. They are strange, in-between places, much like jet bridges, neither one thing nor the other, and therefore somehow sinister. It strikes me that that's also what's wrong with the Stone One, neither entirely human nor entirely monster, and therefore unknowable and terrifying.

But why is the Stone One afraid of me? Why am I able to stop him from attacking? Is it just who I am? Is it because I created the world? I seem to hold a lot of power in the dreaming, when in waking life I am ineffectual, forgettable, invisible. *Or maybe*—I flip again to the picture that scares me, of me lashed to the stake and crosspiece—maybe I am just a scarecrow. Maybe I represent something greater; maybe I am the shadow of some far more powerful force, and *this* is what keeps the Stone One from destroying the wolves when I am there.

I have vowed to finish him the next time I see him. He was approaching Oread's Keep right before I awoke. Will he harm Ash and Willa while I'm not there? Maybe just my return has been protection enough for them, my shadow lingering there, a ghostly imprint, during my waking hours. The scarecrow totem of a scarecrow. Maybe that's enough.

I'm not sure how I'm going to spend this day. I have no one left to see. I will bake Dad that cake, though. So: shopping, baking, waiting. That will be my day. I'm struck again by how different I am in the waking. In the dreaming, I am Artemis, fierce with my arrows, but in Poppy Beach I am merely Hestia, tending the fires. But that's important too. Dad needs looking after. I can't bear the thought of leaving him again tomorrow. I want to bake him enough cakes to fill his freezer, individually wrapped reminders of how much I love him.

He must know, right? He must know how much I love him just by being around me, but what is our human need to have tangible objects as proof? Or maybe that's just me. But Dad and I are so similar that I know it would mean more to him if I could leave something physical behind. When I'm back in Boston tomorrow, it'll be harder for him to feel the love radiating out of me across three thousand miles of cell phone towers and telephone wire, especially when neither of us is in any way good at communicating.

How many cakes can I bake before Dad gets home for the night?

I take a quick shower and think, *This is the second-to-last shower I will take here for a long time.* I'm strangely nostalgic about everything as I pull the brush through my wet hair. I throw on some clothes from my bag, which I never bothered unpacking. Maybe I should have unpacked, put some things back in my dresser drawers. Why didn't I? Maybe I wanted to underline the fact that this is temporary. That I shouldn't get too comfortable, because I'm only going to leave again. I don't want to be the girl who lived here, the girl who Shelly threw away, the girl who didn't exist to Ian Millbrook.

But that also means denying that I was the girl who was so much loved by Peter Larch. The one who still is, and the one who will break his heart tomorrow by going away again, to return…when? Maybe never. Maybe I'll never be brave enough again, and I hate myself a little for being brave for Ian Millbrook and not for my father.

I put on my coat before leaving the house, because in less than a week, my body has already acclimated again to Poppy Beach weather. I'm chilled in the damp now. I shiver just thinking about the bone-aching cold that awaits me when I return to Boston. *When*, I keep reminding myself, trying to be optimistic. I will survive the flight. I will see Vivian again.

I lightly lay my finger in the dent in Bessie's bumper before climbing in and starting the engine. I make a list in my head as I wait for the heat to kick in: eggs, butter, flour, sugar, baking chocolate, cocoa powder, baking soda, baking powder. Basically everything. I didn't check the cupboards before leaving the house, but I know Dad won't have anything but salt. There might be flour, but I can imagine it's infested with weevils. I vow to clean out the pantry and cupboards before leaving. It's the least I can do, just set Dad up so he'll be okay until I come back.

If, I correct myself, unable to be optimistic on that front.

I'm on autopilot as I drive, thinking about my dream, wondering how on earth I'll be able to defeat the Stone One. I go over what I know in bullet points in my head. I didn't create him. He existed before I became aware of the dreaming. When I abandoned the wolves, when I shrieked and destroyed everything beautiful in Oread's Keep, he was not destroyed. So I don't have power over him, not like that. But I'll make him pay for what he did to Joshua and to countless other wolves during my long absence. Somehow. I have to. I'll make it okay in case I have to leave again someday.

I stop the car and am surprised to find myself not at the shopping plaza but at the cemetery again. As much as I know I should take Bessie out of park and turn around to head to the grocery store, my body won't obey. I'm having a tug of war with myself over taking the keys out of the ignition. I want to keep them in there, but my body fights me the whole way. My body wins, and I'm sitting there in my truck with my keys clutched in my hand. Fine. I'll go see him again, or the place where he will come to rest one day—one day soon, I hope.

I don't think I'll run into Meg today. I pick my way through the springy grass, hoping I'll remember where to go. My feet seem to know the way. I stare at them as they carry me through the fields. I close my eyes, surrendering myself completely to my body's control, and I hear the wind, some birds chirping, and an occasional car zipping down the road. I bark my shins against something hard, and when I open my eyes to rub the pain away, I see I'm back at the Millbrook gravestone.

I should have brought something to leave here. I kneel down to trace his name again. *Ian Christopher Millbrook.* His name is here, etched on stone, another something tangible. But how tangible can a grave be if it's empty?

I get up stiffly and walk to the tree I hid behind yesterday when Mrs. Millbrook came to fetch Meg. I put my hand on the trunk and make a slow circle as I walk around its circumference. I feel like I'm looking for something, but I don't know what. And then I see, hidden among the golden pine needles, a little slip of paper just like the one Meg gave me yesterday. I brush the needles aside and extract the note, thinking idly of Boo Radley.

It's folded in half, just like the other one. The outside just says, *Hi.* My hands tremble as I open the note. It could be from anyone, but I'm pretty sure it's Meg, the same paper, the same pencil pressed hard against the paper. I don't know what I'm expecting to find as I unfold the note. All it says is, *I can see you.*

I glance around—can she see me now? Is this note even for me? She could have been leaving a note for Ian, maybe, or maybe her tiny ghost sister, little Emmy. Still, I pocket the paper, knowing I'll tape it into my sketchpad once I get home. Christ, I'm so selfish. This note might have been left here for Ian or Emmy. But then again, even if it were, it would blow away, get trampled on, get thrown away, or become tattered in the wind. I'll keep the note safe for whomever it's truly for.

And maybe I'm the intended recipient. I don't know.

I sit among the dead leaves and lean against the tree, planning out the rest of the day: groceries, then cake. And Dad. We'll do something tonight. Maybe I should rent a movie. I should check the TV listings first—there might be a game. I fiddle with the pine needles around me, smoothing them out, lining them up until they're facing the same way. My hand catches on something, and I sweep the needles away until I uncover a small, smooth rock with jagged edges. It doesn't look like anything that would occur naturally here—someone must have dropped it. It's black with an iridescent sheen, volcanic glass of some sort.

I take my phone out and text Vivian: *Hey, u took Rocks 4 Jocks, y/y?*

She texts right back: *Best gut I ever took. Pretty rocks! Pretty!*

I smile at her use of *gut* to mean *easy class*—a usage I haven't heard since I graduated Longfellow. It makes me feel cozy and young and hopeful and sad all at once. I take a picture of the rock in my hand and text it back to her: *What the hell is this?*

It takes a minute or two, but she texts back: *I took that class CR/D/F, but I think it's obsidian. Shiny. Can I put it in my mouth?*

I laugh. Vivian is always asking to put things in her mouth. I know, that sounds totally bad, but there's nothing sexual about it. She just…likes shiny things…in her mouth. When we first saw ads for the redesigned iPod shuffle, she grabbed my arm so tightly I nearly bruised. "Oh my fucksticks, when does that come out so I can buy it and put it in my mouth?"

"Vivian!" I shrieked while trying to pry her fingers off my arm. "Don't you already have an iPod with, like, a gazillion gigs of storage?"

"Well, *yes*, but not one that fits in my mouth," she said, rolling her eyes and enunciating each syllable as if I were not a native speaker of English.

Oh, I miss her. I can't wait to see her tomorrow. I text back: *No, rock stays here. But thx 4 yr help.*

I'm about to put my phone away when she texts back: *Killjoy.*

I text back: *Skankbot.*

She replies quickly with: *Mother Whoresa.*

I know I can't win this game. I text, *Well played*, and put the phone away before she can insult me again.

"Hello, obsidian," I say to the rock in my hand. "How did you get here?" I hold the rock in the filtered light from overcast skies and watch the colors dance across the surface. "I know—you're not for me. But I know a place where you can stay." And I walk back to the Millbrook gravestone.

I dig the earth a little with my fingers, making a small pocket to nestle the rock in. Before I put the rock down, I hold it to my mouth and whisper against it, "Ian, if you can hear me, I'm leaving this with you, giving you a little something like you did for me a long time ago. Think of it as a housewarming gift, a rock of approval." I rub my thumb over the stone, gasping as a sharp edge cuts me. Instinctively, I bring my thumb to my mouth, tasting salt and metal. It's not deep, but it stings.

My DNA is on this rock now, and as morbid and crazy as it seems, something about that makes me kind of happy, that there's a tangible piece left here with him, not just the fractured hopes that will always linger around this gravestone, around all the unanswered questions and rejections and regrets. I plunk the stone down in the little hole I've dug and pat down the earth. I'm reminded of burying the cigarette butt in my dream world, but I force those thoughts out of my head. I will not let Shelly into this moment. This moment is for me and for Ian Millbrook, even though he doesn't know it.

"Can you see me, Ian?" I ask the air, thinking of the note in my pocket. It's kind of funny to think that he must know now — I mean, if there is life and consciousness beyond our world. My love for him is no longer a secret to him if something exists beyond death. I'm not sure how I feel about that. Embarrassed? Glad? Terrified? Maybe all three. "I guess you know now, Ian. Sleep well," I say, patting the earth down. Still, none of it feels real, and I make my way back to the car, brushing the dirt off my hands.

After my time in the graveyard, I'm barely aware as I make my grocery trip, numbly putting items into my cart, planning out a couple of cakes. As I dig my wallet out at the checkout, I see there's dirt under my nails, Ian's dirt. I curl my fingers up so the cashier won't see them. I stumble back to the car with a couple of grocery sacks on each arm.

There are red marks on my skin from where the bags were looped over my wrists, and I rub them a bit after I start the car. This is probably my last grocery trip here for a long time, my last drive home from the grocery store. Why do I keep trying to attach significance to every little thing I do today?

I don't bother putting the groceries away when I get home, immediately making two different kinds of cake batter. There are still cake pans around, untouched since I was in high school. I'm not even sure of the last time the oven was used before this week. I fill a couple cake pans with chocolate cake batter and one loaf pan with pound cake. We have only the one oven, so I put everything in and hope for the best. I know the rounds will be done first, and then I can adjust the temperature for the pound cake.

As I'm waiting for the cakes to bake, I clear out the cupboards, refrigerator, and pantry of anything that I recognize from before college. The tall kitchen garbage can is soon filled to overflowing with nasty old sacks of flour, expired cake mix, Tupperware containers filled with things so green and mossy I don't think I have the stomach to try to save them. They go right in the trash. *Sorry, Mother Earth*, I think.

I bag up the trash and take it to a can around the back of the house, and I go back inside, wash up the dishes, and sit at the kitchen table, waiting. I pull the note out of my pocket and read it again. *Hi. I can see you.*

The timer buzzes; the chocolate cake rounds are done. I adjust the heat for the pound cake and reset the timer. What to do now? I'm twitchy. I go upstairs with Meg's note and tape it on the page opposite her other note and the sketch of us at the grave. I'm writing before I'm aware, *Who can you see?* I also draw the rock as I remember, but I'm having trouble capturing its iridescence. It's hard to show all the colors of the rainbow with a graphite pencil. When I get home (*when*, not *if*, I remind myself), maybe I'll try with oils.

I try to draw what the bark on my hand felt like, the needles smooth and pliant and fragrant, the sharp edge of the rock piercing the skin on the pad of my thumb. How do you draw sensations? I frown at my pencil in frustration. I can't get my feelings down. Everything I feel inside me is twisted, encrypted, and I can't put it into a form I can touch and share with…well, I don't know. I don't know who will ever see this sketchpad, but it seems important to document. Maybe I'm trying to leave something of myself behind, so someone hundreds of years from now will open the sketchpad and think, *Hmm, I may understand her a bit.* But it all seems so inadequate, the dark mass inside me incapable of being captured in graphite on paper.

I can smell the pound cake all the way in my room, and I'm halfway down the stairs when the buzzer goes off. It's come out with a nice crust, cracked open and showing off its bright yellow center. *Hi. I can see you.*

Dad comes home with Chinese takeout, which is a good thing since I hadn't even planned dinner, too busy filling the house with cake-smell. He drifts into the kitchen dreamily sniffing, and I'm reminded of those old Froot Loops commercials with Toucan Sam, following his nose. "Is that cake? Is that cake…*for me?*" he asks with awe and hope, hands clasped at his chest like an excited child.

"I couldn't very well leave here without baking you at least one cake," I say, shrugging and looking away, smiling to myself. I made him happy. It eases the feeling of guilt gnawing away at my insides at the thought of leaving him. "How was the shop?" I ask, just trying to fill the space with sound.

"The usual." Dad shrugs, getting out a butter knife and cutting into one of the chocolate cake rounds. "Maybe quieter. Fewer people out, Friday the thirteenth and all."

Oh! Oh. It's Friday the thirteenth. I used to be a little superstitious about the date, and I'm glad I didn't know as I went along my errands. Of course it's Friday the thirteenth — it's why I opted to fly back on Saturday and not Friday, not believing a plane with me in it would make it to Boston safely on such an inauspicious date. Oh God, I'm flying again in less than twenty-four hours. I grip the table to keep from floating away, trying to hold my molecules together and not dissipate into the air like a gas.

"Ags, honey, are you okay?" Dad asks through a mouthful of cake.

"Yeah, I'm fine," I say, deciding not to share with Dad my struggle to stay in solid form. "Just thinking about flying tomorrow."

"You'll do great, kid," he says, rubbing my shoulder soothingly. Oh, how I wish I could take Dad with me on the plane to calm me when my inevitable freak-out happens. But I also can't stand the thought of putting him in that kind of danger now. He'll be safe here in Poppy Beach, lonely but safe. And if I had to choose, I'd keep him safe above everything else.

"Do you want to eat here or in the living room?" I ask, eyeing the food on my plate warily. I'd forgotten how bad Chinese is out here, how bland. It may as well be plain pasta with butter. Soy sauce cures most ills though, so I'm glad the takeout bag is filled with many plastic packets of the stuff. I feel disloyal though, thinking bad thoughts about little Poppy Beach. This is my home. I don't want to turn into one of those big city Ivy League snobs, or worse, like Shelly, who hates everything about this place for no reason other than her being a monstrosity of a human being.

"Up to you, kid," Dad says. I hate making decisions. I hate when things are up to me — I feel so responsible for everyone. I ask myself, *What would Dad rather do?* If I know him the way I think I do, he'd be uncomfortable with the silence if we stay here.

"Let's go to the living room," I say, taking my plate, fork, and a few packets of soy sauce with me. Dad follows.

He flips through channels, trying to find something we both want to watch. There's a nature special on primates, a little bit of

Jane Goodall and her chimps and a lot about Koko the gorilla, the one who was taught sign language. Dad sneaks a glance at me, and I know he can tell just from the way I sit up a little straighter and lean forward that I want to watch. He puts the remote control down and starts eating his food in earnest. I cry when it gets to the part about Koko's little cat. I remember learning in school about Koko, about how she wanted a pet, how she'd chosen this little cat without a tail and named him All Ball. Even though I know the end of this story, that All Ball escapes the cage and gets hit by a car, it's still devastating for me when the serious-voiced narrator tells us of All Ball's fate. Watching Koko try to sign her grief with her limited vocabulary feels so familiar, sorrow tearing away at her, and all she can say is "cry" and "sad." Those two tiny words can't possibly convey the immensity of her grief. I sniffle into my lo mein, and Dad pats me on the arm.

"You're such a softie," he says, but he says it with tenderness. He's not criticizing.

"Yeah," I agree, leaning against his shoulder. "I'm a marshmallow."

The food is actually not half bad, and I'm sort of proud of Poppy Beach for stepping up and pretending to be ethnically diverse, at least cuisine-wise. Dad starts watching some old Van Damme movie, and that's my cue to go to bed. I get the plates and kiss my dad on the head. *This is the last time I'll kiss Dad goodnight for a long time*, I think, and I wonder what words I would sign to try to express what I am feeling.

SIXTEEN
BEING ARTEMIS

I make my way up the stairs slowly, trying to memorize the feel of each step under my feet, the banister under my hand. *This is the last time I'll go up the stairs to this bed for a long time*, I think again. I feel like I've squandered my time in Poppy Beach and am trying to make it up in these last few hours home. I should have been bonding, making memories, reconnecting with Tricia and her family, but half the time I moped around or was a lump in the house. My father and I should have, I don't know, gone fishing or something. Done stuff together, maybe taken a walk together on the beach. Hell, why didn't I just go visit him at the shop? But then again, it's the mundane that I miss the most, our daily routines, the silent bonding over dinner and TV in the living room, the security of knowing Dad is sleeping in a room down the hall from me. So would I have lived this week differently? I don't know. I honestly don't.

I hate this. I hate life sometimes, the way that every choice facing me sends me into an infinite loop of indecision, of worrying so much about the consequences of my actions that I become completely inert. I hate the way life seems to slip through my fingers, how I dig my heels into the ground to make time go more slowly so I can savor each moment but then don't ever *do* anything. It seems that all I want to do is live a quiet life, but somehow that seems like a waste of being alive. I think of Ian Millbrook. He didn't waste his life. He pursued his dream. Music was his life, and he went out there and made it happen. I am positive he would have made it big—things were just starting to happen for him. How much more might he have accomplished if he'd been given the chance? It makes me feel ashamed of my sad little life, wasteful.

Because what have I done? I dropped out of art school. I am a cog in the wheels of corporate America—and not even a true cog, but a temporary, replacement one, like a spare tire, inferior to the real thing, a placeholder for something worthy. I draw obsessively, but for no purpose and for no audience. I'm so afraid to fly that I hardly ever see the only man who will love me completely for the flawed person I am.

Before I left for college, I was bubbling with excitement at all the *potential* of what my life would become. I was headed to Longfellow University—that made me *somebody*. It didn't matter how invisible I felt at school—getting accepted to Longfellow was a huge achievement. I think I was the first person in the history of Butler Academy to get in. Longfellow admits plenty of Hollywood stars and children of famous people, but they also seem to look for people filled with potential, people who will Be Somebody someday. Before I left for college, I felt like a mystery seed packet, something that might grow into a rare plant, something either so beautiful that I'd inspire poets, or so useful and healing that I would cure a million diseases. Vivian grew into something like that, brilliant and ready to save the world once she gets her law degree. But me? I don't know if I even sprouted. All those years of careful cultivation in rich soil, and I'm still trapped in my husk, refusing to burst out and become...something else. Something greater. I'm too afraid, I guess, to decide what I am and put down roots. Or maybe deep down I know I'm not special at all.

So I'm just me, nothing more and nothing less. Some days that feels like enough, and others, well...

I start packing my bag, not sure how early Dad will want to leave in the morning to make the long drive to San Francisco. Since I never actually *unpacked* my bag, the task doesn't take long, but I am determined to pack semi-tidily instead of balling everything up the way I did for my trip out here. I fold my shirts and pants neatly, gather up my dirty laundry in a plastic bag, and then open the closet to pack away the black dress I wore to Ian's memorial. When I turn back to close the door, I see the one remaining item of clothing in there, my homecoming dress, alone again as it has been these years I've been away. Set in motion when I removed the other dress, it still sways gently on the wooden dowel, appearing eerily alive like a totem, a scarecrow.

I deliberately did not bring the old velvet dress with me to college, because when I saw it, I could not stop seeing that kiss, Ian Millbrook leaning down, Tricia's surprised face, and dozens of other scenes provided by my overactive imagination. I'd relived the scene so many times in my head, adding in details that I couldn't possibly have seen—his hand cupping her cheek, her fingers twined in his hair, the way her eyes opened in shock before she melted and let her eyelids drop. None of this happened. All of this happened. Schrödinger's kiss.

But now that he's gone forever? I'm not sure I can leave it behind. *He danced with me in this dress*, I think. Nothing separated my skin from his in that moment except this fabric, now carefully hung and swathed in plastic. I shiver, thinking of how physically close he was to me, absentmindedly singing Clapton and wishing I were someone else. How can I leave this dress behind now? Maybe the fabric still holds the memories of his hands. The velvet may remember his touch, the heat of his palms.

Before I know it, I've put the dress away in my bag, keeping it on the hanger and in the plastic, just folding it into thirds and laying it on top of the pile of neatly packed clothes.

I get ready for bed ceremoniously, carefully putting a glob of toothpaste on my toothbrush, watching my mirror-self methodically brush her teeth. It almost feels like a religious ritual. *This is how I get ready for bed in my father's house.* I want to remember what it's like, because by tomorrow night this place will once again feel like it was only a dream.

Once I'm in my pajamas, I walk around the perimeter of my bedroom, trying to commit every last detail to my memory: the scuffmarks on the wall from moving in my desk, the burn mark of a cigarette Shelly had put out on my carpet when she'd come home drunk one night, the bare spot on the window where as a child I'd scratched the paint off into the shape of a tiny wolf while I looked out the window, willing Shelly to come back to us. As I walk around the room, running my hand along the walls, I'm reminded of the circle I made around the tree in Ian's cemetery. My eyes sweep the floor as I walk, looking for another note, another piece of obsidian. All I see is carpet that ought to have been replaced years ago.

I'm getting on a plane again tomorrow. I imagine myself strapped to the seat, and I break out into a cold sweat. I fumble for my sketchpad and flip toward the back, to Meg's notes. *Hi. I can see you.* Why does it comfort me to think this note is for me, that she can see me? That she can see *me*, somehow? Is the comfort just in the fact that *someone* from that family can see me?

But of course the note is not for me, and Meg knows only what I've told her, of my obsessive love. I think of Meg in school, of how rough things must be for her now that she's lost her protector, the boy who could make her laugh and forget whatever horrors took the power of speech from her. My life seems pretty easy compared to that. Surely I can get on a plane if there are people like her living much harder lives. I think of Mrs. Millbrook's pain, of the emptiness she must feel in the space where her ghost children used to live within her, when she was their sole nourishment and protection. It must be so hard to be a mother, once your children are out in the dangerous world, no longer shielded by your flesh and organs.

I am almost too afraid to go to sleep, too nervous thinking about flying tomorrow. What if this is my last night on earth? If that's the case, I'm glad I could spend it here with Dad. I don't think I can go to sleep, but then I remember that the Stone One is waiting for me. I will honor Joshua. I will keep all the wolves safe. If this is my last night on earth, I will make certain that the wolves will be okay after I am gone. I owe them at least that much.

I keep the sketchpad by my bed, feeling braver with Meg's notes taped in there. I shut off the light, lie with my palms up, and prepare to do battle. When sleep doesn't come right away, I close my eyes and picture Joshua's tree, the weeping cherry. "I can see you," I whisper in the dark, and I start saying it again and again in my head like a mantra until finally the feeling of my sheets below me and my blanket on top begins to dissolve, and I'm in between, returning to end the Stone One once and for all.

Every muscle in my body is tense as I become conscious. It's as if I never left, except that I feel the weight of the quiver on my shoulder and back and the longbow in my hand. How did I arm myself while I wasn't here? Did I make it happen just by preparing myself to face him? Willa and Ash are both still pressed against me on either side of my body, and the rumbling continues, growing steadily louder, closer, rocking the ground beneath my feet.

"I am ready for you!" I scream to the air.

The Stone One laughs in his unsettling, scratchy way. I know my fear is sweet to him, ambrosia on his concrete tongue. How, *how* then, am I able to stop him? The last time I faced him, I was able to shut down my brain and let my body's muscle memory take over. For a moment I became the little girl I used to be, the girl who was unafraid and had believed she was loved.

But was that all that saved me? Maybe...maybe in this world he cannot hurt me. Maybe those are rules *he* must follow.

So what happens when *he* breaks the rules?

My mind is spinning a thousand different thoughts and scenarios. There must be some way. I make a show of putting my weapons away.

"*Is that the wisest thing to do, Abdicator?*" asks the Stone One with something like a smile on his face, too grotesque to be truly called a smile. "*I thought you wanted to finish me.*"

"What's the point?" I ask. "It seems that these arrows have done nothing except to keep you away for a time. You're invincible, aren't you?"

"*Your arrows alone cannot harm me,*" he says.

"So, you *can* be harmed," I say, arching an eyebrow.

"*Oh, how amusing, little Abdicator. As if you would be capable of such a thing on your own. You, who are so fearful and feeble and fragile.*"

"Then why do I keep you away? Why are you unable to hurt the wolves while I am here?"

"*I seem to recall that I was able to do away with your Joshua while you watched. Or rather, while you looked away like the coward you are.*"

"You will *never* say his name again; I forbid it. His name is holy now, and you...*nothing* about you is sacred," I snarl, my fury almost unable to be contained in my small frame. If my anger were visible energy, I'd be glowing like an ember. "You are not *fit to speak of him again.*"

He grinds his teeth, a horrible sound that makes the skin on the back of my legs prickle. I feel coiled up like a spring, ready to flee. But I notice he also doesn't challenge me about Joshua's name. Another thing to file away.

I try to capitalize on my fury, still burning hot within me. "You talk about how sweet my fear is to you," I say, trying to keep my voice steady and menacing. "Do you want to taste it? Wouldn't it be more wonderful if you could actually feel my skin in your mouth?"

I have no idea what I'm doing, or who is speaking through me. What am I offering to do? I think of when I tried to offer my life for Joshua's, and how I didn't really mean it. But at this moment, I don't feel in danger. "*I can see you,*" I whisper to myself, and somehow it makes me feel like I have power here. *I* have power, not the Stone One.

"*Princess, what are you saying?*" asks Willa, looking at me with frantic eyes. "*You cannot challenge him. You cannot tempt him in this way. You will doom us all forever.*"

"No. It's going to be fine," I say, taking a few steps toward him. Willa grabs at my dress with her teeth, trying to hold me back.

And like I'm watching my dream-self on my dad's TV, I begin to advance on the Stone One, who stares at me with his mismatched eyes. He crouches down, only slightly taller than I am now. His jaw begins to drop, partly in shock, partly in anticipation as I prepare to do…I'm not sure what. At this point, I'm just watching myself from a distance, strangely disconnected from what's happening.

"*You can't do this!*" I hear Willa scream behind me. "*We* need *you here.*"

"Can't you see?" I say calmly, not turning around. "I'm making sure you will be okay no matter what."

"*Stop her, Ash, please,*" begs Willa.

"*My princess,*" says Ash in measured tones, "*I cannot say that I understand what you are doing. But I trust you. I always trust you.*"

Willa yelps, betrayed by her fellow wolf, the only other one remaining.

I'm still advancing slowly toward the Stone One, and I know now what I need. I see it clearly in my head, the obsidian I found at Ian's grave.

"*Come to me,*" I call in my heart. "*A piece of me remains on you, so you know how to find me.*" I close my eyes, daring to do this in front of the beast, holding my hands out and waiting. I don't sing, because that doesn't seem right for this situation, but I hold my hands out and wait. *"Come to me,"* I say again. *"My blood marks you. Find me. Find the source."* My thumb begins to throb a little where I was cut earlier, pulsing like some sort of beacon.

Is it my imagination? My silly imagination in this dream world? Behind my eyelids flicker images of Ian Millbrook's empty grave, the ground in front rumbling slightly, the irregular slab of obsidian beginning to vibrate, to tunnel up. Maybe it's just positive thinking, wishful thinking. *"Come to me, obsidian,"* I say again in my heart.

And just like that, I feel something cool and smooth in my hand. I close my fist around it. I don't need to look to see that the obsidian has found me. *Now what?* I think.

What did the Stone One say? *Your arrows alone cannot harm me.* I feel the stone in my hand, roughly triangular. Like an arrowhead. Why did I leave my longbow behind me? Now I'll have to get close in order to harm him. I don't think I'm brave enough for that. *I can see you,* I hear in my head, but it's Joshua's voice, and I see pink petals of his tree flutter past me in a sudden, gentle breeze.

"Princess," the Stone One says in that sneering tone, *"is that an offer? Are you allowing me to taste you?"*

"You can't harm me. I can see it now," I say, even though I'm not certain. After all, the wolves are safe when I am here, except when they break the rules. Am I breaking a rule? Can he harm me if I break a rule? *They're only dreams, Agnes,* I try to reason with myself. I can't be harmed here anyway. I can be harmed only in the waking. I think. I think that's how it must work.

Oh God, I'm flying in a few hours. This could be my only chance to make things right here. It's got to be now.

I put my hands behind my back and scrape the obsidian roughly against my palm. I wince as the sharp edge cuts my flesh. I run the edge against my palm again, and the edge bites like fire against my hand. I palm the bloodied rock in the other hand and show the Stone One my wounded one.

"Can you smell the fear in my blood?" I ask, taking another step forward. My heart is racing. I have no idea what I'm doing.

"It is less sweet if it is willingly given," he says, pretending to be uninterested, but I can sense the struggle within him.

"Well, tough shit," I say, taking another step. "Will you take my blood instead of theirs now? Will you stay away?"

"*You don't seem to understand the way of this world. I will always be here. I have been here forever. You cannot ask me to leave for all time. I belong here.*"

"Take my hand," I say, walking closer. I can feel his resolve crumbling. My blood confuses him, somehow. "This is my gift to you, given of my own free will. Payment. A compact." I advance with my arm outstretched, trembling, fearing the pain of his crushing jaw.

"*Princess!*" screams Willa behind me. I hear feet bounding on the soft ground, but I'm too involved in this showdown with the Stone One to know what's happening until it is too late.

Willa jumps on my back, knocking me to the ground, and leaps up to the Stone One. "*You will* not *harm her!*" she screams as she continues to soar up in the air. Unperturbed, he simply opens his jaw wider and snaps it closed as she sails right in.

I can feel the moment she dies, a burning pain inside me. Another part of my heart has been snapped off like a bit of royal icing on a gingerbread house.

"*Do you see now, Princess, what your foolishness has done?*" he gloats.

I get up, not bothering to dust myself off. Fighting the tears in my eyes, I make a mad dash for him as he laughs. *Why did you do it, Willa?* I think. *I'm not worth that. I'm not worth that, especially to you.*

I run up to him and mark him with my left hand, a bloody handprint looking almost like a Georgia O'Keeffe poppy on his chest. It's tiny on his humongous body, but I can feel his stone exterior shift and shimmer. Something has changed when my blood touched him. I take my right hand clutching the bit of obsidian still marked with my blood, and I shove it as far as I can into his mouth, scraping my knuckles against his teeth as I withdraw my hand quickly, leaving the obsidian inside him. He swallows tidily and smacks his stone lips together, making a sound like a crack of thunder.

"*You amuse me,*" he says, standing up again, lifting his foot as if to trample me.

"You cannot hurt me," I say, but I am less certain of it with each second. The obsidian was my only hope, and nothing seems to have happened.

"*Find me,*" I say in my head to the obsidian, now coated in more of my blood. "*Come back to me. Find my blood, which gives you life. Find me. Return to me.*"

"*What is happening?*" asks the Stone One, for the first time sounding afraid.

I think my eyes are playing tricks on me as his whole body seems to vibrate and wobble. Maybe it's the loss of blood. His outlines seem to blur, and his jaw drops again.

The first cracks split out of my bloody handprint on his chest, and they spread rapidly like a spider web woven in fast forward from the center out. I'm unable to move as I watch the cracks climb and circle him. "*What have you done to me?*" he asks right before his jaw falls from his body, his eyes wide with fear.

I almost pity him.

I'm still frozen as he begins to crumble. I look up, and falling grit lands in my eyes, blinding me. I feel something slap into my hand roughly, and even though I cannot see, I know the obsidian has returned. I can hear stone scraping against stone, and a rock or two pelts me on the head. I rub my eyes with the backs of my hands to get the grit out so I can see, but everything is happening too fast.

Something warm and solid slams into me, knocking the breath out of my body, and I'm being dragged hastily across the ground.

"*I have you,*" says Ash, through a mouthful of linen, and I regain my eyesight just as the remains of the Stone One topple over, collapsing in a noisy heap right where I was standing a few moments earlier. *That would have crushed me*, I think, still unsure what would happen if I died here.

After the rubble stops falling and the crashing sounds and echoes fade, it's just me and Ash side by side, looking at the heap of stone and sand that remains of the monster. A cloud of dust rises from the pile and dissipates in the air. I slowly sit up and put my arm around him.

"Thank you for saving me," I say, choked up.

"*You have saved me, Princess,*" he says simply.

"Oh, Willa," I say, looking at the rubble. "She shouldn't have died for this. You're the last one now."

"*It was meant to be. I was the first one,*" he says. "*She will live on as long as you remember her.*"

"Aren't you upset with me? Because of me you are all alone."

"*You sacrificed much to keep us safe. You were not able to save Willa, but I know you never meant to harm her.*"

I'm crying now, my tears falling on the rock in my hand, mingling with my blood. "Thank you, obsidian," I say to the rock. "Now you go back. Go back to Ian and keep his resting place ready. He'll be there soon. Go back. Welcome him, and tell him he will always be loved." I squeeze my hands together tightly, feeling the edges of the rock bite my palms, and suddenly my hands are empty again.

Ash laps at my hands, closing the wounds, and we sit for a long time and watch the rubble settle.

I know the answer already, but I still ask, "I can't bring her back, can I?"

"*It is not the way*," he says.

Still. Still, I can do for her what I did for Joshua. I stand up slowly, hold my hands out in supplication, close my eyes, and open my mouth. I sing the song of Willa, the one who distrusted me, hated me, blamed me so much for leaving her, and yet, when it counted, she gave her life for me. She willingly leapt into the monster's mouth so that I could live. Did she do it out of love for me or for love of her wolf brethren? Maybe both. She did love me a little, at least, and I sing of her bravery, her impetuousness, her anger, and ultimately, her loyalty and sacrifice.

When I open my eyes, there's a cactus, a prickly pear, in a golden patch of sunshine a distance away from Joshua's weeping cherry. What a strange place this is, where trees that should never be able to live in the same climate can all thrive side by side. Sharp spines erupt from the green paddles of the cactus, but brightly colored fruit crowns the plant, red as blood, red as love. It is a fitting memorial, I think.

"I'm so sorry, Ash," I say again. "Will you be all right alone?"

"*You are here, Princess, and that is all I have ever needed.*"

"And you're safe now, now and forever," I say, but Ash doesn't say anything back.

His ears prick up. "*You are being Summoned*," he says.

"Summoned? By what? By whom? I don't hear anything."

"*You must follow me*," he says, breaking into a run.

"Should I take my weapons?" I ask, glancing over at the spot where I laid them down near Willa.

"*He will not harm you*," says Ash. "*He is the Eternal. He merely watches.*"

I run after him, catching up easily, since I am Artemis in this world, goddess of the hunt, fleet-footed and brave and strong.

He leads me to the Bridge Between. *"I can go no farther. You must cross the Bridge alone."*

"The Bridge? The Bridge actually *leads* somewhere?" I ask, stupefied. "I thought it just let me carry my thoughts back and forth."

"It leads to the Eternal, sometimes. When he Summons you. And you have been Summoned."

I don't have a good feeling about this, but I step onto the bridge, feeling the rough wood against my bare feet, resting my hand on the coarse rope. I look back at Ash.

"I will wait here for you," he says, before I can even ask.

I begin to walk across the bridge, disappearing into the clouds.

"Agnes? Agnes, honey? If you want bacon and eggs at the diner before we head to the airport, you should get up now." Dad's scratching at my door, and I open my eyes and stare at the ceiling. *This is the last time I will wake up in this bed*, I think, and I stretch my hands out, noting that my palms are crisscrossed with faint scars that weren't there when I fell asleep.

SEVENTEEN
SUMMONED

As I stare at my palms, I remember the feel of cold, sharp volcanic glass in my hands. I rub my eyes roughly and look again. Is it a trick of the light? I sit there gazing at the spidery scars on my skin until Dad knocks tentatively, apologetically, on the door again.

"Ags? You up?"

"Yeah, Dad." I shake my head and slowly come to sitting. None of this is real. It was just a dream. This is getting creepy. Or I'm going crazy. I must not be entirely awake yet. "I'll be ready in about twenty," I call out, throwing the covers off of me.

"Okay then," he says, and my heart is already hurting a little, wondering when the next time will be that his voice will wake me up in this bed. What person will I be when that happens? Who will Dad be? When will I be brave enough to fly home again? Do we have enough time left together? *Please keep Dad safe*, I pray to no one in particular. *Keep him safe until I can come home again.*

I shuffle to the bathroom, feeling nostalgic about everything, as if I'm secretly being filmed for a documentary about my life. I'm self-conscious about all my movements, trying to make every gesture significant, in case this time is the last. As a result, my motions feel stilted and unnatural. I'm having trouble playing the role of myself.

I turn on the water, thinking, *This is my last shower in Poppy Beach; this is my last shower in my father's house.*

Even the pattern of mildew between the tiles is familiar after my visit here, and I'm already feeling homesick. And I'm still home.

When I get back to my room, I put on my comfy traveling clothes. It's too warm here and on the plane—*oh God, I'm getting on a plane in a few hours*—to put on all the extra layers I'll need to stay warm when I get back to Boston. *When, when, when, not if,* I say to myself. I quickly stuff my pajamas and last bits of dirty laundry in my bag, zipping it closed.

I stop to look at my unmade bed. Should I make it? I crave the normalcy of making it, but I know I'm not going to sleep here tonight. Stripping it bare just emphasizes the cold truth that I am not returning here. But I also don't want to make more work for my father. I don't want him coming back from dropping me off at the airport and having to clean up my mess or spending unnecessary time in my room. What does he do when I'm not here? Does he keep the door shut so he doesn't notice my bare mattress? Does he ever come in here and just sit?

I opt for stripping the bed, choosing Dad's convenience over my desire to make my bed here one last time. I try to pretend it's just a normal Saturday laundry day at home with my dad. I throw the comforter on the floor and reach under the mattress to unhook the fitted sheet. I try to do it fast, like ripping off a Band-Aid, trying to stop my mind from overanalyzing my gestures and making me so homesick that I'll start crying before I have to leave.

I say hi to my dad over my armload of used bedding as I pass by him on the way to the laundry room. He's on the living room couch, watching TV as usual. I bump the laundry room door open with my hip and start the load, thinking it's the least I can do. Dad shouldn't have to spend the rest of his Saturday doing my dirty laundry. It's bad enough it'll take half the day to drive to the airport and back.

Once I hear the agitator begin its soothing, heartbeat-like rhythm, I go back to my room and fold up my comforter neatly, leaving it at the foot of the bed. I put my bare pillows on top of the comforter, because seeing them uncovered at the head of the bed makes me uneasy—it's something in-between again, of only resembling a bed ready to sleep in, a skeleton or a scarecrow imitation of a real bed. With the pillows piled on top of the folded comforter, it no longer pretends to look like a bed in use, and I am okay with that.

Once I have all my things, I shut my bedroom door behind me, saying a silent goodbye as the door clicks shut, almost unable to let go of the small ceramic doorknob in my hand. I clomp down the stairs awkwardly, and my bag bumps against my leg just as it did on the way down the subway back in Boston almost a week ago. It feels like that happened to a different person. I know so much more now, about me, about Shelly, about my wolves. Oh, Willa. Willa, who sacrificed herself for no reason. I was not worth saving, and worse still, I was never in danger in the first place. I look at my palms again in the dim light in the foyer. They are red from carrying my suitcase down the stairs, so I can't see if the scars I thought I saw when I woke up are still there.

I think of Willa's memorial tree, so different than Joshua's, but so fitting for her. I think of Ash all alone in my dream world, but tell myself, *Well, at least he is safe. Alone, but safe.* Like my dad. Even if something happens to me on that plane (*but it won't, it won't, it won't*), Ash will be safe forever.

"I'm ready," I call out to my dad, who turns to look at me with a small, resigned smile and shuts off the TV.

"All right, Ags, let me carry your suitcase out." He pats his sides to make sure he has his keys, and the gesture is so *Dad* that I'm missing the hell out of him already.

I follow him out the door, locking it behind me—already I'm falling back into my big-city habits—and I put my backpack in the front seat as he holds open the truck door for me. Here we go.

No.

Not yet.

Before climbing into the truck, I run back to the front yard, looking up at the house for the last time, trying to force myself to remember every detail, every shingle, every smudged windowpane. Home. *My home.* When will I return?

"Okay, I'm ready," I say in a small voice that Dad probably doesn't even hear. I turn back and walk to the truck, the door of which my father is still holding open patiently. I slide in, and he waits until he sees my feet are safely inside before shutting the door for me. I'm already choked up as he opens his door and starts the engine.

I want to do nothing but stare at my dad as we drive, soak up his essence as if my eyes were sponges, but I get distracted, looking out the window at the trees blurring like charcoal smudged under my fingertips. I feel a sudden pull in my heart, and I don't need to look out of Dad's side of the car to know we're passing the cemetery. *Goodbye, obsidian.* *Goodbye, Ian,* I think, pressing my palms together and hoping our obsidian is safely buried, waiting for his arrival.

This is the third time I've been at the diner this week: the first with Tricia, when she admitted she remembered nothing of Ian's kiss; the second with Shelly, when I learned that I was a result of a drunken revenge fuck; and now with my dad, the man who fills up all the parts of my universe not already filled with Ian Millbrook. We walk slowly to the diner entrance, and I lean my head on his shoulder. I feel like a little girl again, and I want to; I want to cling to this feeling as long as I can, because no one makes me feel as safe as Dad.

The same waitress who served me last time is waiting at the door to seat us. "Pete Larch!" she says brightly, flashing him a smile and seating us immediately. She glances from Dad to me quizzically, trying to figure out how we know each other.

My dad clears his throat. "Roxy, this is my daughter Agnes." I wave awkwardly, embarrassed that she associates me with Shelly.

"Agnes and I are good pals, aren't we, hon?" she says with a wink. I smile at her gratefully.

"Roxy's been working here a few years," Dad says. He puffs his chest out and says to Roxy, "My girl graduated from Longfellow University!"

Roxy whistles through her teeth. "Wow! Now that's somethin'. You must be *smart.*"

I smile, looking down, happy that I can still make Dad so proud, but also embarrassed because I feel like a fraud. Yes, I did the coursework and graduated, but what am I doing now? I may as well have stayed in Poppy Beach; answering phones doesn't require a degree from a fancy school. And yet, that degree is all I have that makes me ever think I'm special. It's the one thing Ian Millbrook ever noticed me for, telling me himself, "You're *smart.*" But college was a long time ago, it seems like, and I can't trot out my Longfellow sweatshirt every time I want people to think I'm worth anything.

Roxy begins to lead us to the same booth I've been sitting at all week, but I shake my head slightly, and she understands immediately, seating us on the other side of the diner. I'm so grateful to her for being able to see me, to understand me without words.

My father orders the biggest breakfast platter they offer, and I say, "Dad, your cholesterol, remember?"

But he just says, "I'd rather die than give up bacon."

I can grant him that, although I don't like hearing him even joke about dying. I wrap my arms around myself tightly, trying to keep my insides from falling out.

"I think I just want a big glass of orange juice," I say to Roxy, pushing my menu away.

"Ags, you sure? It's a long flight," asks Dad with concern.

"I'll be okay, Dad, really. I'm just not very hungry." I clench my jaw so my chattering teeth aren't obvious to him. I don't want to let on how afraid I already am. He'll just worry about me. I want to cause as little disruption to his life as I can.

We hardly exchange words during breakfast, but that's as it always is, and everything my dad does makes me miss him before he's gone, the way he picks up the bacon in his fingers, the impatient way he blows on his coffee, the way he gets frustrated at the unwillingness of the ketchup bottle to give up its precious contents. I sip my orange juice, tiny sips, trying to make this moment last.

The orange juice is watery, probably from one of those big dispensers like we had in the dining halls at Longfellow, and there's some pulpy scum on the top of the glass. My last meal in Poppy Beach.

"Well, Ags, you ready?" asks Dad, giving his mouth a final wipe before tossing some well-worn bills on the table. I nod and stand up, adjusting my clothes and trying to get my arms in the sleeves of my heavy coat. Dad's right there, helping me. I guess I'll always be his little girl. I kind of wish he'd zip up the coat for me too, but I know that's silly. I am a grown woman.

I am his little girl.

Something squeezes my heart as we drive outside Poppy Beach's city limit, the wooden sign rushing past in an illegible blur. Goodbye, Poppy Beach. Goodbye, Tricia. Goodbye, unworldly Meg and grieving Mrs. Millbrook. And goodbye, Dad.

Shelly does not get a goodbye.

We hit a rare sunny patch on the 101 about halfway through the four-hour drive to San Francisco. I'm staring at my hands, looking for the scars. I see them. At least, I *think* I see them.

"Hey, Dad?" I ask, turning to my side to look at him.

"What is it, Ags?" he responds, never taking his eyes off the road.

"Do my hands look different to you?" I hold my palm up near his face for inspection.

He quickly glances over between checking the road, the rearview mirror, the side-view mirror, the speedometer. He drives according to the driver's ed. handbook. "Huh, I don't know. Do they feel different?"

"Kind of."

"They look the same to me, hon," he says, again giving his full attention to the road.

What was I hoping him to say? That he could see it too, the new spidery lines? Do I want my dreams to be real? Maybe I just wanted it confirmed, because otherwise it would mean I'm seeing things that no one else can see. And in our cold, logical world, seeing things that other people can't see doesn't equal special; it equals insane.

In the sunbeam, I can see my hands lined with filaments that reflect the light. I stare at them until the sun hides once again behind the clouds. I fold my hands and put them in my lap, wondering what on earth is going on in my brain. And all the while I can hear a clock ticking inside me, each second slipping away from me, the last slivers of my remaining time here with my father.

I want to make it count, but I don't know what to say to him.

"I've had a great week with you," I start, unable to convey adequately how much it's meant to me to be here.

"Me too, Ags," he says, his eyes crinkling with his smile. "Hope it wasn't too boring after all that excitement in the big city."

"Are you kidding? There is no Pete Larch in Boston. *There can be only one*," I say goofily.

He chuckles, but there's something behind his eyes that tugs at me, and I'm too chicken to ask the questions that are pressing on my heart: *Dad, will you be okay alone? Are you sad? Dad, should I stay?*

But that's not how we operate, my father and I. We are quiet, or we make jokes, or we talk in code.

I want to make this drive last forever, and not just because I know there's a terrifying flight on the other end of this journey. This is all I have left with him, this tiny remnant of time. And now I've started crying. I look out the window, hoping to shield my dad from my tears, but soon I'm sniffling audibly, and Dad takes one hand off the wheel and claps me on the shoulder. "You all right, Ags?"

I press my lips together and wipe my eyes with the back of my hand. "Yeah," I manage to get out, trying to smile. "I just...I'm going to miss you."

He swallows, and I watch his Adam's apple bob. He continues to stare at the road. "Aw, Ags, you'll be back before you know it. And we always have the phone."

Yes, I think, *but we never* say *anything*. It's not the same as sitting shoulder to shoulder with him on the sofa. Our voices are mere shadows of who we are when transmitted through wires and speakers. It's not the same.

"Maybe Easter?" I offer, knowing full well that I cannot possibly make the trip back so soon.

"Sure, kid. We can have Peeps exploding races in the microwave like old times."

"Thanks," I say, smiling weakly but still feeling this hole in my heart.

When Dad drops me off, I look enviously at the people streaming out of the airport's automatic doors, walking with purpose, seeking taxis or shuttles or pick-ups. They're already home. They're already safe. They've already survived their flights. They already know the end of the story.

Dad gets my suitcase out of the back while I put my backpack on. We hug briefly at the curb, and the tears start up again. I sob for a while into Dad's shoulder, and I feel so damn selfish, because I know my crying is tearing him up inside. He holds onto me, whispering, "It's going to be fine, Ags. You'll be back soon. I'll see you soon," over and over until I nearly fall asleep on his shoulder at the soothing lulling of his voice.

"Your jacket is all wet now," I say stupidly as we pull away from each other.

"Ags, I work in a bait shop, remember? I'm used to being covered in slime," Dad jokes, winking, but he looks away quickly. He's already put my bag on the curb, and all I have to do is turn around, grab the bag's handle, and roll it through the automatic doors. That's all.

But I'm frozen. I can't do it. "Agnes?" Dad asks after I don't move.

I turn and run to him, throw my arms around his neck, and say, "I love you, Daddy. I miss you so much already."

"It's going to be fine," he says again.

"Okay," I say, exhaling loudly. I'm ready now. I grab my bag, go through the automatic doors, but turn in the vestibule to watch Dad drive away.

It's only when the truck is out of sight that I remember that I forgot to make frosting for Dad's cakes.

I travel so seldom that I irritate everyone in line behind me at security, forgetting to take off my shoes, going through the metal detector with my watch on. The TSA officer rolls his eyes at me, but the embarrassment feels like a vacation from my slowly building panic.

When I get to the gate, I rifle through my backpack for my lorazepam. I take two to start off with. I desperately want to go to the bar in the terminal and pound a drink, but if I'm too unsteady on my feet, they won't let me on the plane. *Would that be such a bad thing?* I consider. But no, once I set my mind to do something, I have to follow through. I booked this ticket, and I am going home. I miss Vivian. I miss my apartment, my corner of the world that isn't colored by ghosts of Shelly.

My phone buzzes with a text: *When r u coming back, u h00r?*

It's Vivian, of course. *ETA 12:30A,* I text back.

Gimme yr flight #. I'll track u.

Bless her. I don't know why it helps so much to know that Vivian is tracking my flight as it makes its way across the sky. Maybe because she's thinking of me on the plane, it'll keep the plane in the sky. And at the very least, if something goes wrong, at least someone will know right away. I text her the info right as they start the boarding process.

My heart is whirring, but my legs don't quite feel like jelly yet, and I step onto the jet bridge like it's a passageway to the underworld. I think of Ian Millbrook again, walking through a jet bridge like this—it would be the last time he walked anywhere. I try to make each step count, even as my footfalls sound hollow against the jet bridge floor.

I manage to get my bag into the overhead without help, and I pull out my sketchbook and pencil before pushing my backpack under the seat in front of me. I lift the window shade and let the light shine on my palm. I try to sketch what I see is there, delicate etching. *I destroyed the Stone One,* I think. *So why am I afraid of a little flight?* But I know that I am far braver in my dreams than I ever will be in waking life, and I let the panic wash over me, pulling me under, making me gasp for breath.

A mother with a small child is in the seat next to me, and part of me wants to shriek at the woman, "Why would you bring your baby onto this flight? Don't you love her enough to keep her safe?" But the child cheerily sucks on the ear of her stuffed bunny toy and pulls on her mother's hair. Maybe it's easier when your mother's arms are around you. Maybe it's easier when you don't know the danger that lurks outside and all around you.

"Daw!" she says, pointing at my sketchpad.

"Excuse me?" I ask the child's mother.

"Daw pony!"

"Dahlia, we don't demand art from strangers," she says, looking at me apologetically.

"No, no, that's all right," I say, laughing a little, glad to be commissioned by the world's youngest art patron. Her comical, tiny bossiness distracts me from my terror.

I draw a cartoonish pony, humanized, wearing overalls and holding a pitchfork.

"Dat's not a pony," she says with toddler contempt, reminding me a little of my portfolio critics in art school.

I try again on the back of the page. This time I do it as realistically as I can, except I'm not sure I know the difference between a pony and a horse. I make him short and cute and chubby.

"Pony," she says, nodding. "Dah-ya can hab it?"

"Of course, Dahlia," I say, ripping the paper out of my sketchpad.

"Thanks," says Dahlia's mom. "She's got a mind of her own, this one," she says with so much pride and affection that I can't help but feel wistful. I turn back quickly to look through the sketches, all the new ones I did this week in Poppy Beach, the impossible cigarette butt, the notes from Meg Millbrook. I begin to draw Willa's prickly pear and the rubble remaining of the Stone One. I try to draw the feeling of the obsidian cutting into my hand, but my pencil feels as clumsy and primitive as caveman's tools. I tuck the sketchpad in the seat pocket and clutch the pencil in my hand, waiting for takeoff.

Dahlia and her mother sing little songs as I squeeze my eyes shut. I try to get lost in the sounds, focusing on the parallel voices with only a generation holding them apart, focusing on the sweet sounds of breath over vocal cords instead of the angry whirring of engines. They sing "You Are My Sunshine," and Dahlia breaks off at the end of the second verse, the bit about waking up and being all alone. "Dat part too sad," she says solemnly.

"All right," her mother soothes, "let's just sing the refrain again."

Mother and child sing only the happy words again and again until we're in the air. The flight attendants soon come by with the drink cart, and I rush to force oblivion upon me. As soon as the flight attendant passes me my gin and tonic, I gulp it down so quickly I get brain freeze from the ice cubes. I clutch at my head, not caring how much of a crazy alcoholic I look to Dahlia and her mother, and I feel it, the heaviness in my limbs, the slowing of my breath, and my eyes falling closed as I hear mother and child begging the sunshine to stay.

I'm standing on the Bridge Between, exactly where I was before Dad woke me up this morning. I turn back to look at Ash.

"Are you sure this is safe?"

"*Nothing is ever truly safe, is it?*" he responds in his traditional question form. "*But you cannot ignore the Summons.*"

"I'll...be back soon," I say, not really believing it.

The planks of wood are damp from the spray of the river below, and the coarse rope digs into my palms. I try not to look down. I put one bare foot in front of the other, feeling the unspoken danger of the air beneath me, much like on the jet bridge. The bridge keeps going higher and higher, and soon I can no longer see Ash waiting for me on the riverbank below. It's like I'm walking into a cloud. Everything is misty and cool, and the roaring of the river fills my ears.

Something on my left catches my eye, and I see a dark wooden door with strange gold markings. Just that: a door, floating in the mist—possibly a door made *of* mist. I'm not sure I'm really seeing it, the way a rainbow that appears in a garden hose's spray in a sunbeam is *there* but not a thing you can hold. There's nothing around it, nothing behind it, just more white fog and haze. I shake my head and continue, filing it away to ask Ash about later. Soon the bridge levels out and ends on a plain of white. I can't make anything out but brightness. I cautiously step off the bridge onto cool stone, and the bridge disappears behind me.

"Archer, you have heard my call," I hear someone say, the most beautiful voice I have ever heard. It's not quite human. It must be an angel. "Come through the archway."

The archway appears before me, where before there had been nothing but light. I step through, looking around for the source of the beautiful voice. I feel my body pulled down the bright hallway, pillars and sconces appearing as I pass, as if someone is animating this background just one step behind me.

Finally I reach a grand room. I look up to see the ceiling, and I'm not sure if it's the sky overhead through glass, or a ceiling far away and white, or no ceiling at all, looking straight up at the heavens. There is a golden-haired man standing with his back to me, in a gown so bright I have to squint.

"Ah, Agnes Larch. Maiden. Little archer. You have done well," he says.

"Are you the Eternal?" I ask.

He laughs lightly. "They call me that here, your silly, superstitious wolves."

My hands clench into fists. "They are *not* silly."

"Oh please, Archer, do not be upset. I mean it with affection." But there is something in the way he holds up his finger, something in the darkness of his eyes, that gives me pause. As bright as his gown is, his eyes are dark, unreflective.

"Who are you?" I ask. "And why have you Summoned me here?"

"So many questions, little one," he says. "Shall we sit?" Immediately two chairs form from the light, not quite as bright as his robes. I climb into the seat cautiously. The chair is overstuffed and enormous, and my feet don't quite reach the floor.

"I'm sitting," I say, looking him square in the face, into those inky eyes.

"Who am I?" he says, making himself comfortable in his chair. His feet reach the ground. "I am the creator of what your wolves call the 'Stone One.'"

"Oh!" I say, wishing I had my weapons. "I'm...I'm sorry about that."

"No, I have Summoned you not to punish but to thank you. I created him to protect the land, since I am forbidden to interfere directly in the happenings below. I thought I was doing the right thing, outsmarting the rules. But the rules will be enforced, no matter how you try to outsmart them. He was not under my control—but such is the danger. I cannot breathe life into anything while denying it free will. He had a killer's nature, choosing to destroy instead of protect. Once I create something, I cannot unmake it myself. This world has been waiting for you, Maid Agnes. I didn't think it was possible to stop him."

"But…but why was *I* able to stop him?"

The Eternal's laughter sounds like the pealing of tiny, handcrafted bells. "I'm not entirely sure myself, little archer. Blood has powerful properties, especially freely given."

"Can you bring the lost wolves back?" I ask, gripping the armrests of the strange white chair.

"Why would you ask me to do that?"

"I miss them. It's my fault they are gone."

"That's part of what comes of being a creator, Archer. You can't stop what they do once you call them here. You can't protect them from all danger. You may only sit back and watch them destroy themselves. That is our gift and our burden."

"But…but they *didn't* destroy themselves!" I shout. "Your monster took them! And Willa, Willa was just trying to protect me. Doesn't that count for something?"

"Nothing is stopping you from making another…Willa," he says, tasting her name carefully, "but she wouldn't be the *same* Willa, not the one you knew. She might have her memories, but she wouldn't be the same. But that is up to you."

"Are you a god? An angel?" I ask. I can't stop looking at his face, having never been so close to the divine.

"I suppose you might call me that in your limited human vocabulary. It's close to what I am. I am Eternal. I was here before the land was here, and I will be here long after."

"Do you have a name?" I think of poor Joshua, dying because he was named and then unnamed.

"My celestial name cannot be formed with human tongues, but the last little archer called me *Samuel*. And you may do the same."

"Hello, Samuel," I say, holding out my hand.

He laughs again, another tinkling of bells. "You amuse me, little one, with your strange little customs." He leans forward to bring his hand close to mine, and it feels like I'm holding hands with a sunbeam, warming but immaterial. I'm not entirely sure we actually touch. "There, now have we done the ritual properly?"

"Yes." I'm still not sure what I'm doing here.

"You wonder why I've Summoned you here, dear one, do you not?"

I nod slowly. "I thought maybe you'd be upset that I destroyed the Stone One."

"And you came anyway? My, that was brave." He smiles, his teeth as bright as his robes, sharp as knives.

"Ash said you wouldn't harm me. That you just watch."

"That's an approximation of the truth," he says, and I'm not sure what he means. "I do watch, but as you don't come from this world, I *could* harm you, if I desired."

I start to get up from my chair, but Samuel stops me. "No, no, little one, do not fret. I was merely being up-front about that. I have Summoned you here, as I said, to thank you for dispatching of the beast, the product of my own hubris."

"Well, you're welcome," I say, still confused.

"I don't think you understand. I can grant you a boon as long as it is in my power. I wish to grant you this boon in thanks for protecting the land, for fixing my mistake, my failure in judgment."

I know, immediately, what I would wish for, if I could have anything in the world. I want to bring Ian back. He should be alive. He needs to return. If Samuel didn't create him, he can bring him back, can't he? I remember the haunted Meg Millbrook weeping silently at his gravestone and feel my heart breaking all over again.

I'm trying to figure out how I can ask him. I mean, I don't know how to identify Ian, from another world, to this Eternal, who may not see me when I am awake. He could bring back the wrong person.

"I see you puzzling, Maid Agnes," he says, a smile curling on his lips. "You wish to waken someone."

"Yes," I say, even though that's not the language I would choose. But things work differently here.

"You wish to waken the Sleeper," Samuel says matter-of-factly, not asking.

My heart nearly stops. "I do," I whisper.

"Then you must ask me, in those words."

"I…I wish to waken the Sleeper."

He smiles wider and wider like the Cheshire Cat, until the light from his smile is so painfully bright I have to shut my eyes and turn my face away. Behind my closed eyes, I see the afterimage of Samuel's smile and am reminded of a grinning skull.

EIGHTEEN
THE SLEEPER, THE SINGER

When I dare to open my eyes again, Samuel is drumming his fingers lightly on the armrest of his chair.

"So, little archer, little maiden, little lamb. You wish to waken the Sleeper."

I nod. For a second I wonder if I should clarify, but I can sense from his piercing gaze that he's able to look directly into my heart and see the face that haunts me day and night, that has haunted me long before he was ever dead.

"You realize that this request will not be easy to grant. I have some power, but not enough for such a complex request. I will need your assistance to get around my—*ahem!*—limitations."

"I'm not sure what that means," I say, trying to untangle the strange knot of his facial expression. He doesn't seem like he wants to harm me, but I'm not convinced he cares one whit about my well-being. I'm no fool. He's not being altruistic. He just has to hold up his end of the bargain because I unwittingly did him a favor. He's beholden to me, and I have a feeling he doesn't like to be beholden to anyone.

"Will…the Sleeper…be whole?" I ask. "Not, you know, not somehow *wrong?*"

"Maid Agnes!" remarks Samuel with something like offense. "What agenda do I have? Why should I lead you down such a path? I will grant you your boon, but I need help."

"Why? I thought you were the Eternal."

"Just because I have been here since before the beginning does not mean I have all the power. My role here is to observe, nothing more. I interfered by creating the Stone One, thinking I could outsmart the rules that have been set down since before time existed. This is my dominion, Archer, but I must only watch from a distance, never get my hands dirty. Do you think Eternals have it easy? In a moment of weakness, I had pity on the land and wanted to use my power to help. See how I was punished?"

It doesn't seem like he's really been punished, since he's still here in his crazy, IKEA-esque, stark-white palace and my wolf friends are dead. He doesn't seem too broken up about it either.

Something deep inside me tells me I am not to trust him, but a louder, more persistent part says, *Do whatever you can to bring Ian Millbrook back. He did not deserve to die.*

I know full well that it would not change anything. He wouldn't suddenly be in love with me. I think of Gillian and her perfect cork-screw curls at the memorial. I don't know one thing about her except that they were living together. But she should be happy, shouldn't she?

Oh, forget her — *he* should be happy. Maybe she made him happy, and they are not together now. And that is tragedy enough. Bringing him back so I can continue not having him seems a small price to pay for his happiness. Perhaps it would be reward enough for me knowing that he's *out there* in this world, stepping on the same soil, feeling the same heat from the same sun. I would feel less empty just knowing we were on the same dimension, the same plane.

I think also of Mrs. Millbrook's grief, the phantom pains in her womb, and if I can help this loving mother somehow, be a balm for her, I will do it. As for me, there always will be a question mark, a *maybe*. A second chance. A possibility that one day he may know who I am, even if he never knows — or, shit, *remembers* — who brought him back to life. Instead of what I have now: a full stop, a bricked-in fireplace, a yellow *No Outlet* street sign.

"So what do you need me to do?" I ask.

He smiles again, but I'm ready this time, turning my head away. Strangely enough, it reminds me of when my dad taught me to swim, getting the breathing pattern down for the freestyle. Head to the side and breathe, head in the water, head to the side and breathe.

"Amongst the rubble of the creation you call the Stone One is the thing which once gave him life. A thing I fashioned but may not touch again, or else it will lose its power. Find this object and bring it to me."

"What does it look like?"

"Ah, little maiden, there are rules. You will know when you see it, I am sure, the same way some part of you knew that your blood would make him vulnerable. The air of this land fills your lungs, is carried in your bloodstream. You are as much a part of the land as the Bridge, as the Source, even if you come from elsewhere. I trust you will find what you need."

"And the Sleeper?" I ask. "The Sleeper will be awakened?"

"Upon my honor, if I receive all the pieces."

"All the pieces? There is more than one?"

"My dear," says Samuel with an amused clucking of his tongue, "you should know by now that things are never so simple."

He stands up, and I know the meeting is over. The room begins to fade, and I am running to stay ahead of the vanishing marks in the stark white background. I don't want to be erased by whatever is happening here. I run back the way I believe I came, the sconces and pillars again disappearing behind me. The white world a few footfalls behind me seems to shatter into blinding flares of magnesium, and I find myself on the Bridge Between again, with nothing but nothingness behind me. If I stepped off the bridge toward the whiteness again, I'm not sure my feet would hit solid ground.

Confused and dizzy from everything that has just transpired, I slowly make my way back down the Bridge, holding onto the rough rope to steady myself. The strange dark door is no longer there, or perhaps the mist has grown so thick I can no longer see it. Maybe the light has shifted. My knees are shaking. Ash is standing alert, a sentry, as I come off the last few steps of the Bridge.

"*Well?*" Ash asks.

"That was…different," I say, feeling groggy and slow-witted, my head clouded from the brightness of Samuel's smile, the cloying perfume in the air through the archway. My head is swimming with thoughts, and the first thing I think to say is, "There was…I saw a door."

"*In the Eternal's kingdom?*"

"No, when I was walking on the Bridge Between. It was just floating there. And then when I came back, it was gone. Did I imagine it?"

"*I have heard talk of a door that appears only sometimes.*"

"Do you know where it goes? Does it open?"

"*All we know of it is that it leads Beyond. But we wolves, we do not use it. There is legend that the previous Archer may have gone through it.*"

"Will I see it again?"

"*The wolves do not know much about the Door Beyond. I do not believe it often appears.*"

"Oh." I shake my head, still muddled. I'm so sleepy. What was in that perfume?

"*I am glad you have returned safely.*"

"Me too," I say, crouching down to give him a hug. He lets me scratch him behind his ears and gives my face an affectionate lick. I can't believe this is the same wolf that frightened me so much when I returned to the dreaming, the nameless, terrifying wolf.

"Ash?" I ask.

"*Yes, my princess?*"

"Why is it that I could see you even before I remembered your name, when I couldn't with the others?"

"*Ah, that is a story for another time.*"

"Are you different from the others?"

"*In most ways the same, but in one important way, quite different.*"

I sit down with my legs out in front of me, listening to the river roar behind me, my head still full of fog, waiting for Ash to explain.

"*What did the Eternal want?*" He changes the subject instead, looking at me with his head cocked to the side.

"He, well, I guess he wanted to thank me for killing the Stone One. You know like in *The Wizard of Oz*, when Dorothy thinks all the Winkies and flying monkeys are going to hate her for killing the Wicked Witch of the West, and instead they're all cheering and celebrating?"

"*I...cannot say that I do. This is part of your history in the other world?*"

Right. There is probably no *Wizard of Oz* here. "It's a famous movie," I try to explain, still thinking fuzzily from my encounter with Samuel.

Ash looks at me blankly.

"Nevermind—you'll have to take my word for it. He was just… grateful instead of upset. He…he wanted to grant me a wish, or something. No, wait, he called it something else."

"*A boon?*"

"Yes. How did you know?"

"*It does not surprise me. The Eternal does not grant wishes. He merely maintains the order. There would be unbalance if he did not grant you a boon for what you have done for the land.*"

My mind is reeling, thinking about Ian and wondering how it would work. Would time be slowly cranked backward, the jack-in-the-box coiled up again and pushed back into its metal chamber, and the plane would never have crashed? Would Ian miraculously not get on that plane? Would he be plucked from the water, barely clinging to life, but alive? And would I remember? Would the entire world's memory be wiped for these awful eight days when we believed him dead? Maybe I would wake up last week, and none of this would have happened, and I'd never know, which would mean he'd also never know. But still: I'd have done it. Maybe I could leave a note here in the dreaming so at least I would remember, like my name carved in the rock. *I was here. I can see you. I, Agnes Therese Larch, brought him back.*

"*My princess?*" Ash asks, nudging my shoulder with his wet nose.

"Hmm?" I say dreamily, still trying to work out the possibilities. I'm absolutely giddy about being able to save him, if Samuel is a man—an Eternal, I correct myself—of his word.

"*What did you ask of the Eternal?*"

"I asked him to bring back the boy I've loved forever, to awaken the Sleeper."

"*And who is the 'Sleeper'?*"

"He…I'm guessing he's the reason I came back here. Yes. That must be why," I say, the realization slowly dawning. "I started dreaming again only after he died. That's why I was returned. This must be my purpose," I say, winding my fingers into the damp grass by the riverbed as if it were the hair of my Sleeper, soon to return to the living.

I returned to the dreaming around the time Ian Millbrook died, before I even knew he was dead. That can't just be coincidence. He brought me back to life in this world, somehow, and maybe that's why I was called to bring him back alive in the waking.

"I thought I was the one you have loved forever," says Ash, sounding vulnerable for the first time that I can remember. And not just since returning—in all my memories of my childhood here, Ash has always seemed strong and secure.

"Oh, Ash," I sigh. "You know it's not the same thing. You have always been and will always be a part of me."

He lays his head down on his crossed paws, not looking at me.

"I swear I'll never leave you again, no matter what. You are my lifeline in this world."

"I guess I should not be jealous of your affections in your other life. But it was hard when you went away. It wasn't even the danger. A piece of me was missing. And knowing the spot where we had buried you...I visited you every day. Did you know that? Some days I would steal away from the rest of the pack and sleep on top of your grave, just so I could be near you."

"Oh, Ash," I say, my eyes filling with tears. "I'm so sorry I hurt you."

"Did you feel me visit you?"

Should I lie? I don't remember feeling anything. "I don't know," I say finally. "All I know is that I couldn't stop drawing you and the others, but I didn't know why, or who you were."

He turns to look at me dolefully, and I wrap my arms around him and hug him as hard as I can. "Part of me must have felt your absence. And it wasn't anything you were lacking that made me not remember. It wasn't your fault." I think about all the lies I told myself when I was a kid, trying to convince myself that I wasn't the reason Shelly had left Dad and me. I never was able truly to believe it had nothing to do with me. I wonder if Ash has felt anything like that during my long absence. My chest hurts as if it's collapsing on itself, thinking I've hurt him the way Shelly hurt me. "I'm so sorry," I say yet another useless time.

Ash nods, looking away from me again, and I feel like a total heel when I say, "I need you, Ash. I need your help."

"You know I cannot deny you anything. What do you require?"

"Samuel—the Eternal—told me I have to find something from the Stone One. He said I'd know it when I saw it. I'm supposed to bring it back to him or something. In order to...waken the Sleeper."

"Tell me about your Sleeper," he says with a heavy wolf-sigh.

Now I'm faced with a dilemma. Here is, finally, someone I can tell the whole truth to without worrying about word getting around to Tricia or Dad or the Millbrooks. I can unburden my soul without fear of repercussion or embarrassment. But I can sense Ash's pain, his wish to be the center of my life. He is the center of my life *here*, for sure. But I don't carry that with me in the waking. And Ian is with me in both worlds now, always. I can't bear to hurt Ash any more than I already have.

"I loved him because he was kind to me when he had no reason to be — when he didn't even know who I was. I loved him because he could sometimes see the worth in me when no one else could. I loved him because he always stuck up for the vulnerable. I loved him because when he played music, he was transfigured, almost painful to look at, like a celestial being." I feel the hole in my heart again now that he is gone, and that he never was mine to lose.

"*That sounds like you*," says Ash.

"What do you mean? Like, you just figure I'm the sort of person who'd obsess over someone with no basis in anything?"

"*No, you sound as though you are describing yourself. You are the Singer here, the one who names and creates, who transforms and is transformed.*"

"I'm nothing like him," I say, wrinkling my brow. "He was bold. He feared nothing, no one's words or bad opinion. I'm afraid of everything and can be cut down with a look."

"*That is not the princess I know and serve*," disagrees Ash.

"You don't see how I am out there," I say, gesturing broadly with my arms.

A sudden jostling of the plane in turbulence wakes me up in a panic, and I cry out. My voice is loud and embarrassing in the relative quiet of the plane. Dahlia and her mother look over at me. "Bad dweam?" asks Dahlia.

Looking around the plane, I think, *This part* is *the bad dream*, wishing I were back on the riverbank with Ash. I know I'm still on the plane when I'm there, still in danger of plummeting to my death, of burning up when the plane bursts into a fireball on impact from the jet fuel, but at least I'm unaware. I know I should be afraid when

I am in the dreaming, but it's like this world and its dangers melt away. "I don't like to fly," I say quietly. I don't want to give the girl a complex or anything.

"Why?" she asks automatically, the way children her age often do.

"Because..." I stop, trying not to frighten her, carefully constructing my response. "I just don't like being in between places. I'd rather be far away, or I'd rather already be home."

She nods, my half-truth believable, sufficient. Her mother gives my hand a comforting squeeze. "It's going to be okay," she says, putting the pieces together—the desperate way I slammed back my drink, my inappropriate, cowardly scream. "It's just a bit of patchy air," she says. Her hand is cool and soft, and I wish it wouldn't be considered weird to clutch her hand for the rest of the flight. Blushing, I mumble, "Thanks," and reluctantly extract my hand from her unfamiliar maternal grasp. I don't want to take too much. This small gesture is comfort enough, as much as I deserve.

Dahlia is looking at me still. "Mama," she says, "maybe sing her da special song wid da funny words."

Dahlia's mom glances at me and smiles kindly. "Well, Dahlia, sweetheart, not everyone wants songs flung at them by strangers."

Dahlia pouts. "She need it. Sing it."

I want her mom to sing to me. Their singing helped me fall asleep at the beginning of this flight. Maybe it would work again.

Dahlia continues to squirm and command. "Dat lady need it, Mama."

The mom looks at me again, smiling apologetically. "I'm sorry. Are we disturbing you? I'll try to get Dahlia settled so you can get back to sleep."

"No, Mama. Dahlia no seddle. You sing. Sing for lady."

"I'm sorry, I don't know what's gotten into her. I know, I sound like every mother when I say, 'Oh, she's never like this at home.' But I mean it. This is strange, even for her."

"What's this song?" I ask, curious.

"Well, she usually doesn't let anyone else hear it. It's my special lullaby to her."

"And it has funny words?"

"Well, 'funny' to her means German."

"No talk, Mama," Dahlia interrupts, pulling on her mother's sleeve. "Sing! Sing now."

I remember her cool hand on mine, her comforting squeeze, and I have a flash of pressing a lipstick-stained cigarette butt to my cheek. "Would you?" I ask hoarsely.

"Would I what?" asks Dahlia's mother.

"Sing the song? I took German," I say, as if that makes it any less weird that I desperately want a mother to sing to me while I am terrified in this plane as it shakes and wobbles, just a few loose bolts away from disintegrating in the air.

"See? Lady want it," says Dahlia smugly.

"Gosh, this is a bit embarrassing," begins Dahlia's mother, but she opens her mouth and, quietly, so as not to disturb the other passengers, starts to sing the most beautiful lilting melody. I don't catch all the German, but her voice is like a tangible thing that cloaks me. I do understand, somewhat, the repeated refrain:

Schlaf, Kindlein, Süße,
Schlaf nun ein!

Sleep, little child, sweet one,
Fall asleep now!

I let her voice wash over me, swaddling me, stilling my racing thoughts. *Schlaf, Kindlein, Süße.* The movement of the plane now feels like clumsy rocking, reminding me of fishing with Dad as a kid, falling asleep to the gentle waves. I try to turn to thank her for her song, but I'm already slipping away, back to Ash, back to my first task.

Ash waits for me with twinkling eyes like the star-filled night outside the cold oval pane of the window by my true sleeping body.

"Where do we begin?" he asks.

NINETEEN
THE FIRST TASK

I can't hear Ash's silent footfalls behind me, but I know he is there, following me to the rubble, as he would follow me to the ends of the earth. There is a connection between the two of us that I can feel growing stronger every time I return to the dreaming, as if our hearts are tethered by a myelin-sheathed cord, thick and unbreakable. He is like my shadow in this world, and maybe in waking as well. I wonder if we mirror each other when I am awake, two sides separated only by the thinnest veil of consciousness.

"We're here," I say as we both regard what remains of the Stone One: pebbles, dust, sand, craggy rocks, and something else, something hidden and magical. What gave this monster life? And will I know it when I see it, as Samuel has promised?

"I guess we're supposed to look through here until we find the object, or whatever it is," I say, shrugging. Ash walks around the pile of rubble slowly, sniffing the perimeter. I pick up the smaller rocks and toss them aside. What am I even looking for? I think of what Samuel said about my blood, rich with oxygen from this land. I'm a part of this place as much as it is a part of me. I kick away the pebbles aimlessly, not caring that I am barefoot. I have no idea what I'm doing.

"Does anything smell...different, Ash?" I ask, watching him circle the rubble again.

EDEN BARBER

"All I smell is decay, danger, despair."

I don't know if he's pouting and being melodramatic, or if that's truly what the scent of the Stone One's remains brings to his mind. Aware of his hurt that he isn't the center of my life as I am his, I feel tremendous guilt even asking him to help me find the object that will bring Ian back—in whatever form. *No*, I chastise myself. *I have to trust Samuel, as much as I don't think I can.* He promised Ian would be whole and not "wrong." Not some halfway thing. I have to trust that. I want to believe it so much. I can bring him back. I just have to find this object. Which could be...well, anything.

What gives the Stone One life?

Could it look like the rest of these drab, colorless rocks? Is it some kind of stone as well? Or did he have a life force in him that was flesh and arteries and sinew and tendon? I shudder, imagining what slimy thing I might find, perhaps still pulsing under my touch.

Ash is picking up rocks in his mouth and dropping them onto a new pile. I wonder what he thinks of tasting the creature that destroyed his friends and family—odd satisfaction? Revulsion? Or does he not think this way at all?

"How are you doing there, Ash?" I ask, hunching over to pick up one of the larger stones.

"This is a strange task, my princess."

"I'm sorry. You don't have to help."

"No, I must. How often do you ask anything of me? And so, I must serve you."

"Please. Please, Ash, don't say it like that. You have freedom. You have free will. You can do what you please."

"I have free will, but I am tied to you. Your pain is my pain; your longing is my longing."

Has there ever been a creature so selfless? And so we continue searching through the rubble. I don't tire, but I do get a crick in my neck, and soon I'm telling Ash that we should take a break.

We walk over to the weeping cherry tree. I put my palm against the trunk and say, "Hi, Joshua." I could swear the swaying fronds reach forward to kiss my cheeks in greeting with pink petals soft as silk, delicate as tissue paper. I nod toward the prickly pear cactus and say, "Hey, Willa." I sit down with my back against Joshua's tree. Ash lies down next to me, his head on my knee. I scratch him behind his ears, and his tail thumps happily against the ground. This is all

194

he wants from me, this quiet life, this innocent affection. But I can't even give him this simple thing. First I abandon him, then all my actions here seem to do nothing but take his friends away. And now I ask him to do something that surely will disturb the order of his world. It's so easy to make him happy, so why can't I just do it? I should just sit under this tree and scratch his head forever.

But it's not about me. It's about Ian Millbrook. It's about bringing him back so he can live out his life, as by all rights he should if there were any fairness in the universe. Even forced to observe from afar, I would find joy in each beat of his heart because it would mean he was alive. It would mean the people around him would no longer be hurting. It would mean I could still dream that one day we would meet and that he might know me. I think of these things and say with fresh determination, "I'm ready to start again." I brush off my dress and head back to the impossibly tall pile of rubble, when I feel a rumbling like an earthquake. What now?

I look around in panic over to Ash, who shimmers and begins to fade. As I slip back into the waking, I hear him — or perhaps just the wind in the trees — calling, "*Goodbye, Princess.*"

The plane touches down roughly, and my eyes snap open. I look out the window out at the clear Boston night to make sure that we're on the ground, that the rumbling I feel isn't of the engines falling off of the plane. I see runway lights, feel my weight against the seatbelt as the aircraft brakes hard. I made it. I can't believe I made it. I start to cry with relief. I'm glad I'm far back in the plane, because I'll need the time to will the blood back to my legs. I'm not sure I'd be able to stand up right now.

Dahlia's mom is already reaching into her purse to hand me a tissue, just like Tricia at Ian's memorial. Moms. There must be a training manual. "Thanks," I say sheepishly.

"Don't worry about it," she says, patting my hand. Dahlia is sleeping in her arms, all floppy like a doll.

"She's wonderful," I say, nodding toward the sleeping child with my head.

"She's my treasure," she says, brushing away some matted curls and kissing her on the forehead.

"Thank you for the song," I say, feeling a little awkward and wistful at this personal motherly display.

"Oh," she says, gazing at her child. "Dahlia can be pushy sometimes."

As the aisle slowly clears, I ask, "Do you need any help?"

She smiles gratefully and motions toward the overhead compartment. "I've got a bag up there. Could you help me get it to the jet bridge? The stroller should be waiting, and then my hands will be free again."

I put my sketchpad back in my backpack and stand up slowly, testing out my legs. They'll hold. I put the pack on and take down both my suitcase and her duffel. It's not too hard to get everything through to the jet bridge. Her duffel reminds me of Shelly's, though, and it's hard not to feel cold and empty. Or maybe it's just the chill seeping into the jet bridge from outside.

I unload the duffel next to the pile of gate-checked strollers and car seats. "Do you mind holding her a second while I pop up the stroller?" she asks.

"Of course not," I say, holding out my arms. I worry the transfer will wake Dahlia, but she merely sighs and snuggles against my neck. Her relaxed body weighs me down, but it's not a burden. It's a feeling like security, a feeling like love, a feeling that my life *means* something. My heart aches for reasons I can't describe, and I'm lost, closing my eyes, breathing in her little-kid smell, listening to her shallow, little-kid breathing. *Tiny lungs*, I think, and finally I hear a voice say, "I'm ready now."

Dahlia's mother has finished unfolding the stroller. I hand Dahlia back, and she doesn't even twitch as her mother lays her inside. Dahlia's mom takes the stroller handles, and I hand her the bag.

"Nice meeting you," I say, holding out my hand, and she takes it for a moment, smiling kindly at me.

"You have a big heart," she says, and I watch her push the stroller away, the duffel over her shoulder. I hope someone's waiting to pick her up. The thought of her taking a cab or shuttle with her baby this late at night just seems wrong. Someone should be looking after these two.

They're already far out of sight by the time I walk down the stairs out of the secure area and into baggage claim. Since the *T* has stopped running for the night, I start weaving through the lower level of the airport to the exit closest to the cabstand. I'm groggily walking, eyes half closed, when I hear someone shriek. "Agrippina!"

Vivian is here. I look around to find her, and she's over by the Dunkin' Donuts by one of the luggage carousels. She's the tallest woman here, her glossy black hair like a beacon guiding me home.

"Viv! Viv! You dirty whore!" I yell, barreling into her. My legs feel like jelly, but she's solid. It's like running into a tree. People are looking over, too tired to be more than mildly shocked at my language. "What are you doing here?"

"I was tracking you, loser. And I thought you might be wobbly from flying, and I figured, what else do I have to do on a Saturday night than wait for my bestest Aggie-Boo to come home?" She picks up my rolling bag and says, "Cab's on me, beeyotch."

I loop my arm through hers as we march outside. "Holy *fuck*," I say as the automatic doors slide open and the cold air hits my face.

"Boston, fuck yeah!" She suddenly breaks into the Standells' "Dirty Water" at the top of her lungs, her breath visible in the biting cold. "*Oh, Boston, you're my home!*"

Vivian's outburst, the song played in Fenway Park every time the Sox win a home game, makes me wistful. Baseball season seems impossibly far away as I look out at the piles of snow, dirty, frozen, melted, and frozen again into slick and ugly shapes like gargoyles or imps. It's like Narnia before the Pevensies appear, when it's always winter but never Christmas. This winter feels endless. Always winter and never baseball season.

Jesus, it's cold. I can't believe how quickly my body has forgotten how to stay warm. How can it be so easy for me to forget everything? My teeth are chattering, and I clutch Vivian's arm while we get into the taxi line. "Muff up!" Vivian says, removing her Hello Kitty earmuffs and clapping them over my ears. They help marginally, although I must look stupid. When Vivian wears them, she looks like she did it on purpose. I'm pretty sure I just look crazy.

"Augh, it's *cold*," I say because my brain isn't working in the arctic wind.

"Almost there, Aggapotamus," Vivian says, rubbing my arms up and down, trying to keep me warm. The next cab is ours, and I shrug off my backpack, gratefully stumbling headfirst into the back while Vivian and the driver get my crap into the trunk. The air inside is thick and heavy, almost viscous, with incense and artificial vanilla, reminding me of the perfumed haze of Samuel's kingdom. Still, I'm thankful for the blasting heat, not caring that the cloying air will probably give me a headache.

"Where are we headed?" I ask, my teeth still clenched together from the cold.

Vivian gives the driver my address. We sit in silence for a while as we both try to warm up. As we get onto Storrow Drive, Vivian asks, "Okay if I stay over?"

I'm thrilled that I don't have to spend the night alone, but I say, "I don't know," scooting away from her slightly. "I'm going to have to prorate the rent, split it between the two of us, plus there's the twelve-point-four-five-percent state room tax…"

Vivian pulls something out of her enormous purse and bops me on the head with it.

"What the hell is *that?*" I ask, rubbing my forehead.

"It's a present!" She tosses me a book, a glossy new paperback. I angle it toward the side window, trying to make out the picture on the cover by the orange light sweeping over the book as the cab zips dangerously fast past the streetlamps around the curves on Storrow.

"Vivian? Is this a…naked…Native American? Sitting on a horse?"

"Uh, *no*," Vivian says, offended. "*Clearly* he's wearing a *loincloth*." She taps it on the cover, and I feel she's violating this unfortunate noble man's dignity.

"Leave poor Sitting Bull's junk alone," I say, snatching the book out of her reach.

"His name is *Dusky Sequoia*," Vivian corrects.

"Okay, what the hell is this?"

Vivian snickers. "A One-L told me that every airport bookstore has at least one romance novel with a mostly nude Native American hero on the cover, sometimes holding a white woman, sometimes on a horse. Sometimes on a horse while holding a white woman. I thought he was making that shit up, so I had to check while I was waiting for your flight to come in. Now I owe him five bucks. Anyway, I thought maybe we could read this out loud to each other tonight."

I lean my head against the cold, smudged window and laugh softly. "That sounds great," I say, closing my eyes for a second. "But who's Juan? Have I met him? Is he a friend of yours? Or a conquest you've forgotten to tell me about?"

"*Juan* who the what now? Are you high?"

My whole brain feels furry. "You *said*," I say between yawns, "that a Juan El something told you about these superbly Natively and nudely American books."

There is cackling, and the next thing I know, Vivian has me in an affectionate (if slightly painful) headlock. "Oh, you innocent, beautiful woman, I just adore you. Not Juan. A one-L, like, first-year law student?"

"Of course, *durr*. I'm idiotic. Sorry, I should know that by now," I mutter, trying to free myself from the bear trap of Vivian's arms.

But she's having none of it, none of the squirming free and none of the self-deprecation. "I squish you," she says sternly. "Now you hold still while I squish you with love, you refreshingly un-law-school-jargoned specimen." I submit to her squishing, and when she finally lets go, she grabs the book back from me.

"Listen!" Vivian uses her cell phone as a flashlight to read me the back cover. She puts on her best phone sex voice. "'*Dusky Sequoia throbbed in a relentless summer heat for the love of Marianne. He prayed for rain for the parched earth, which longed for water as much as his mouth ached for the wetness of Marianne. Would she yield to his mighty firmness? Or would she leave him longing in the endless drought of his sorrow?*' Doesn't that sound *awesome?*" Vivian fans herself with the book, swooning as melodramatically as a Tennessee Williams heroine.

Halfway through the description, I am cackling right along with her. "It does. But is it okay if I replace 'Marianne' with 'Vivian'?"

Viv gives me a death glare before busting out laughing. "Hmm, *Mrs. Vivian Sequoia*," she muses. "Yes, I like the sound of that."

"You just like the sound of *Dusky Sequoia's relentless throbbing heat*. Or whatever."

"Hey, I'm not going to look a gift Dusky Sequoia under the loincloth," she says, as the cab driver coughs uncomfortably. We're in front of my apartment, and Vivian pays him before he runs outside to put my bags on the curb.

My apartment smells stale and institutional when I unlock the door and flip on the lights. I think of the home I left behind. *Oh, Dad,* I think, wondering what he's doing right now. I picture him in front of the TV in the living room, maybe with a dry slice of cake that I've forgotten to frost.

Vivian brings me out of my funk as she whacks me on the ass with the Dusky Sequoia book. "Come on, sweetcheeks. Let's get this show on the road." She kicks off her boots and flops on the couch.

Vivian begins to read as I pull my boots off. When I unzip my bag, the smell of Dad's house comes wafting out. "Oh," I gasp to myself, taking out my pajamas and smelling deeply. If I close my eyes, I'm back in my room with Dad just down the hallway from me. How could I leave? Why am I not there?

There's nothing for me in Poppy Beach but *Dad*, I remind myself. I listen to Vivian continue reading as I peel off the clothes smelling heavily of airplane and slip into the pajamas that make me feel small and protected under my father's roof. I join Vivian on the couch. When she finishes the chapter, she passes the book to me, and I read, being sure to replace the heroine's name with Vivian's. As I reach the end of the chapter, I'm yawning every other word. "I don't think I can get through much more of this tonight," I say, handing the book back to her.

"Of course, Aggala. You must be exhausted. You get in bed now. I'm on couch duty tonight, me and Dusky Sequoia." I'm about to protest, because I'm so tired that I could probably fall asleep under the kitchen table, but Vivian pulls me to my feet and points me toward my bed.

I unpack my toiletries with limbs like stone, feeling like I'm about to fall asleep standing up. But I manage to brush my teeth and get under the covers before passing out to the sound of Vivian's quiet chuckling and the fluttering of cheap paperback pages.

"You've been busy," I say to Ash as I open my eyes. While I've been gone, he's moved aside most of the rocks and rubble.

"I am not sure what I am looking for."

"I'm not either," I say, shaking my head. "Why don't you take a break? This must have taken a long time."

He nods and shuffles off, his tongue hanging out of his mouth. He looks tired. I scratch him behind the ears as he stretches out.

"You should sleep, maybe," I say. "You shouldn't work so hard for me. I'm not worth it."

"*What else am I going to do?*" he murmurs. "*There is no one else left.*" He must be falling asleep, because I know he'd never bring up the lost ones to me that way. Even so, I'm eaten alive by guilt. I stay a long time, patting his head, rubbing his belly, until I can tell from his steady wolfy breathing that he has fallen asleep. I wonder briefly what he dreams about, if he's got a special world where maybe he's not even a wolf. Maybe he's an enchanted prince in his dream world. I wonder how many worlds nest inside each other, if creatures in his secret world dream in an even smaller world. The thought of it makes me dizzy.

Maybe he doesn't dream at all. I'll have to ask him when he wakes up.

He's cleared away a flat place in the center of the rubble, and as I step inside this circle, I feel a pull in my stomach and fall to my knees. Whatever this object is, it's close now. It's so close that it causes actual physical pain, prickling pulses of something like electricity, heat, fire. I start crawling toward the pain, using my stomach as a compass. It's hard to force myself to move *toward* the pain, sharp and stabbing now as I near the object, but I visualize Ian Millbrook's face as he leans over his guitar and loses himself to the music as I get closer. Away from the pain, I picture him, lips blue, frozen in Lake Michigan. It gives me the strength to keep crawling, nearly blind now from the agony. I must be close now.

I feel like I'm going to lose consciousness, but in my delirium I think I can hear Ian's voice say, "Hold on—I can see you." It gives me the strength to make the final push toward the origin of the pain, and I make a desperate grab with my eyes shut. My hands close around something ice cold, cruelly sharp, and heavy. It throbs like something alive, and the minute it touches my skin, I'm screaming from the intensity of the electric pulses. My stomach feels like it's being pierced.

"*My princess! My princess!*" Ash shouts, awake at once and circling around the rubble. "*Are you all right?*"

I try to answer him, but I can't stop screaming, and his voice fades away. I can no longer feel the coarse rocks under my knees. There's smooth, cold marble now.

I hear laughter, and though my eyes are still squeezed shut in pain, I can tell through the delicate skin of my eyelids that the light has grown brighter.

"So you have found it, little maiden, as I thought you might."

I force my eyes open and find myself in Samuel's strange white palace again. Here the pain is no longer, and after a few moments to catch my breath, I stand up shakily. I look at my hands and see a dull stone knife. I turn it in my hands, and when the light hits it a certain way, the knife pulses red and is murderously sharp. It looks alive and vicious.

"Here," I say, offering the knife to him.

"No," he says quietly, folding his hands behind his back. "I may not touch it. And this is only the first task."

"So what now?" I ask, exhausted. I can't imagine doing another task.

"You must use the knife."

"I? What am I to do?"

Samuel takes a moment to consider his words. "Part of your heart is hidden away in this world. You must find it, sever it, and bring it to me. You must use the stone knife to do it."

"Where is it hidden?" I ask.

"I cannot tell you. But you already know, deep within yourself, where you have hidden it. You must remember. That is all," he says, dismissing me.

"But wait!" I call, before his world begins to disappear. "How can I complete the second task if I can't even hold the knife without screaming?"

"Does the knife truly cause pain, or do you imagine it does?" he asks.

"I…I don't know," I say, suddenly confused. "If it didn't cause me pain, I wouldn't have been able to find it."

"Maybe. Or maybe you believed you needed the pain to find the knife."

Why would I believe that? "I don't think I can bear that again," I say, shuddering at the memory of the pain, the burning, the sharp pulsation.

"There are no consequences if you decide to withdraw your request," Samuel says, turning to walk away.

In my mind I see Meg and Ian again at the swings, her silent laughter. I see Meg at the memorial, staring directly at me from across the room. I see Meg's haunted face at the grave. I can endure pain for her, for him, for everyone who loves him. "I don't withdraw my request. I wish to waken the Sleeper," I say again. "I'll endure the pain."

"The pain that may be only in your head, Archer."

I'm pretty sure it's not in my head, but I don't contradict him.

"Hurry back now," he says, and his palace begins to shatter away again like shards of glass. I run with the knife, letting it pull me along. I'm not even looking where I'm going, but I find myself on the Bridge Between, Samuel's land once again a blank slate of blinding light. I clutch the knife in my hand without pain at first, but as each step down the bridge takes me closer to the land, the pain grows.

It's still bearable as I step off the bridge onto the springy grass, but as I approach Oread's Keep again, I have trouble breathing through the stinging in my hand. I have chills all over, cold sweat on my forehead as if I have a fever. I can see Ash under Joshua's tree, waiting for me anxiously, pacing.

"I'm all right!" I wave to him, even as I have to struggle for air. I try to breathe through the pain, to focus on memories of Ian's face transfigured through music. That lessens the pain somewhat. If I can keep my mind focused on something else, maybe I can bear it.

"*Will he waken your Sleeper now?*" asks Ash.

"Not yet," I say, trying to keep my thoughts focused on Ian's face.

Ash strides toward me and leans his warm body against me. I feel complete, full in my chest, when he is so near.

"*What now, then? What is the second task?*"

"I have to find my heart."

Ash is suddenly still and silent, and all I can hear is the wind rustling the pale pink petals of Joshua's tree, sounding less like gentle whispering and more like a death rattle.

TWENTY
HER HEART

The pain in my hand lessens as an incessant ringing pulls me out of the world. I open my eyes to darkness and fumble around for my phone without looking at who is calling. "Hello?" I say in a voice thick with sleep. I shake my right hand out. I must have been sleeping on it funny, because it's numb, coming back to life slowly and painfully, all prickly with pins and needles.

"Ags? You okay?"

"Dad?" Oh *shit*, I forgot to call him when I got off the plane, too distracted when Viv surprised me at the airport. "Oh, Dad, I'm home. I'm so sorry I didn't call right away. It slipped my mind." As soon as the words are out of my mouth, I want to reach out and pull them back through the phone. I know my father will think I've forgotten about him, and I guess I *did*, but it wasn't because he's forgettable. He was on my mind the whole time, the way he is part of the fabric of my skin. He's *always* on my mind, my body always feeling his absence. He's there in my macro-world, but in the micro-world of walking through Logan Airport in a daze, I didn't think of pulling out my phone and taking thirty seconds to ease his worries. I am a terrible daughter.

"Vivian — Vivian Park, Dad — she surprised me at the airport, and I was so tired when we got home."

"Oh, sure, Ags, I understand," he says, and I tilt my head and listen to his voice again and again in my memory like a prospector panning for gold. Are there any trace elements of hurt? Or is it just relief?

"I'm *so* sorry, Dad," I say again, bunching up my blanket in my fist, frustrated and angry with myself.

"Aw, Ags, it's just fine. I know you must be tired. Was the flight okay?"

"Yeah, I met a nice little girl named Dahlia," I babble, yawning.

"That's my Ags, always making friends," he says, and I can just see him bobbing his head while he's saying it. I feel doubly guilty that he is trying to soothe me, when I'm the one who's upset him. It's not enough that I've made him worry that I'm all right; I've made him think that he's forgettable, an afterthought, when he is an indelible mark on my skin, an invisible tattoo.

I look at the clock—three a.m. I can hear Viv snoring softly from the couch, and as my eyes adjust to the light, I see that she's fallen asleep with Dusky Sequoia on her face. I make a mental note to mock her in the morning for sleeping with her nose nestled firmly beneath Dusky Sequoia's loincloth.

"Just midnight there, huh, Dad?" I ask.

"Yep," he says, and I know he is stretching, arching his back the way he always does before he heads up to bed. "House is real quiet again."

"I'm sorry," I half-whisper. My heart hurts. I wish I were there.

"I'm fine, Ags. Don't you worry about me; I'm going fishing tomorrow."

"Well, you'd better get to bed then," I say as cheerfully as I can. "Hope they're biting tomorrow."

"You know me, kid. They can't resist the *professional*, no, *artisanal* lures of Pete Larch, master angler," he says, chuckling.

"Of course they can't. No willpower, those fish. Goodnight, Dad," I say, yawning again. "Miss you already."

There's a long pause, and I think I've lost the connection until I hear my dad say quietly, "You too, kid."

He hangs up, and it's just my heartbeat, the hum of the refrigerator, and Viv's snoring keeping me company in the dead of night. I flop over onto my side under the blankets, and my right hand begins to tingle again even before I'm asleep.

"*Your heart?*" asks Ash in a steady, measured tone.

"He said I've hidden part of it here, in this world," I say. My speech is labored as I try to speak through the pain in my hand. I focus on Ian Millbrook's face, his smile in the parking lot, his bandaged hand after defending his sister. The pain is dulled, like sharp edges of a beer bottle shard battered and smoothed by the ocean until it is a beautiful piece of sea glass. "I'm…I'm supposed to sever it with the knife and bring it to him."

"*Oh,*" says Ash. I notice he hasn't moved an inch, even when I disappeared to answer Dad's call. He's stiff by my side, ears back, not looking at me.

"Do you know where it might be? Where I might have hidden it?"

Ash is silent and still.

"I'm sorry, Ash. I shouldn't even ask you."

I let the knife slip out of my fingers onto the grass and immediately feel relief in my whole body. I can feel the relief travel through Ash's body by my side as well. I walk back to Joshua's tree with Ash behind me. He lies down again as he did earlier, his head on my knee, and I scratch behind his ears. "Sweet Ash," I murmur. "You're my friend," I say, stroking the short hair on his face with the back of my hand.

"*You are my princess,*" he says in a sleepy, satisfied rumble that vibrates all the way through my stomach.

We sit for a long time as I pat him. I want to spend time with him, quiet, together time, appreciating him. I grab handfuls of his fur and lean down, sniffing his wolfy, woodsy smell, and my pulse slows as we begin to breathe as one. He is peace here, warmth, security, identity. He remembered who I was when I had forgotten. I think of all the years he slept where I had been buried, trying to feel near me, remembering me while my dream body remained below. Where did I go?

I try to remember all those years when I did not return to this land but my dream-corpse remained. I know it's been only about a week since I've been back (*has it really been only a week since we lost Ian Millbrook, since my world ended?*), but now I barely remember the years of blankness, of brain static. Even with the sorrow of losing Joshua and Willa and my terror facing down the Stone One, I am glad to be back here. It's dark and confusing and frightening, but it's also kind of wonderful. I am confident and powerful here, graceful, strong, courageous, and vital to the land's survival. The land needs me. Ash needs me. I continue to stroke the coarse fur, humming a little as Ash's breathing slows.

"What do you dream about?" I ask suddenly, stopping my humming.

"*Dream?*" he asks, half-asleep.

"What happens when you sleep? Do you dream?"

"*I am not sure. It feels as though I return to the others, my lost brethren, the one mind with which we think. Or thought,*" he corrects. After all, as he has reminded me, he is the only one left.

"Do you feel, you know, *yourself* when you are there, or are you just part of a whole, like a cell in an organism?" As I ask him, I wonder myself what it's like to be a cell. Does it know it's only a cell? Does it feel like an individual, unaware that it helps make up something bigger, greater? Am I just a cell myself? Would I even know if I were part of something greater? My mind is spinning as I contemplate this, wondering if I only believe I am an individual with choices when in reality I'm only a minuscule part serving some sort of larger being. Ash interrupts my train of thought before I can start to panic at my feeling of insignificance.

"*To be honest, my princess, I do not really think of it in such concrete ways. I just let myself be. I live in the history, our history, with our fallen, with the ones not yet born. They live around me. We all just* are."

"Is it peaceful to think that way?"

"*It is restful. It is restorative.*"

"Ash, why *is* it that I could see you when I didn't remember your name?"

"*I want you to remember that for yourself,*" he says.

"But you know why."

"*Yes.*"

He *wants* me to remember, he says. He doesn't say he *can't* tell me. I curl up next to him on the ground, scratching his head. I let my hand rest against his side. His ribs feel so delicate and surprisingly fragile as his skin and fur slide between his bones and my hand as he breathes. I'm pretty sure he's asleep now, his mind in his greater wolf consciousness. I watch my hand on his side rise and fall, rise and fall.

I'm not tired in this land, but something about the rhythm of his breathing, his pulse fluttering under his warm skin, puts me in something like a trance. I rest my head against his side, my head now rising and falling with the tide of his breath, and the world slips away.

I am Princess Aggie. I am brave and strong. Nothing scares me. I march in my pretty dress around my castle. Once I saw a spider and almost screamed, but then I remembered that I am the princess. I told the spider that this was my land and the spider was not to frighten anyone. The spider apologized and did a little dance for me. He spun a little top hat out of spider silk and floated in the air, and I laughed and clapped my hands. I twirled around and around in my pretty dress until I was dizzy. Dizzy, swirly Princess Aggie!

I come here all the time. It is my secret place. No one knows about it, not Mama or Daddy or the other kids at school. I can do things here that I can't do anywhere else. I can make things appear or disappear. I can close my eyes and build things. There's a stream, and I am never tired.

I'm the only one here, the only one like me. The only little girl. Maybe I shouldn't have made the spider go away.

I would like a friend.

Maybe that's asking too much. I can do so much here. "Don't be greedy," Mama says sometimes when I ask for more dessert, and her eyes look like beetles. I don't want to be greedy.

I'm looking into the stream, and I can see my face in the water, and the face in the water talks back to me!

"Aggie, Aggie," she says in her watery voice, "I know you are lonely, because I am you."

And I say, "What can I do?"

She says, "Reach in here," and she puts her hand on her chest. And since she is me, I do the same thing. My fingers go inside my chest, and it hurts, but only a little, like when Daddy took that splinter out of my toe.

She says, "Reach inside and keep on pulling," and because she is me, I do. I look at my hands and see a small purple rock, like a kind of jewel.

She says, "Now whisper your wish to your hands. Cup them, like this." And she shows me. And because she is me, I'm already doing it.

I whisper to my hands, "I want a friend. Send me a friend."

"Squeeze your hands together," she says as she does it, and because she is me, my hands are already pressed together. My insides hurt a little,

and there is a rumbling like I am holding the world in my hands and it's breaking. I feel like I'm going to fall down, but I don't know if the shaking I feel is in my hands or under my feet. Is the world in my hands or am I inside the world?

I fall down on my bottom, but it doesn't hurt because the grass is always soft here. I open my hands, and they are empty. But I can hear something beating. I hear something little crying, a little-scared-baby kind of sound. Something that needs help, that is looking for its mommy. I crawl around toward the noise, the quiet crying. "Don't be sad," I say, and I reach under a bush because I know the baby thing is under there.

Under the bush is something warm and furry, and it licks my hand. I pull it out, and I can hear the beating louder now. It's a little wolf cub, a puffball, so cute that I want to squeal and jump up and down. I hug him to my chest, and my heart matches the beating I hear all around me. Everything is beating, like I am locked inside a grandfather clock.

"You are beautiful, my little furry wolfy thing," I say to the baby wolfy in my hands. "I love you. My name is Aggie. What is your name?"

He looks at me with big, wide eyes, clear like the water in the stream where the other me is. I can see me in his eyes, like I saw the girl in the stream. I expect him to bark or howl or do something else that is wolfy.

But he doesn't. He doesn't open his little mouth at all. I just hear a voice in my head. "You must name me," *the voice says. Was that my little wolfy friend who spoke?*

"Is that you talking, little wolf?" I ask the little furry baby in my hands.

"Yes."

"I have to give you a name?"

"That is why you are here," he says, *and I don't understand. I thought I was here because...well, this is where I go. This is my special place.*

"Where did you come from, little wolfy?" I ask my cupped hands.

"I have always existed with the other ones, but not in this body. But you called me here. And now you must name me."

"I'm not good with names," I say, thinking hard and wrinkling my eyebrows together. I don't like naming my dolls. They just stare at me.

"I will not just stare at you," *the little wolfy says.*

"Can you read my mind?" I ask.

"I know what you think sometimes, because part of you is in me," *he says.*

"If part of me is in you, maybe I already know what your name is."

"Maybe *you* do, but I do not."

"Let me think," I say, and I sit up with him in my lap. He opens his mouth and nips at my hands with his little baby teeth. "You are a little monster," I say, laughing and rubbing his belly. He has a really cute little wheezy wolfy laugh. He must be ticklish.

And then the name comes to me like the girl in the water is talking to me again. "Ash," I say. "Your name is Ash."

"Of course it is. Thank you, my princess." *And he grows right in front of me and is suddenly as big as I am, still with a little wolfy baby face, but not so breakable. I stand up and chase him, and he turns around and chases me, and we fall and tumble down a grassy hill, laughing and laughing the whole way to the bottom. I screech in that loud voice that makes Mama say, "Use your indoor voice, Aggie," but here it doesn't matter. Ash, my special wolfy wolf, laughs too, that same wheezy laugh that I can feel all around me like a fuzzy blanket.*

"I love you, Ash," I say, touching noses with him. I won't be lonely here anymore. He is my Ash.

A sudden snuffly break in Ash's breathing wakes me up from… well it wasn't a dream, but whatever it was, this living memory. I gaze at him sleeping there so peacefully.

I look at my cupped hands. I touch my hands to my chest. I touch one hand to my chest while resting the other on Ash's side. Our hearts beat as one. Exactly with the same beat.

Oh God. Oh God, no. This can't be right.

I crawl to where I've dropped the knife in the grass and pick it up again. Even though I mentally prepare myself for the painful electrical jolts, the sting as my hand wraps around the knife's handle still surprises me, making me gasp. Just to confirm my fears, I hold the knife near Ash. It begins to hum and whirr, and the stone transforms into that strange, red, glass-like substance, appearing sharper, deadlier.

Oh God, no.

I won't do it. I won't! I toss the knife away from me. I'm crying, thinking, *Don't make me choose. You know I can't do that.*

There's a rustling in the woods, and I look up and see something like the shadow of a man, or a beast. I'm not sure. I think I see a camelhair coat, but…no, that's impossible. I pick up the knife again and run after the shadow, which I'm now not sure if I've really seen. I'm led to the Bridge Between.

"Samuel!" I shout. "Samuel! I request entry to your kingdom."

I can feel the Bridge vibrate, and I know in my heart that the gate is open. I run across the damp wood, but I do not slip. I'm clutching the knife in my hand until my fingernails turn white. "Samuel!" I shout as I reach the other side. I run as fast as I can, flying under the arch, the columns and sconces that appear as I run past.

"Little maiden," Samuel says coolly as I reach the room with the chairs. "Have you brought me your heart, then?"

"I found it. I know where it is," I say breathlessly. "But I can't. That's impossible. You...you *can't* be asking me to..." I'm crying too hard to finish what I'm saying.

"Dear one," he says, and a shiver runs down my spine, "you knew that your request would come at a high price. It's not for my pleasure; there are rules that even we Eternals must uphold. You are asking for something large. These are the items required."

"How do I know that you are right?"

"Why, whatever do you mean, Maid Agnes?"

"How do I know you are telling the truth?"

"Archer, what reason have I to lie to you? My job is to watch, to observe, not to interfere. As you know, I once interfered in this world out of pity, and I was punished. You delivered me from that, and so I owe you a favor, but still, there are costs to everything."

"Show me I can trust you. *Show me*," I hiss.

Samuel chuckles. "Oh, little maiden, you are so fierce. You are a good guardian for this land."

"Show *him* to me," I demand. "Show me you can do this."

"Hmm," says Samuel. "Let me see." He strokes his chin thoughtfully and whirls his hands around in the air.

There's some smoke that begins to spin in the corner and starts to take shape. I hear a shrill chirping sound to the side that I choose to ignore. I'm staring at the smoke, hoping to see a familiar form. Could it be? I see an outline of hair, a pair of hands. The chirping won't stop, and I look at my hand, and there is a silver cricket that's just landed there, rubbing its wings together. "Be quiet," I say sternly to the cricket, but it's some sort of mechanical thing, and it won't stop. I'm trying to look at the swirly smoke, desperately trying to make out Ian's face, but now the cricket stings my hand as it chirps.

Crickets don't even sting, I think crabbily, trying to crush the thing in my hand, but the metal doesn't give under the pressure of my squeezed fist. The mechanical thing just stings me more. The chirping won't stop. The chirping is regular, like breathing, and I cannot, for the life of me, focus on the swirling, almost-Ian shape.

I am pulled into a consciousness that I do not want. My eyes pop open in the darkness, and I hear it again, the shrill chirping. I'm crying, because I was so *close*. I could almost see him. Ian would have formed in the corner if not for that distracting chirp. *Chirrup!* I hear again, but I'm awake.

It's the goddamn smoke detector. The battery must be dying. I sit up in bed, wiping away my tears, and every twenty seconds or so, the smoke detector chirps again. Damn it, I don't have time for this. I almost *saw him*. I rip the covers off me, get the stepladder out of the closet, and climb up to the smoke detector. I have to go on the highest step and stand on my toes and reach my fingers out so far that I think the edges of my soul reach beyond the fingertips to twist down the detector and take out the battery in the back. I toss the dying battery onto the blanket Vivian has kicked onto the floor in her sleep, put the detector back on the ceiling. After I shove the ladder into the closet, I crawl back into bed, praying that I'll wake up again where we left off in Samuel's palace, with the swirling, dancing smoke. *Please*, I whisper to myself, tears streaming out of the corners of my eyes. *Please, please, please*, I beg to no one in particular.

I'm still whispering, *Please, please, please*, as I open my eyes in a stark, white place. Good. I must still be in Samuel's realm. I look in the corner for the smoke, and it's just ordinary smoke again, dispersing into a frustrating haze.

"What happened?" I ask.

"Your mind wasn't focused," he says. "I could not bring him forth before you disappeared."

"Can you do it now?"

"Little one, I'm afraid that magic works only once. I don't have infinite power. But you saw what you wanted, did you not?"

I'm not sure. I'm not sure what I saw, but I can hear Ian's voice like a great wind blowing my hair and giving me his message: *Trust.*

"You must leave here now," says Samuel. "Remember, it is always your choice. You may refuse the boon."

"No," I say, feeling the wind in my hair. "I do not refuse. The boon remains unchanged." There's a chance. There's a chance that he's right. I try to remember the swirling smoke. Yes. Yes, I am fairly certain now that I saw the overcoat, the hair, the outline of long, beautiful fingers, the ones I remember feeling on my back, forming Clapton chords on my trembling skin through velvet. It was him. I can ease the pain of so many by losing my biggest comfort here. The cost is dear to me, but so insignificant to the others whose lives were thrown into turmoil the moment Ian died.

It's not for me, I remind myself. It's for the others. What does my happiness matter?

But what about Ash's happiness? a part of my brain demands.

"I don't know!" I cry out loud.

Samuel looks embarrassed at my outburst. "It would be best if you left now," he says almost gently. The world begins to shatter, and I run with the knife in my hand back the way I came, just barely making it back to the Bridge before his world explodes into white, into void.

I stand on the top of the Bridge, the clouds swirling below, reminding me of the almost-Ian I saw in the corner of Samuel's hall.

What am I going to do?

My happiness, or the happiness of the Millbrooks, of everyone who loved Ian? And the happiness of Ian himself? He deserves to live out his life. He shouldn't have been taken from us.

What is my happiness? It is just in this world, my dreaming. Ash isn't real. But now I picture the tiny, helpless cub in my cupped hands, asking me to name him. I feel our hearts beating at the same time, two halves of the same heart.

My happiness? Or everyone else's? How can I possibly choose?

With a heavy heart, an aching heart that feels it may soon lose a part of itself, I walk slowly back to the land. I look at the knife in my hand, trying to picture the act. How could I possibly…? No, it is unthinkable. *Unthinkable.*

I am selfish, after all. I will not harm him. I cannot. I choose *my* happiness. *Ash's* happiness.

Trust, the wind seems to say again as it ruffles my hair. And now I don't know again. The knife hums in my hand, and I walk back to Ash, who still sleeps peacefully under Joshua's tree.

He is my Ash, I remind myself. *I won't be lonely here anymore. He is my Ash.* I clutch the knife in my hand and watch his chest rise and fall, rise and fall, his breaths lined up with mine. We breathe as one; our hearts pump blood through our bodies in synchronized beats.

I'm frozen, trapped as if between two panels of glass, as the knife hums in counterpoint to the tide of Ash's breath, and all the while, the wind blows through Joshua's tree. In my head I hear, *Trust*, but the blossoms rain down as Joshua's tree slowly is stripped bare, the remaining branches like stark, bleached bones against the clear sky.

TWENTY-ONE
HER DECISION

Ash stirs, and I hide the knife behind my back.

"*My princess, you are back,*" he says, and his voice in my head sounds a little...sad, maybe? Disappointed?

"Hi, Ash," I say, trying to sound normal.

"*What is it?*" he asks, getting slowly, gingerly, to his feet, as if his joints ache. He shakes the petals from Joshua's tree off of himself, his fur going in two directions at once. It's a puppy-like gesture, but there's such solemnity and fatigue about him that it hurts my heart.

I can't keep up the façade. I start to tear up. "Oh, Ash," I whisper.

He seems to understand right away. "*So you know, now, why you could see me.*"

I nod. "My heart. Part of it is in you." I lay my free palm on my chest, feeling the heart underneath my fingertips quivering in fear as its mate beats away in the faithful vessel — *no*, I correct myself, *not a fucking vessel, but my* friend — across from me.

"*I am glad you remember,*" he says simply. "*I wanted you to remember on your own.*"

"It was being so close with you, laying my head on your side," I say, unable to look him in the face. I close my eyes. "I could feel your breath, your pulse, and it was like your memories flowed through me. I was a child again, your Princess Aggie."

"*I miss her,*" he says.

"I couldn't stay that way forever, you know."

"*I know.*"

"I had to grow up. But I'm sorry I went away for so long, that you didn't see me change. I'm sorry we lost so much time. I'm sorry we're strangers to each other now."

"*It was what you wanted, my princess. I could not say no to you.*"

The knife in my hand is throbbing. "But, Ash," I say, hardly daring to let the air escape my lungs, "I can't do it. I won't." And the knife slips from my fingers and clatters onto a flat rock behind me.

Ash looks sternly at me. "*I serve you, my princess. Do what you must.*" He stands his ground, looking me squarely in the face, his eyes filled with determination and not even a shred of fear.

"I won't!" I say, backing away from him, stepping on the knife and cutting my foot. The pain is excruciating, and I fall onto my side, holding my foot and gasping, watching the blood ooze, thick and nearly black as it mixes with the dirt on my sole. It's as if there is poison in the knife. This isn't like cutting my hand with the obsidian. This knife, this thing which gave the Stone One life, it is an evil object. I can feel it. I can feel the hatred coursing through my blood. I don't want it to reach my heart.

I run for the stream, the Source, limping, trailing blood behind me. Ash follows at a comfortable distance, silent. I reach the water's edge and plunge my foot in. The stream is ice cold, pure, numbing. When I pull my foot out, there's a trickle of blood from the cut, scarlet now, no longer like tar. Is the poison gone from my blood?

"Am I all right, Ash? Is there poison in me?"

Ash comes over and sniffs my foot, giving it a careful lick, closing the wound. "*You taste clean.*"

"What am I going to do?" I ask myself as much as I ask him.

"*You will be fine. There is no poison. You will live.*"

"You know that's not what I meant, Ash."

He is silent. I put my arm around him, and we lean, heads together, listening to the rushing water. I think of when he pushed me in here before I remembered, when I was afraid of him, when he told me he could not promise not to kill me.

"*What do you want me to say, my princess?*"

"Agnes," I say. "My name is Agnes. I am no princess. I don't deserve to be a princess. I'm just…Agnes. And that's all I'll ever be."

"*Do not speak that way,*" says Ash. "*I can bear many things, but not that. Please let me call you my princess. It is the one thing that has not changed. I need this.*"

He's never asked me for anything, at least as far as I can remember, and I think again how selfish I am, how selfish for running away from this land, selfish for being too afraid to offer myself in earnest to the Stone One in exchange for Joshua, selfish for considering cutting the heart out of Ash, and now, even now, selfish for wanting him to call me Agnes. How little he wants, and yet I would take it from him.

"Of course, Ash. I'm sorry. I am your princess. Always."

I let my foot dangle in the cold water again, and even though Ash has said my blood is clean, I feel like I am poison. I am poison because I know deep down I would trade Ash's life for Ian's in a heartbeat. As much as I tell myself it's for Meg and Mrs. Millbrook, deep down I know it's because of me. Because *I* need him alive. And for what? So he can continue to know I don't exist? Because I need him for my stupid fantasy world where maybe one day he'll know who I really am?

In a heartbeat, in one beat of the heart we share, I'd give up Ash forever for Ian Millbrook. I would give him up *if* I didn't have to do the act myself. And that makes me worse than a traitor; it makes me a coward. And Ash knows I'd give him up. I can tell. He knows the darkest things that I feel because we share the same heart.

"*Let us walk back,*" he says, looking toward my foot. "*I think you are all right now. It was not a deep cut.*" And resignedly, head down, he leads me back to the courtyard, to Joshua's tree, to Willa's prickly pear cactus.

And to the stone knife, which glimmers in the light streaming through the branches of Joshua's tree, stripped bare by the wind.

A bright ray of sunlight falls across my eyes through the blinds, and I am lit awake like a candle. My foot aches, but when I sit up to examine it, nothing seems to be wrong. A heaviness in my heart makes it hard to breathe. Oh, Ash. What am I going to do?

I rub the sleep out of my eyes and try to get my bearings. Vivian still snores from the couch, her face buried under her precious Dusky Sequoia's muscled thighs. It is Sunday. A week ago, Vivian slept here, keeping me company during my vigil, my personal agony in the garden, before I flew back to Poppy Beach. And she is here now, to celebrate my return. There was a part of me that didn't believe I'd make it back. And she waited for me on both sides of the journey, not even asking why, exactly, I was going home.

I take a shower, glad to be back in my familiar bathroom, but feeling sad, missing the cracked soap dish, the security of the smallness of the bathroom in Poppy Beach. I put my hand on the cold, industrial tile of the impersonal apartment bathroom, half-wishing I were a reflection, that my shadow-hand could meet my real hand in the bathroom in my father's house in Poppy Beach. I wouldn't mind being only a reflection if my other self could be there with Dad. I close my eyes as the water streams down my hair, washing the smell of airplane and panic off of me. With my eyes closed, I picture myself in the bathroom of Dad's house. When I open my eyes again, my reality is jostled; I am startled to find myself back in my shower in Boston. I feel cheated that I am not still in Poppy Beach, not still under my father's roof. When I close my eyes I am still there. Why can't I make the image stay when I open my eyes, make it reality?

I wash my hair numbly, trying to choke back tears. I'm not sure why I am so sad. Is it because of Ash? Is it because I miss Dad? Is it because I fear I'll never see my father again? Is it because I don't want to accept that Ian Millbrook truly is dead?

I let the streams of water wash the shampoo out of my hair, my arms folded across my torso, water pooling where my hands are tucked inside my elbows. I feel like a tree in a sudden summer downpour, immobile, unchanging, unfeeling. I want not to feel. I'm feeling too much; I'm sad about everything. I'm missing everything, everybody. I think of Joshua's tree and imagine myself cocooned inside the trunk, enveloped in its delicate willow bark. I'd be safe there, maybe. I'm so tired of feeling.

I don't want Viv to end up with a cold shower, so I stop my thoughts long enough to shut off the water, shivering already from the cold air creeping around the frosted-glass window. She's still snoring softly when I come out of the bathroom wrapped in a towel and begins to stir only once I've pulled on my long johns and several layers of clothing.

"Good morning, loser," she says cheerily, once she's tossed Dusky Sequoia to the coffee table, stretching her arms languorously over her head.

"Dusky Sequoia rode you all night, did he?" I ask, bending over and twisting the damp towel into a turban around my dripping hair. "He sat on your face pretty hard," I add, straightening up and jumping away just in time to miss Vivian's hand attempting to swat my ass.

"You're just jealous." Vivian sniffs, tightening the ponytail holder in her hair. "You're jealous Dusky Sequoia didn't choose *you*. He's such a thoughtful lover, and he has days-of-the-week loincloths."

Thank God for Vivian. I'm snickering, and that morose girl in the shower already is slipping back into the shadows. *This* is me, this snickering girl, the one Vivian brings out; *this* is Agnes Larch.

So why do I still feel this dread in my chest? A twinge in my foot brings me back. *Ash. What will happen to Ash?*

"Trader Joe's?" Vivian asks, untangling her iPod earbuds and putting them back in her bag.

"But it's not Saturday," I say.

Vivian shrugs. "You weren't here yesterday. Being with the Agnes of Larch is more important than going on the proper day of the week."

"Sure." To be honest, I did feel a certain sadness yesterday morning, knowing I was missing our weekly ritual. "Are you going to shower first?"

"Nah, they like me ripe there," says Vivian, sniffing her armpits and making a face.

We both gird ourselves to face the bitter cold, and despite the chill that assaults us as we exit the building, I feel warm in my heart as I march down the icy sidewalk next to my friend Vivian. It's good to be back.

We walk down Boylston Street, and as the wind numbs my cheeks and blasts sand and salt from the sidewalk into my eyes, I feel that this place too is my home. The Prudential Center is a friendly, familiar giant, and I am tempted to wave at it as we head inside to the TJ's. But then I see a truck just like Dad's rumble by, and suddenly my heart is split in two again, one piece aching three thousand miles away by Dad's side. I'm not sure if the part of my heart with him is trying to find its way back to Boston, or if the part in me now is trying to jump out of my chest to join its mate in Poppy Beach. I try to focus on Vivian's brightness, but it's hard when half of me feels as though it's missing.

I sigh because I will never have everyone I love in the same place at once. The world is too wide, my body too small, too finite. I blink back my tears and try to make the most of my afternoon with Vivian, my vibrant Vivian.

Vivian and I head to the back corner with the samples, and I drink paper thimble after paper thimble of organic limeade while she loads up on coffee. Today the pleated cups are filled with tamari-flavored almonds, so we each take about five cups of them and tip them back like they're tequila shots. It's almost like our usual Saturday ritual, except my body knows that it's Sunday. It's not the same, and I feel cheated somehow.

As we go up the escalator back to street level, Vivian asks, "So, do you want to do anything today?"

I want to stay by her and borrow her light to avoid this feeling of being split in two, everyone I love spread far and wide like shrapnel after an explosion. But something tells me I need to be alone; I can't avoid my head forever. I'm going to find something important today.

"I think I need to be by myself for a bit." I watch my feet carefully so they don't get eaten by the top of the escalator.

"That's cool," she says, zipping up her retro ski jacket before we exit into the wind tunnel of Boylston Street again. "I've got a shit-ton of reading to do, but you know where to find me." She hugs me when we're outside, and my balance is thrown off by her embrace. But Vivian is solid like a tree, just as she was in baggage claim last night, and she rights me before I can fall to my knees. "Easy there," she says, grasping my elbows. "Hold onto my dusky sequoia."

"I'm fine," I say, straightening up. "Thanks."

"Anytime, whore," she says, cheerfully patting me on both cheeks.

I watch as she heads back toward Mass Ave. I know her afternoon will be filled with reading and taking notes in the warm, cozy library at her law school. I've visited her out there with Hostess cupcakes smuggled in my backpack to get her through some late-night study sessions, trying my best to look casual so the library guards won't search my bag before I can deliver the goods. When I go, it's nice to be back in the womb of academia and gothic architecture again, but it's a false sense of warmth because I know I don't truly belong.

The dark, musty books on the shelves stare down at me severely, and I can almost hear them hiss, *Imposter*.

Once Vivian disappears around the corner, I just start walking. I'm not sure where I'm headed, but I know I need to go somewhere. I let my feet, already numb with cold, lead the way. I reach up to feel my damp hair peeking out from under my knit cap, and my hair is frozen into icy branches. They don't even feel like part of my body. I know hair's not living, but it's still disconcerting to feel them this separate from me. I'm not going to touch my frozen hair any longer. I already have such a bad feeling in my stomach.

I walk, just gazing at my feet, and I stop when I think I hear organ music. I look up, and I'm at a church. No, not just *a* church, but *the* church.

It was a day like today, and I was still a student at Longfellow, a junior, and I was having one of those dreamy days when I just wanted to wander. I'd overslept and missed brunch, but Viv had thoughtfully grabbed a breakfast sandwich for me and left it on my desk. I dressed and went walking, eating my cold English muffin, letting my feet take me where they wanted. I just had a feeling about the day. I was being pulled by something deep in my belly. I got on the subway and rode it awhile, watching the Sunday tourists with their maps and newly purchased Red Sox hats. I got out at Hynes because I knew that was where I needed to be.

My body felt out of my control, as if I were some sort of preprogrammed robot, or maybe a sleeper operative set into action. Barely watching traffic, I crossed streets and wandered sidewalks until a lilting melody wrapped around me and tugged me toward it. It was as if the melody were an actual string tied around my waist, a ball of yarn leading me out of the Minotaur's labyrinth. I had no choice but to follow. And I found myself in front of this church, the Church of Our Lady of Sorrows. Masses were over for the day, but the most beautiful melody was playing on the organ inside.

It had been years since I'd been inside a church — I guess the small chapel at Butler Academy was the last time, if that even counted. I pulled open the heavy doors, and I could smell the rich incense, the oiled wood, the birthday-cake scent of newly extinguished candles. And here was this melody.

I crossed myself with holy water and genuflected, acting like a Catholic after having gone to Catholic school for so long. Even if I wasn't sure what I believed, I respected these buildings and the people who worshipped inside. I respected anyone who could believe so much in something unseen, who could find comfort in such blind faith, especially since I was unsure of who I was and afraid of everything. I envied the people who found comfort here.

I followed the music toward a choir stall on the side of the church. A young man, his back toward me, was playing the organ. Even as he played this melody again and again, his feet working the traveling bass on the foot pedals, I could sense such joy radiating from him. I was drawn to him like a moth toward candlelight, and, before I knew it, I was at his shoulder. My hand reached up and grazed his arm.

He stopped in surprise, leaving the melody hanging thickly in the air like smoke, unresolved, and he turned to look at me.

My heart stopped. *Ian Millbrook.*

"Wha…uh…I'm sorry," I said, snatching my hand away and staring at my feet.

He laughed, not unkindly, and ran his fingers through his hair. "Oh. You just startled me, that's all."

"What…what are you doing here?" I asked. Ian Millbrook wasn't supposed to be in Boston. He'd gone to Northwestern after graduation; I was sure of it. It's what Tricia told me the minute she'd heard he'd been accepted, and it's what was listed on our graduation programs.

He smiled again. "I'm just practicing. I'm sorry, was it distracting your praying? I'm almost finished."

He didn't remember me. I know I was different; my hair was cut in an ill-advised asymmetrical bob, and I was experimenting rather unsuccessfully with liquid eyeliner, but still, I wasn't *that* different.

Should I ask him why he's not at Northwestern? Or will that seem stalkery? I wondered. I chickened out. No way would he understand, especially if he hadn't recognized me.

"What was it you were playing?" I asked, speaking softly in the large, echoing space. "It's beautiful."

"It's Bach," he said. "It's called '*Wachet auf, ruft uns die Stimme.*'"

"Wake up, the voice calls to us," I murmured, translating.

"You speak German?" he asked, smiling a little as he flipped pages in the score.

"I'm taking it in school. Aren't you awfully…young to be the organist?" I decided if I were a stranger to him, I could ask questions without seeming too odd.

When he smiled, his eyes crinkled, just how I remembered. He had new glasses, slightly smaller John Lennon specs. They suited him. Even after three years away from him, the sight still sucked all the air out of my chest. "I just work here on the weekends. I'm a student at the conservatory."

"Have you…have you been there long?" I quickly added, "You play so beautifully; you must not need much more school."

"Oh, I have a few years left yet. I transferred from Northwestern this year, see." He laughed. "I have no idea why I'm telling you my life's story."

"I'm sorry for interrupting you," I said, shifting my weight uneasily from foot to foot. "Please don't let me stop your practicing. Do you mind if I listen for a bit? That melody…I can't describe it, but it does something to me here." I pointed at my heart, feeling foolish, my words so clumsy and faltering, jagged against the smoothness of his playing and the tranquility in the air of the dimly lit church.

"Of course I don't mind," he murmured, looking back at the score. He shook his hands out rapidly for a few seconds before adjusting the stops on the organ and beginning again. There was that beautiful lilting line again, gently rocking me, and then the melody would come in strong and triumphant. I had no idea what the piece was about, but it was so full of joy and hope, the meter pulsing through solidly like a heartbeat. It was a living piece of music, and I hungrily watched Ian Millbrook bent over the keys, his blond mop of hair in his eyes, and that look, that *look* on his face of the ecstasy created by such great music flowing through him like electricity. I remembered that look. I missed that look.

He finished the piece and swiveled on the bench toward me. "So, hey, I'm Ian Millbrook," he said, holding out his hand.

He really didn't remember me, not even one whit. Not even a glimmer, a wrinkle in his brow, a ghostly feeling of déjà vu across his face.

I started to reach my hand to press it against his but stopped halfway. "I'm…I'm nobody," I said, and I turned and ran out of the church, leaving, I'm sure, a very puzzled Ian Millbrook in my wake.

Why didn't I stop? Why didn't I say, "Ian? Is that really you?" It was too late by the time he was introducing himself. I felt foolish, like a stalker. He would have thought I followed him there or something. And then, then the humiliation of having to remind him that he knew me, that he'd known me since I was thirteen years old, that I had loved him for about as long...it was too much.

Of course I never get what I want, because I'm too scared to fight for it. I'm too afraid to put myself on the line. I predict that I'll be rejected, so I take myself out of the equation first. Because deep down I know I'm not worth anything. Who would choose me? Who would want me? Who would find value in me? It's why I quit art school, and it's why I could not introduce myself that day to Ian Millbrook, who had no memory of me.

This afternoon, I stand outside the church for a while, just listening. I realize that no one is playing music. My mind was playing tricks on me. As I did many Sundays ago, I enter the Church of Our Lady of Sorrows, looking around at the paintings on the wall of the Stations of the Cross, stopping at the painting of the Fourth Station: *Jesus Meets His Mother*. I study the image of his mother standing there, weeping, watching him pass her for the last time, knowing he is condemned to death, that he will soon die right in front of her eyes. The same baby she felt grow and stretch and move inside her. I think of Mrs. Millbrook and the sorrow she has faced twice already in her relatively short life, and I know I have to do everything I can to bring him back.

I stop by the organ, covered and locked, before leaving, pressing my palm against the wooden bench. *He was here once, many times*, I think to myself as I leave, not running away this time, just quietly sorrowful.

As I walk back to my apartment, I think of that long-ago Sunday afternoon again, of going back to my dorm in Longfellow and rushing to my computer. I went online, looking for news, Googling "Ian Millbrook" to see what I could find. He was listed for a few recitals at the conservatory in the last few months, and before that, for events at Northwestern. To think, that he had been in this city, *my* city, that entire year. If I had been special, I would have felt his presence here.

If I had been special, I reminded myself, he would have recognized me.

After that day, I looked for Ian Millbrook everywhere because now I knew he was living in my city. He was here. He was near me.

He was close by, but still a world away. I never stopped looking for him, though. Some days I thought I spotted him, but I was always too shy to approach. And now it is too late.

I'm back at the apartment and exhausted already, probably still worn out from my terror on the plane yesterday. I want to sleep so desperately, but I'm afraid too, because I don't know what I'm going to do about Ash.

Don't make me choose! I scream internally, scream as if Samuel could hear me. And I'm not sure if it's me answering, or Samuel, when I hear a voice in my head say, *But you have already chosen.*

I sigh, tugging off my boots and socks, and I head wearily to my bed, sleeping on top of the covers.

I'm at Joshua's tree, its dark, naked branches stark against the sky. *What have I done to you, Joshua?* I ask silently, patting his trunk. Did I bring the wind that stripped him bare? My eye falls on the knife, that hated knife.

"I won't do it!" I cry out, hoping Samuel can hear me. I know he said I could refuse the boon at any time. I don't have to do this.

"*My princess.*" Ash is at my side.

"I won't," I whimper, letting my head fall to my chest.

"*You know what you need to do,*" he says. "*Do not be afraid.*"

I'm crying like crazy now. "Why are you comforting *me*, dear Ash?"

"*It is all right. I...I think this is why you made me, all those years ago.*"

"What? What do you mean?" I can barely see him through the scrim of my tears.

"*I have been thinking while you have been away. And why should you have made me different from the others? Why should you have given me part of your heart?*"

"Because you were the first. Because I *needed* you. Because you are a part of me, and I needed a part of me here."

"*Or maybe you somehow knew that this day would come,*" he says.

I don't really believe him. I think he's trying to make me feel better, trying to lessen my guilt over what I need to do. *NO, NO, NO,* I say to myself, *what I WILL NOT do.*

"*You know you must*," he says, as if he is reading my mind.

"I can't. You know I can't do that to you. I can't lose you. I *love* you," I say, weeping.

"*You have not said that in so long*," he said. "*That makes me brave. I know I will not feel the bite of the blade.*"

"You're talking crazy, Ash. I'm not going to do it. I'm selfish. I'm scared. But I can't do that to you."

"*Princess, you will. If you do not, I will leave this place. I will leave and never come back. I was made for this, and I am ready.*" He stands by me and nudges my palm with his nose. "*Thank you for loving me.*"

"Why? Why are you making me do this? You know what this means, don't you? You'll be gone. We won't see each other. We will never play again."

"*But you will have him, will you not? And that will make you happy, will it not?*"

"I…I'm not even sure of that, dear Ash. And you would give up your life for this? For this *indefinite?*"

"*If it is an indefinite that would make you happy, that you have waited for your whole life, who am I to stand in your way? Who am I but someone you created to keep you company? I would not exist if not for you, and if you decide I should exist no more, then I will go. I will go, but first I will thank you for giving me life.*"

I sink to my knees, sobbing into my hands. "No, Ash. I won't. I won't do it."

"*I will leave you. You will not see me again either way.*"

"I know that's just an empty threat, Ash. You didn't leave my side when I begged you to bury me and forget me forever." I glance at the knife. "I know you're just trying to get me to do *this*." I can't even breathe the words of the second task out loud.

"*I will live on. I am not afraid,*" he says, sniffing my hair before lying down by my side.

I raise my head and hold his face with my tearstained hands. "Ash. Look at me. Listen to me. I will not harm you. I want Ian alive more than anything else in the world, but I cannot harm you."

"*You must. Or I will do it for you.*" He trots over to the knife and picks it up with his teeth.

"What are you doing, Ash?" I shriek, backing away until I'm against Joshua's tree. "Keep that away from me!"

Even with his mouth around the knife, I can hear his voice clearly in my head. "*You* will *do this, my princess. I have never asked you for anything. I ask you this now. Cut out my heart. Let your Ian live. I live, I die, only to serve you.*" He presses the knife into my hand, and pain shoots through my hand, all the way up my arm.

Something is different. With his saliva on the handle, the knife fuses to my hand. I couldn't let go of it if I tried, and it burns. It feels as though I am getting electrocuted, current and heat and pain pulsing through me. The knife transforms again to that deep, blood red glass, and Ash lies on his back, waiting.

"I won't harm you, Ash!" I cry, but my arm swings out against my will, the blade finding Ash's chest.

"*Do not be afraid, my princess,*" he says, even as the blade cuts through his flesh easily, goes right through him as if he's already a ghost.

"No!" I cry out, but my arm and the knife work together as one, and I have to look away. "I love you, Ash, forever!" I can feel my arm working swiftly. I am an angel of death. The knife cuts deeply, cruelly, and I feel warm stickiness on my skin, like the warm stickiness of the tears drying on my face. The air is thick with the smell of blood and iron and the sound of my half of our shared heart breaking into a million pieces.

And then the knife hits something hard and falls out of my hand. My hand, still not quite my own, wraps around the hard object and pulls it out of his body.

I force myself to look at the jewel in my hand, the hidden part of my heart. Ash's heart.

He is still alive, panting. "*I knew you could do it,*" he gasps. "*Thank you.*"

"Ash! Ash! Stay with me!" I cry. "I could never give you up for him—you *know* that!"

"*But you already have, my princess,*" he says. "*Do not mourn. I understand.*"

I drop the jewel in the grass next to the knife, which once again is dull and stone. I gather Ash into my arms, patting his head, kissing the fur I've bloodied with my hands. "Don't go, Ash. Please. You don't need my heart to live. What is my heart? It is nothing. Who wants my heart? It is worthless." I squeeze my eyes shut in grief and rock him back and forth in my arms, praying, praying, praying. *Save him. Please let him be all right.*

But I know even before I open my eyes that Ash is gone.

I look at his lifeless body in my arms and sob all over again, wetting his fur. "I didn't choose this," I say, but I know in my heart that I did. I chose Ian. It would always be Ian, even if he didn't remember who I was.

I gently lay Ash's body on the grass and stand up. I will at least make him the most beautiful, noble, majestic memorial there is. I can at least give him that. I can almost hear Willa scoff and tell me such gestures are meaningless, but they are not meaningless to me.

I close my eyes, hold my arms out, palm up, at my sides, and open my mouth to sing. I sing of the little puffball of wolfy I found under the bush, the brave beast who stayed by my side. I sing of his loyalty, his vigil over my dream-corpse when I begged to leave this land. I sing of his fierceness, of his finding me when I awoke in this land again, of his unwavering belief that I was his Princess Aggie, even if I remembered nothing. I sing of his selflessness, of his sacrifice to give me the thing I want most in the world. I sing of his heart, my heart. I sing all my love for him, the sweet, wild, loyal, vulnerable beast. I sing of Ash. My Ash.

I open my eyes, wondering what fine tree will stand as memorial to this great wolf.

I open my eyes.

Nothing. There is no tree for Ash. There is nothing.

I look down, and his carcass lies in a pool of blood at my feet.

I gather Ash in my lap, not caring that my white garment is soiled. He is still warm. I weep over his lifeless body, remembering the painting of the Fourth Station, and I think, *Was I not, in some way, Ash's mother?*

The wind whistles through the trees, through the empty space where Ash's tree should be, and I cry into his fur, kissing his head, stroking his ears. I rock him gently as if to sleep, and I find myself singing "You Are My Sunshine" as a final lullaby.

But I can't bring myself to sing the second verse.

TWENTY-TWO
BANISHED FROM THE GARDEN

I'm rocking poor, brave Ash's broken body like I'm the goddamn Pietà. I don't know how long I've been here, but his body is getting cold. There's nothing I can do. I can't revive him; I can't even erect a memorial to him.

The least I can do is give him a decent burial.

I ease Ash's body onto the ground and get to my feet. *Please give me the strength*, I think as I grab Ash's forepaws and pull. I know I can't carry him—he is easily at least twice my weight. Amazingly, I am strong enough to drag him slowly toward the woods. I will bury him where I was once buried, I think. There's a kind of symmetry there; it seems fitting, somehow. It's what Ash would want: to rest forever where I once rested.

I'm sweating, and my back is beginning to ache as I near the area where I was buried. There's no marker here, but I know the place by the pulling feeling I have when I stand over the ground. It's shady, and a breeze is blowing. In the hollow of the tree nearby there is a scrap of linen from my shroud. As I pull it out of the hollow, the fabric grows and grows until it is large enough to wrap Ash up, swaddling him tenderly as if he were a newborn baby. The fabric helps hold together Ash's flesh, helps to give the illusion that he is whole and perfect, unmarred. But then his blood seeps through the cloth, leaving a shape like a heart or a lipstick stain over his fatal wound.

Ash is now a tight, neat bundle, white except for that bloodstain. I lean down and kiss the bloodstain, whispering, *Thank you*, against it, as if I were whispering right into Ash's ear. I'll never be able to thank him enough for his sacrifice, not if I live a hundred lifetimes.

I realize I have no way to dig a hole for Ash's grave. The wolves dug my grave once, much as dogs hide their prize bones. But there is no one left to help me. If this had happened to Joshua or Willa, Ash would have helped me dig their graves. I look for a stick, a rock, anything that might help. I can't find anything, so I sink to my knees and weep. I can't do *anything* for him.

When my tears splash on the earth, something strange happens. The dirt begins to shimmer and swirl, and I step back before I'm swallowed by the large, deep hole that suddenly appears. The land itself has taken mercy on me, somehow, and I am grateful. I try to lay Ash's shrouded body gently into the cavity in the earth, but he's far too heavy. He slips from my fingers and free-falls into the hole, a sickening thud sounding when his body hits the bottom. I cringe even though I know he can feel no pain now.

I wearily get to my feet and sprinkle a handful of earth on top of Ash's body. *Oh, Ash, I did not deserve such a noble friend as you*, I think as fat tears continue to slide down my cheeks. The skies overhead turn black, and for the first time since I demanded to leave the dreaming, it is raining again. I throw clods of dirt on the body, muddying my hands. *"May the choirs of angels come to greet you; may they speed you to Paradise,"* I sing softly. My heart aches so much; a part of me is missing now, gone forever.

It doesn't take long to fill the hole in the earth, but even as I pat down the dirt on top of Ash's grave, I know nothing will ever fill the hole in my heart. For now it is a sharp, stabbing pain; the sensory memory of the feel of the knife in my hand against the resistance of his flesh runs over and over in my head on a loop. Even if the feeling fades to a steady, throbbing ache, I know I will carry this grief forever. As well I should—a permanent reminder of my selfishness, my trading an innocent life for an *indefinite*. I should be in pain. I should never forget. He'll live on in my heart because of the hole carved there, a phantom pain. *Maybe this is what Mrs. Millbrook feels*, I wonder before stopping myself—she doesn't feel this way because she never would have made such a horrible choice.

I look around, wishing I had something to mark his grave, something like the obsidian I buried at Ian's gravestone. I search through the brush, my eyes sweeping across the damp, rotting leaves. *Please, please, please*, I pray silently to the land, *please grant me at least this, one thing to make this grave a sacred place.* I see nothing, so I trudge back to the clearing, to Joshua's bare tree.

The knife still sits there, dull and stone, looking deceivingly innocuous. I pick it up, no longer feeling electric prickles up and down my arm. Perhaps its malevolence has been released now that it has fulfilled its brutal task. The knife begins to drag me to Ash's resting place, and my heels leave shallow trenches in the mud where I try to fight the magnetic pull of the knife. Eventually I give in and run to keep up with the pulling.

The knife wants to burrow into the dirt, and I fight with all my power to keep it from contaminating my sweet Ash's grave. "This is a sacred place," I hiss to the knife, and my arms are shaking now from fatigue. "Was it not enough that you stole him from me?" I cry, still fighting against this tremendous downward force. As I fight, the blade slices my left palm. Gasping in shock and pain, I lose control over the knife.

Sticky with my blood, the knife pulls me to the ground, sinking easily into the dirt to its hilt. And then the strangest thing happens. As I watch the skin on my sliced palm knitting shut again cleanly and with no trace of poison, the hilt grows and branches out, transfigured, gold and shining, and little flowers bloom, the same ruby red as my blood. I kneel by this strange little shrub and gently brush my fingers against a branch. It is cold to the touch, stiff, metallic. I cup a blossom in my hand. It is glass, perhaps even pure ruby. If this existed in my waking world, it would be priceless, in a museum vault watched over by armed guards twenty-four hours a day.

Only Ash's unconditional love and complete selflessness could have the power to transform this object of evil into something so beautiful. But I remind myself that jewels and gold are not alive. This magical shrub, no matter how valuable monetarily, is worth nothing in comparison to my friend lying under this earth.

But at least his grave is marked. He will not be forgotten. I could not create his memorial, but it seems that Ash took care of that himself; he always could. I lean in to kiss one of the ruby blossoms, but the gold leaves beneath the blossom clamp around my lip like a vise. I pull back, using my fingers to unhook the sharp leaves from my lip. The pain is like a bee sting, and my lip is bleeding. I run my tongue along my lip, tasting the iron in my blood.

I don't know if it's the true, dark nature of the knife that makes the shrub attack me, or whether it is Ash's disapproval. My blood glistens on the center of the ruby-flower before it is absorbed, and the shrub stretches and grows just a tiny bit larger. It is a wild memorial, unpredictable, untamable, a more fitting tribute to Ash than one I could provide.

I hear rustling behind me, and I whip my head toward the sound. It feels as though there are eyes on my back, but as I scan the area, I see no one, nothing. *There is nobody left.* I look at my mud-caked hands, the mud mixed with blood: Ash's blood, my blood. These hands are impotent now, unable to call forth a memorial. Am I also unable to create? Maybe I just need to be cleansed, to atone. *Go to the Source*, the wind seems to say.

I leave Ash's grave and walk, head bowed, back to the stream, to a shallow part where the current isn't likely to sweep me away. I step in carefully, washing my hands, kneeling down and letting the cold water puff up my bloodied dress. I'm momentarily floating inside a fabric mushroom. The water is freezing, but it is a relief, because it shocks my body, temporarily halting the pains in my heart. I take a deep breath and dip down lower, until my head is below the water's surface.

I remember being under this stream before, the water burning into my lungs, and Ash's sharp teeth pulling me out. The current is not dangerous here, and I hold my breath as long as I can in the shallow water, my eyes closed, memories of Ash dancing behind my eyelids. When I stand up straight, breaking the surface of the rippling waves, I gasp for air. I emerge reborn and, I hope, clean again.

My dress is as bright as a full moon reflecting the sun, without a stain upon it. My hands are red from the cold but clean, the cut on my left palm now just a pale white shadow of a line. My lip still bleeds, but it doesn't even feel like part of my body anymore, numb from the iciness of the water. I step onto the riverbank, my long hair streaming rivulets of water down my bare arms, my feet finding warmth on the springy grass.

It has stopped raining.

I stand in the clearing by Joshua's tree, by Willa's prickly pear cactus. I hold my arms out at my sides, palm up. I close my eyes. I open my mouth and sing, trying to bring new wolves into my world.

Images flash and blur in my head, more and more quickly, the puffball of wolfy, Willa's haughty tilt of head, Joshua's sweet smile. I see my charcoal sketches of all the forgotten wolves, the nameless ones, the lost ones. They are all lost ones now.

When the song stops pouring from me, I am afraid to open my eyes, afraid I have been banished from the Garden.

I wake up to complete darkness, in complete confusion. It could be midnight; it could be just after sunset. I have my barrette clamped in my left hand, clenched so tightly that it's made a deep groove in my palm. My lips are parched, cracked in the middle, and caked with dried blood. I shiver from falling asleep without the covers on and curse my old apartment building's faulty, unreliable heating and wiring. That's Boston for you — everything is so historic but falling apart. It should be warmer than this in here.

As I stand up in the dark to stretch, I trip over my sketchpad. I don't know how it got here, but I shakily turn on my desk lamp, the closest light to my bed. I am shocked to see my right hand blackened with charcoal, and I am afraid to look at the new drawings. If they were drawn while I was sleeping…I don't think I could bear to relive what has just happened in my dreams. "Oh, Ash," I sob out loud, wiping my face with my soiled hand. My tears mix with the charcoal, and I drag my finger across a blank patch of the open sketchbook page, leaving a long, inky smudge. Here is Ash's noble face. I turn the page to see the knife in my hand. The sketch after that is almost completely blackened out. As soon as I make out the knife tip disappearing into Ash's flesh, I flip past it quickly, feeling queasy. The last picture is of his tightly shrouded body, a wolf-shaped mummy. Stifling a sob, I bite my lip, reopening the wound on my chapped mouth. I hold the fingertip of my pinkie to my lip to stop the bleeding, then press it on the sketchbook to mark the spot on his shroud where his blood seeped through the linen. The red is startling on the mostly white page, and I can't tear my eyes away.

But it's wrong. It's wrong because the blood on the page is mine, but the blood on the real shroud, on the *actual* object versus my inadequate paper representation of the object, is Ash's. It only highlights what I was unable to do, to save him. He did this for me. I wonder if my own heart would have fulfilled Samuel's requirements. Should I have cut out my own heart to save him *and* Ian? But no, Samuel said he needed the part that I'd hidden away in the dreaming. Should I have at least tried to cut out my own heart first?

I shake my head. I'm getting too mired in these dreams. The dreams are not reality; *reality* is reality. I look over at the glowing numbers on my clock. It's still early, dinnertime. Maybe I'll go for a walk, try to clear my head.

I flip on the overhead light, squinting a bit, reminding myself a little too much of the prickly feeling behind my eyes when Samuel smiles, showing me all of his teeth. The light is painful, but I need it to see what I am doing. It must be even colder outside than it was when Vivian and I walked around earlier today. Layers. I need more layers.

I pull another sweater on my head and dig in my purse for lip balm. Should I call Viv again?

She can't save you from yourself, I think, and I wonder what I need saving from as I walk to the bathroom to wash the charcoal and tears off my face.

I bundle up, pull on my knit cap, and go outside. The blast of cold on my face reminds me washing in the stream, and I wish for the numbness again to still my mourning heart. I suck on my lower lip, running my tongue against the crack in it. My lips taste like petroleum jelly and salt and iron. Why iron? It bothers me suddenly, thinking of trace amounts of metal running through my body. I imagine all the iron sucked from my body and fashioned into a weapon. That was in a movie once—*X-Men 2*, I think. My blood would certainly contain something that kills. I want it all out of me. It must be Shelly's blood in me—her share of my genetic makeup—that makes me this way.

I walk down Newbury Street and look into the boutique windows, steal glimpses of happy couples enjoying dinner on this chilly Sunday night. I want the cold to deaden me, cleanse me, make me not feel my heart pumping this killer's blood inside me. There's laughter spilling out of the bars as drunken college kids stumble out into the night. It occurs to me that I'm always on the outside looking in. I also realize that it's my choice, this self-isolation. I think how easily I could have called Vivian before leaving the house, but I couldn't make my hands obey my heart. *How very fitting*, I think, as this is the same dilemma I had with Ash. How could my body betray me like that? I didn't want to harm him, but my hands worked of their own volition.

Or were they just acting out my basest desires? Did they kill him because as much as I cried out that I couldn't harm Ash, that I of course would choose the maybe-Ian over him? Does that also then mean I actually *want* to be alone, as much as I feel lonely? I shake my head to all these thoughts. I'm reading too much into everything. I wish I could stop my brain from all this useless and confusing churning.

I stop in front of the bar on Newbury where I saw Ian once, where I almost had the courage. I won't go in this evening. I *want* to keep myself on the outside tonight; my head is muddled enough as it is. I don't want to walk inside, because the last time I walked into this bar, Ian Millbrook was here.

It was his birthday, his twenty-first. It was early July, and the weather had just gotten hot but not so much that the air was thick with the stench of overflowing Dumpsters. I never forgot his birthday. I never will, I don't think. Even before I knew he was living in Boston with me, I'd still think of him all day on the fifth of July. I would imagine tiny newborn Ian, helpless, eyes shut, in the arms of his mother. He was an *indefinite* then, too, if you think about it. If you saw this tiny baby, you'd never think that one day he'd save me from school humiliation with a tiny fruit sticker, that he would touch enough people in his short lifetime to fill an auditorium with mourners.

Junior year had just ended, and I figured that Ian might be home for the summer break, but I still thought, *Maybe I will see him.* That night, Vivian and I were out prowling. We were both in Boston for the summer because she was taking summer school classes and I… well, I had nowhere else to go. I'd just finished up dorm crew and working the reunions at Longfellow, and now I was looking for a temp job. We'd found a cheap sublet though, made cheaper because we were sharing the small, vacant bedroom. "You're my bed-buddy bitch now," Vivian had said when we woke up accidentally spooning the first morning in the sublet. We'd shared a dorm bedroom for three years already, but we'd always had separate beds, obviously. I was surprised that I'd snuggled into her in the night, especially in the third floor walkup without air conditioning. Maybe she reminded me of sleeping between my parents after a particularly intense night in the wolf world when I was small. I used to do that, right? I didn't make up that memory? Would Shelly have let me in her bed?

In any case, Vivian didn't care. She just rumpled my hair and said, "No Rear Admirals unless you take me for steak dinner first."

I sputtered, "I'm not even going to ask what…that…is…"

Patiently, Vivian explained, "That's when you take me to a restaurant where they make delicious steak. Then you pay for my meal. Then…Rear Admiral." She slipped out of bed to claim first shower, shutting the bedroom door behind her just in time to miss the pillow I'd hurled at her head.

When Vivian had asked if I wanted to go out that early July night, maybe cross the river to walk along Newbury Street, I'd said yes, because it was Ian's birthday, his twenty-first, and maybe he was out celebrating. Vivian had already turned twenty-one that year, and she'd also hooked me up with a good fake ID that worked a majority of the time. I was only a few months away from twenty-one myself, and most of my underage drinking took place in dorm rooms. But Viv had insisted I needed the fake ID to get into the over twenty-one shows that she liked to drag me to.

So we wandered up and down Newbury in our cute summer clothes. I was still pale from my thermal cocoon for the harsh winter and Boston's cold, damp spring, but I didn't care if I looked like a corpse. I was thrilled to be wearing a halter top and a short skirt and not shivering in the night air. She hustled me into an Irish pub, my ID not even raising an eyebrow from the gruff bouncer, and announced, "Let's celebrate Cinco de Julio."

She ordered us a couple of tequila shots, and I slammed it back, making my usual cat-coughing-up-a-hairball post-tequila noises. "I fucking love that, Agnancho Villa," she said, patting my back and offering me another lime wedge.

"You *know* Pancho Villa had nothing to do with Cinco de Mayo," I slurred. "You're a fucking history major."

"And you know how much I love how you fact-check even when you are hammered. And besides, how do you know what happened on Cinco de Julio?"

"*Important* shit happened Cinco de Julio." I tilted slightly on my seat. "Yanmilk was born," I burbled into my glass of water.

"Isn't that something from the *Legend of Zelda*?" asked Viv.

"Huh?"

"Yan-yan-milk?"

"The fuck is that?"

"*Legend of Zelda*, fool."

"Why are we talking about video games, Viv? That's pretty stereo-typically Asian of you. But I thought you Koreans were only allowed to play *Starcraft*."

"That's racist, Caucasian pocket-buddy!" Vivian roared, leaning in to bite my shoulder.

"I am not a sparerib, Vivian. Christ, you must be drunk." I laughed really close to her face, nearly falling off the barstool.

"I think we need another round," she said, and she waved over the bartender as we laughed sloppily at each other.

I was pleasantly numb and cozy when I felt white-hot heat and prickles on my back. *He's here*, I thought, even through my boozed, hazy mind.

"Who's here?" asked Vivian, eyes slightly glazed over.

Oh, crap. *Inner voice, Agnes, inner voice.* I'd said it out loud. "Zelda elf. S'is birthday."

"Agnes, my darling, you are speaking in tongues."

"Tongues," I repeated, sticking mine out at her. "Yanmilk's here. Birthday."

I turned and saw him surrounded with a bunch of friends whoop-ing it up. "Our boy's legal today!" I heard one guy say, clapping him on the shoulder. "Halfway through the pub crawl!" The friends all roared, drunken cavemen.

I heard Ian murmur something. He seemed embarrassed.

"'M gonna go over an' say hi," I said, steadying myself slightly as I hopped off the bench.

"To the elves of Hyrule?" asked Vivian, eyes half closed. "But they're not really elves, I think. I forget. Wait, where are you going?"

"Pay attention," I said, my back already to her.

I tottered to the table. If I hadn't been goofy on tequila, I never would have walked to the circle of rowdy boys with Ian Millbrook as its nucleus. "Hi." I waved as I stumbled over one of Ian's friends. "'S your birthday. Happy birthday."

"Hey, cutie," said one of his friends, snaking an arm around my waist. I slapped at his hand clumsily like I was shooing away a mosquito.

"Not *your* birthday," I said. I swung my arm around wildly and pointed at Ian, nearly poking him in the nostril. "*Your* birthday."

Ian's eyes were closed. "Is the whole room spinning, or is it just me?" he asked.

"I'm-a give you a birthday kiss," I said. Part of me was horrified, but Tequila Agnes had Sober Agnes good and tied up. I plunked myself on his lap while his friends hooted, put my arms around his neck, and planted a big kiss on his cheek. It was stubbly and smelled like heaven. My cheek hit his eyeglasses, leaving a greasy print. I whispered in his ear, "Love you, Yanmilk."

He opened his eyes. "Do I know you?" he asked, his eyes crossing slightly. "Is the room wobbling? Are we on a boat?"

"I'm a princess," I said, "'m Zelda. You are a Yanmilk."

"I'm pretty sure we're on a boat," he said, scrunching his face and holding onto his head.

I hopped off his lap and took a tiny plastic monkey off his drink. "I'm-a keep this. You're my Yanmilk."

"Where's this boat going?" I heard Ian demand loudly as I stumbled back over to Vivian.

"I kissed him," I said.

"The Hylian?"

"No, pay *attention!*" I said, and we both erupted into giggles before settling our bill and cabbing it back home.

The next morning I woke up with a killer hangover and a taste in my mouth like I'd licked the inside of the Park Street subway elevator. I was still in my clothes from last night. I groaned as I rolled over, and something sharp poked into my leg. I dug my hand into my skirt pocket and found the little plastic monkey.

"Vivian!" I shook her awake.

"The *fuck*, slore?"

"What happened last night?"

"Cinco de Julio, remember?" she said, yawning and rolling over, sticking her butt toward me.

"How did I get this monkey?"

"Oh, that was when you were mumbling about elves and you sat on that guy's lap. Cute. Slore." She was already asleep again and snoring.

I stared at the monkey in my hand. Was that…did I…? I guess I'd never be sure if I had really kissed him on the cheek. I was kicking myself for being too drunk to remember. But at the same time, I knew I never would have had the courage to walk over there unless I was drunk. And maybe it wasn't Ian anyway. Maybe it was some other kid whose birthday was yesterday. I scanned my memory for details—had anyone actually said "Ian"?

But then I remembered the prickles I'd felt when he'd walked into the room. It was real. It had to be. I touched my mouth hesitantly, thinking, *This mouth touched his cheek.* I clenched the plastic monkey in my hand tightly, wishing it were Ian's hand. There was a cracking sound, and I opened my fist to see the plastic monkey broken into several pieces.

As I stand outside the Irish pub, I can remember the taste of tequila on my tongue and his stubble on my lips. I look into the darkened windows, trying to see the table where Ian sat with his buddies that night so long ago. The night is a hazy memory rebuilt collaboratively with Vivian over the years, and she doesn't even know why it matters so much. I think she just chalked it up to another of our drunken adventures. I can't even remember what the sun's warmth feels like on my bare skin; how could I remember a night years ago when I was drunk?

I breathe on the glass and take my mitten off, using my bare fingertip to trace in the fog, *You were here.*

I turn around and head back home.

I peel off layer after layer as I stand in the now-stifling heat of my apartment. It's always this way, either too cold or too hot. Never Baby Bear just right. Once I've achieved the proper temperature-to-clothing ratio, I sit cross-legged on my bed with my laptop. I know I shouldn't, but I power it up to check Ian Millbrook's music website. I haven't looked since before the plane crash. The familiar banner loads onto my monitor, and then his artsy publicity shot of his head inclined in profile, dark-blond hair falling in his eyes, and then his voice and guitar surprise me, as they always do, streaming from the music player embedded on the page. I scroll past the songs heavy on guitar and cello until I settle on my favorite, one of just him and the piano. I close my eyes and pretend I'm in the music room at Butler

Academy on a Wednesday, just me and Ian, and he is singing this to me. *I'll get to know you someday*, he sings, and I get chills until I realize the song is called "Sweet Emmeline." Emmeline. Emmy. Emmy Elizabeth Millbrook, his baby sister, forever a baby. I should have put that together when I found the Millbrook gravestone. Well, maybe they are together now, I think. Maybe that's why he was called home, to take care of her. I don't know.

I feel like a voyeur, but I can't stop myself from reading the most recent comments on his last blog entry, written just days before the crash. It's filled with condolences, people who knew him better than I did, retellings of experiences of which I never knew, memories I never shared.

I dig a shoebox of college mementos out of the closet and lift up the lid, taking out the broken plastic monkey pieces from Ian's twenty-first birthday, trying to fit them together, trying to make them whole. The monkey smiles at me, as if being broken into pieces is perfectly normal. Tiny shards of plastic have been lost in the years since I woke up with the monkey in my pocket, and even if I had Krazy Glue, the seams would always be imperfect, with missing bits like chipped teeth.

I shake my head at my foolishness and prepare myself for bed, afraid of what I will find when I fall asleep, afraid I'll discover that I am an exile in the dreaming.

TWENTY-THREE
THE NATURE OF STERILITY

When I first open my eyes, I think I must still be in the in-between, that limbo between waking and sleeping, the jet bridge to the dreaming. In-between places. I hate them. I try to open my eyes wider to wake up here in the dreaming, because I know I'm not awake; I can't be. If I were in the dreaming, I'd feel more alive. I'd feel less afraid. I'd feel different, somehow.

I rub my eyes hard and blink a few times. Everything is gray and misty, bleak like the landscape of my heart without Ash. I look down at myself. I'm wearing my white gown. I'm here. I'm in the dreaming. But where are the wolves? The last thing I remember before waking was singing more wolves into creation in this world. I can't hear a sound. I must be too far from the Source to hear the rushing water.

I walk through the mist. I can barely see the hand in front of my face. I try to recognize where I am by the ground under my feet. But the grass looks the same everywhere. I decide to close my eyes and let my body guide me. Heel, toe, heel, toe, I softly step through the damp grass, cool under my feet, hoping that at any moment I will hear new wolves barking, scurrying, calling to me.

I am met with nothing but silence. But I won't give up hope. I can't.

I follow the pull of the land, trusting my body not to lead me into danger, and collide with Joshua's tree. I open my eyes. My eyes are stinging from the pain of my nose hitting the trunk. I look around with trepidation but with still a tiny flicker of hope. If there were wolves, they would be here, surely. This is where they would gather. Joshua's tree is still bare, and the only brightness is the hot pink of the flowers growing out of Willa's prickly pear cactus. So it's true, then: my powers here are gone. I have no authority to build, to rebuild, to repair. *Why am I here, then?*

Facing away from the woods, I feel a strange tingling on my neck as if I'm being watched. I turn around and try to look through the fog and mist to the trees. Of course I can't see a thing.

I circle Joshua's tree, my hand on the bark, three slow circles. On my third revolution I stub my toe on a root clawing its way out from the ground. Nestled in the crook of this root is the iridescent jewel: Ash's heart, my heart. It sickens me to see it, to remember how I cut it out of Ash's chest. I sicken myself. I look at my hands, and I want to damage them. I feel the sore spot on my mouth where the shrub at Ash's grave, made of the very knife that killed him, pierced my lip. I deliberately pinch my lip, pinch it until my eyes are watering from the pain.

I deserve this pain. I deserve *more* than this pain.

I reverently bend down on one knee and scoop up the jewel, the heart. Our heart. It belonged to both of us. Now that Ash is gone, truly gone, I don't know what I'll do without him. I don't know what was so important to me.

Ian Millbrook, my mind whispers immediately.

When did the land become so gray, so dead? I'm chilled in my sleeveless linen dress. I sit down, placing the heart in my lap. I rub my hands over my bare arms rapidly, trying to warm them. I would almost prefer the bite of the knife in my hand again. I'd gladly feel that pain if it meant Ash would be here with me.

Ian Millbrook, my mind urges once more. Right.

I have to do this now. I am committed. Because if I let my grief and guilt over Ash consume me, then he will have died for nothing. He sacrificed himself so I might have the thing I want most in the world: just the *hope* that one day, Ian Millbrook might know who I am. I'm not even asking that he fall in love with me — I just want him to know I'm so much more than that girl who was so shy and tongue-tied and awkward. I graduated from Longfellow. That's got to count for something, at least to some people. I have passion for art, just like he does—*did*, I correct myself, still finding it hard to think of him in the past tense—for music. I'm not dull. I'm someone worth knowing—aren't I?

Don't I matter?

I'm not deluded. I know I can't be what he wants. But just having the *hope* there, the *maybe*…

I break my train of thought, because it strikes me how sad it is that *this* is all I want. I'm pathetic. A genie comes out of a lamp and grants you a wish, and most people would figure out a way to change their whole lives or save the world. And I'm focused on this one person who won't even know who I am. I lie to myself and say that it's because I want to save his loved ones from pain. And yes, that is a part of it. I can't bear the thought of a loving mother aching for her much-wanted child. Or a sweet girl, who has probably seen enough horror in her young life to fill several lifetimes, forever without a fierce and loving guardian, a boy who tirelessly did anything to make her laugh. What will her life be now? What could her life have been, had he not been killed?

If these were my reasons for my wish, I would be foolish, but still noble.

No, I've bet everything, given up everything in this world just so *I* will know that he is *out there*. That at least I can say, "We both live. We both live on this earth." Is it selfish to want that? Or should I have asked for more? Should I have asked that Ian come back *and* that he'd know me? Love me?

I don't know how to ask for things. I don't know what's too much. I feel so selfish all the time. I know I don't deserve much, and here I've asked for this enormous thing—a huge wish that, even if it were possible to fulfill, will yield nothing but more longing. I'm a fool.

I've asked the Eternal to bring back the dead, or to turn time backward, or to create an alternate reality where none of this ever happened. It goes against all logic, all reason. I'm amazed that I have wished for something so large and impossible, yet at the same time so small and sad. I never know how to ask for what I want. Maybe it's because I don't know who I am.

In this moment I wish I'd never returned to the dreaming. *I was fine all those years, you know*, I think. When I was tired, I'd just close my eyes. There was nothing to fear in sleep, because there were no dreams, only rest. No one was in danger. No one was dying. No one was being killed by my hand. *Yes they were*, my mind interrupts me again. *Just because you chose to leave doesn't mean life stopped here. The wolves died because you weren't here to protect them.* All those wolves, the nameless ones, all gone. And the three I remember, they are gone too. It's only me now. *The cheese stands alone*, I think, remembering a Robert Cormier book from long ago, a dog-eared, creased paperback tucked in the front pocket of the book bag by my feet in the music room while I stared at Ian Millbrook bent over his guitar.

Was it my choice to dream again? Did I do something that made this happen, the way it was my choice to leave the dreaming? I look down at my lap, at the gemstone that fills me with piercing sorrow.

Ian Millbrook. Save him.

Do I think my thoughts, or does someone else think them for me? I don't even know whose voice is in my head anymore. I feel that prickle on the back of my neck again, but I don't bother looking. I know I won't see anything.

I stand slowly, our heart in my hand. It's time to go back to Samuel. We must finish this. I've already given up so much.

And Ash? Ash has already given up everything.

It takes me a minute to remember where I am, who I am, as I lie in bed, staring at the ceiling. Home. I am home. Which home? Whose home? I have only one home, and that's with Dad. Why am I even here? I feel like I've been asking myself that a lot lately.

I miss Dad so much. I want to call him, but it's too early. I know it's too early without even checking the time. I can tell from the angle of the sunbeams through my blinds that I shouldn't even be awake yet. I should still be on Pacific Time, at least for a few more days. I hate my body for adjusting so quickly, for forgetting so easily my true time zone. Couldn't it wait even a few days before setting back to this, the zone of my solitary, adult life in Boston? Why can't my body let me at least pretend I am still in Poppy Beach?

Today is Monday. If I were working this week, I could at least get up and take a shower, maybe tidy up my place or change my sheets, anything to fill the time before I'd have to leave. But I haven't called my temp agency yet. I'm not even sure if I want to work. I'm a little short on cash, but I've got enough for next month's rent, and I think I'll be okay on food and utilities as long as I work next week. This week, though...I just can't go back. I don't want to talk to anyone but Viv. I don't think I can put on a normal face and try to be helpful and pretend my world isn't falling apart—no, not fall*ing*. Has already fallen. Both my worlds, awake and asleep, destroyed. In frustration, I punch the mattress with both fists, sending up little clouds of dust that remind me of the mist now covering the dreaming. Did I make that happen?

God, I want to mourn Ash. I thought it was hard enough to lose Ian Millbrook, but he was never mine to lose. Ash, though—Ash was mine, all mine. He lived only in my world, lived for me, died for me. He was my *friend*. I'm sitting up now, sobbing, hating myself. I hold my head in my hands. *Pull it together*, I tell myself. *You're weeping over dreams.* My thoughts are erratic and irrational, and I just...I just don't sound sane.

I reach by the bed for my sketchbook and my drawing pencils. I page through the book, looking for new sketches. Nothing, no new material, the same way there were no new wolves by Joshua's tree. I haven't drawn anything while I was sleeping last night. What if I've lost it all?

I sit up with the sketchbook, looking at a blank page. I put the graphite tip of the pencil to the paper and let my mind wander. My hand works furiously, a blur against the page, and when I stop, I see the grove of trees where Ash is buried and a pair of eyes like lit coals staring back at me. I remember the prickly feeling on the back of my neck. "*Who's out there? Who are you?* What *are you?*"

Prickly feeling aside, drawing the picture has calmed me, and I roll over onto my side and try to sleep again. I put one hand under my pillow and let the other rest on the cover of the sketchpad.

I'm standing with our heart in my hand, turning it this way and that, trying to see the different colors glinting off, but it's still too hazy here. Maybe the sun will never return. Maybe I destroyed that too.

I square my shoulders and walk to the Bridge Between. My teeth chatter from both cold and dread. I've come to learn that nothing good ever comes of these meetings.

"Samuel?" I call out, my voice faltering. I'm trying to be brave. "May I cross?"

I don't hear an answer, but I step onto the bridge anyway, feeling the wetness in the air from the spray as the Source crashes against the rocks. The wooden slats creak, and I hold Ash's heart in one hand and the rope in the other. I check to see if the Door Beyond is there today, but I see nothing. I am inside a cloud, so far above the ground, and I think of being on a plane, my terror of being that high. I'm not afraid like that, though. I know the bridge will hold. I know I will not slip. I know, because I have Ash's heart with me.

I reach the end of the bridge, and everything is still white, a blank canvas. "Samuel?" I call again.

"Archer, have you returned?" His voice is everywhere, not in my head, but just part of the air.

"I have come with my heart," I say, gripping the gem more tightly in my hand.

"Then by all means, enter," the voice says, and the columns and sconces and arches reappear, swiftly sketched by an unseen hand.

I step off the bridge and follow the familiar path to the room where Samuel and I conduct our business.

"Welcome," he says, and he smiles, gesturing to the white chair that has appeared from nothingness.

"I'd rather not sit right now," I say. Sitting here, casually, holding Ash's heart, as if we are about to have tea…it doesn't seem right. It doesn't seem respectful.

"Up to you." He shrugs, as if this angel-like body could make a gesture so common, so mortal. It's an approximation of a shrug, practiced but not quite organic, as if he's Jane Goodall trying to fit in with the chimps after ages of observation.

I hold out Ash's heart. I don't want to give it to Samuel. I don't know what he will do with it. But I know Ash would want me to do this. He died so that I might live. If I hold onto the heart, then it all was for nothing. "Here is the part of my heart which was hidden in this land, cut by the knife which gave life to the Stone One."

"I see," he says coolly. I don't know what I expected from him, but these curt answers are confounding.

"I've completed both tasks. Now, will you do it?" I'm agitated, impatient.

"Do what, little maiden?"

"Will you waken the Sleeper?"

"Tsk, tsk," he clucks—again, a divine being's too elegant imitation of our clumsy human behavior.

"What have I done wrong?" I demand.

"Nothing, my dear," he says, mouth pulled taut into a grin. I think he is trying to smile benevolently, but somehow…it feels false to me. I don't trust him. I wish I'd never asked for this boon.

"You do not want the boon any longer?" he asks, reading my mind. "You wish to end the journey here?"

I look at the heart in my hand. I think of all I've already done, all I've already destroyed. Do I keep going forward on this path? What else will be ruined? Or will stopping now make everything that has come before this moment meaningless?

Ash would not want me to turn away. He *died* for this. He gave himself up for this. As scared as I am of what might come next, I owe it to him not to give up.

"I wish to continue the journey," I manage. "Do you…do you need this?" As much as I hate to do it, I hold out the heart to him.

He hisses and backs away. "I may not touch it, if you want the boon. But lay it over there." He gestures toward a small, blindingly white dais under a glass bell jar. I walk toward it slowly, not wanting to lose this part of Ash forever. As I approach, the jar floats upward just enough for me to slip the heart onto a white pillow on the platform, white on white. It looks sterile. Sometimes *sterile* is a good thing, like for bandages and gauze and medical instruments. And sometimes it means that nothing lives here. Nothing *can* live here. Sometimes, *sterile* means death.

As I'm thinking about the nature of sterility, the jar swings back down, nearly slamming down on my fingers. I barely get my hands out of the way in time.

I feel even sicker than I felt before, seeing his heart on the pillow, encased in glass, in this strange place. This was a mistake. I feel it in my bones. I try to touch the glass, but there's a sharp, electric pulse when I get too near. His heart is lost to me now, forever.

"Now," says Samuel.

"Yes?" I wish my voice sounded bigger, stronger. It is a mouse squeak, tiny and insignificant.

"Your journey is almost complete."

"What now?" I ask, filled with dread.

"There is a third task. The final task."

There's something about the way he says "final" that makes me shiver.

"Just tell me." I gather handfuls of my dress, crinkling the linen in my fists anxiously.

Samuel glides over to me, almost cupping my face with his radiant hands, but he stops just shy of touching me. "I'm sure you must have guessed by now, Maid Agnes."

"Are we playing games now? Guessing games?" I turn my face away from him. I don't want him to touch me.

"This is not a game, and you know it," he says, letting his hand drop by his side. "Don't act ungrateful, Archer. It's unseemly."

"I'm sorry," I say, although I'm not at all. "It's been a rough couple of days here. You know, having to dissect my friend and everything."

"Hmm," he says, studying me. "I don't recall forcing you. Everything you do here is your choice, little one."

It sure doesn't feel like it. I think how alone I am, of the bleakness that awaits me on the other side of the Bridge Between. "Why are there no more wolves?" I blurt out. I don't mean to, but it just spills out of me. "I tried to create them the way I always have."

"Ah, Maid Agnes. Consequences. Did you think you would escape unscathed from such a large request? You took life that you created. Your hands are no longer clean."

"I washed in the stream," I say, knowing I'm grasping at straws.

"Don't insult us both by pretending I am speaking literally."

"Why didn't you warn me this would happen?" I look over at the dais, at Ash's heart under the glass. It seems like a contradiction that being unclean has rendered me sterile. These hands, my voice, no longer create. And they will not create again. I know this now, without needing further confirmation from Samuel.

"My dear, you never asked. When will you learn to ask the right questions? All actions have consequences. You asked to waken the Sleeper. I am helping you down this path. You knew it would not be easy; I told you that from the start. You are asking me for something nearly beyond my power to grant."

He acts as if he's doing me this big favor. I guess he is, when I think about it. But he's doing me a favor because I inadvertently did him a favor. Then why does it mean I have to give so much up?

"Do you wish to know the third task or not?" he asks calmly. How can he frighten me so much with such a quiet voice, such a beautiful face?

"I do," I whisper.

"You do not wish to guess?"

"I do not."

"Well, then. Remember that you asked."

"I will. Just tell me, Eternal."

"Isn't it obvious? I am surprised you haven't figured it out yet."

"Just *tell* me." I am tired of his games. As much as he says he doesn't play them, I can't help feeling like a mouse trapped under the paw of a giant cat. I just wish he'd deliver the final blow instead of toying with me, making me twist in the wind.

"My dear Archer. Since this involves the human realm, there needs to be an exchange, a life for a life. You need to give up yours."

The room spins around me, and I feel like I'm on that ride at the amusement park where the barrel spins and the floor drops and you're pinned to the wall with nothing beneath you. "What?" I manage to gasp.

"Agnes Larch, you need to die."

I wake up screaming, my hands tangled in my hair.

My sketchpad lies open on my lap covered by my comforter. It lies open to the picture that has scared me since I drew it, the one of me tied to the stake, a scarecrow, my arms pinned to a crossbar. And for the first time, I see it for what it truly is. I'm not a scarecrow.

I am a sacrifice.

TWENTY-FOUR
THE ANSWER TO A RIDDLE

I hold my head in my hands. What am I going to do? This is fake, right? He can't mean that I actually have to *die*, can he? But...oh, God.

I'm at a crossroads; I can feel it. I can take the sane person's route and say that they are just dreams, or I can take the crazy person's route and say they are real. The sad thing is, I often feel so much more alive in these dreams than I do in my real life. I look out the window, and Boston stares back at me, colorless, cold, dead. I close my eyes and think of the dreaming, lush and green and very much alive. Alive, that is, until I came back and ruined everything.

I idly wonder if it's me, if I'm the factor that brings ruin. I ruined two lives in Poppy Beach for sure, and every winter in Boston I feel like the world has ended just by my being here. I know it's a silly and unhealthy way to think, and of course I don't think I'm responsible when the world is reborn in the spring. Only the bad things feel like they're my fault.

Consider the dreaming: I reappeared in the dreaming, and now it's drab, desolate, colorless. Empty.

When in my life did I see color around me? I think of my old car Bessie, her bumper covered in fruit stickers, a patchwork quilt in harlequin's colors. There was color then, gaudy perhaps, but still vibrant. Definitely not in-between. But that's the only place in my real life that I remember that intensity of color. So who's to say that this world is real and the dreaming is the false one?

But...dying. Yeah. I...no. I am scared. I've been scared my whole life of dying. It's the reason I'm afraid to fly. It's the reason I'm afraid to *try* anything or make any sort of real decisions. That's my biggest problem, I think—I'm so afraid to die that I never actually *live*.

So what's the big deal, then? If I'm not really living, does it matter if I die?

Ash's words come back to me: *You are always given a choice. You may take it, or you may not. Your path is always changing.* But I'm not so sure, as I look at this drawing I made before I knew the third task—before I knew there *was* a third task at all. Yes, I could choose not to follow this path, could choose not to complete the journey, but didn't my body somehow know when I drew this picture how this journey would end? I don't really feel like my path is always changing.

What's the alternative? To keep living my life, to flounder in the temp world, never figuring out who I am? Go home to Poppy Beach for good and admit to the world that I gave up, that everyone was wrong about expecting so much of me? To acknowledge that I'm just a cookie-cutter carbon-based life-form who will never make a difference, who might as well have never been born?

Or is this my chance to do something great? To *be* great? For my life to have meaning? I can save someone. I can be a hero. I can make a difference, and—for once—in a *good* way. Me.

If it's real, I remind myself. And it may not be. Would it still be worth it?

I'm thinking in circles, so I throw the covers off and begin pacing around my small apartment. I stub my toe on my suitcase, which I should have unpacked by now. All I've done is fish my pajamas out when I first got home. I unzip the bag completely and flip the lid open. It looks like a gaping mouth, reminding me for a second of the Stone One preparing to devour my dear Joshua and my complicated Willa.

The monster's gone now, I remind myself, plunging my hands into the bag and tossing my clothes out. Even with the bag partially open for a day or two, the clothes still hold onto the scent of my father's house, the way I never stop longing to be with him. Eventually the fabric will release the scent molecules back into the air, will give up their hold to absorb the smell of my barren apartment. The clothes will lose their memory of their time in Poppy Beach, but I, I never will. It would be easier if I could forget, I think. My heart wouldn't hurt all the time.

I toss my dirty clothes into the laundry basket, put my shoes away. I reverently lift out the homecoming dress, still on its hanger in the plastic bag, and hug it to myself. I stand in front of the full-length mirror and remember trying it on for Dad. I hold the hanger with my hands and pretend to dance with it, my body as a stand-in for Ian's. *My body for his.*

I wonder if the dress still fits. I consider trying it on just to see, but this dress is a relic. If I open the bag, something, some essence, will be lost. I don't want to do that. His hands were the last thing that touched the velvet here. I touch the dress only through the plastic, protected from the elements, from the oil in my fingers, from anything that would cause the dress to age or disintegrate.

It's kind of like me, living in plastic. Shielded, trapped in time, inert. Inert, as in not interacting with others, not mixing, not becoming part of some greater whole. Not living. It's funny that inert gases on the periodic table are also called *noble*. I certainly don't feel *noble*. I feel…sterile. Like I am now in the dreaming. Sterile. Noble. Inert.

Who am I?

I sigh heavily and slide the hangers in my closet aside to make room for the dress. All my other clothes are out, messily hung on their cheap hangers. I don't have anything dry-cleaned, like, ever. Seeing the one dress in plastic among all the other pieces of clothing, I can't help but think of introducing a new fish to an aquarium, letting it float for a while in its own plastic bag to get used to its foreign surroundings.

"Welcome home," I say to the dress and put my suitcase back in the other closet.

I have slept past noon, and I decide to give the apartment a thorough scrubbing. I can't think of anything else to do, and I can't bear to get out of my pajamas. It's just one of those days. I have to turn on every light because the sun sets so early, and the light that does filter through is pale and weak. There's no warmth in this light. False light. Light should be warm, life-giving. In-between things again.

My nose is getting cold, so I put on a fleece and my slippers. I feel like I'm home sick or skipping school. I keep the TV on so I don't feel so alone. I thumb through a few books, but I can't focus enough to read more than a paragraph of anything. I leave chores half-finished, dropping a paper towel smudged with Windex and dust on the kitchen table, picking up discarded socks and dropping them on the bed, distracted by something on TV. I drag my vacuum across the floor but leave it there running when I stop to eat some crackers.

As the sun sets, I'm not sure the apartment is any cleaner than it was when I started. At least I've put my suitcase away. I look at the spot on the floor where it used to be, and my heart aches a little because my apartment looks completely ordinary. It's as if my trip home never happened. There's no indication, no memory that says, "Agnes Larch went back to Poppy Beach. She saw her father. She held hands with Ian Millbrook's sister."

Maybe the trip was never real.

In a panic, I run to the closet and throw open the door. The dress hangs there like an old friend, like it's always been here. I touch a sleeve of the dress through the plastic. "I was there," I murmur to myself. "It happened."

I call Dad's shop. A strange woman's voice says, "Larch Bait and Tackle."

"M-May I talk to Pete Larch?" I stammer, confused. I thought I knew everyone at the shop, but I remember that I never even stopped by while I was home.

"I'm sorry," she says, "but he's not here at the moment."

"Okay," I say.

I'm about to hang up, feeling stupid, when the woman says, "Do you want me to take a message for him?"

"Can you tell him that Agnes called?"

"Agnes? Is this Agnes Larch? Pete Larch's daughter?" she asks.

"Yes," I say politely, fighting my urge to hang up the phone. My thumb hovers over the "end call" button, twitching anxiously.

"It's nice to meet you. I mean, I know we haven't *really* met, but we're talking on the phone, so it's like we're meeting, and, oh gosh I'm babbling all over. Your dad talks about you all the time. He's so proud of you, you know."

"Yes?" I say, my heart swelling with pleasure a little, but also feeling like any minute I'll be exposed as a fraud. *They don't really know how little you've made for yourself. And what happens when they find out who you really are? When they find out you're nothing?*

"All the time! I feel like I know you. Oh, I'm sorry," she chatters on, "I haven't even introduced myself. I'm Diana. Pete hired me a few months ago."

"Nice to meet you," I say, smiling. I know she can't see me, but I hope she can hear it in my voice.

"I hope you'll stop in the next time you're in Poppy Beach so I can see Pete Larch's famous daughter."

The next time I'm in Poppy Beach. When will that be? I try not to sigh directly into the phone.

"It was good to talk to you," I say. "I won't take up any more of your time."

"All right, sweetheart. I'll make sure to tell your dad you called. Take care now."

"Thanks. Bye," I say, finally letting my thumb end the call and staring at the phone in my hand. Dad barely says two words to me in person or on the phone, but it's always like this. When I meet new people who know him, they always say he talks about me all the time. I know he's got pictures of me in his fat, battered wallet, baby pictures, school pictures, even my graduation photo from Longfellow, and I'm pretty sure he trots them out for everyone to see, laying them down with a little smile on his face, as if he's got a winning hand of poker.

I know he must *really* be proud if he talks about me when I'm not there to hear it. And I guess I know deep down that he doesn't care that I'll never be anyone *important*, at least the way I define *important*. But still, I wish I could be the person he thinks I am. I wish I could make him proud the way he thinks he's proud of me. It's all based on this false image he has of me, the confident, successful graduate of Longfellow, someone who can weave in and out of these Ivy League social affairs, who knows which fork to use, who knows which wine goes with what kind of meat. He knows I won't be sitting at a fancy dinner with my hands awkwardly folded in my lap, not knowing what to do or say to fit in.

It would be nearly impossible to come out of four years of Longfellow *not* knowing those things, but that doesn't make me particularly special. I'm more like a trained parrot. Anyone could learn this stuff. I haven't been able to make good on the other side of things, the part where I actually make the world a better place. The part where the world is better off for my having lived in it. My footprints will be washed away by the tide, and there will be no trace that I ever was here. It's not like Neil Armstrong's footprint on the moon, there now and forever. The world will always know where he's been. But me? I'll have never existed. I'll be eraser shavings brushed aside and swept into the dustbin.

But you can make something of yourself. You can be a hero.

Not this train of thought again. These are dreams; they aren't real. It won't make a difference.

Right then, a commercial comes on TV, and my heart nearly stops, because it's *his voice*. It's a commercial for car insurance, and there's a song playing faintly in the background. It's not one of the songs on his webpage, but I would recognize his voice anywhere. I can hear Ian Millbrook's music as a car drives slowly home in pouring rain, a toddler asleep in the backseat. *"I'm coming home to you, coming home,"* he sings in the background as the car arrives safely at the house, where the porch light is on against the darkness, the grandparents waiting by the door.

I don't think it's a coincidence.

I sit on the couch with my sketchbook, much as I did a little more than a week ago, before Tricia called me and ended my world. I stare at the drawing of the eyes in the woods. "Is that you?" I whisper. "Are you ready to wake up?"

I begin to sketch, not paying attention, and when I look down, I see I've drawn myself, but my dress has changed. It's longer, not looking like a huntress's garment. What does it mean?

I know I've done nothing today but sleep and wander and eat crackers, but I start nodding off. I'm afraid to go to sleep, so I try to fight it, try to force my eyelids open. But I can't, hearing only in my head *his* voice, *"I'm coming home to you, coming home."*

I'm curled up on my side beneath Joshua's tree. Samuel must have returned me from his realm. I get up slowly, my muscles stiff and sore from the cold ground. My dress has changed. The skirt flows down past my ankles, skimming the grass. I have sleeves now, long, diaphanous sleeves, like moth wings or moonlight.

I can be a hero, I think.

Willa's prickly pear cactus shifts in the wind. The hot pink blossoms sway back and forth like heavy heads shaking *no*. She doesn't think I should do it. But why have my clothes changed? Am I now dressed for this sacrifice? The wind whips my long sleeves around, and I feel light as a bird. I am not afraid.

I climb the highest tower of Oread's Keep, where I often faced down the Stone One. I bested him, and now it's my turn to meet my end. *They're just dreams*, I think. *Don't be afraid.* I stand on the ledge but make the mistake of looking down. It's like being in a plane again, this height. I shouldn't be afraid here, not in this moment. If I'm afraid, maybe it won't count. I don't know. I scramble to get back from the ledge, but my toe catches in a gap in the battlements, and I lose my balance.

I windmill my arms to try to stay on top of the castle's keep, but it's no use. I plummet headfirst to the ground, my sleeves and skirt fluttering after me. I think that I must look beautiful in this moment, like a falling star. I don't make a sound as I fall.

The ground is hard and unforgiving, and I feel so much pain that I no longer can see. Then the world turns to white, and I fade away.

Everything hurts. I can barely breathe. I feel completely broken. But if I'm breathing...maybe I didn't do it right. I hear a low chuckling.

"Archer, did you think it would be that easy?"

I know that voice. I push myself up to sitting and open my eyes. I'm on the floor of our meeting room in Samuel's realm.

"What?" I croak. I keep swallowing and clearing my throat, trying to make my voice work.

"You can't give up your life here. You can't be harmed here, not permanently," he says. "But an *A* for effort." He does this little golf applause thing that seems obnoxious coming from him, since he's not even human. Doubly obnoxious, because it's carefully studied behavior, applied sarcasm and mockery.

"I had to try," I say, trying to stand up.

"Then you are not truly ready," he says, turning his back to me.

"But I am. I *am* ready," I insist, walking up to him and straightening out my skirts.

"You're not afraid?"

"I…I am afraid, but I am still ready."

"Hmm," he says, turning back to me and tapping his finger on his chin. "It's an awfully big thing you need to do, Archer."

"You promise me you can waken the Sleeper?"

"I already have promised."

My head is spinning, maybe from the fall, maybe from everything I've been through here in this world where I used to have power, where I used to find companionship. I look over at the dais and Ash's heart under the bell jar.

I say in a tiny voice, "I don't want to die." And I begin to cry.

I don't want to cry in front of him. I don't want to seem weak. But it's the truth; I *don't* want to die. Even though my life feels worthless, I still want it. I want to hold onto it. I think of Anna Karenina and her little red purse right before she throws herself under the train. The tower thing was just an experiment, a test to see. And deep down I knew it wouldn't count.

"What would give you courage, pet?" he asks, crouching beside me, still looking all too divine in his attempt to appear human-like.

I try not to focus on the intense creepiness of Samuel's calling me *pet*. "I need to know this is real," I say. "I *need* to know. I want to see *him*."

"I can't do that," he says. "But I may be able to send you a sign. Would you like a sign?"

"A sign?" I repeat stupidly.

Samuel appears lost in thought, eyes unfocused as he thinks. He murmurs quickly to himself, his eyelids fluttering, his fingers twitching in the air. Slowly his eyes refocus on my face, and he says, "You will meet someone in your world, someone close, and then you will know that I keep my word.

"Remember, dear lamb, I ask you these things not because I relish your pain or wish to see you suffer. You have asked me a favor, and these are the things the universe requires. I am not all-powerful. I make mistakes. I have weaknesses. These tasks, as painful as they are for you, are merely the requirements, the *ingredients*, if you will, for me to grant you your wish. I am beholden to grant you your wish, and this is why I ask these things of you."

I nod glumly.

"Now, come. Stand up. Ready yourself," he says. "I'd offer you my hand, but I may not touch the elements involved in granting your boon."

"Ready myself?"

"You need to go back down the Bridge. And you need to hurry."

"Why?" I'm tired of his riddles and rules and commands.

"Because your father is calling. Go!"

He exhales loudly, and the room starts to crumble and disintegrate, becoming brighter and brighter as I run for the Bridge Between, my dress fluttering behind me like a ghost.

I can hear the phone ringing as I sprint across the Bridge, trying not to trip on the hem of my dress. My bones no longer ache, healed already by the air here.

I wake up on the couch, my face on top of the sketchbook. The phone is still ringing. "Hi, Dad," I say sleepily without even looking at caller ID.

"Ags?" he says. "Is everything all right?"

"Yeah, Dad," I say. "I just…missed you. I wanted to hear your voice."

I can hear my dad swallow hard, even through the phone. "Well, here I am," he says a little too cheerily.

I laugh sleepily. "Dad, you sound like you're making jazz hands."

He barks out a laugh in reply. "Now, Ags, you know I don't even know what those are."

"Ask Diana to show you," I say. "I bet she'd know. She sounds nice."

"Yep," he says. "She's a real nice girl. Hardworking."

"Who's a nice girl?" I hear Diana say in the background.

"Kind of *nosy* though." I can just see the patented Pete Larch glare. Diana blows him a raspberry. She must be standing right at his elbow. "Now, that's disgusting, Diana," Dad says, but I can tell that he's smiling.

I'm glad he's having a good time in at the shop. It makes me feel less worried about him. "I miss you, Dad," I say again.

Dad is silent for a long while, and then he sighs, "Me too, kid, me too."

"I'll come home again for Easter," I say, not knowing why. It just comes out.

"That would be real nice." I'm not sure he believes me, either. I've made these promises before.

I wish I could hug him, feel his five o'clock shadow on his cheek, like that page in *Pat the Bunny* with the sandpaper. Voices alone aren't enough. They're never enough. They aren't the same as a warm body in front of you.

"Well," I say, "I guess I should let you go."

"It's real nice to hear your voice, Ags."

"Love you, Dad."

"You too, kid."

I hate to do it, but I hang up the phone. Otherwise we'd be sitting in silence for hours, listening to each other breathe, wanting to say the things we really mean but are unable to put into words. I don't want him to feel awkward in front of other people like that, so I spare him the embarrassment.

I've got a huge lump in my throat that won't go away, and I blink back tears. *How can you think of leaving Dad?* I berate myself. *What would he do without you? You're all he has.*

It's too much to have to make another choice like that. Ash was hard enough. It's not being selfish to hold onto my life. I can live for my father. But then I look at the new picture I've drawn while I was sleeping. I'm wearing the new dress from the dreaming, but I'm out in the streets of Boston — no, wait, over the river on the Cambridge side of things. I recognize this street, right in the middle of Longfellow Square, a side street paved with cobblestones. *I need to be here. Now.* I don't know how I know, but I do.

Maybe this is my sign.

I peel my fleece and pajamas off and get dressed as quickly as I can, rushing out the door to catch the *T*, the Green Line to the Red Line, right into the Square. I slam the door behind me, not realizing until I'm halfway to Hynes that my hands are smudged with graphite. I pull my mittens over my dirty fingers, already red from the cold, and I find myself thinking of that old riddle, "What's black and white and red all over?"

Maybe my problem is that I keep wanting to know the answer to all my questions, when I am the answer. I'm not sure what I'm the answer to, exactly, but it feels important. I am the answer. *Me.* Whatever that might mean.

I run into the swinging doors of Hynes station, hearing the screech of trains as they arrive. "*Er kommt! Er kommt!*" I find myself muttering. That's odd. German. *He comes?* I don't understand half the things that go through my head these days. But I do know one thing:

My sign is waiting on the other side of the river.

TWENTY-FIVE
THE SIGN

It feels like the gods are with me as I travel to Cambridge. When I get to Park Street, the Red Line is waiting on the platform, and it's even one of those rare express trains going straight to Longfellow Square, which happens only when there's a backlog of trains stuck behind this one. *Hurry, hurry, hurry,* I seem to hear in my head as I stare at the floor of the subway car, slick with melted snow.

The car is crowded, so I stand, facing the left-hand windows. It's my favorite view of Boston, looking toward the Prudential and the Hancock Tower as we cross the Charles River. I remember the first time I took the Red Line into the city from Longfellow's campus, and I couldn't believe there was such beauty for free, visible from something so common, so *mundane,* as a subway car. I love looking out the window in the spring and summer when sailboats dot the river, looking like doves on the glimmering blue water. As we cross now, however, the river is frozen, covered with snow. I can barely see the Boston skyline because of the fogged windows of the subway car.

I wish I could see sailboats.

I take one of the side exits once we get to Longfellow Square. It's always a little strange for me to come back here. Since moving to the other side of the river, I rarely come back, preferring to compartmentalize my college experience. It was a special time; I felt I was on the cusp of something wonderful. When I come back here, I get tiny flashbacks of hope, of awe, twinges that I still might transform into something greater. If I came here every day, I'd lose that, I think. This place would become integrated with my present self. I don't want to combine the memories of this place with the person I am now. *Diagnosis: Failure to thrive.*

So I save these visits. I rarely even walk through Longfellow's quad, because I want it to remain like a museum, or a time capsule, or like Colonial Williamsburg. When I step through the wrought iron gates, I want to feel transported, like walking through a time machine right into the past, back to a time when I believed anything was possible. I avoid the main quad even now, heading instead for the cobblestoned alleyway I recognized from my drawing.

I've got a sign to find. And if I find it, I will have to trust Samuel. Everything in me screams that I should not, but I am giving him a chance. Not because I want to believe the best of him, but because I desperately need *something* to help me complete this final task. He said it would give me courage, something I am sorely lacking.

I clench my jaw to keep my teeth from chattering as I take careful steps down the snow-packed sidewalk to the cobblestoned alleyway in my dream-sketch. As soon as I pass the movie theater, I can hear it: strains of music in the otherwise quiet, cold night, rays of warmth reaching out like tendrils of smoke into the street. I close my eyes and follow the burn, right to Club Flotsam, a small venue for folk and acoustic rock.

It's not the typical folk music I've heard the off times I've wandered down this street during a concert. I'm used to guitars, maybe a keyboard, but tonight I hear the mournful velvet tones of a cello. The rich threads of music pull me from my belly, much like I was pulled into the church where Ian Millbrook was playing, and I find myself going down the stairs to the entrance of the club.

The concert is just starting, and I pay for a ticket at the door and squeeze inside. As I walk into the main room, I lock eyes with the man with the cello on the tiny stage at the far wall. He's got chiseled features and a probing stare, reminding me of a young James Dean, and he looks at me with such intensity that I look behind me, certain he must be seeing someone else.

But there is no one behind me. He's looking at me. *Me.*

He finishes the song to polite applause, clears his throat, and thanks us for coming. "This is my first concert since...the accident," he says, still looking right at me. "I don't know if you heard on the news, but my good friend and colleague, the amazingly talented Ian Millbrook, was killed in a plane crash about two weeks ago."

All the air escapes my lungs, and I have to hold onto the back of the nearest chair. I know him. I know *of* him, rather—Ian Millbrook's friend playing cello on songs I've heard on his webpage.

"Once again, my name is Glen Fordham. Thanks for coming tonight." And he starts his next song. He plays the cello in a way I've never seen before, his fingers flying around, the bow on the strings at times, at times tapping against the wood of the cello, turning the beautiful instrument into an ersatz drum kit. He stomps his foot on the ground, his hair falls in his eyes, and I get a shiver as I see his neck inclined like a statue of the Madonna, bending over the cello and wringing out his grief through strong strokes of his bow.

Everyone else can feel it too, I think. The atmosphere is quiet, meditative, respectful, like at a Good Friday service.

I'm crying just listening to his song, his voice wrapping around the sorrow pouring out as horsehair touches string. It's like we are connected. *He understands what it's like to lose Ian Millbrook, to lose him as an outsider*, I think, except I'm aware that at least he *knew* Ian and that Ian knew him. Still, it makes me feel less alone to feel his pain expressed in song. Maybe it's not the same as my pain, but they are from the same family, the same tree of grief. Just different branches.

I feel like we are the only people in the room, and I think Glen knows it too. He starts playing a familiar riff on the strings in that rich lower register that seems to rumble in my chest. His notes spin and wrap around me like a mantle, like swaddling clothes, and when he starts singing, I am completely immobilized. He's doing a cover of "Wonderful Tonight," and he ends the first stanza singing about a woman with *long brown hair*.

Now, I know those lyrics are wrong. I know it should be *long blond hair*. I know, because over the years I have listened to "Wonderful Tonight" over and over and over again, trying to remember the feeling of Ian Millbrook's fingers on my back, wondering if his fingertips were rough and callused, wondering what they would feel like clasped in my hands or brushed along my cheek. But Glen won't stop looking at me as he sings, and I wonder how he can play the cello without seeing what his fingers are doing.

As he stares at me, I wonder if the lyrics flub is a mistake, a slip of the tongue, or a deliberate change. I find myself swaying from side to side, as if I'm back in the gymnasium, swathed in secondhand velvet, dancing with the back of the chair I've been leaning on in the club, clutching tightly so I don't float away from this room. I don't even feel like I'm really here.

His Clapton cover ends, and there is a brief, awed hush before the audience applauds enthusiastically but respectfully—no hooting or table pounding. We all know that *something* has happened just now, something important, spiritual. We've witnessed this moment.

He balances his bow on his knee and says, "I, um…that wasn't part of the set-list. I just, wow, I don't know what came over me." He is silent a second, trying to collect himself, closing his eyes and breathing deeply long enough that people in the audience grow uncomfortable, shifting in their seats and coughing. Finally, he raises his head and takes the bow back into his hand.

He plays his own music for the rest of the set, and I am amazed, again, at the different tones, the different styles of music he's able to coax from his cello. I wish I'd gotten to see Ian Millbrook and this Glen Fordham play together live. It must have been incredible, each of them feeding off the other.

When the concert is over, I linger. I wait for his fans and well-wishers to disperse, and he looks up at me as I lean against the exposed brick on the other side of the room. The jolly club manager comes over to congratulate him on the show, but he shakes his hand briefly and says, "I have to get going."

He makes a beeline for me. He grabs one of my hands and says, "You knew him, didn't you?"

I nod. Neither of us needs to say Ian's name out loud.

"I could see it in your face when you walked in. I knew that look. I…I felt something, almost like a whispering in my ear."

I slip my hand into his, and my face crumples into tears. "Your playing, it was so beautiful."

"Did you have something to do with that Clapton cover?" he asks, clutching my hand to his chest and searching my face.

"I…I don't know," I finally say, my voice faltering and timid.

He pulls me with him to the stage as he packs up his cello and amp. "Do you have anywhere to be right now?"

"I, uh…no, I guess not." *I never have anyplace to be*, I add in my head.

"Do you want to get coffee or something? I can read the grief on your face. It's like looking in a mirror. You loved him too, didn't you?"

I normally would lie, dissemble, change the subject. But something is different about him. I look him square in the face and say, "Yes. I loved him. I *love* him. I wish…" But I can't finish my sentence.

"He was my best friend, like a brother to me," says Glen, and he blinks back a few tears.

"Did he…did he feel the same about you?" I ask, looking away.

"What do you mean?" He's absentmindedly wrapping a long cable around his arm.

"Just…did he think of you as a brother too?"

"Of course he did," he says, sounding almost offended. Of course Ian knew *him*.

"Oh," I say.

"Come on, let's go," he says, picking up his cello case. "Just give me five minutes to pack all this back in my van."

I sit on a rickety wooden café chair as I wait for him to clear the stage. I should probably have offered to help him, but I'd probably drop his amp into a puddle, shorting it or at least smashing some important component inside.

I'm lost in thought, hearing Clapton in my head, when I hear someone say, "I'm ready now." I jump, startled, but of course it's just Glen. I nod and follow him out of the club.

I grimace as the cold air hits me and pull my clothes around me more tightly. "Jesus," I hiss under my breath. "Are you from here? Does the cold bother you?"

"Went to school here, but I'm from New Mexico, so I never got used to it."

I'd say something back, but my jaw is clenched too tightly from the cold.

"Are you a coffee snob?" he asks, and I shake my head. "There's a Starbucks across the street. Let's just duck in there so we don't have to be in this monkeyfucking cold anymore."

We dash across the street and up the stairs into the Starbucks. I stamp my feet by the entrance, trying to kick all the snow off, and

Glen looks at me with a sad smile, shaking his head. "Finished?" he asks as I stop stomping.

"Yeah."

He gestures to let me pass in front of him to order. "Can I get a hot chocolate? Like, whatever is large? Is that the venti?" I say to the bored barista behind the counter.

"Just give me the House Blend, black, venti," orders Glen smoothly. He turns to me. "Want anything to eat?"

"No, I'm good," I say, even though I'm pretty sure I didn't eat anything but crackers today.

As the barista rings us up, I reach for my wallet, but Glen shakes his head and says, "I've got this." The amount comes to something and two cents, and Glen digs in his pockets. "Fuck, I hate pennies," he mumbles, coming up empty-handed.

"I've got some," I offer, and I put two pennies in his hand.

The coffeehouse is fairly empty, as it's almost closing time, so we're able to get some of the comfy chairs. I wrap my hands around the cup and breathe in the steam from the hot milk. I still feel cold. I feel like I'll never be warm again.

I think how strange it is that I'm sitting in a Starbucks with Ian Millbrook's collaborator, within spitting distance of Longfellow University. There are too many worlds colliding at once. I don't know what to say, so I stare out the window.

"How did you know Ian?" asks Glen.

"I, uh, we went to school together, sort of," I say. "Junior high and high school. He gave me an apple sticker once," I add stupidly. "How about you?" I know exactly how he met Ian, but I ask anyway, because I don't want to creep him out. I want him to keep talking to me about Ian Millbrook.

"I met him at conservatory, in a jazz improv class," he says. "We ended up playing a wedding together through the school gig office, and then we decided to keep collaborating. He was a genius."

"Yeah, he was." I'm looking at the reflection of the overhead lights in my cocoa, still too hot to drink. "I loved watching him play," I admit. "I would sneak glances when I thought no one was looking. It was the most beautiful thing in the world to see the kind of passion he had…the way his face would light up when he was *in it*. You could tell the rest of the world disappeared for him."

"Music's like that," Glen nods. "It's funny. It's when I feel the most alive, when I can escape the grief. But it's also when I feel the grief the most, when I can hear the parts in my head that Ian would have been playing." His voice starts to waver. I don't want him to cry in front of me, so I put my cup down and reach for his hand.

"I'm sorry," I say, as if those words can adequately describe what I'm feeling.

"I just can't believe he's gone. Just like that. And you know something crazy? I was supposed to be on that flight too."

I let my shock settle before I ask, "Where were you going?"

"We had a gig in Philadelphia. We'd just finished up a mini-tour in Chicago, but I'd gotten food poisoning and missed the flight. I was going to fly out later, catch up with him there." He shakes his head. "I don't know why I'm alive and he's not."

"Why does anything happen?" I say, letting go of his hand and drawing my knees up to my chest in the armchair.

The Starbucks manager comes to our table and says, "Sorry, guys, we're closing now."

Glen and I nod and hurry to finish our drinks. My cocoa is cool enough to drink down in one big gulp, but Glen leaves his coffee almost untouched. I bundle back up, wrapping my scarf around my neck several times.

"Where are you going now?" Glen asks.

"Home, I guess."

"Need a lift? My van is just back there, behind the club."

I'm about to decline, but he's my first living, speaking connection with Ian. I can't bear to leave him. "Sure, that would be great, thanks."

Glen's van is littered with fast food wrappers and empty soda bottles. "Sorry about that," he says as he holds the passenger door open for me.

The van is freezing, and Glen cranks the heat on full power. We don't try to talk over the whirring of the fan. As the heat begins to kick in, he turns it down to a reasonable level and begins to drive down the cobblestoned alleyway. I don't say much except to give him directions back to my place. We drive over the Charles River back into Boston, and I try to look at the view. I can make out the old Citgo sign and the steady blue light on top of the old Hancock building. No snow tonight, then.

"I hope I never get tired of that view," I say. Glen nods, focusing on the road.

It always amazes me how small the city is when you travel by car. It usually takes me an hour to get from Longfellow Square to my apartment, but even with the roads narrowed by piles of plowed snow, we're at my front door in about twenty minutes.

"Thanks," I say, unbuckling my seatbelt. "It…it was good to talk to you, I mean, about him."

"Yeah," he says. "I haven't been able to talk to anyone else who understands, so thank you for that."

My hand lingers on the door handle. "Do you want to come inside for a minute?"

"All right," he breathes, leaning his head for a moment on the steering wheel.

If I wasn't sure he was the sign promised by Samuel before, there's no doubt in my mind now when a car pulls out of the one visitor's spot in front of my building as we're talking. He parallel parks the van, and we both hop out.

I don't know what is going to happen when we go inside. I don't know what I want to happen. But I do know that I feel this connection with him, that *he* is my sign. I need courage; maybe he'll be able to make me brave.

We get inside, and the heat is almost unbearable. "These old apartments can't seem to hold a steady temperature," I say, peeling off layers and dropping them on the floor. "Just drop your crap anywhere. It's cool."

Glen folds his coat and sweater carefully and places them on my desk chair.

We sit on my sofa. "Tell me about him," I ask. "Tell me what he was like as…you know, all grown up."

"Jeez," Glen says, running his hands through his hat-flattened hair, "I don't know. He was wickedly funny, a nice guy, and the best musician I've ever met."

This isn't enough. "Tell me something that no one else would know about him. Not like a secret, but just something mundane."

Glen thinks a minute. "He…he really liked Spaghetti-Os right out of the can. We called him Boxcar Will-Ian because of it."

I laugh, even though my eyes are welling with tears. "Boxcar Will-Ian," I repeat. "I love it." I blink, and the tears streak down my face.

Glen brushes a tear away with the back of his hand, and I lean into him. "Tell me something else," I say with desperation as he inches toward me. I close my eyes and picture Ian Millbrook eating Spaghetti-Os out of a can.

He whispers against my forehead, "He liked to play pranks on people."

"Yeah?" I sigh as he brings his mouth to mine. "What kind of pranks?"

He kisses the corners of my mouth and says, "Before an orchestra concert, he once replaced my bow with a riding crop."

"Oh shit," I laugh, even as I keep crying. "What happened?"

"Oh, as soon as he saw me panic, he gave me my bow back." Glen's face is wet, and I think I must have cried all over him, but when I open my eyes I see that he's crying too.

"I didn't know he could be such a prick," I say, smiling. "Did you get him back?"

"I *may* have stolen all his boxers while he was in the shower and left him only a pair of exceptionally fabulous manties I'd purchased especially for him. He was getting ready for a date," he explains.

I know it's not rational, but I feel a pang of jealousy thinking of Ian on a date when I was living in the same city. But still, the image of Ian in some crazy male underwear model manties has me laughing and sobbing at once. I know it's a losing battle, but I try to clean my face up, rubbing my hand over my cheeks.

"Wait, you just got something on your face," he says. He looks at my hands. "What's this?"

"Oh." I realize I never washed the graphite off my hands. "I was drawing before I went to the club."

"You're an artist?" he asks.

"Not really," I say. I get up to wash my hands and face. In the bathroom, I stand on tiptoes to study myself in the tiny mirror above the sink. My eyes are red-rimmed, my cheeks splotchy. I'm a mess. *What are you doing, Agnes?* I ask my reflection, but she shrugs back at me.

"Better?" I ask, and Glen nods.

"Now, you tell me something," Glen says.

"I...I didn't know him enough to tell you something," I say, twisting my hands in my lap. He lays his hand on top, stilling them.

"Please," he begs. "Talk to me about him."

"I loved him," I say. "I don't know why. I think about him all the time. I wish I'd had the guts to walk up to him and say, 'You amaze me. Every day, you amaze me.' And now I'll never have the chance."

Glen plays with my fingers, and his fingertips are callused on one hand, smooth on the other. I cry more because I wonder once again what Ian's hands were like, how they'd feel on my bare skin.

"I'm terrified of flying, but I went back to California for his memorial," I offer. "His parents, his family—they all looked at me, and they didn't even know who I was. They knew who you were, didn't they?"

"I went home with Ian for Thanksgiving once. My folks were in Europe, and his parents couldn't bear the thought of my being in Boston alone for the holiday. So, yeah, I guess they knew me," he says almost guiltily.

"Yeah," is all I manage to get out before I'm sobbing again.

"Shh," says Glen, holding me against him. "It doesn't matter. You loved him. This?" he says, brushing another tear away from my cheek. "My heart rips open the same way every day. So it doesn't matter if his family knew or not. Somehow, the universe knew. Somehow, I'm sure he knew too."

"Ha," I say bitterly.

He talks past me, as if I'm not even there. "Every day I wake up thinking I'm going to see him."

"Me too."

"I keep thinking it's a bad dream that I'll wake up from. I think of all the songs we had left to write together, all the gigs we were going to do..." He trails off, his face twisted with grief and regret.

"Do you know Gillian?" I ask. I'm partially trying to distract him, but I also really want to hear about her from someone who has met her, seen her with his own eyes.

He nods.

"Oh," I say, gulping. "Is she nice?"

"She's great, actually. We all went to school together. They were pretty much inseparable."

"Oh," I say again, but in a really small voice.

But before I can feel more sorry for myself, Glen has pulled me up to standing, and we're kissing. He leads me to the bed. This sudden passion is weird, but it's like he was talking about his playing—that it makes the pain less, but at the same time all I can think about is the pain. Just the human contact, the physical act of being loved, distracts me from the ache in my heart, and the whole time we are kissing desperately, all I think about is Ian. *Ian, Ian, Ian,* my heart beats against Glen's chest.

I've never done anything like this, had a moment of intimacy so tinged with mutual sorrow. But I think we understand each other. This is our way to grieve, our way to remember, our way to honor. The only thing that connects us is our love for Ian, and when I look into his eyes, I can almost see Ian. Or maybe it's just my grief reflected back at me.

"Tell me something else," I ask, even as we're a mess of unbuttoned clothing and sweat.

"He was afraid of blue food," Glen whispers.

"Blue food?" I barely am able to pant out.

"You know, like blue Gatorade and stuff. It freaked him out. Something about the Smurfs? I don't know."

"Thank you." We cling to each other like we're on a capsizing boat. With each thrust, I can see Ian more clearly, Ian the adult, Ian the prankster, Ian the beloved. "Thank you," I say again as Glen groans and flops on his side away from me. "I know this didn't mean anything," I say before he can try to make up excuses. "I know this wasn't about me. I know this wasn't about love."

Glen dresses, straightens his clothes. He's about to interrupt me, but I stop him.

"No, really. It's all right. I was meant to see you. You were meant to find me. I think this had to happen. I understand now, and I think I'm ready."

"It's...that's not..."

"You know this was about him. It's okay," I say, pulling on my pajama top. "I'm glad. I really am."

"I miss him," he says, giving up trying to explain. He stares at his socks.

"I know." I turn to look out the window for a minute at the Boston night sky, strangely lit orange and purple all at once. "You should go now."

He gathers up his things, and I just stay on the bed and watch him. He fumbles with the deadbolt on the door, so I finally get up to let him out.

"Thanks for finding me tonight," I say, holding the door open.

"Wait, I don't even know your name," Glen says, almost touching my cheek but drawing his hand back.

"It's Agnes. Agnes Larch," I say, and he has a strange look on his face as he nods, taking in the information.

"Goodnight, Agnes Larch," he says, turning and starting down the stairs.

I watch out the window as he gets into his van and drives away, leaving me in silence and darkness again.

I understand now. And I am ready.

TWENTY-SIX
SHE COUNTS, TASTING OF SUGAR

After Glen leaves, I straighten the sheets, tuck the corners in, pick up my comforter from the floor. We must have kicked it off while we…my mind gets fuzzy when I refer to Glen and me as a "we." We aren't a *we*. And yet, there *we* were, he and I, in this bed, still warm from when our two bodies joined.

"Did you feel anything, Agnes?" I hear a voice in my head. Is it my voice? Is it Samuel's, taunting me? Is it…someone—or some*thing*—else?

It *just happened*, and I am unable to remember what I was feeling, at least physically. Certainly I felt, in that moment, that my grief had found a mirror, that his grief somehow completed my grief. It was nice to know I wasn't alone. I'm reminded of an old Greek folktale I read long ago about a woman made of sugar and a man made of salt who often quarreled. One day he'd chased her out of their salt home, so she was forced to live in a house of clay. And then the rains came, washing away his house. The salt man almost melted away too, but the woman took pity and let him into her home. He apologized, and they kissed passionately. But they were fused together from rain and tears. When they finally were able to pull apart, he tasted of sweet, and she tasted of salt, and they never fought again.

I'm nearing the end of this journey; I can feel it. All the lights are off, but I've drawn up my blinds so the light from the streetlamps outside filters in. I look at my hands, ghostly in the artificial light. It seems a waste to go to sleep, when I know what I have to do, and yet, I slip under the sheets and lay my head upon my pillow, which smells slightly of Glen, of *other*. His salt on my sweet.

I don't know why I bother coming back here. There's nothing left for me now. The dreaming is a wasteland again, once again through no one's fault but my own. Why was I brought back to rebuild, only to destroy everything again? What was, or is, my purpose here? In coming back? In remembering the pain?

The sun is hidden, the skies gray, and a chill is in the air. The color is fading from here, leached out, like an untouched coloring book. Even the grass is looking gray, almost as if it were made of stone. I'm still dressed in this long gown, the sleeves fluttering behind me in the constant breeze. "Hello?" I call out, knowing no one will answer me.

"Hello?" I say louder, wishing even for just my voice to echo back. I hear rustling in the woods where Ash is buried, and I'm not sure if it's a person, a thing, or just the wind waiting for me there.

I should say goodbye to him, I think, making my way into the forest. Ash's strange tree, the instrument of his death, is still there, blooming its ruby blossoms, undulating strangely in the wind. I hear a twig snap, and my head pops up, trying to make out anything, a shadow, dark eyes, a silhouette.

But there is nothing here. I am alone. I pat the earth on top of Ash and kneel, not caring if I muddy up my long gown. "I miss you. And I am sorry. But I'm going to make it worth something. Thank you. I couldn't have done any of this without you. I don't deserve your love."

I look up one more time to see if there's anyone here, if by chance someone has stayed behind, has survived. I wait a few moments, folding my hands as if in prayer, hoping. But eventually I get up, brush the dirt off my dress, and head back to the courtyard, back to Joshua and Willa, or at least, my memorials to them. Willa's prickly pear blossoms have faded, too. They look frosted over. Joshua's stark, bare branches against the dull sky remind me of a skeleton, and I have trouble reconciling this barren, colorless place with the rich land where I first returned to the dreaming. Even though Oread's Keep had crumbled away, nature was still wild, free, alive.

The dreaming is now just a graveyard. A waiting place. Another in-between. I wonder if this is what *forever* is like, me stuck alone in a place like this, without any visible joy or color. I guess I'll know soon. The thought of it, how soon it's all going to happen, makes my head all swirly. But you know what? At least I won't be afraid anymore. At least I'll *know*. At least it will be over. And that, in itself, is a comfort. *Cowards die many times before their deaths; The valiant never taste of death but once.*

Only one more to go.

Against the cold, I wrap my arms around my middle, remembering the feel of Glen's body pressed against mine, skin to skin, grief to grief. Salt to sugar, sugar to salt, fused together. Momentarily complete.

Lines of Eliot's "The Hollow Men" float into my head, the bit about the space between *desire* and *spasm*. I say the two words over and over again, *desire, spasm, desire, spasm,* until they blend into one jumbled word that means nothing. It's my way of whistling in the dark, giving my fear voice through old words that existed long before I was born and will live on long after I am gone. I whisper the words over and over like an unintelligible prayer, *desirespasm.*

I can hear low chuckling.

"*So you* did *enjoy that, didn't you, Archer?*"

Samuel.

I look around, behind me, up and down, trying to find him. "Where are you?" I demand.

"*I'm where I always am,*" he says.

"But I can't see you."

"*You don't need to see me, because I can see you.*"

It occurs to me that his words are no longer *spoken*—now they seem to form right in my head. Since when could he do that?

"*Oh, I always could, you know. I just thought it would be more…comfortable for you if I spoke aloud.*"

"And now?" I ask, trying not to show my fear and unease that he seems to be able to peer into my mind and pluck out thoughts as if he's making a selection out of a box of chocolates, taking little half-bites to see if he wants to take the whole thought or keep looking for a better one.

"You're nearly done now, aren't you, lamb? Your comfort, well, it's going to be irrelevant soon enough. I thought taking away this part of the charade would help you in the transition."

I lean back against Joshua's bare tree, trying to find strength, trying to let his trunk be my backbone. "I…I am ready," I say, not sure if I mean it or not.

"Good. Because time is running out. And, as I can hear you realizing, there's no need for you to voice your thoughts. I've always been able to hear them."

"I would prefer to speak them out loud, if you don't mind," I say, my hands balled into fists. "I'm looking after my own comfort, thank you." I can feel the bark of Joshua's tree through the thin fabric of this white gown, and the pain of it somehow makes me feel stronger: a fighter, a warrior. I *am* a warrior, aren't I?

More chuckling. *"Of course, little maiden, little archer. It is funny, though, the difference between what you say out loud and what tinkles around in that complicated little mind of yours."*

I hate him. I hate him for invading my privacy. I want to blame him for everything that has happened here. I want him out of my mind.

"'Desire' and 'spasm,' Archer?" he mocks. *"There wasn't too much time between the two, was there? That is, if what I'm seeing in your memories is accurate. Still, I was true to my word, was I not?"*

"Did you make that happen?" I gasp. "Was he real?"

"Of course he was real." Samuel sounds irritated. *"Do you doubt what I am capable of?"*

"I suppose not," I say.

"There's not much time left," he says. *"You need to wake up now. And you need to finish your journey."*

The wind whips up, pinning me against Joshua's tree, the white silky fabric wrapping almost all the way around, blowing stronger, until the tree cracks in half with a sound like a bat breaking at Fenway Park.

I wake up with my arms wrapped tightly around my middle. I am freezing. The wind is rattling the old windows, letting February's bite seep right through. I touch the radiator by the bed. Ice cold.

The heat's shut off again. Always too hot or too cold. Strangely, it's the one "in-between" thing I wish I had: the temperature inside this apartment. But again, no matter; soon these things will be irrelevant. Soon I'll feel nothing.

I *hope* I'll feel nothing.

What do I do? Am I supposed to leave a note, an explanation? No one would believe me if I did. I think of Dad. I think of Vivian. Am I strong enough?

I glance at the time. It's late, but maybe not too late to call Dad. I need to hear his voice one more time, because I don't want to forget. I don't want to forget the sandpaper of his always-present stubble on my face as I peck his cheek. I don't want to forget how safe I feel when my hand is in his. His hands are always warm, powered, no doubt, by his huge, loving heart.

I dial the house, and the phone rings and rings and rings. I get voicemail, Dad's awkward message. "This, uh, you've reached the Larches. I can't figure out this dang thing." Muffled fumbling. "I guess you're supposed to leave a—[*beep*]." It's so *Dad* that I never tire of listening to it, never fail to smile when I hear his technophobic befuddlement.

I hang up. I don't know what to say. How do you say goodbye forever? How do I sum up in sixty seconds how much he is my hero, my rock, my life? How can I leave him?

You already left him, I tell myself. *You left him the minute you walked out of his truck at the airport. You knew you'd never be brave enough for him, never brave enough to come home again.*

It's true, and I know it.

Vivian. It's too late to call her for sure. Against my better judgment, I send her a text: *Viv, u r my fave dirty h00r.*

I get out of bed and stretch, jump up and down a few times to try to warm up. My phone pings as Vivian texts me: *u shd know, u connoisseur of dirty h00rs.* I text back: *Shouldn't that be "connoiseuse"?*

She responds with: *u r a dirty French h00r.* She's awake. I could call her. But…if I call her, I'll want to cling to life, like Anna Karenina and that stupid red bag again. She makes me escape my head and, while I need that most days, right now it won't help me do what I need to. But this exchange seems fitting for us, for our goodbye. It feels right.

I am ready.

I know I've been saying that a lot, out loud, in my head, to myself, to others. I still don't entirely believe it. But maybe if I say it enough, I will begin to believe.

I've thought about the *how* ever since Samuel told me what the final task is. And everything seems so painful, so frightening. It's like having to fly every day for infinity.

And just like that, I know the answer—what do I do to get on the plane? What gives me strength, or at least oblivion, when I most need it?

I scramble in the half-dark of my apartment, looking for my backpack. I dig around it, finding Vivian's scrunchie. I slip it over my wrist. The bottle of lorazepam is still in the front pocket from my trip to Poppy Beach. My physician gives me sixty at a time, because he believes that I would never abuse them.

I thank him in my heart for trusting me, even though I know in this moment that I am not worthy of his trust. I count out how many are left in the bottle as I sit on the bed, letting the streetlights illuminate my hand and the ghostly white pills. I'm tipping them out little by little, and my hand starts shaking. The rest of the pills tumble to the floor, bouncing off the wooden floorboards and sounding like the scuffling and scurrying of little mice feet.

"No, no, no," I cry out in frustration. *Not now.* I let the pills in my hand trickle slowly onto the center of my bed, the covers pulled back. They glow against my dark sheets, like the pebbles Hansel leaves behind him to find his way home. I think of the airplane safety announcements at the beginning of every flight, when the attendants talk about the floor lights that will glow in the event of an emergency. *White lights lead to red lights, which lead to the emergency exits.*

Where will these lead me?

I crawl on my hands and knees by the bed, searching out the little pills and dropping them on the sheets. Does this fall under the five-second rule? Does the five-second rule even apply in this situation? I pat around under the bed, under the couch, reaching as far as my arm will allow.

Even though it would be easier, I don't want to turn on the light. My knees start to ache, and I decide to take a break to count up what I have. I sit on the floor and slide pills from one side of the mattress to the other, almost like an abacus. Counting, counting, counting.

I have forty-five pills. Will it be enough? Why do I feel like I'm counting out bus fare? *Is it enough for the journey?*

I go to the kitchen and fill a glass with tap water. I don't bother letting the water run for a few minutes to get cold, so when I take a sip, it's warm and tastes of the metal pipes. This is it. Here we go. And...*I can't.*

Oh, I'm scared. I'm so chickenshit. *Worthless Agnes. Coward Agnes.* NO.

I am Warrior Agnes. I can do this.

Maybe if I take some pills first, I'll feel calmer about it. I throw a few in my mouth and gulp them down with another sip of water. Then a few more, maybe five at a time. The pills are small, so it's not too horrible.

It's slow, methodical, the pills lined up. *White lights lead to red lights, which lead to the emergency exits.*

By the time I drain the glass, I'm feeling too wobbly to get up to refill it. I'm worried I'll drop it. My hand, already heavy and clumsy, tips the empty glass over as I try to set it safely on the floor, and it rolls back and forth slowly like a pendulum.

Not much time left now. The last few pills I put in my mouth without water. They dissolve readily enough, sweet and powdery. *My sweet to his salt, his salt to my sweet.*

I'm swimming through thick air now, but I know there is one more thing I need to do. I crawl to the closet and try to pull myself up to standing. I'm unsteady, but if I lean against the doorjamb, I'm okay.

Time to unwrap the dress.

My limbs feel like they belong to someone else as I rip open the plastic. *Will it still smell like him?* These stranger's arms touch the holy velvet, carefully unzip the dress. I get the dress off the hanger and stumble to the floor. I hold the fabric up to my face and inhale deeply.

It just smells musty, that's all. It smells like me, and neglect, and years of confinement. There's no evidence that Ian Millbrook ever touched this dress, that he ever sanctified it with his hands.

I'd cry about it, but I can barely form thoughts, my brain feeling as if it's at the bottom of the ocean. I ease my uncooperative legs into the dress while I'm on the floor. All I know is that I have to put this dress on. It's the last thing I have to do. I get up on my knees to pull the dress up more. I peel the pajama top off and toss it aside. I slip my arms through the sleeves, the lining a cool caress. I tug a little to free Vivian's scrunchie from under the velvet. I'm so dizzy now, so dizzy.

Again, it's like a stranger's—or manikin's—arms behind me, zipping up the dress. I can't reach all the way to the top, so the dress lies open in the back, making, I'd imagine, a deep V of my skin, ghostly in the half-light of the fading moon and streetlights.

There. Infinity awaits.

I start thinking of forever, and of nothingness, and I feel the fear again. It's sheer instinct now, like a wounded animal seeking shelter, as I pull myself on my elbows toward the bathroom. The bathtub beckons to me. *Come rest here*, it seems to say, so I crawl to the place where I began this journey a little over a week ago.

The cold porcelain is like a compress on my panicked skin. The solidness of it gives me strength. *I'm still here. I'm still here.* The side of the tub seems so tall. I peer over the edge, my hands on either side of my face. I lean my face into the scrunchie on my wrist, which still smells like Vivian. I gaze into the deep tub: white, cold, an arctic landscape. How will I ever get in?

I think of Warrior Agnes, and I pull myself up, throw a leg over the edge, and fall into the tub. I've done it. This is it.

In my fuzzy head, I think I hear Dad's outgoing voicemail message again. "This, uh, you've reached the Larches. I can't figure out this dang thing. I guess you're supposed to leave a— [*beep*]"

What message should I leave for him? But that's impossible; the phone is by my bed, out of reach, practically a world away from this secure space, my final destination. Still, what would I say to Dad?

I whisper, "I am Warrior Agnes," again and again as I try to force my eyes to stay open. My head is heavy, and I let it rest against the side of the bathtub, my lips against the cool, solid wall of the tub. I look up and notice for the first time that the underside of my soap dish is cracked. I continue to mouth *I am Warrior Agnes* against the side of the old bathtub.

Vivian's scent in my nose, my own name on my lips, Ian's velvet shrouding me, a sweet taste on my tongue: these are the last things I remember before everything goes white. Like an arctic landscape.

I am ready. I am ready.

I am Warrior Agnes.

TWENTY-SEVEN
WARRIOR

If I'm gone, I shouldn't be able to think anything, should I? I shouldn't have a concept of *me*. And yet, here I am, still sort of *me*. Everything is white, and there's not another soul around. It looks like Samuel's kingdom, except he's not here. I can tell; I can't feel him in my head. I don't hear his mocking.

"*Oh no, Archer?*"

"Samuel!" I grind out, no longer afraid. What have I to fear now? I've done it. I've confronted death, *my* death, head on. And I walked through the other side. "I know this isn't your domain."

"*True, true,*" chuckles Samuel. "*You're an observant one. But foolish. Quite foolish.*"

"Where is the Sleeper?"

"*Impatient, are we?*"

"I did what you asked. Now do what I ask. Where is the Sleeper?"

"*Have you? Have you done what I asked? I wouldn't be so sure.*" He clucks his tongue at me, an unsettling, otherworldly clicking sound, like a child's marbles dropped on a stone floor.

"I'm here now, aren't I?"

"*Are you, now?*" he says, amused. "*Are you? Can you see yourself?*"

And I realize that I am just my thoughts. I look for my hands, for my body, and there is nothing.

"How can I speak if I have no body?" I ask.

"Are you really speaking? Or do you just believe you are?"

"I…I don't know," I say, trying to see or identify anything. But it's all white and brightness around me. How am I even *seeing*?

"Where is the Sleeper?" I demand again.

"Still sleeping," he says, laughing. *"You haven't completed the third task, Archer. You're stuck."*

"What?" Now I am getting panicky. "What do you mean, I'm *stuck*? Where am I? What is this?"

"You're in between, my dear."

Fantastic. I'm on some sort of jet bridge to eternity. Maybe this is my own version of hell, never to be one place or another, and to have failed in my mission. And it *was*—it *was* a mission. I believe it's why I was brought here. I am the instrument to relieve the pain of this grieving mother, this haunted girl.

Why couldn't I live for Dad, for Vivian? I'm not sure.

Maybe part of me wanted to save the me that died when Shelly left. If I could prevent the heartache and destruction of abandonment for someone else, then my life will have had meaning. Everything I lived through, suffered through, it would be okay, because it would have led me to do *this*. It would have led me to bring Ian Millbrook back from the dead, to bring back Meg Millbrook's brother from the grave. My pain, my loss, finally would have meaning and worth. If I save Meg's brother and save her, that part of me would live again too.

Except I haven't. And now I'm stuck.

"Am I going to be here forever?" I ask, dreading the answer.

"I cannot tell you that," says Samuel. *"You're out of my domain. I can only observe."*

"That's all you ever do," I snap. I wish I had a body so I could find him, so I could make him feel everything he has put me through. Make him feel what it was like to kill my most loyal friend—not just physically, but make him feel what I did in my heart, that soul-rending pain. But even if I had a body, I'd have to find him first. I know it would be impossible to harm him emotionally—he has no heart. He has no emotions. I don't know for certain, but I am pretty sure I would not be able to harm him physically, as much as I'd like to wrap my hands around his perfect, blindingly white throat...

"Nasty, spiteful—these thoughts don't suit you, Archer," Samuel scolds.

I don't know if it's an hour, or a day, or a year, or several lifetimes that I am aware of *being*, just quietly *being* in this white light. Sometimes I imagine I can see a door, a dark wooden door with mystical gold markings. I let my mind float to it and try to open it, but I have no hands. I see the front and the back of the door at the same time, but it doesn't seem to go anywhere, and the cracks in the panels of wood aren't wide enough to see anything through. *"Are you the Door Beyond?"* I ask, not expecting a reply. Sometimes Samuel talks to me, and sometimes I find I am quite alone. If I had a body, I would mark down the days, scratch them into the wall with a pebble, but there is nothing, no body, no wall, no pebble. Just my mind. So I can only count in my head, but then I lose count, and then I begin again.

"It's time," says Samuel, maybe centuries after I climbed into the bathtub, maybe only seconds.

"Time for what?" I ask, my voice still sounding clear, even from not having been used for—minutes? Days? Weeks? Time has no meaning here. Then again, it's probably not my voice I'm hearing. I have no voice, no ears to hear.

And even though I have no body, I suddenly feel pain, true pain, throbbing, pressing down, like I've traveled from the bottom of the ocean and have the bends. My head feels as though it is going to explode, but I know I have no body. How can I have a head?

"Time to wake up, Agnes Larch. Now."

My head. Oh, my head. I thought death was supposed to be painful and then over. Not like this. I'm cold and wet, and I realize that I must have a body again, to be able to feel these things. It's bright behind my closed eyes, but a different kind of bright than the nothingness of that in-between place. I wiggle my fingers, realizing I have fingers to wiggle. Wherever I am, I'm no longer stuck.

My mouth—*I have a mouth again*, I silently rejoice—is dry, my tongue stuck to the roof of my mouth. I breathe in and out a few times, trying to muster up the energy to open my eyes and find out where I am.

Do it. Do it now, Agnes. Everything feels so heavy; it's taking every bit of strength I have just to pry my eyes open. It's so bright, and even after being in that in-between place of light, my eyes still hurt. It takes them a few moments to focus, and I slowly realize I'm still in my bathtub, staring at the ceiling of my apartment.

"No!" I cry out, slamming my fists on the cold porcelain. *It didn't work.* I can't even do *this* correctly. I'm cold and damp, and I realize I've peed myself. What day is it? Or is this my afterlife?

I doubt this is the afterlife, because it looks just like, well, *life.* And that doesn't make sense.

I'm still wrapped in the old velvet dress, clumsily half-zipped. I stand on unsteady legs and undo the zipper. The dress is ruined. I step out of the soiled velvet and toss it onto my bathmat. I desperately need a shower.

I have no idea what day it is or how long I've been lying here. But I'm here. I'm alive. I'm still here. It really starts to soak in: *I'm still here.* I looked death in the face and said, "Yes, I will. I will take your hand."

So what if I didn't succeed?

I stand right in the stream of cold water, being grateful even to feel cold enough to make my teeth chatter—grateful just to have teeth to chatter. When the water warms up, it's like my body is waking up. *I* am waking up.

I am Warrior Agnes.

I'm scrubbing off my identity in this shower. When I leave this bathtub, I will be a new person. Old Agnes died. Frightened Agnes. Failure Agnes. Only Warrior Agnes is left.

I towel off, avoiding touching the old dress, my old skin. That girl is dead. She died here, in this bathtub.

Wrapped in a towel and with my hair sopping wet, I walk out to my room, leaving steamy foot outlines, ghostly footprints, on the cold wooden floor. I pick up the glass from where it rolled under the bed and gather up the few pills that I missed in the dark. I put them back into the empty bottle, but then I decide to chuck it all in the trash.

What does it matter now? What do I have to fear? Part of me is already dead, and the only part that remains is the warrior, like Achilles held over the fire, his humanity burned away.

I sit on the edge of my bed in the towel. I can hear my hair dripping onto it, a dull, irregular drumbeat. The comforter is still pulled back, and I can see evidence of *whatever* that was with Glen on the dark sheets. *That did happen. He was my sign.*

I turn on my laptop to read the news, hoping against hope that somehow, in some way, that Ian Millbrook is awake. I check the news sites, look at the date. I have been unconscious for two days. I'm lucky to be alive.

There are no news developments on the crash, and when I Google Ian's name, I still see memorials, messages of shock, news articles covering the crash. I see that the Millbrooks have set up a scholarship fund at Butler Academy in his name. I realize, as my heart sinks, that I'd still been hoping that what I did, what I was brave—or stupid—enough to do, would have had an impact. But of course, there is nothing. Of course, because these were just silly dreams. I've been letting these dreams rule over me, make me willing to abandon the people here who I know *do* love me.

Why do I seek only the love of those who don't?

While I'm online, I look up airfare for Easter. I'm going to go home. I *will* see Dad again. No more false promises. I don't have to sit here and *miss him* so much. I can do something about it. I can see him as much as I want, as often as I want. I book a ticket.

I am no longer afraid.

I consider putting my pajamas back on, but I get dressed instead. I'm going to do this right. My legs are still a little unsteady as I go to the kitchen. I fry up some eggs and toast a few slices of bread. I take everything to the table. I will not cram my mouth with hot eggs while standing up at the counter, nor will I balance a plate on my lap while I watch TV. I resolve to sit at the table with my hot breakfast, because I *deserve* to be eating here, as if I'm a special guest in my home. Food has never tasted so good. Maybe that's what happens when you've been unconscious for two days.

I call Dad as I'm mopping up the last of the runny yolk with my toast. I don't even know what time it is. "Ags!" he answers on the first ring. "I was just about to check in with you."

"What time is it?" I ask. My voice is hoarse, sounding wholly unlike me.

"A little after five," he says, yawning. "Sorry, haven't had my coffee yet. Was about to go open the shop, but I...I just really wanted to hear your voice."

I'm almost uncomfortable at the raw honesty and open affection in his words. We don't speak this way. "Me, too," I say, remembering my desperate need to hear just his outgoing voicemail message when I thought I'd never see him again.

"You catching a cold, Ags? Your voice sounds kind of scratchy."

"No," I say, love seeping through me from my heart all the way to my fingertips and toes just from the concern in his voice. I'm still his baby. I will always be his baby. "But hey, Dad, I booked a ticket home for Easter."

"Did you, now? Really?" Dad sounds confused, surprised, skeptical.

"Really. I…I don't think I'm afraid anymore."

"Well, Ags, I don't know what to say."

"I can't wait to see you again," I say, and I'm grinning.

It takes Dad a moment to process, but then he announces, "We are going to have the best Easter ever. You still like chocolate bunnies? I'm going to get you the biggest chocolate bunny you've ever *seen*." I've never heard him so excited.

I laugh, wiping some tears away at his child-like enthusiasm. "You know me. Chocolate anything is good. But don't go overboard."

"Define *overboard*," says Dad in his "serious father" voice.

"If it's bigger than my head, that's too big."

"I'll take that under consideration," he says solemnly, and I can almost see his fingers crossed behind his back. "But it's a good thing your head is really, really big," he adds.

"*What?*" I say, indignant.

"Well," he says, unable to conceal his laughter, "that's my cue to go. Can't wait to see you."

My smile is so wide it hurts my face. "You too, Dad. Love you."

"Yup, you too, kid."

"And I'll have you know my head is perfectly average sized," I blurt as I end the call. I notice I've missed a bunch of texts from Vivian. There's nothing important, and she knows that sometimes I like to keep to myself. Still, I ache to see her. I tap into the phone: *Where r u, u dirty h00r?*

A moment later, she texts back: *Class — looking busy, cuntmuffin.*

I laugh and text: *WTF is a cuntmuffin?*

Beep. *Look in a mirror, cuntmuffin.*

I tap back: *Want 2 have lunch w/this cuntmuffin?*

There's a bit of a pause, and I'm guessing Vivian is waiting until it's safe to text back. *Duh, CM. Meet me @caf?*

She doesn't have much time between her classes, and my day—my life—is completely open. *Today's special: Cuntmuffin. See you @1?* I write back.

Just one word in reply: *Sweet.*

While I wait to meet Vivian, I look through my sketchbook, mourning the loss of my wolves. But it feels different to me somehow, now that I've gone through what they have. Sort of. Maybe they passed through. Maybe they're all right. *Maybe they are imaginary, and you should put them away.*

Where will I go tonight when I sleep? Will I return? Will the dreaming be the same, or will it be different because *I* am different?

Before I leave my apartment, I consider the velvet dress. It is my burial shroud, my old self, my old skin. I shouldn't leave it here. I should be finished with it. I get a plastic grocery bag and pick it up gingerly, trying not to touch any of the wet patches. I'm about to tie the bag handles tight to throw it away, but I can't. My hands won't allow it.

Ian Millbrook touched you through that fabric, I tell myself.

I know it's not good for me to hold onto it. But I also can't bear to throw it away. I reach into my desk drawer and find my scissors. Carefully, as if trimming a delicate bonsai, I cut one perfect square of velvet from the back of the dress where it's still clean, where his hands touched me. I use a glue stick to put the square on a blank page, a patch of dark on this stark, white page. I wonder what I'll draw around it, but I don't have time now, because it'll take me nearly an hour to get to Vivian's school.

Tonight. Before I dream. If I dream...

I finally feel all right tying up the bag, and I toss it in the Dumpster behind the apartment. I feel a twinge of guilt, wondering if I should have made more of a ceremony of it, said some words, left a note inside the bag. But it's too late now. Since it's daytime, I walk through the Fens to the Museum of Fine Arts subway stop. There's a little bridge over a creek I have to cross to get to Huntington Avenue, and I linger a little at the railing, thinking of the Bridge Between.

This bridge is tiny, modern, nothing like the majestic and somewhat terrifying Bridge Between. But it's real, and it's mine, and it's home. I stomp across, owning it, feeling the metal vibrate through my bones.

It's still cold today, but the sun is shining so brightly that I can barely open my eyes. The glare off the snow is blinding; it scrapes against my retinas. Still, I am glad to see the sun. I'm glad to smell the cleanness of air so cold. That is one nice thing about the chill — everything smells fresh, untouched, even though there's litter on the sidewalks, even though we are as unclean as we always are. But in the February cold we all seem pure.

Vivian is waiting just inside the cafeteria, wearing a red puffy vest that makes me think of Marty McFly. I wave madly as soon as I see her, and she sticks her tongue out and flips me the bird. But that's Vivian for "I'm happy to see you, you cuntmuffin."

I still have snow in the tread of my boots, so when my feet hit the linoleum, I skid a little, but Viv is there to catch me. I give her a bone-crushing hug. She's a good head taller than I am, so this means I'm sort of nestled in her boobs, which are encased in the Marty McFly vest.

"Missed you too, you slore," she says, tugging on my hair. "Jesus, Aggles, did you go out with wet hair again?" The tips of my hair are frozen. I didn't even notice, too busy sniffing at the air and squinting.

"Meh." I shrug. "I can't be bothered with hair dryers."

"One of these days you are going to catch your death of hypothermia," she says sternly, and I feel that warm rush seep through me the way I did when Dad was worried I'd caught a cold. I am loved.

I am lucky.

Viv talks my ear off about the latest law school scandals, and we reminisce, as we often do, about the crazier things that happened at Longfellow. "Remember when you kissed that elf guy when we were off our nut on tequila? What was his crazy elfin name?"

"Yanmilk," I say, blushing. I wonder if I should tell her about the other night with Glen, but it feels too private. She'd make too much of it, or too little, and somehow it would cheapen what we experienced. I shake my head again, thinking of Glen and me as a *we*. But *we* were, sugar and salt, fused together through grief, just for that moment. I fiddle with the sugar bowl on the table, slide over the saltshaker, and make them tap together. They don't stick — they clatter, reminding me of Samuel's clucking tongue. "Who was that asshole who used to dump the salt into the sugar bowls?" I ask, trying to clear my head of the memory. *I was dead—no, in between, I* correct myself. I shudder.

"*God*, I never found out," Vivian says, thumping the table. "Do you have any idea how many perfectly good grapefruit halves he ruined for me?"

"Did we ever figure out for sure the salt hooligan was a he?"

"It was a dick move," she says. "Dick moves equal penises, which equal dudes."

"Let's not cast aspersions on penises and those who possesseth them." I say. I hold my hand up before Vivian can interrupt me. "I believe a wise woman once told me that penis biology isn't penis destiny. Or, maybe minus the *penis* part."

"Are we playing *Penis* now?" asks Vivian excitedly.

"No. Oh, no," I say, shaking my head. "Let's not—"

"Penis!" she shouts in her clear, cutting voice. The objective of *Penis* is to yell "penis" the loudest in a public place. Needless to say, I'm fairly certain Vivian is the reigning world champion.

I sigh with resignation. "Penis," I say halfheartedly.

"PENIS!" Vivian counters. The entire cafeteria is now staring at our table.

I wave weakly. "Nothing to see here, folks," I say. "Just a casual lunchtime game of *Penis*."

Vivian takes my response as a cue that the game is continuing. "PEEEEEEEEEEENISSSSSSSSS!" I'm pretty sure I see birds fly out of a tree outside, startled by the noise.

"I yield! I yield! I yield to your mighty *Penis!*" I say, trying to shush her.

Vivian takes a deep breath. Afraid how loud the next outburst will be, I clamp my hand over her mouth. "MRRRRFFFFNRRRRF!" she says, and I can feel the bones in my fingers vibrate.

I should be embarrassed, but I lay my head on the table, unable to stop laughing. I wipe my hand, damp from Vivian's mouth, on her sleeve. "When will I learn that the only winning move in *Penis* is not to play?" I wheeze.

"You taste like ham," she says.

Once we both recover, I get suddenly serious. "Hey," I say, tugging on her arm. "What are you doing for spring break?"

"Not sure. Why?"

"You know how you always talked about going to Europe? We should go. Pick a city. I don't care which. I'll save up the money."

"Shit, Agnes, are you serious?"

"Yeah."

"The flying?"

"I'm going to be okay," I say. And I will. I know it. I think of the dress with one square removed, in its plastic bag, waiting in the Dumpster. *That other girl is dead.*

"I'm going to be late for class, but let's talk about this later. I'm thinking, since you're such a dirty French whore, maybe Paris? But we don't have to decide now." Viv has to run off to class, so she gives me a quick peck on the cheek and rushes out with her bags, her crazy legwarmers, and her Marty McFly vest.

I walk two stops past the closest stop to Viv's school, because I'm just happy to have a body again. As I tromp in the snow, I think of getting on a plane with Vivian and going to Paris, of drunk-flirting with French men and eating crepes and waiting in line to see the Mona Lisa.

I'm finally going to do all those things that I was supposed to do.

The light is already fading as I unlock my front door. I turn on the desk lamp and flop on my belly on the bed, pencil in hand, staring at the square of black velvet and the nothingness around it. I touch the velvet with the pad of my finger, then with the tip of my nose.

For the first time, my hand is still, not drawing. Not knowing what to draw. Maybe this is it, one square of velvet on a white background, one moment of Ian Millbrook. I don't know.

When I sit up, my back is stiff and night has fallen. I must have stared at that page for hours. Even having been *in between* for two days, I'm already tired, so I ready myself for bed. The apartment is cold again, too cold, so I wear my thermals under my pajamas and put the sleeping bag on top of the comforter. I keep the sketchpad by me, tucked under the blanket. My eyelids grow heavy as my head swims with questions.

Will I dream tonight? Will I return?

I don't know, but I do know that if I see Samuel again, I will make him *hurt.*

I am Warrior Agnes.

I'm here, in the dreaming, in Oread's Keep. Joshua's tree is split in two, and the blossoms have fallen off Willa's prickly pear cactus. I'm still in the long white dress. I wonder if I'll ever get the archer's dress back. The color is nearly all gone now from this world, making me wonder if something is wrong with my eyes.

I'm going to go see Ash. I run into the woods to his grave. I remember Samuel's voice in my head when I was *stuck*, and I am suddenly filled with fury. The pain, the mocking…I am done with him.

Ash's strange gold tree glints, the one thing still holding color as everything else bleeds away. It seems to pulse at me, and I think that it is wrong for this vicious plant to mark the spot where such a noble soul lies. I grasp it in both hands, and the stinging is almost unbearable. The ruby blossoms nip mercilessly at my bare hands, begin to snake under my sleeves, burrow under my skin, but I keep pulling. "You are not *worthy*," I hiss, leaning my whole body's weight back. The tree begins to give, loosening its hold on this sacred dirt, and my blood seeps through the white gossamer sleeves where the treacherous blossoms have bitten me.

When I pull the tree out, roots and all, it turns back into the knife. There is pain from the bleeding and that same electric pulsing, but I am no longer afraid of any of it. I think I hear footsteps behind me, so I turn around. "Who's there?" I call.

I must be mistaken. I must be hearing things because I don't want to be alone here. But even the loneliness doesn't frighten me so much now. I march to the Bridge Between with the knife in my hand, blood trickling down my arms.

"Samuel!" I shout at the top of my lungs. "I am back. You *will* receive me." I no longer ask. No more politeness. He deserves nothing.

I run across the Bridge, my bare feet cold but sure, unwavering. As I reach the other end of the Bridge, the white greets me, but there is no sign of Samuel.

"Samuel!" I shout again. "Eternal! I am here, and you *will* receive me."

"*My, my, my, aren't you a little tigress?*" I hear him say in my head.

"I am entering now," I say, setting foot on the nothingness. I'm not afraid. "And you *will* speak out loud. I hold the knife, and I command it."

"How curious," Samuel says aloud. "For once what you say and what you think are exactly the same. What has happened to you?"

I step farther into the white, and Samuel begrudgingly allows the pillars, the sconces, the torches appear. "You were there. You know what happened. I thought you could see everything," I taunt.

I finally reach our meeting room, where Samuel stands calmly, waiting. "Welcome," he says, but there is no friendliness in his eyes. He's not even trying anymore. I've seen what he is, and he knows I no longer believe. He can feel my hatred.

I look over to the dais, to Ash's heart. "This heart does not belong here," I say. "It belongs to me. It is my heart."

"What about the Sleeper?" asks Samuel.

"Were you really going to waken the Sleeper?" I say, inching toward the bell jar.

"Archer, I do not quite understand your lack of trust. I do intend to waken the Sleeper, but you have not completed the third task."

"You take too much pleasure in my suffering for me to trust you. In good faith I tried to take my life, to offer it for the Sleeper's own. And you mocked me."

"Perhaps, Archer, something is lost when I try to speak your language." He's backpedaling.

"I've seen the dark, the malevolence, in you," I say, moving ever closer to Ash's heart. "You try to mask it with this brightness." I gesture around me at his kingdom, at him. "But I know now. I know."

I turn quickly, running for the bell jar. I know I couldn't touch the glass before, but somehow, in my heart, I know the knife will let me pass. I use the hilt to smash the glass.

"What have you *done?*" shrieks Samuel.

"I'm taking this back. It doesn't belong to you." My hands are cut up from the glass, but I don't care, because I'm holding the jewel by my heart again. I don't know what I'll do with it, but I won't let it stay here with this cruel god.

"Foolish, foolish Agnes Larch. It was never about you. And it was never about me. The rules —"

"I'm tired of the rules. I am a princess. I am a warrior."

"Are you? How brave you are now, little maiden." There's something almost like pride in his voice.

I cradle the heart near my own, and it seems to gleam a little, almost seems to beat again with mine. At the same time I find myself struggling to take a breath. "What's wrong with me? What did you do?" I gasp, choking.

"Believe it or not, my dear, you can't blame me for all your problems." His face is unperturbed, his shock at my actions smoothed back away.

The room seems to grow even brighter, and I cough and squint. "Are you doing this to me?"

"You begin to tire me, Archer, with your petty accusations."

The room is brighter now, even brighter, and my skin starts to burn. The knife has been pulsing in my hand this whole time, and maybe the shocks have ramped up in such small increments that I haven't noticed how intense they've become. But I can't ignore it now. I writhe in pain. I'd scream, but I can't draw a breath.

With the last of my strength, I lunge at Samuel, trying to sink the knife into him. But he easily dodges me. Of course. He can read my thoughts.

"Little lamb, you disappoint me with this anger, this blame. I only wanted to help you."

I'd laugh, but I have no more strength, and I sink to the floor, gasping for air. How is it that dying in the bathtub was so painless? This is agony. My skin, my skin, I claw at myself trying to find relief, and Samuel looks down on me with a smile, a gentle smile.

"My goodness, little warrior. I didn't think you had it in you." His voice is filled with...admiration?

"What do you mean?" I manage to croak out in between coughing fits.

"You're completing the third task." I'm vaguely aware he is standing before me, his hands folded neatly before him, but my vision is going blurry, and he looks like a child's watercolor picture dropped into a rain puddle, like an eyeless reflection in a fogged bathroom mirror.

In front of me the Door Beyond appears, solidifies, and I crawl toward it, every part of me aching. I clutch Ash's heart to me as I crawl, pressing it so hard into my chest that it leaves an impression on my skin. I don't understand him. I don't understand anything. The pain, the pain is indescribable, unbearable. "*Why does it hurt so much?*"

"It hurts because you're dying, dear one," he says gently, crouching near my head.

I can't keep my eyes open. I just want this—whatever *this* is—to end. "Please," I whisper through parched lips. "Please." I don't even know who I'm talking to or what I'm asking. My free hand reaches up, reaches to try to touch the handle of the Door Beyond, and I think I feel it in my palm, the same, cool ceramic doorknob as my bedroom in my father's house. Do I see the same tiny roses painted on the handle?

Do I imagine it when I hear Samuel say, "I will waken the Sleeper"? Do I imagine when he says, "Rest now, your journey is finished"? I feel something brush my cheek tentatively, then tenderly, and I think I see…but no, it couldn't be. That face. *Oh, sweet one*, I think. *It was you? It was you all along?* I should be upset, but instead I find I'm glad. I clutch Ash's heart to me, and then…

And then there is no more.

TWENTY-EIGHT
THE SLEEPERS AWAKE

In a small apartment by the law school, Vivian Park sleeps. She usually sleeps soundly — "like the dead," she's been told by friends, family, and lovers who have tried to rouse her from slumber before she was ready. She's been told she snores. She's slept through all kinds of things — even an earthquake when she was visiting her grandmother in Los Angeles. But this day, she wakes up, afraid. Vivian Park is not used to feeling terror like this, silly monsters in the dark. Even as a child she slept without fear of what might be lurking under her bed or in the closet. But this early morning, so early it may as well be night, she bolts up in her bed, where she's fallen asleep with a law textbook under her pillow.

"Agnes," she says out loud, not knowing why.

She gets up and fumbles with the remote control. When the TV warms up, she sees a breaking news report about a fire. These are fairly common in the winter here — so many old buildings with faulty wiring, so many space heaters foolishly placed near curtains or bed skirts. But she has a terrible feeling in the pit of her stomach, and she is not as surprised as she should be when she recognizes the building, the apartment where her best friend in the world lives.

Without thinking, she puts extra layers on over her pajamas and bundles up. There's a cabstand near her place, so she hops in and tells the cabbie to head to the Fenway. Her coat is half-buttoned, and the cabbie looks her over, thinking she's doing some Cab of Shame after a tryst she already regrets. There's little traffic at this hour of the early morning, so it doesn't take long before they are there, but the street is jammed up with flashing lights, ambulances, police cars, and the tall masts of news-vans' broadcasting antennae.

"I cahn't get you closah," the cabbie says in his thick Boston accent, and Vivian fumbles in her jacket pockets, finding a crumpled ten-dollar bill and slipping it through the partition. "Is that yah house on fiyah?" asks the cabbie, but Vivian shakes her head, unable to speak.

"Take keeyah now," he says kindly before pulling away, worried about the look on her face.

Vivian nods, not really processing his words as she wraps her arms around herself and rushes forward past the parked cars, the emergency vehicles, the news reporters scoping out the best spots to deliver their reports. The apartment residents are huddled in blankets, looking up in shock as the building smokes, flames still licking around the roof.

Vivian starts pushing through the crowd of residents, searching for Agnes. "Has anyone seen Agnes? Agnes Larch? Really tiny, brown hair? Lives on the third floor?" She grabs people indiscriminately, overcome with panic. The residents shrug, some of them quietly weeping, worried about losing their possessions, not having a place to live. They know who Agnes is, but no one has seen her. They all shake their heads, murmur "no" and "sorry."

Vivian continues to scan the crowd, her back to the smoking building, when she feels it. Suddenly, she stops in her tracks and her blood runs cold. After she musters up the courage, she turns slowly around and is not surprised when she sees firemen exiting the building with a stretcher covered in a sheet.

"No, no, no," Vivian sobs, rocking back and forth. She doesn't need to get closer or ask the firemen to know who is under that sheet. She knows. She realizes she's known since the minute she was shaken from sleep. She puts her face in her hands and weeps, her ragged breath leaving clouds of steam in the cold air, puffs of visible grief as the sun begins to rise in the east, blood red, giving not even a shred of warmth as it climbs into the pale sky.

In a large house in a small town on the Lost Coast of California, five grieving people sleep: four members of one family, and an outsider. A husband and wife cling to each other in the center of the king-size bed, his arms wrapped around her middle, even in deep slumber. She had been crying herself to sleep for days until her husband begged her to take the Xanax the doctor had prescribed her. Now every night she drops to sleep placid and blank, numb and slurring, but at least she is getting the rest, short, merciful bursts of forgetfulness. The husband lies awake next to her most nights, listening to her drugged breathing, wondering how many times his heart can break before it stops beating entirely. Eventually he places one hand on the thin fabric of her nightgown, watching it rise and fall on the tide of her breath until his eyelids grow heavy. With closed eyes, he focuses on her breathing, feels the unevenness of the skin on her belly that stretched and grew taut and shrank back again three times. Only one of those three souls that began under this skin still lives, sleeping tonight under the same roof.

The jangling phone makes the husband sit up, panting and clutching his chest. He never sleeps well, and he won't take the Xanax he too has been given. He feels that one of the two should be alert, irrationally afraid that if they both sleep too soundly, that more tragedy will find them. *Vigilance.* The wife merely groans a little and flips over, but he picks up the phone, hand trembling, reminding himself that everyone he loves most is under this roof. *It's okay, it's okay.* What more bad news can come in the middle of the night?

"Millbrook residence," he answers, voice shaking. He quietly takes in the voice on the other end of the line, brusque and professional. He exhales in exhaustion, squeezes his eyes shut, and says, "Thank you. Yes. I understand." He places the receiver back on the cradle carefully, trying to make as little noise as possible. He leans against the headboard with his fist pressed against his mouth, fighting his urge to sob out loud, trying not to wake his wife. But then he realizes that he needs to wake her. She should know.

He shakes her gently, and she whimpers a little, a tiny crease forming between her eyebrows. He shakes her again, a little less gently, and her eyelids flutter open and closed a few times before she too wakes in a panic.

"What's wrong?" she whispers, her voice tinged with fear.

He holds her to him. "They found him. They found his body."

The two of them weep together in the dark, the pain as fresh and raw as when they got the first phone call. Neither of them realized until this moment how much they'd held out hope against all odds that the whole thing was just a bad dream, that they'd find him alive, that it was a mistake and he had never gotten on that plane. That he'd call them or walk through the front door as if none of this had happened. "Mom! Dad! Why are you looking at me like that?" he'd say.

After the first wave of sobbing passes, the man cups his wife's face in his hands and wipes her tears away with his thumbs. He kisses her softly on each cheek, and then on her mouth. Her breathing calms. Finally she speaks. "Our baby can rest now," says the wife in a quiet, calm sorrow, her hand resting on her belly, remembering the life that once fluttered under her fingertips.

"Should we wake Benjamin?" asks the man.

"He'd want to know," decides the wife.

They get out of bed, put on bathrobes and slippers. The house can be drafty and cold. Hand in hand, they creep out of their room, down the hall, and knock softly on their living son's door.

Gripping the down comforter in tight, angry fists, Benjamin fitfully sleeps. He doesn't live here anymore, but he's taken a leave of absence from college for the remainder of the semester, wanting to make sure his mom and dad are okay. At least that's what he tells himself. But deep down, he's afraid he's going to fall apart without them now that his best friend is gone. He knows they don't expect him to fill his brother's shoes, but he feels his brother's absence all around him in the house, in the whole goddamn world. Some days he forgets that Ian is gone; other days he can at least pretend it never happened. But then he walks by the empty space where the piano used to be, a cavity in a rotted tooth. And then he remembers. *Ian's gone. Ian's gone. Ian's gone.*

He grinds his teeth in his sleep now, some mornings waking up with so much pain that he can't even speak for the first few hours of the day. He'll pour himself some coffee and hold the hot mug against his face until he feels his jaw loosening up again. What would Ian say? He used to grind his teeth as a child, in the old house they lived in before they moved to Poppy Beach, where they shared a bedroom. Ian used to lob pillows at him in the middle of the night to make him stop grinding. If he woke Benjamin up from a particularly nice dream (at that age, it usually involved a never-ending supply of ice cream and cake), Benjamin would leap out of bed and tackle Ian. They'd wrestle and punch each other, all in good fun, until their parents would pound on the door and demand to know what the hell was going on in there. They didn't understand. You could punch your brother in the stomach or sit on his face and fart and hold him down until he was begging for mercy, tears of laughter running down his face. It didn't mean you hated him. It was just part of what brothers *did*.

In his half-asleep state, he's remembering wrestling with Ian in the middle of the night in the old house, his hands mistaking his blanket for Ian's funny old-man button-down pajamas. He's remembering how they'd grapple with each other, laughing and shushing the other. They didn't want to wake their parents. Neither brother wanted to get the other in trouble.

So when he hears the knock on the door, he mumbles into his pillow, "Honest, Mom and Dad, nothing's going on in here. We're just playing."

The knocking is louder, more insistent, and Benjamin wakes up fully, momentarily confused that he's in this *other* room, this *other* house, this Ian-less world. He looks over to his left, where his brother's bed would have been in their old room. He swings his legs around the side of the bed and places his feet on the cold floor. "Be there in a sec," he says gruffly, and he opens the door to see his mom and dad with tear-streaked faces. "What is it?" Benjamin asks, eyes wide with concern. "Is everything okay? What's happened?"

"No, Benjamin, it's good," his mother says, placing a cool hand on his cheek.

"They've found Ian," says his dad, swallowing hard. "They've… identified his body."

He takes a few steps forward and enfolds his parents into his arms, squeezing them tightly. He's much taller than either of them — he'd outgrown his mom while he was still in junior high, and he easily overtook his dad when he hit his second — or was it third? — growth spurt in high school. Now he wishes he were small again, small enough to crawl into his mom's lap while she'd rub his back and sing lullabies into his ear. But instead he crushes them in a hug.

"Easy there, Benjamin," says his mom, her eyes glittering with tears but a sad little smile on her face. "I'm your mother, not a squeak toy."

Benjamin laughs through his crying, and the three of them are just one big mass of arms and backs and tears, holding each other, a strange celestial body. Ian is coming home at last. They found his body. It'll make it real, final. And as much as that hurts, to be forced finally to say goodbye, it's still better than the not knowing, or thinking his body was lost forever.

After a moment, the good father says, "Should we tell Gillian?"

Benjamin says, "You guys go back to bed. I'll tell her." They nod, grateful, and shuffle off to bed, although they know they will not be able to sleep now.

Benjamin creeps down the hallway, then down the stairs to the guest room. He raps lightly on the door.

In this strange bed far from the apartment she once shared with her best friend, Gillian sleeps. She'll never get used to this mattress, the smell of unfamiliar detergent in the sheets. When she has trouble sleeping here, she thinks of herself as the princess and the pea, and then corrects herself, the *widow* and the pea. Only she never was married, or engaged, or, hell, even *dating* Ian in the first place. Why don't they have a word for someone whose best-friend-but-I-wish-we-had-been-more has died? All the same, the Millbrooks were kind enough to let her stay here after the memorial. She dreads returning home. She doesn't feel brave enough to be faced with the *already was*, let alone the *might-have-beens*, the life she had in the past and had fantasized about in the future. Benjamin has said that he would go with her, whenever she feels up to returning, to help sort through Ian's things and look for a new roommate. He said that between two broken people, they might make one strong person.

Benjamin has been wonderful to her, not making her feel like it's too weird that she should be hanging around so long after the memorial. It's not as if Mr. and Mrs. Millbrook have been deliberately cold — no, she knows the shock on their faces, that lost, frantic look that you get when you find yourself trapped in the worst nightmare of your life and you just can't wake up no matter what. So she doesn't blame them for seeming to look through her. They're barely holding the pieces of themselves together. But Benjamin…he's been the only one she can — or wants to — talk to, the only one who seems to understand. Some nights he sneaks down to her room with late-night snacks if he sees the light seeping out from the crack underneath the closed door. Sometimes they'll just sit there in their pajamas, stuffing Oreos in their mouths, sharing their favorite Ian stories.

So as Gillian is awoken from her dreams of princesses, widows, unrequited love, and peas, she isn't too frightened or surprised at the light knocking. She creeps to the door, placing one hand against it, leaning her forehead against the polished wood. "Benjamin?" she asks. "Is that you?"

"Yeah. Can I come in?"

She opens the door, gesturing Benjamin inside. He doesn't have cookies tonight. He pulls her blanket up neatly, and plunks himself down near the foot of the bed. She sits near the headboard, hugging her knees to herself. After a bit, she pulls the pillows out from underneath the comforter, putting one behind her back and offering the other to Benjamin, who takes it from her with a grateful nod. He doesn't put the pillow behind his head or back, just clutches it as if it were a basketball he's getting ready to pass.

"What's up?" she says.

"Mom and Dad just woke me up," he says, squeezing the pillow like an accordion. "They found him…his body."

"Oh," says Gillian in a small voice. It's less a word than it is her breath just expelled out of her, as if she is a deflating balloon.

"Yeah," he says, peering up behind the pillow to see how she's doing.

"I…I guess that's a good thing, right?" she says, looking up at the ceiling. She's trying not to cry again. She's cried so much the past few weeks that her eyes are constantly puffy, her skin splotchy. She blinks quickly a few times, and two fat tears roll down her cheeks. "Fuck," she says, angrily brushing the tears away. "I'm so fucking sick of crying."

"Yeah."

They sit in silence for a while. She rests her head on her knees.

"You loved him, didn't you," Benjamin says, watching her.

"Of course I did," she mumbles into her knees. "You know I did."

"I mean, you *loved* him."

So Ian's brother has figured it all out, how she wanted so much more from him than he was willing to give. She kept thinking he'd come around eventually. Humiliated and despondent, she can't bear to look at Benjamin. Tears slide out of the corner of her eyes in a constant, slow stream. But she looks so beautiful to him, like a sad garden sculpture, a trickling fountain. Without thinking, he scoots over closer and strokes her hair, just letting her cry.

She closes her eyes at his touch, so familiar yet so not. She hates that she hates him a little for *not* being Ian, and she hates herself a little that sometimes, like right now, she doesn't really care, that she's okay with his being just Benjamin.

She sits up, and he jumps away, afraid he's crossed a line. "Sorry," he mumbles.

She shakes her head, letting her curls fall into her eyes, and takes his hand in hers. He doesn't pull away. They sit, side by side, legs straight out. They lean against the headboard. She rests her head on his shoulder, and they hold hands, not speaking.

They don't need words.

In a large house in a small town somewhere on California's Lost Coast, four people in two bedrooms now lie awake, and only one, the child, remains asleep. The husband and his wife hold each other, both feeling drained but strangely calm. Maybe it's just temporary numbness. Or maybe their souls have calloused. In any case, they will be okay. They will make it through this, the same way they've gotten through so many other sorrows. There is enough love to hold them together.

Downstairs, the brother and the best friend lie next to each other on top of the covers, fingers intertwined. *What would Ian think?* the brother wonders.

Is it possible to be unfaithful to someone who was never yours? wonders the best friend.

The brother leans down and kisses the top of the best friend's head chastely. She squeezes his hand in response. *I think he'd be happy,* the two of them think, separate from the other but of one mind.

All is quiet in this large house in a small town on the Lost Coast of California where four people lie awake and one child sleeps. The man and his wife, the brother and the best friend, they all are alert and watchful, listening to the breathing of their respective companions.

Their loved one will soon be at rest. They are full of sorrow, yet still thankful that the heavens have at least found their lost one, that he will finally be home. It's painful that it is real, but it's a good kind of pain, like the pain as your skin mends itself back together after a bad cut.

There's no sound in the large house in a small town on the Lost Coast of California, no sound but the inhale, exhale of four people beginning to close doors and move into new rooms of their lives. Quiet, still, a formal and stoic grieving. No sound but the inhale, exhale of a child still asleep.

The man and his wife, the brother and the roommate, breathing, grateful for the warm body next to them, grateful for the beginnings of closure. They, all four, begin to drift back to sleep.

And then...

And then a shriek fills the air, an otherworldly shriek. It's a voice no one in the house has ever heard before, and the man and his wife, the brother and the roommate, all are awake again, wide-eyed and fearful. The brother drops the hand of the roommate, worrying it is some sort of alarm, that somehow Ian disapproves.

There is another shriek, and the wife gets up again out of bed, puts her slippers back on. "Henry," she says, "something's wrong."

Henry says one word, one word only, before he bolts out the door, his wife on his heels. "Meg."

They run to their daughter's room, just a few doors down from their own. The shrieking is coming from inside. "Oh no," murmurs the wife. "My poor baby, what's happening to her?"

"Gretchen, it's going to be all right."

"How do you know?" Gretchen angrily whispers in the dark.

"I don't," admits Henry, hanging his head. "I just needed to say that."

They take hands, and Henry opens the door. The two cower as the door opens wide, as their eyes try to adjust to the utter darkness of Meg's room. She wants all the light shut out in the dark, too afraid of shadows on the walls. They had to order the blackout curtains for her room online. Eventually, the *something* light from the hallway is enough for them to see her small form.

She is sitting up in bed, holding her head in her hands, her fingers tangled in her long matted hair. The shrieking is coming from her mouth.

They have never heard her scream.

Then she starts to cry: loud, body-wracking sobs. She's always cried silently before. She is mumbling something—*actually speaking!*—repeatedly.

"What's she saying?" whispers Gretchen, afraid to come any closer. "*Gag?* What's gagging?"

"No." Meg surprises them by looking them in the eye and speaking—*speaking!*—out loud to them. "Not *gag*."

Henry and Gretchen take a step back at the fierceness in her voice—*her voice.*

"*Aggie*," corrects Meg.

"Aggie?" asks Henry, the first to recover from the shock. "What is *Aggie?*"

"Not what. Who. I can't see her anymore," says Meg. And she screams again.

The brother and the roommate listen, looking up at the ceiling. Two screams. Then scurrying of feet, and then silence. At the third scream, the brother stands up. "I'm going up there. This isn't right."

"I'll come with you," says the roommate, reaching for his hand. He doesn't pull away. He lets her slip her elegant hand into his clumsy one. They are both a little braver when their skin touches, and they squeeze hands tightly as they climb the stairs up to the second floor. The roommate understands now what Benjamin means when he says that two broken people might be able to make one person strong enough. She'll be able to deal with the apartment if Benjamin comes with her.

"I think it's Meg," says Benjamin, and Gillian nods.

"You're all right, Meg," he hears his dad say. "You're safe."

"*Aggie*," weeps Meg, "*Aggie, Aggie, Aggie, Aggie, Aggie.*"

Benjamin and Gillian walk into the room. "Did...was...was that Meg talking?" asks Benjamin.

"*Aggie*," wails Meg again.

"What happened, Dad?" He touches Henry on the shoulder with his free hand. The good father turns around, his eyes drawn to where Benjamin and Gillian hold hands. In the dark, no one can tell that

Gillian is blushing. She feels confusion from her roommate's father, and embarrassed, she tries to pull her hand out of Benjamin's grasp. Benjamin shakes his head and holds on more tightly. With a squeeze of his hand, he seems to say, "You don't have to explain. Apart, we are two broken people, and together we are one strong one."

"Meg…" answers Henry finally. "She's…*talking* now. She woke up screaming, and now she's talking."

"What happened, kidlet?" asks Benjamin, pushing past his dad to see Meg's wide, frightened eyes. His mom sits next to Meg, trying to smooth down her hair.

"I'm awake now," she says. "But I can't see her anymore."

Benjamin finally lets go of Gillian's hand. She understands. Family first. Benjamin gets on Meg's other side, wraps his long arms around her. "You're talking, Megapixel. It's nice as heck to hear your voice."

She throws her arms around his neck and squeezes hard. "Thank you."

"Big bro Benjie is here," says Benjamin. "I know I can't be like Ian, but it's you and me now. And the Millbrook kids stick together, right, Megatron?"

"Uh-huh," she says, pressing her wet face into the side of his neck.

"Are you going to be all right?" he asks solemnly, pulling back and touching the end of her nose.

"I'm fine," she says. "But *Aggie*…" And she begins to weep again.

Still, each word that passes her lips is a treasure for her adopted family. They don't understand what has happened tonight, if finding Ian's body has somehow unlocked her, if the events are at all related. But she can't have known about finding the body. They hadn't even gotten to tell her the news yet. They're not going to question it too much, though. They will take it for what it is: a gift. One bright spot in this living nightmare of the recent past.

"Well," says the mother. "Who wants to go downstairs for some hot chocolate?"

"Mommy, please," says Meg, exhausted, leaning on her adopted mother's shoulder.

Gretchen can't explain the feeling in her chest, the aching in the parts of her heart that are gone forever, nor can she explain how that simple word, *Mommy*, spoken out loud to her for the first time by a daughter, seems to fill in the cracks and make her feel whole. "Oh, Meg," she says, cradling her littlest baby. "I love you so much. You know that, right? So much?"

And in a large house in a small town on the Lost Shore of California, five people traipse downstairs for hot chocolate, none quite understanding what has happened this night. But they know their lives will never be the same. They know when the hand of the divine has intervened, even if they don't know how or why.

The investigating officers walk through the smoky wreckage of the third floor apartment, the one where that girl died. No one else died in the four-alarm fire—everyone else got out of the building on time. So why this one? Why this one girl? She was young—she shouldn't have had trouble escaping on time. She shouldn't have slept through the fire alarms, the knocking on the doors, the sound of sirens outside.

There's not much left here, and it's hard to imagine this used to be someone's home. Everything is smoke damaged, waterlogged. It could take days to get to the bottom of this mystery. Officer Williams's eye travels to the young woman's bed. This is where she died, where she was found. Smoke inhalation, the coroner's office had said.

In a room that is mostly in blacks and whites and smudges of gray, an intact notebook of some sort draws attention. What…what is this? Officer Murray is busy checking one of the other rooms, so Williams picks up the notebook with his latex-gloved hands. A sketchpad. How did this paper not burn or at the very least get drenched and warped? It's bone dry and completely intact.

Curious, he opens it to the first page. On the front cover is written a note, a name, and an address. He's moved by what he sees, and he can't get the image of the fragile, sad girl they kept flashing on the local news and running in that free paper they give outside the *T* in the mornings. This was her last request. It's not procedure, but…screw it. He slides the notebook and the small object he finds beside it into a large evidence bag and tucks it into the back of his pants, under his policeman's jacket. He could get fired if anyone finds out, but it's not as if there were anything criminal about this fire. The police dogs could smell no accelerant, and the landlord checked out.

He may still be held accountable because of the faulty wiring in the building, but most likely it was the space heater on the second floor that caused the initial blaze. Hell, it could have been something as simple as someone falling asleep while smoking in bed.

How can he deny that sad girl her last request? Her eyes still haunt him. He can see them when he closes his eyes at night. If he doesn't do this for her…even the thought of turning this sketchbook in as evidence makes his heart heavy, saturated with sorrow.

Let them fire him. He knows what's right.

"How you doing in there, Williams?" asks Officer Murray from the other room. "Find anything?"

"Oh, just fine, nothing new here," he replies, patting his back to make sure the sketchpad is secure and not bulging enough to arouse suspicion. He thinks it will be okay. These extra-long Boston Police winter jackets hide a multitude of sins — and in his case, evidence.

"Seems pretty open and shut, this one," says Officer Murray. "See this? Batteries missing in the smoke detector. She must have been unconscious from the smoke before she could hear the rest of the noise anyway. Damn shame."

"Yeah." Officer Williams nods.

"Are we done here? I want to get some coffee."

"I don't think we're going to find anything here," Officer Williams says, packing up the evidence kit and putting it back into the large duffel.

He's sweating a little, nervous about what he's doing, but he thinks about those sad, dark eyes. She was barely an adult. He thinks of his own sweet daughter, around her age. If she'd died in something like this…he swallows thickly. He'd want her last wish to be carried out.

He glances over at Murray, who seems to be dreaming already of donuts. Yeah, he'll be able to do this. He just needs to ride around with this sketchpad tucked under his jacket for a few more hours. He'll go right to the post office on his way home, the one by South Station that's open all night.

Poor girl. It's the least he can do.

It was nothing like the memorial they'd had before there even was a body to prove that their beloved son, their beloved brother, was gone. This one was just for family. Henry had flown out himself to Chicago to pick up what remained of his son's body, identified only by DNA samples. He'd had what was left cremated there, tucking his son's ashes in his carry-on bag. He'd wanted to cradle the silver canister in his arms the way he did when his Ian had been born, so tiny and fragile, wrapped in the hospital's rough cotton receiving blanket. But the metal was cold, the canister rigid, not at all like that warm little bundle that gurgled and cooed and rooted around the father's shirt, looking for milk. "Hey, buddy, you're barking up the wrong tree," he'd said, handing the precious bundle back to his amazing wife. She was positively radiant as she sat in the bed, waiting to nurse the baby, their baby. Their first child. He was perfect.

The metal canister…how could it contain that beautiful boy?

They stood shoulder to shoulder, all dressed in black, in the light rain. More like mist. More like being inside a cloud.

Henry appreciates that the cemetery is small and quaint enough to have the option to hire a guy to dig the hole, instead of having some big construction machine make the space in the ground. For sweet Emmy, they'd had no choice, even though her casket was heartbreakingly small. But Ian's ashes are so tiny, tinier even than his newborn body. And he worries that a machine might hurt Emmy's casket. He knows his fears are irrational—what could harm her now? But still. He doesn't want anything to disturb her slumber.

They don't have to dig a hole too deep—the canister is small, after all. The undertaker's shovel hits something hard the first or second time he pierces the earth. It's a small rock, a shiny thing, triangular, unusual.

"Meg, isn't that the rock you lost?" his wife asks, leaning down to examine the object.

Meg nods. She runs forward and picks up the glinting rock from the freshly overturned earth. "This stays here," she says, her chin jutting out. Henry still hasn't grown accustomed to his daughter's voice. It startles him every time, despite how thankful he is that this miracle has happened.

They lower the canister in, and each family member takes turns dropping a handful of earth into the hole. When it is Meg's turn, she drops her tiny handful of dirt and then falls to her knees. She brings the rock up to her lips and says, "Goodbye, obsidian," before dropping it with a loud *clunk* into the hole.

Her stockings are muddy when she stands up again, and she takes her mother's hand. The husband, his wife, and their daughter head to one car, but the son and Ian's roommate go to the son's. Henry has noticed the two have been spending a lot of time together, but he's also noticed the way the tiny worry lines in their foreheads seem to go away when they are by each other's side.

Good, he thinks. *I bet Ian would have liked that.*

In Henry's car, everyone is quiet as they drive back to their house, each one, the mother, the father, the sister, lost in thought, in sorrow. But when they drive down a stretch of street, Meg screams. "Stop here!" she demands. "We have to stop."

"Meg, honey, what's wrong?" her mother asks.

The daughter bangs her fists on the window. "We have to stop here! Please! Please stop!"

Henry doesn't understand it, but he doesn't understand much of anything of the last few weeks. As requested, he stops the car. "What do you need, Meg?"

But Meg has already unlocked the door and dashed out. "Meg, wait!" shouts Gretchen, opening her door.

"No!" she shouts. "You stay there. I'll be back in a second. I'm safe. I'm okay."

Gretchen watches her daughter dash across the street. There's an old, beat-up Oldsmobile in the driveway parked by a truck from Larch's Bait and Tackle. This must be Peter Larch's house. She'd heard the news reports about the horrible tragedy that had happened to that girl, his daughter…what was her name? Amelia? No, no, that doesn't sound right. A-something, something old fashioned. Agnes—that's it. She looks up at the windows of the house. She knows how he feels. She wishes him some peace, some comfort.

"No, Meg, don't bother him," she begins to call out, but her voice fails her. She watches Meg stop by the old sedan. She's running her hand along the bumper. Meg reaches into her jacket pocket and pulls out an apple. What on earth is she doing?

She watches her daughter carefully peel the sticker off the apple and place it on the bumper, which seems to be littered with them.

Meg climbs the front stairs in her muddied stockings. Gretchen wants to stop her, to run across the street and tug her back, but something, a twinge in her belly where she feels the emptiness, tells her to stay where she is.

Meg stands on the front stoop, her back to them, and rings the doorbell.

It's the middle of the day, but still, Pete Larch sleeps, half-drunk, on his sofa. He hasn't shaved in days. He's shut down the shop ever since he got the news. *Closed indefinitely*, he'd had Diana write on a note on the door. He's slipping. This is what would have happened to him when his wife left him, but back then he'd had his daughter to live for, his daughter to be strong for. And now, now she is gone.

Who does he live for now?

He didn't think anything was out of the ordinary when the phone rang in the shop last week. He wasn't even alarmed when Diana had said with a hand on her mouth, "It's the Boston Police on the line for you." He'd been too busy daydreaming about giant chocolate bunnies. His little girl was coming home again.

Smoke inhalation. A fire. The investigation had found there were no batteries in her smoke alarm. He'd already had a few vulture lawyers come to him to ask if he wanted to try to sue the building owner for negligence.

He doesn't care about money. He just wants his baby back, his beautiful Ags. She was going to come home for Easter. He hadn't known how much he'd been lying to himself when he said he was okay without her. He'd believed it was the truth until she'd come home suddenly a few weeks ago. Sure, it was for some boy she'd gone to school with, but he still got to have her under his roof again for a few nights, right? He didn't know he could sleep so soundly, knowing that his baby had returned home, if only for a visit.

When he watched her walk away from him at the airport, he fought the urge to shout out, "Don't leave me!" But he didn't want to embarrass her. And besides, this was what he was used to — the people he loved the most just walking away from him.

The funeral was yesterday. It had all happened so quickly. He'd had to do all the paperwork involved to bring his baby's body home. Diana had helped a little. She was a smart one. The funeral was small, but that Colby girl was there with her two kids. He couldn't stop looking at them, and his heart broke all over again realizing he'd never have grandkids of his own, never would be called "Grandpa Pete."

He'd stood in his one good suit, the same one he used to wear when he visited Ags out in Boston, the same one he'd worn for Longfellow commencement. How he'd hooted and cheered then, wanting to stand up in his seat as she walked across the platform and received her degree! He'd never been prouder.

But it was always like that. Every day, he'd never been prouder of his beautiful Agnes. He could never believe how such a beautiful, smart, loving young lady had come from him. Sure, he missed Shelly. He still dreamed of her most nights. But all that hurt went away whenever he could see Agnes's shining face, the way she'd look at him like he was the best daddy in the world. She made him feel worth something.

And just like that, one phone call could take that all away.

He's startled from slumber by the doorbell. "Goddamn it, who is it now?" he mumbles to himself as he rubs his face. All week it's been nosy ladies coming over with casseroles, as if a Pyrex dish of cream of mushroom soup and some noodles is going to make up for the fact that his baby is gone, that he is all alone.

He stumbles on his way to the door as the bell rings again. "Keep your pants on," he calls out.

He's ready to bite the head off of whoever is at the door, but he is shocked when he sees that it's just a little girl. He opens the door on autopilot, not aware of any of his actions. His whole body feels numb.

"Pete!" the little girl says to him, and she bursts into tears.

He's not sure what to do as she runs forward, hugging him around his waist so hard, nearly squeezing the breath from him. "Aggie, Aggie, Aggie," she sobs. He waits a moment, looking around, seeing a well-dressed couple across the street in their car. Oh, the Millbrooks. He remembers seeing them at the big memorial for their son. They look as bewildered as he must look. So this strange creature hugging him must be the Millbrooks' little adopted girl. But that can't be right—he'd been told she was some kind of mute. But look here — she is clearly talking. "She saved me, Pete, she saved me," she weeps. "She didn't even *know*."

He freezes, but then he pats this strange girl awkwardly on her back. "There, there," he soothes, pretending for a moment that it's his own little girl. She used to be this small.

"May I come in, Pete?" she asks politely, even with her face buried in his shirt.

"Huh?" Is he still asleep?

"Please," she begs, tipping her face up, looking at him with big, shining eyes.

Pete tries to clear his mind of the beer buzz. He feels like he ought to be at his best for this girl. He can't explain it, but there it is. "Well, now," he says, "check that it's okay with your folks over there."

The girl turns around and bellows, "Mom, Dad, is it okay if I go inside to talk to Pete for a second?"

Pete looks at them and shrugs. "Is she bothering you?" asks Mrs. Millbrook, concerned. He can hear the sorrow in her voice. He feels a kinship with these two, even if they live in one of the newer McMansions in Poppy Beach, because he knows they've lost someone recently too.

"Nope, it's all right," he says. "She's not bothering anybody."

"Okay then, Meg, if Mr. Larch says it's okay."

"Well, come in then, little lady," Pete says, bowing courteously, as if she's a princess. "Now, what's your name?"

"Meg," she says.

His face is already a little different, a little softened. "Well, Meg, how do you feel about chocolate bunnies?" he asks as he closes the door.

Glen sits by the window of the Starbucks across from Club Flotsam, a little past three in the afternoon. He can hear bells tolling, probably at the big church in the middle of Longfellow's campus just a few blocks away. He's not sure why the bells make him feel so solemn. He gazes into his coffee cup, the placid surface shifting and rippling when he brings the cup up to inhale the steam. It had started here, at this Starbucks, that strange night he'd that...*whatever*...

it was with that girl with the sad eyes, the one who had loved Ian too. Agnes Larch. Her name…when she said it, it was as if bubbles started fizzing up from the bottom of his brain and all the way to his scalp, the way it feels when you eat a big hunk of wasabi. *Agnes Larch*. Had Ian ever talked about her? As he'd gone down the stairs of her apartment, brain lit with activity, he'd tried to remember but had come up with nothing.

He still can't place it. And her face, it hadn't been familiar. But something had happened when she walked into the club that night, almost as if Ian had been there shaking him by the shoulders and saying, "Wake up! Wake up, wake up, wake up!" And then, they'd just… collided. He certainly hadn't planned for it to happen — that wasn't his thing, to pick up girls at gigs. But she knew *him*. She missed *him*.

Glen had tried to call Gillian after the crash to talk about Ian, but she wouldn't pick up the phone, maybe too grief stricken. He couldn't think of anyone else who'd understand in the same way, the magnitude of what it felt like to lose Ian. And so when Gillian refused to answer his calls, he'd felt utterly alone with his grief, and then Agnes Larch had appeared with her smudged hands and haunted eyes. She understood, and she wasn't afraid to talk about it. He was grateful for that, at least, and to have found a way to mourn in a language deeper than speech — deeper, even, than music. What happened between them, it wasn't physical. It wasn't about lust or flesh.

He thinks again of what he felt when he first saw her across the crowded club, that look of loss. And once they'd gone back to her place, what it felt like to press his hands to her face, her skin delicate like an eggshell, and then her grief coming out in her words and her tears, the egg cracked open, the yolk exposed and broken, golden, and kind of beautiful. Who knew there could be so much inside one person?

And then he remembers Ian and his silly rocks, the ones his little sister sent him, the ones he sent her, how he was always wandering into science museum gift shops and New Age stores when they were on the road. "What *is* it with you and the rocks?" he'd asked as Ian pawed through a bin of rocks and crystals in a shop smelling heavily of patchouli. Glen's stomach was growling, and he was eager to find some lunch.

"Meg's birthday. I promised her."

"Yeah, but why rocks? I mean…you are paying money for rocks and then paying for bubble wrap and mailers and going to the post office to mail…rocks. You know, like, *rocks?* Those hard things in the dirt that you can find anywhere?"

Ian had shrugged. "It's our special thing."

"It's. A. Rock."

Ian smiled and shook his head. "Look, Glen." He took out a lumpy gray rock and showed it to him. "What do you see?"

"Uh, dude, I see a rock."

"Now look," he said, turning the rock around. It had been cut neatly all the way through, exposing its hollow interior. All along the insides, every surface glittered with purple crystals.

"Whoa. The fuck?"

"It's called a geode. I like to send them to Meg because they remind me of her."

Glen took the geode and felt the heft of it in his hand. "Yeah?"

"You know, how people might have seen the outside and thought, 'Oh, hey, ordinary old rock,' and tossed it aside, but someone came along and knew there was a lot more to it. Inside is this whole universe, and no one ever would have known. Maybe we all have universes in us. Maybe our purpose in life is to find the universes inside each other."

Glen had felt a twinge of guilt for not seeing the potential for beauty in the deceptively dull rock. "Sorry, little geode," he'd said, and Ian had laughed.

"People are like that," Ian had said, almost talking to himself. "The ordinary ones are never quite ordinary. The ones you think are ordinary often turn out to be the most extraordinary of all."

A student bustles by Glen's table, dropping a newspaper on the floor. "Hey, your paper!" Glen calls after her, but the girl is already out the door. Glen reaches down to pick it up, intending on putting it in the recycling bin. It's the *Longfellow Daily News*, the college's student paper.

He glances at the front page. *Longfellow Remembers Deceased Alumna Today*, reads the headline, and Glen's hands are shaking when he sees Agnes Larch's face above the fold. He'd heard about the fire in passing, of course, and had heard someone had died, but he hadn't been paying enough attention. He skims the article and reads that a memorial service is being held for her *right now.* He gulps down the rest of his coffee and sprints toward Longfellow's campus, toward the sound of the still-tolling bells.

Vivian trudges home after class. She knows they buried Agnes yesterday, and she hates herself for not being there. But she also knows Agnes wouldn't have wanted her to miss lectures. She has a shot of being at the top of her class, and Agnes wouldn't want her to risk it. All Vivian could do was arrange a memorial service at Longfellow University. It had taken just a few phone calls to their old residential college and to the university chaplain's office. Word got out quickly, and the large church in the quad had been overflowing with people, all holding lit candles, illuminating the huge space with tiny flickering tongues of flame, made of the same stuff that took her life. How can love and death look the same? Vivian wonders if Agnes ever knew how many people had been touched by her, by her quiet, unselfish love.

She was loved.

Vivian can barely see her front door through her tears as she pushes it open, and her foot catches on something, a package.

She hasn't ordered anything online recently, and she's not expecting anything, but she still checks the label to see who it's for. It's addressed to Vivian Park, in handwriting she doesn't recognize. She tucks the package under her arm and lets herself into the main entryway.

Her hands are shaking so much that she can barely open her front door, dropping her keys twice. "Fuck, come on, Viv, pull it together," she hisses under her breath.

As soon as she's inside, she fights the urge to rip the package open immediately. Something tells her to take her time. She removes her jacket slowly, removes her hat and gloves, unlaces her boots. She makes herself a cup of tea.

Finally, finally, she sits on her bed with the package. She pulls on the little easy-open strip, sending bits of newspaper dust from the padding around her as she tears the package open, bits of lint catching the light like the fake snow in a snowglobe all shaken up. She reaches her hand in the package, and it wraps around a wire coil, heavy cardboard. It feels like a notebook. She pulls it out. No, it's a sketchpad.

No, it's *Agnes's* sketchpad.

She sees Agnes's familiar handwriting: *Please mail this to Vivian Park.* And there's her address.

What can this all mean?

She opens the sketchpad slowly. Wolves. Of course there are wolves. Agnes was always drawing those creepy things. She smiles to herself through her tears. So Agnes.

There's a picture of Agnes herself, some crazy self-portrait where she's tied to a stake, and then strange things taped in: a cigarette butt, a folded note, a square patch of black velvet.

It's this page that she lingers over the longest, the page with this square of black velvet. There's a drawing all around it. It's Agnes again, she thinks, even though Agnes's drawn herself from the back. But Vivian recognizes the hair and her tiny frame.

Agnes wears a long gown, her unkempt hair cascading down her back, and she's holding hands with someone in a slim, tailored jacket. She can't see the face, but she sees a mess of floppy hair. They're standing together under a doorway, a large, dark door covered with strange symbols, swung open to the side. There's so much charcoal on this page, but not a spot around the two figures under the door-frame. The paper seems almost to glow around the two of them, whiter than white. She wishes she could see past them, wishes she could see what was on the other side of that door. Wishes she could see what's beyond the page.

"Who are you?" Vivian whispers to this mysterious boy.

She touches the velvet, and words float into her head. She doesn't know what they mean — they sound German. She didn't take German. Agnes took German. *Bräutigam und Braut.* What on earth does it mean?

She checks the padded envelope again to see if there's anything else. Probably not. She sweeps her hand inside and is surprised to find something small, pointy, that fits in the palm of her hand. She closes her fingers around this mysterious object, reminded of the "touchy-feely" box in kindergarten, when you'd stick your arm into a dark box and try to guess what was inside. She can't figure out from touch what this object is, so she pulls her hand back out slowly, her fingers still wrapped around the mystery.

She takes a deep breath and opens her fingers.

A tiny, red plastic monkey, the kind bartenders hang from girly mixed drinks. She stares at the velvet, the monkey, and the drawing of Agnes and this mystery boy. She doesn't understand any of it, but still, she whispers, "Thank you, Agnes. Thank you for letting me know you're okay."

She holds the monkey in her hand, places the sketchpad underneath the pillow, and stretches out, suddenly exhausted.

Vivian sleeps.

ACKNOWLEDGMENTS

How do any words get written? How does language happen? How do we convey our emotions in a way that another person can drink in our thoughts and say, "Yes, I have felt that too"? Communication is a kind of miracle, and to think that everything we feel can be attributed to electrical pulses and neural receptors makes me dizzy, a little frightened, but mostly grateful. It makes me think of a line I once heard about the entire universe being in a drop of water. It seems sadly inadequate then, this action of my fingertips tapping on this keyboard, the cursor blinking as if to tell me, hurry up, hurry up, hurry up, my words clumsy and unable to express my gratitude fully.

Great thanks to P-the-K, who told me that creativity was just a part of who I was; to my cousin, who one Christmas gave me a blank notebook "to write down your pretty thoughts" and told me I was a writer before I knew I had anything to write; to my writing instructors, especially the one who told me that he became a writer "the day [he] began thinking like one" — that it was merely a different way of seeing that could define who we were.

So much love to my old friends who have seen me through this journey and those I met along the way, all who read my words and took the time to tell me that they had meaning outside of my head. I would not be here without my online writing cohort: Algie, AC, Phila, and K.

I am also indebted to the writers who have stirred my imagination and shown me new worlds. I cannot write about the dreaming without owing much to Neil Gaiman, nor allegorical fantasy without C.S. Lewis or Madeline L'Engle. I doubt these words will ever find them, but thank you, thank you, thank you.

Thanks to the MAFssiah for telling me about the Lost Coast of California, not even knowing that it would be the kick in the pants I needed to transform this work. Thanks to smands for reasons too many to list, and to Carla for reading through this story in its many incarnations and being my biggest cheerleader when much of this project was still a secret. Thanks to the Ravicorners for being there when this story was just a little idea wearing someone else's clothes.

And to the dear ones who have gone Beyond: I still remember. I still think of you. I still miss you.

ABOUT THE AUTHOR

Recluse by day and recluse in pajamas by night, Eden Barber enjoys a rich life of snacking, knitting, and hamboning. She wrote and illustrated her first book of short stories in the fourth grade and has been writing and drawing ever since.

check out these titles from
OMNIFIC PUBLISHING

◂─ພ─▸Contemporary Romance◂─ພ─▸

Boycotts & Barflies and *Trust in Advertising* by Victoria Michaels
Passion Fish by Alison Oburia and Jessica McQuinn
Three Daves by Nicki Elson
Small Town Girl and *Corporate Affair* by Linda Cunningham
Stitches and Scars by Elizabeth A. Vincent
Take the Cake by Sandra Wright
Pieces of Us by Hannah Downing
The Way That You Play It by BJ Thornton
Poughkeepsie by Debra Anastasia
Burning Embers by Hannah Fielding
Cocktails & Dreams by Autumn Markus
Recaptured Dreams and *All-American Girl* by Justine Dell
Once Upon a Second Chance by Marian Vere
The Englishman by Nina Lewis
Tangled by Emma Chase
16 Marsden Place by Rachel Brimble
Sleepers, Awake by Eden Barber

◂─ພ─▸Paranormal Romance◂─ພ─▸

The Light Series: Seers of Light, Whisper of Light, and *Circle of Light*
by Jennifer DeLucy
The Hanaford Park Series: Eve of Samhain and *Pleasures Untold* by Lisa Sanchez
Immortal Awakening by KC Randall
Crushed Seraphim and *Bittersweet Seraphim* by Debra Anastasia
The Guardian's Wild Child by Feather Stone
Grave Refrain by Sarah M. Glover
Divinity by Patricia Leever
Blood Vine by Amber Belldene
Divine Temptation by Nicki Elson

◂─ພ─▸Romantic Suspense◂─ພ─▸

Whirlwind by Robin DeJarnett
The CONduct Series: With Good Behavior and *Bad Behavior* by Jennifer Lane
Indivisible by Jessica McQuinn
Between the Lies by Alison Oburia

◂─ພ─▸New Adult◂─ພ─▸

Beside Your Heart by Mary Whitney

← ⤍→Young Adult← ⤍→
Shades of Atlantis and *The Ember Series: Ember* and *Iridescent* by Carol Oates
Breaking Point by Jess Bowen
Life, Liberty, and Pursuit by Susan Kaye Quinn
Embrace by Cherie Colyer
Destiny's Fire by Trisha Wolfe
Streamline by Jennifer Lane
Reaping Me Softly by Kate Evangelista

← ⤍→Historical Romance← ⤍→
Cat O' Nine Tails by Patricia Leever
Burning Embers by Hannah Fielding

← ⤍→Erotic Romance← ⤍→
Becoming sage by Kasi Alexander
Saving sunni by Kasi & Reggie Alexander
The Winemaker's Dinner: Appetizers & *Entrée* by Dr. Ivan Rusilko & Everly Drummond
The Winemaker's Dinner: Dessert by Dr. Ivan Rusilko

← ⤍→Anthologies and Singles← ⤍→
A Valentine Anthology including short stories by Alice Clayton, Jennifer DeLucy,
Nicki Elson, Jessica McQuinn, Victoria Michaels, and Alison Oburia

It's Only Kinky the First Time by Kasi Alexander
Learning the Ropes by Kasi & Reggie Alexander
The Winemaker's Dinner: RSVP by Dr. Ivan Rusilko
The Winemaker's Dinner: No Reservations by Everly Drummond
Big Guns by Jessica McQuinn
Concessions by Robin DeJarnett
Starstruck by Lisa Sanchez
New Flame by BJ Thornton
Shackled by Debra Anastasia
Swim Recruit by Jennifer Lane
Sway by Nicki Elson
Full Speed Ahead by Susan Kaye Quinn
The Second Sunrise by Hannah Downing
The Summer Prince by Carol Oates
Whatever it Takes by Sarah M. Glover
Clarity by Patricia Leever
A Christmas Wish by Autumn Markus

coming soon from
OMNIFIC PUBLISHING

The Runaway Year by Shani Struthers
Romancing the Bookworm by Kate Evangelista
Cry by Linda Kage
Blood Entangled by Amber Belldene
Good Ground by Tracy Winegar
Keeping the Peace (A Small Town Novel) by Linda Cunningham
Until Next Time by Justine Dell
Hold Tight by Cherie Colyer
Forced to Change by Stephanie Caldwell
Hydraulic Level 5 by Sarah Latchaw

www.ingramcontent.com/pod-product-compliance
Lightning Source LLC
Chambersburg PA
CBHW020329120726
47904CB00002B/334